BLOOD ORANGE

Book 1 - The Dracula Duet

KARINA HALLE

Cover Design: Hang Le

Edited by: Laura Helseth

Proofed by: Chanpreet Singh

To anyone who has felt alienated, unappreciated and misunderstood: There's nothing wrong with you. You just need to find your people.

And I guess I just wanted to mention

As the heavens will fall

We will be together soon if we will be anything
at all

— "ZERO SUM" - NINE INCH NAILS

PLAYLIST

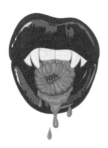

You can find the playlist to Blood Orange on Spotify HERE. Otherwise I have included a few songs below to help set the mood.

"Zero Sum" - NIN
"Bitches Brew" - +++ (Crosses)
"Corrupt" - Depeche Mode
"The Lovers" - NIN
"Red Right Hand" - Nick Cave and the Bad Seeds

PLAYLIST

"World in My Eyes" - Depeche Mode
"Vampyre of Time & Memory" - Queens of the Stone Age
"Digital Bath" - Deftones
"Tear You Apart" - She Wants Revenge
"The Perfect Drug" - NIN
"Loverman" - Nick Cave and the Bad Seeds
"The Becoming" - NIN
"This is a Trick" - +++ (Crosses)
"Welcome to my World" - Depeche Mode

CONTENT WARNING

Blood Orange is a book I personally consider to be a dark romance (though I realize there are levels to dark romance and what I consider dark may be considered grey to other readers) and as such there are content warnings that I think readers should be aware of to protect their mental health. It contains the following potentially triggering situations:

Explicit language and graphic sex, graphic violence, pregnancy loss (on page), blood, murder, death of a spouse, M/M, M/F, Non-con (minor/not between the hero or heroine), dubcon, exhibitionism, BDSM-lite elements, and certain kinks including breath play, fire play, blood play, cum play, anal play, instrument play, impact play, primal kink, chasing, bondage, degradation, praise kink, and feeding (vampire style). The majority of these content warnings are in regards to the sexual acts in the book.

It must be noted that this book is for adults only. This is not Twilight. Please heed the warnings if recommending this to those under 18.

Blood Orange is book 1 in The Dracula Duet. Book 2— Black Rose—releases December 29th.

CHAPTER 1

VALTU

I WRITE this down because I don't trust Bram to write his novel without twisting my story around. I'd seen the wheels turning in his head in that peculiar way writers get when an idea starts taking off on them like an ornery horse. I'm sure the countless days and nights we spent together in Cruden Bay where I opened myself up and poured my heart out to him paled in comparison to what Mr. Stoker's brain could conjure up. Thus, I'm not relying on his tale to be accurate in any way, shape, or form (He told me his title is *The Un-Dead*, I was hoping it would be called Valtu or Count Aminoff).

Besides, over the centuries, my memories have begun to fade. I used to pray for the day I would forget all the pain, for the day I could burn my memories of her to ash. But I know that one day I will have to remember her. To forget her would be to forget what it's like to be human, and I'm dangerously close to losing myself all together at times. And so I will write down all I remember of her, in hope that our love might bring about my humanity.

One can only dream.

I have been doing a lot of dreaming.

THE GREAT WRATH 1714
The Kingdom of Sweden
(the land currently known as Finland)

I WAITED FOR HER THAT MORNING LIKE A STARVING MAN for a crust of bread. Nothing would ease my hunger, not the sunshine on my face, the call of the meadow larks from the thicket, nor the wind rustling my humble field of wheat, all things that would normally bring me pleasure, even on the saddest of days.

Mina. Even her name felt like a song, like an answer from God to make up for a past awash with grief. Losing my first wife Ana and the child, a child we never had a chance to name, then having the country invaded by the enemy, the burning of Helsinki, then most of my land taken away from me, even all of that felt trivial whenever I thought about Mina. She was my redemption, my second chance at life. She was a salve on the deepest wounds of my existence, and those wounds ran deep.

Even the harsh reality of this new world didn't have a chance against the way she made me feel, the hope she brought me. If I thought about it even for a moment, I would have known how impossible our love was, how there was no future for us, not when I was a lowly farmer, just a peasant in his mid-thirties, and she was the daughter of the general, the very monster who took over the countryside and made it his.

But I never dug deeper. I didn't want to think. I was content to live on the surface of love, letting it sweep me from one day to the next on an unyielding current, no fear of the turbulent water and jagged rocks that lay ahead ready to flay me to pieces.

The sound of hoofbeats came from beyond the line of birch trees and a flock of starlings suddenly flew above the leaves, frightened by Mina's approach. I was standing at the start of the forest, my cottage barely visible from around the bend. If anyone else were to approach, they would come along the road, not from behind through the birch and berry shrubs, where there was no trail. That's how I knew it was her.

I found myself running now to meet her, leaving my wheat field behind and disappearing into the trees. I was almost to the pond, our meeting place, when I saw her horse between the tree trunks, the eyes on the white bark watching me. Perhaps even judging me.

Mina was cloaked, her gray hood covering her head, and I watched in awe as she lifted it off, her face becoming visible.

She saw me approach and smiled, so joyful that it nearly brought me to my knees.

She would always be the most beautiful woman I had ever seen.

Mina's hair flowed around her like a cape, red and chestnut, shades of burnt bark and raspberries, strands of blonde catching the light as the wind pushed it off her face. Her hair was the color of the fiery light from a dying sunset, one last burst of crimson before it faded into night. Her skin the color of fresh cow's milk, eyes the color of unfurled leaves. Her smile was sunshine.

She was my everything.

I felt a sudden warmth in my chest, a feeling so strong it was an almost physical pain. I could see all of her beauty then, in the way the light shone on her face, and I knew then that I loved her beyond measure.

"Hello, Valtu," she said in broken German.

"Hello, my dear Mina," I said, my German only marginally better than hers. Language had been difficult for us—with Sweden's rule over Finland, Finnish was largely forbidden and I had learned to talk, read, and write in Swedish, as well as a bit of German for trading purposes. But in my early days, I didn't understand Russian and Mina only understood some German. It didn't matter though, because when I was with her, words didn't mean as much. We communicated in other ways.

She dismounted but I was already at her side to catch her, taking her in my arms and lowering her to the ground.

There was a shy moment when we were too close, when it felt formal and we didn't really know each other, but I erased it by leaning over, grabbing her by her shoulders, and kissing her hard.

She let out a cry of surprise—sometimes I was rather rough with her, my passion unbridled—but that disappeared into one of lust. At any rate, we didn't have much time with each other. Over the last two months we had met every morning for mere moments, all of it in secret, and did all we could with the time we were given.

Feeling this urgency, my fingers pressed into her skin as my kiss deepened, like she might dissolve if I didn't hold onto her, like she was a mere leaf in the wind.

She responded eagerly, her arms winding around my neck as she pulled me closer. We kissed like that for what felt like hours, exploring each other, tasting each other, wanting more and more. I had never craved anyone or anything like this in all my life, and the more I kissed her, the hungrier for her I got.

Finally, we pulled apart, both of us panting for breath.

"I missed you," she said, her voice a throaty whisper.

"And I have missed you," I replied, brushing her strands of strawberry hair off her face.

We didn't need to say anymore. We both knew what we wanted, what we needed, what we dreamed about in the hours and days we were apart.

I took her hand and led her through the trees to the pond, my heart racing in anticipation.

The sun was filtering through the birch, casting a beautiful flickering light over everything. We reached the edge of the water and I turned to her, taking her in my arms once again.

We kissed, our bodies pressed together, and I was hard as wood. She slid her hand down, grabbing me by my cock, and I gasped in pleasure. She had become more and more bold with me over time, her curiosity lowering any inhibitions. There were so many things I yearned to do to her, blasphemous, unspeakable things, and I knew over time that she would let me. She would even enjoy it. I would make her see stars.

She started to stroke me through my trousers, her hand moving up and down, and I couldn't take it anymore. I needed her, right then and there, or else I would explode.

I grabbed her and set her down on a soft patch of moss and she leaned back, her legs spread wide as she beckoned me closer, the many layers of her dress billowing around her like clouds.

I didn't need to be asked twice. I pushed up her dress and undid my pants, sliding between her legs, pushing myself inside her in one smooth thrust. She was already wet and ready for me, as she always was.

She cried out and I started to move, grabbing her hips and pounding into her. The water stirred near our bodies, wind rustling the trees, and I felt everything so clearly, it was as if I was ascending into something new, a higher version of myself, like I was closer to that God I once cursed for taking my wife and child away from me. Being deep inside Mina was like stepping onto another path, toward another life, a better one.

I could feel my orgasm building, could feel her tensing up around me, and I knew it was time. I slipped my hand between her legs and rubbed where she was slick and slippery until she let out a long moan. Her orgasm started to build, her body tensing up and then exploding around me. I grabbed her hips and shoved myself in as deep as I could go, holding her there as I came, my body jerking with pleasure so encompassing, I felt like my head was put on backward.

I stayed there until we both finished, her body going limp beneath me, and then I withdrew, rolling over to my side and staring at her.

She was breathing hard, her chest heaving, and a satisfied smile playing on her lips, their color a deep red, bruised from my own lips. I felt a sense of calm wash over me, a sense that everything was going to be okay.

She looked at me, her eyes deepening in color as the sun shifted, the pink of her cheeks fading. Then a look of fear came across her pale brow.

"What is it?" I asked, my voice hoarse.

She rubbed her lips together, the line between her delicate brows deepening. "I have to tell you something..."

"Tell me what?" I sat up a little, propped up by my elbow.

She swallowed, her throat moving softly and I was struck by the most unbecoming notion, that I should bite her neck, that I should sink my teeth into her tender flesh, and drink her blood.

I had to swat that feeling away, it was too far gone from any of the other lewd thoughts that would pop into my head from time to time. It felt dangerous in ways I couldn't understand, but soon would very well.

She didn't seem to notice how I was staring at her neck. "I'm pregnant," she said.

The words hit me like a fallen tree. I could scarcely believe it.

"Pregnant?" I repeated, feeling like the world was tilting on its axis and I was given yet another path to go on in this life. "Are you sure?"

She bit her lip and nodded. I could sense in her the conflict she was feeling, like a sixth sense was suddenly bestowed upon me. She was happy it was my baby, for it *was* mine, but she was scared of how I would react, and scared what to do about it after.

But the honest truth was, I was happy. I was ecstatic. I should have felt the fear she had, the impossibility of the situation, but I didn't feel that way at all.

"I don't know what to do..." she said, trailing off, looking away.

I sat up and reached for her, fingers under her chin, making her look at me. "You don't know what to do? You're going to have our baby, Mina. Isn't that what you want?"

She nodded, a bright sparkle returning to her green eyes. "It is. But I don't know how I can. I want you to be the father but...they can't find out. They would kill me."

Normally when one says their father would kill them, it's an exaggeration. But with Mina, I knew the general would do it. I'd seen him slaughter women and children alike. His own daughter would not be spared.

"Did you tell anyone other than me?" I asked.

She shook her head but then stopped. "Only my hand-maiden. I didn't tell her but she knew." My eyes went wide but she rushed on to assure me. "Don't worry. I have known her since I was a baby. She would never tell. She is like a mother to me."

I could only hope that was true. Either way, I didn't want to stick around and find out. I grabbed her hand and put it to my mouth, kissing her palm. "We will find a way. We can escape to where they won't find us." I didn't know where that could be, considering the Russians had taken most of the country, but that didn't seem to matter at that moment.

I watched as her shoulders lightened and tension left her jaw. "Okay. We will have to leave soon before they can tell." She reached down and rubbed her belly. Under her layers of her dress, you couldn't tell and even when I put my hand there it felt normal to me. That was until I felt a surge of warmth and electricity come up from her belly and into my hand. I had never felt anything like that before, it was like I was feeling life itself. I could practically see lightning traveling up my arm.

"Where do you think we'll go?" Mina said, oblivious to what happened.

"I don't know," I said after a moment, distracted by the feeling of pure life beneath my hand. What was happening to me?

"Were you born here or did your parents come from elsewhere?" she asked.

"Uh, I was adopted," I told her. "I never knew my real parents."

"Oh? That is interesting," she said.

"I don't even have a birthday," I said absently, still feeling that energy surge through me, enough to make the hair on my arms and back of my neck stand straight up.

"We will have to change that," she said, moving so that my hand fell away from her stomach. "Perhaps you can have the same birthday as our child. I do hope wherever we go, I can play my music. The only problem is, I will be too fat to play the harp."

Mina was an accomplished musician, according to herself, but her voice was so clear and melodic when she sang to me, that I believed she had a natural talent. In a way, it was her passion for music that made me take it up over the years.

"We will have to leave without the harp," I told her.

"Without anything that won't fit on a horse's back. But I promise I will buy you anything you want once we are safe."

I was such a fool. I had no money. All my wheat crop went to her father, and he barely gave me anything to survive on. I must have known that we would never be able to run away without being found, that there would be no happy ending for us. I must have known that it would only end in death.

But I believed the words I was saying, like only a fool would.

And Mina was happy. She grinned like the sun coming through clouds and she reached for me, pulling me down so I was on top of her, kissing me deeply. My hands went up her legs, eager to feel her again, and that was the last time I would ever feel her skin.

Even though it all happened so fast, I knew it was going to happen moments before it did. I could hear the footsteps creeping through the brush, I could hear whispers. I looked around, startled, but there was nothing around us at all. I didn't quite understand what was happening to my body. I didn't know then what I really was, or the change that was about to be underway, as it is for anyone with my background who turns thirty-five. I didn't even know how old I really was.

And then they appeared across the pond. Five soldiers belonging to the general. They saw me with my hands on Mina and that was all they needed.

They started running for us, swords drawn, and I got to my feet and hauled her up so that she was over my shoulder like a bag of wheat. I had never moved so fast in my life and it was like I had a preternatural grace about me, like an animal taking flight from a predator. Little did I know that I was becoming the predator.

I ran to Mina's horse, flung her over its withers, then pulled myself astride, urging it into a gallop through the woods.

The men were on foot, but there was no doubt they had their horses nearby and were trying to catch us by surprise. I wondered how far we could ride, if we could actually escape this way. It was September, but we could ride into the north of the country for at least a month until the snow set in. Perhaps the native peoples near the North Pole would shelter us in the unoccupied spaces.

The horse went as fast as it could, jumping over logs and streams, dodging trees and rock, and neither of us spoke. Mina gave out the occasional whimper or sob, and I knew she was crying because her handmaiden turned her in and that our lives had changed quicker than we were ready for.

I didn't even know where we were going, but then I heard it over the thundering sound of Mina's horse—the hooves of other horses, racing fast.

Coming toward us.

It was too late.

When the forest opened up to a meadow, a river cutting through it, there was an army of mounted soldiers on the other side.

A roar came out of my throat, something deep, dark and feral. It scared Mina, startled the soldiers. But it wasn't enough to deter them. I turned the horse on its heel but now the soldiers were coming up from behind and we were surrounded.

"Mina!" the general's voice came from the pack and the horses parted as he came through. He was a tall thin man with an imposing face, like it was carved out of pure rock. He put his hand forward as if to reach for us. He said something in Russian to her, something I couldn't understand and yet I understood. He was making me out to seem like I was a bad man who captured her, raped her, impregnated her. He coaxed her as if she were a skittish puppy hiding under a bed, offering it scraps.

But Mina didn't fall for the scraps. She shook her head, her hands buried in the horse's mane, and didn't move.

"She isn't going with you," I said to the general in German. "She is staying with me."

The general raised his chin with a sneer and spoke German back to me. "I forget you're so primitive that you don't even speak Russian. I would be careful if I were you. If you cared for her, you would admit to your crimes. You would sentence yourself to death so that she may go free."

"And what of the baby?" Mina asked.

"Of course you can keep it if you choose," he said, a blatant lie.

And while this was happening, my bones started to burn, like I was on fire from the inside out. I felt like internal flames were being fused to my veins, that I was growing stronger somehow, unnaturally so, and that's when the hunger started to kick in. A deep growl from my stomach that made the horse snort and dance nervously underneath us, as if we were going to take off.

We should have, in hindsight.

At any rate, the horse's movement was enough for the soldiers to spring into action, coming toward us.

Mina's horse spooked further and suddenly reared back with a loud whinny and Mina was thrown to the ground.

I jumped off just as the horse took off at a gallop and grabbed Mina, hauling her to her feet, standing in front of her to protect her.

I snarled at everyone like I was a wolf in human form.

A few soldiers laughed nervously, eyeing each other in cagey amusement, but their horses were so disturbed that they wouldn't advance further. They started pawing the ground, throwing their heads, and then rearing when the soldiers kicked their flanks.

It was at that moment that I understood.

The horses were afraid of me.

I was afraid of myself.

But I didn't know why. How could I? There was no word for what I was becoming.

The soldiers got off their horses, some of them taking off in the direction that Mina's horse went, and they approached me slowly, spooked as well. It wasn't until the general barked at them in Russian that they suddenly lunged like the trained monkeys they were.

I did my best to fight them off but it was impossible to do when I was trying to protect Mina. In the end I covered her like a blanket in a futile effort to keep her safe.

But then there were too many soldiers, from all sides, crossing the river to get us and then they were ripping us apart.

They dragged her off, her heels making tracks through the ground, and she screamed for me, hands outstretched and I couldn't reach her, not with so many men around me, holding me in place.

All the anger, all the rage, the pain, the anguish swelled inside me.

I felt myself transform into something.

The fire in my bones, the hunger in my gut, the pure animalistic urge to kill and fuck and eat. The soldiers felt it too, and all the horses were gone, and even the general had dismounted before his stead took off on him.

He grabbed hold of Mina by her hair, making her scream.

Threw her on her back in the dirt.

"Stop!" I screamed, another inhuman voice that was ripped out of me, tearing apart my throat.

"What will happen to the baby?" the general sneered in German.

He raised his boot.

Brought it down.

In horrific slow motion.

He stomped right on Mina's stomach.

I howled in pain, panting, clawing, trying to do what I could to stop this nightmare from unfolding. "Mina!" I cried out.

She had the wind knocked out of her, his boot still pushing down and she was trying to reach up for her father to help her, gasping for air, face contorted in pain and terror.

But he didn't help her.

He just said something in Russian. A word I understood.

Whore.

Then he brought out his sword.

I was done with feeling helpless.

I started to fight harder as the fire in my bones threatened to drown me in pain, but the pain was nothing compared to what was about to happen.

I remember I was calling her name, screaming it until my voice was hoarse, as if that alone could stop things. But I know now that fate is stubborn when it is set in motion.

Nothing can stop it.

The general raised the sword above Mina's head.

Her eyes widened until the glint of the sun on the sword made her blink.

He hesitated for just a moment.

A moment for the world to slow down.

A moment for Mina to realize she was going to die.

A moment for me to realize that I was going to lose her.

The same moment I knew I would kill everyone in my path.

"My heart will always find yours!" she screamed at me.

He brought the sword down.

Sliced through her neck, decapitating her.

Her head rolled my way, stopping at my feet.

Beautiful, lifeless eyes staring straight up at the sky, the color of unfurled leaves in spring.

There was no time to feel broken at the loss, at the horror. No time to weep, to grieve, to even feel shock.

I became a monster.

I fully gave in to what I was trying to hold back, that last piece of humanity running away from me like the blood from Mina's severed head.

With a surge of fiery power, I let out another roar, inhuman enough to make blood run cold, loud enough to shake the earth, and I fought. I surged forward, clawing, biting, like a ravenous bear.

The soldiers stabbed me with their swords, but they didn't kill me, and the pain only felt sweet and I kept going until I had their swords in my hands. I worked my way through the soldiers, biting into their necks, tearing out their throats, stabbing them in the chest, the face, the head, leaving them to bleed out while I destroyed them all.

The general at this point was trying to get away. He was running on foot for the hills. He had no one left to protect him.

I gave chase after him, this time it felt more like a game, like I was actually enjoying this, predator and prey. I laughed maniacally as I went, slowing down and speeding up, letting him think he had a chance of escape when I already knew he didn't.

Finally he fell down, too exhausted to get up, and I was on him.

I took my fingers and plunged them into his eye sockets, ripping out his eyes until his eyeballs were in my hands, then, while he was screaming, forced his eyes into his mouth. Grabbed his jaw and made him chew and choke on them.

Then I put my body over his, bit into his neck with newly sharpened teeth, and drank down his blood until that hunger

I had was finally satisfied, until his screams vanished into death.

It was the end of me.

It was the beginning of someone else.

Something else.

It took decades of killing people and animals, drinking their blood, and hiding my true self as I traveled south, taking a boat across to Estonia, then disappearing into Eastern Europe where it was easier to hide, before I finally met others that were like me.

When I discovered there was a term for what I had become.

A vampire.

And that my birth parents had been vampires too. If they had raised me, I would have known that at age thirty-five I would transition from human to vampire.

But I didn't know.

I found out in time to save my own life.

But too late to save Mina's.

Too late to escape a cursed life, one that will follow me into all of eternity.

CHAPTER 2

DAHLIA

I'M DREAMING AGAIN. A nightmare.

Same one as always.

I'm on the ground, cold and frightened. Chaos surrounds me: the sound of thundering hooves, horse's whinnying, clashing metal, and the feeling of so many people on the precipice of violence. A man stands above me, dressed in some type of armor, his face full of malice and contempt as he stares down at me. He has his boot on my middle and is pressing down on my uterus and though I don't feel any pain in my dream, it hurts all the same. There are vague feelings that come and go, that he is going to kill my lover, that I am pregnant and he's trying to kill the baby, that he means to kill me. The most disturbing feeling of all is that he is my father.

He raises his sword in the air and I know he means to cut my head off. I scream but it's caught in my throat and I can't make a sound and as much as I struggle, I can't move. His boot has me pinned and I am weak in the way that dreams make you. I am frozen in place.

Then there's another scream. From a man. It's my name,

even though I can't understand it, I know it's my name. Something so blood-curdling and primal that it makes my skin erupt in goosebumps. I turn my head to see the man who screamed but I can't see him. He is being held back by soldiers and as much as I try to focus on him, he is just a blur of a man.

But I know he wants to stop what is happening.

He just can't.

I feel his anguish and his love for me and my love for him and in that moment I will do anything to escape, to be with him, to run away.

Yes, I have to run away.

And as I turn to look up at the man above, the devil who I think is my father, the blade lowers and it catches the light of the sun until the glare makes me close my eyes.

I wake up in a cold sweat right before my head is cut off.

Sometimes I feel the blade go in, just a tickle, and then I'm gasping for air.

As I am right now.

This time it takes me a moment, my head reeling, to realize it was just a dream and that I still have my head and I'm safe.

Except I'm not safe, not really.

I've never been more unsafe in my life.

I am sitting upright in an unfamiliar bed, the sheets tangled around my legs, my body shivering. The window is open though I swear I closed it before I went to bed, and the curtain is billowing as a cold, damp breeze wafts into the room. Venice has a peculiar smell to it, not as unpleasant as I was warned, but still dank and musty, with a hint of the sea, like exposed tide.

You're okay, I tell myself. *You're safe in your new apartment. Just breathe.*

I push back at the end of my nose to get more air in and breathe in deeply a few times until I feel my heart rate returning to normal. But even though I'm calming down, my head is swimming. Fucking jet lag. It's been years since I've traveled to Europe, I'd forgotten how bad it can be. Even with certain herbs and spells to ease the jet lag, nothing seems to work on me. I'm sure if I tried, I might find some success, but since I don't have any excess energy to spare on this mission, I'll just have to deal with it the old-fashioned way, via melatonin and coffee.

I pick up my phone and glance at the time. Three-thirty a.m. Now I'm too wired to go back to sleep and I decide to do the worst thing for dealing with jet lag: I look at the time back at home in Seattle. Seven thirty in the evening. The sun would still be up. In my mind's eye I can picture the way the sun glints off Puget Sound, how my friend Kathy would probably text me and ask if I wanted to go to the bar after dinner. I'd appreciate the gesture, even if it's one of pity, and I'd probably turn her down to spend another night alone.

This was a mistake, I think, twisting the rings on my fingers around and around. *I shouldn't be here. I should be back at home, trying to live a normal life.*

And yet I am here. I'm here because this is my last chance to prove myself, to the witches, to the guild, and to Bellamy. If I fail, I lose everything for good. And then, yes, I can go and try to live a normal life again. But what good is a normal life when you know you're anything but?

The curtain suddenly flutters as another strong breeze comes in through the window and I'm about to get up and close it when mist starts flowing inside, like a stream of vapors suspended in the air.

I stop and watch for a moment, confused at how fog can just enter through the window like that, until I get an uneasy feeling in my gut, like someone poured cold liquid in my veins. Perhaps this isn't fog at all.

"Be gone," I whisper harshly. Even though I have a corner unit in the apartment building, facing onto the lagoon between Venice and Murano, I don't know how thin the walls are. "You are not welcome here."

Anyway, if anyone could hear or see me they'd think I was a crazy person talking to mist, but I know it's not just mist. I can feel it's something else, the way it sits in the air like cobwebs, like it's searching the room for something.

Me.

"Dahlia."

My name is whispered like an exhale of air.

I suddenly get to my feet and push the air toward the window with my palms out and the mist disintegrates, the leftover particles flowing back out the window. I quickly slam the window shut and while I do so, I glance outside. There is a small dock that juts out from the main floor of the building and though there are no boats tied up there, I swear I see a dark figure standing at the end. Except there's something wrong with it. At first glance it seems like a human, but the more I press against the glass, trying to get a better look, the more it seems to shift, as if it's lowering itself onto the dock, spreading in directions that shouldn't be possible. Almost as if it's on four inhumanely long legs.

My breath fogs up the glass and I quickly rub it away but when I look again, the dark figure is gone. The dock is empty.

Okay, what the hell was that?

Jet lag, a voice inside me says. *You're tired. It's jet lag.*

I know that voice is only saying that so I won't think too much about it, so I won't worry. Because honestly, I can't worry. I can't afford to. All my energy has to go into my magic for tomorrow morning and for every day after that until my blade has tasted blood. One slip-up and I'm fucked. Vampires are too good at reading people and they can smell a witch from a mile away. If my mask were to slip for a moment, he would end me.

The one they call Dracula.

The one I must get close to.

The one I have been sent here to kill.

I DIDN'T END UP GOING BACK TO SLEEP. I STAYED UP UNTIL I saw dawn lick the horizon, painting the lagoon in shades of pewter and pink. I decided to go headfirst into the spell, thinking my energy might wane as the morning went on. It took an hour of standing in front of the mirror, whispering my intentions while I lit bunches of dried lavender from back home as well as copal resin, hoping it wouldn't set off any smoke detectors.

The problem with doing a glamor spell, which is essentially putting a mask or shield over you so that others can't see your true intentions, is that you don't know if it works until you actually put it to the test and meet other people. Thank god my contact here from the guild, Livia, is going to meet me for an espresso on the way to school so at least I'll know if it's in place before I put myself in direct danger.

At that thought, I feel a little thrill run through me. I smile at my reflection, taking comfort in it. I had feared that perhaps I lost my competitive drive, the fun part of the game. The thrill of the hunt. The desire to deliver justice, to exact revenge. It's what has been drilled in me since I was thirteen, to kill the enemy, to do a good job, and take pride in it.

During the last two years though, trying to live that elusive normal life, I started to think perhaps I had been brainwashed all this time. I felt that side of me drain like an open wound and that scared me, because to lose my slayer instincts meant facing the fact there was something seriously wrong with me, the fact that I enjoyed killing vampires so much, even though it's what I have been trained to do.

I keep smiling to my reflection, then bare my teeth, checking to see that they look clean and white. I decide to add a little more eyeliner to my face. He might not recognize me as a witch, but if I'm to get closer to him I need to up my beauty game. I'm sure most students at the conservatory aren't wearing a full face of makeup to class, but I have to stand out in some way.

I add some blush to my cheeks, ever so pale, and wish my foundation could have covered up my freckles. The eyeliner is a dark bronze that brings out the green in my eyes and I run my fingers through my hair, separating the loose curls. I'll never be a sexy bombshell, I'll always have this look about me that belongs in old paintings and statues—a chin too strong, a Roman nose—but I know I have what it takes to bring a man to his knees if I must. If Dracula is anything like his counterparts, he'll pick up on the fact that I'm easy prey and he'll be the one compelling me, not the other way around.

Satisfied with my appearance, I take in a deep breath and grab my backpack, slinging it over my shoulder. With my Birks, wide-leg jeans, and blousy green top, I think I look the part of being a student.

I head out of my tiny apartment, locking it behind me, and head down the narrow winding staircase and out of the building, the soles of my sandals echoing on the tile. The guild found this place for me, in the Cannaregio district, the north section of the city. The building is a little run down and very basic, but it fits the profile of what a music student would be able to afford in this city.

I bring out the map in my phone and plot course for the coffee house that I'm meeting Livia at. I'm the type that doesn't like directions and usually just uses instinct to find my way, but Venice is a strange beast. I've been here for two days and I've gotten lost every time I've gone for a walk. Alleyways and streets converge and circle, leading to dead ends of buildings and canals. Even when you swear you've been down a street before, it ends up being another street and you're in the opposite direction you hoped to go in. There's a vibe here, an energy that is dark and light and mercurial.

The sun is just starting to peek over the buildings now and though the streets are sleepy, the canals are alive with motors, boats heading every which way. Every now and then I get a glimpse of the Grand Canal between the buildings and see boats loaded with fish or vegetables, bringing their wares to the shops, markets and restaurants, and of course the ever-present vaporettos coasting through the water.

I'd never been to Venice before, so I'm still getting used to the fact that I'm in such an infamous city. It feels a little like a dream and if I wasn't so worried about my glamor or the mission, I'd be able to enjoy it a lot more. As far as I know, I'll be masquerading as a student at the Benedetto Marcello Conservatory of Music until my job is done, so I might not even have enough time to properly enjoy being here before I have to go. Get in and get out is the essence of the job.

The coffee shop is tiny, with a few tables and chairs crammed between the shop and a canal. I spot Livia sitting down outside with a macchiato and she waves me over.

"I hardly recognized you," she says as she gets up, grabbing me lightly by the shoulders and giving me a kiss on each cheek.

"So it works?" I ask, feeling anxious.

She looks me over again and nods.

"It works," she says, sounding impressed. "Sit, have a coffee. I can get you an espresso? What would you like?"

"The biggest coffee they have," I tell her, taking a seat.

She gives me a wry look, her brow quirking up. "You Americans never learn, do you."

"Hey, at least I know I can't take it to go."

That's something that will take some getting used to. I drink coffee like a fish and I'm so used to grabbing a Starbucks and nursing it for a good hour. To-go coffee is relatively unheard of in Italy, and most drinks, even lattes, fit in a teacup. You slam back your coffee and then you go on with your day, which is insane to me.

Livia comes back with the coffee, carrying the cup and saucer with ease.

"Grazie," I tell her, carefully taking it from her.

"Prego," she says, sitting down. Livia's background is Lebanese but she's part of the Italian guild of witches having lived in Italy for most of her life, and though I've only met her once, I really like her—and that's coming from someone who starts off disliking people as a default. She's probably in her late thirties, with long dark hair and lush eyelashes and has this graceful way about her that I know comes from a deep understanding of witchcraft. When you really become immersed in it, wizened like a mage, you start to become one with the earth and all the realms above and below—or so they say. My craft has primarily been about killing. I'm good with a blade, I know how to attack, but any of that etherealness and grace I seem to sorely lack.

I take a sip of my espresso, eyes widening at the strength of it. I quickly plop in a sugar cube to mellow it.

Livia chuckles at my reaction, then her expression turns serious. "How are you feeling?"

"A bit jet-lagged still," I tell her. "But I'll be okay."

"And with the magic? How are you feeling with the glamor on?"

I think about that for a moment, taking stock of my body.

"It feels a little effervescent. Like I have tiny champagne bubbles dancing on my skin."

"But this isn't the first time you've used glamor to hide yourself, is it?"

I shake my head and have another sip, the espresso already cooled and slightly sweet. "No. It just feels different this time."

I don't want to tell her about the last time I used glamor to disguise the fact that I was a witch from a vampire. To talk about that would be to talk about the very reason I was kicked out of the guild for two years. Why this is my one and only shot to make my way back in.

"Well, it's working," she says. Her dark eyes narrow, looking over me with scrutiny now. "You seem like a normal human, a student. And your power is strong, I'll give you that." She pauses. "But I do worry a little. How long will you be able to keep it up without it waning?"

"Long enough to do the job."

"But your job is going to take you a lot longer than you originally thought."

I sit up straighter and frown. "How do you know? I'm to get close enough to Dracula to kill him somewhere private. That shouldn't take more than a few days, a week? Maybe a couple of weeks if it's hard to get him alone."

"Bellamy rang me last night," she says gravely. "You can—and should—call him to hear for yourself. But Dracula, Professor Aminoff, he's now just part of a much bigger picture. A much more deadly picture. In the last couple of days, the vampires Saara and Aleksi have taken up shop here in Venice. Where, I don't know. And they reportedly have a book that they recently stole from Lisbeth, a witch from Wales. The book went missing after Lisbeth was found dead."

"She was found dead? Did they kill her?" I don't know Lisbeth—I don't know most witches to be honest—but the death of a fellow witch is a hard pill to swallow. There are only so many of us left.

"Saara and Aleksi did," she says, her tone sharp. "Professor Aminoff has an alibi, he was here. And it's possible he had nothing to do with it. But we won't know that until you get close. What Bellamy wants you to focus on now is using the professor to get close to Saara and Aleksi. Find out where they are staying. Find the book. Then kill them all."

I blink, trying to take the new information in. In my job, being adaptable is an asset but this new plan is throwing me off. "I'm going to need more time to process this," I admit, hoping I don't sound weak. The last thing I need is for her to report me to Bellamy and pull me from the mission.

"It shouldn't change anything," she says. "You'll just be at the school for longer. You'll need your glamor for longer. When you feel it weakening, take your time to do another spell. You'll want it strong enough to not only pass Dracula's inspection, but Saara and Aleksi too. And anyone else. Who knows how many vampires truly live in this city. Sometimes it feels like hundreds."

I swallow the rest of my coffee, the caffeine mixing with the adrenaline. "What's so special about the book?"

"It's a spell book."

"So? I know plenty of vampires who have their hands on one." There's one in particular, Absolon Stavig of San Francisco, who has a whole library of them, but he is a little different from the rest of the vampires. He's not loyal to his kind, or really anyone except himself, and he does a lot of deals with witches. As far as I know, the magic he gets from the books doesn't really leave the house he lives in.

"This isn't an ordinary spell book," she says, her eyes looking grim. "It can open portals to other worlds."

Okay. Now she has my attention.

"I'm sorry...*portals*?"

Livia nods. "The witch was in charge of it for safekeeping, so really no one should have been able to find it. But perhaps curiosity got the better of her. Either way, Saara and Aleksi learned about the book, journeyed there, killed her, and took it. Now they have the ability to open portals themselves."

The skin on my scalp prickles uneasily. "And do what with them?"

Livia gives a slow shrug, looking around her as a flock of pigeons land nearby. "I don't know. Bellamy fears they may be opening a portal to the Red World, where their king resided."

"But Skarde is dead."

"He is. But there may be other vampires or creatures that live in that realm that they can pull out." She pauses, shifting uneasily in her seat before she fixes her eyes on me. "Even monsters."

Suddenly the flock of pigeons take to the air, as if hearing her. They probably did.

"Why?" I whisper.

"I don't know," she says. Then she gets to her feet and smooths out her sundress. "But your job is to find out. I will help you in whatever way I can as your guide and fellow witch on the ground, but this is your mission, Dahlia. Bellamy entrusted you with it."

I open my mouth to protest. To tell her that originally my mission was just to come to Venice, enroll in the music school, get close to Dracula, who happened to be a professor there, then kill him. He was a vampire who had killed many over the years and the job of a slayer is to seek out the vampires that kill humans and deliver them justice. After a job well done, I would go back to the Pacific Northwest and resume life in the guild again as a slayer.

But now I have three targets, not one, I have to get close to my professor in order to access the other two, and then there's this magic book that opens portals to vampire worlds that I have to find, then kill all the vampires, and then bring the book back to Bellamy.

I didn't sign up for this.

Yet you did, the voice inside my head says. *You signed up for this when you were thirteen years old, the moment Bellamy became your guardian and you pledged to avenge your parents.*

"You're going to do great," Livia tells me, tapping the table. "Trust me. Just give me a text when you're done with school and keep me updated, okay?"

I nod then yell, "Thank you for the coffee!" as she walks away. She gives me a little wave with her hands and then disappears down an alleyway.

I sigh and spend a few moments sitting in the chair, watching a few boats go past down the narrow canal, listen to the melodic sounds of spoken Italian fill the air. The longer I sit here, the safer I am. The longer I sit here, the less I have to pretend.

I can sit here all day, just avoiding my job. I don't even have to do this job, I can back out, tell Bellamy that this wasn't what we had agreed upon. But part of me knows that this is a test. It's possible that he knew all of this for a while and wanted to spring it on me at the last minute, when I was already here.

He may have been my guardian growing up, but I didn't trust Bellamy most of the time. There was always some lesson for me, some ulterior motive.

A pigeon suddenly lands on the end of the chair across from me and tilts its head.

"Hey," I whisper to it, taking some of the sugar and sprinkling it on the table. "You can have this if you do me a favor."

The pigeon tilts its head again and then jumps onto the table with clean pink feet.

What's the favor? It seems to ask me.

"Just watch over me," I tell it. "I think I'm in over my head."

The pigeon seems to think that over then it takes a grain of sugar before flying away. Hmmphf. No answer.

I take that as a sign to get going. In all my life I have never backed away from a fight. I've always done what was expected of me. This is no exception.

CHAPTER 3

DAHLIA

I BRING out my phone and get out of my seat, using the GPS to find my way to the conservatory. Once I get to Ponte de la Cortesia, tourists already crowding the pretty bridge, it's a straight shot to the school.

The Benedetto Marcello Conservatory of Music is located in two buildings a stone's throw away from the Grand Canal. They blend in with the rest of Venice in the way that it's both elegant and ubiquitous, the type of buildings that seem a fitting home for musicians. I already received my welcome package online, so I enter the school with confidence, only briefly checking a map on the wall before heading off to my first class of the day.

Inside, the school is opulent and grand, with soaring ceilings and ornately carved moldings. There are also a few modern touches, like large display screens in the hallways, and a garden area nestled in between two of the buildings, as well as inner courtyards that I've seen decorated with fairy lights during concerts on YouTube where guest musicians or students play. The floors that surround the courtyards are open to the air, supported by pillars, giving the school the feeling of being in a grand palace.

I eventually find the classroom, passing by the entrance to the library on the way. If I had more time I would duck my head in—the library is one of the most important in all of Italy, with over fifty thousand books as well as important historical artifacts, and it seems the perfect place to hide a stolen book of magic, especially if the professor is involved.

Instead, I go and wait outside the classroom, watching as students go in, pretending to check my phone. Some are in pairs, but most don't seem to know each other. They all look at me but not in an odd way, more in wondering if I'll be joining their class, which is a relief because it means I'm not standing out.

I take in a deep breath, watching the time count down on my phone. I don't want to be too early, but I don't want to waltz in late either. I have to do everything just right, to snag his interest without tipping him off that I'm doing it on purpose.

With two minutes before class starts, I walk in.

This is my music history class. I have a few academic classes while the rest are practical, and Professor Aminoff happens to be my teacher for both this one and the practical. That wasn't an accident of course. Even though this is my last chance according to the guild, I think the reason they picked me (they probably felt they *had* to pick me) wasn't because of their generous nature in giving me a second chance, but because I was probably the only slayer who had musical experience and talent, particularly when it comes to the keys, which is Dracula's speciality.

I immediately scan the room for the right seat, though I don't have many options with only two left by the front. I glance quickly at the professor, just to make sure he's there, and in that quick glance I feel like I've gotten the wind knocked out of me. Which is weird, since vampires usually leave me with an angry, disgusted feeling bordering on primal rage. It doesn't matter how compelling, how sexual, how otherworldly they are, I see past all of that and am only struck by how depraved, feral, and horrific they are. I see them for what they really are: immoral, monstrous killers.

And staring at Professor Valtu Aminoff, the one who inspired Dracula, I see him for what he really is while he takes my fucking breath away.

He's leaning over his desk, staring down at something on it—maybe his phone, maybe the curriculum, but I have no doubt that his attention is on every person that walks in his class, even if he doesn't look like it. For better or worse, my attention is surely on him.

I've seen his picture before so I knew what to expect: a tall, well-built man with dark hair and strong features suited to another century. But seeing him in person is something else entirely.

To start, yes he's tall and well-built but he's more than that. He's wearing dark charcoal jeans and a white dress shirt that shows a hint of his chest, the sleeves pushed up to his elbows in a haphazard way that makes him look like he got dressed in a hurry. His forearms aren't as pale as most vampires, as if he was born with a slightly golden sheen to him. From the way he's leaning on the desk, the veins and muscles on his forearm pop, showcasing the supernatural strength that he would naturally have.

His shoulders are broad, curving into his shirt, chest wide, biceps taking up the bulk of his sleeves, and I'd have to place him at six-foot-two. Despite his height and how well-muscled he is, he's not bulky. He's still quite lean with a lot of length in his limbs, a strange sort of elegance that might be the result of him being a vampire or it might just be him.

Then there is his face. A thick head of black hair, wavy,

that falls long, almost past his chin, the kind of hair you want to run your fingers through. His brows are low, naturally arched and dark, harboring deep-set brown eyes, framed by long lashes. Nose is aquiline, like mine, but suits him so much better, mouth wide, lips full, a strong chin. He's clean shaven but I can tell he'll have a five o'clock shadow by the time the day is done.

To every student walking in the class, no matter their gender, they would be enthralled by this man. I am sure his nickname here is Professor Hottie, or Professore Bello or something. But they would all chalk up their attraction to him on the fact that when you put all his pieces together, he ends up being an extremely attractive, sexually magnetic, charismatic human being. Who wouldn't look? But if they could see below the surface, see the life experiences of a 300 year old, plus being the world's deadliest predator, and having the gift of the supernatural at their whim, they would understand why Professor Aminoff has such a pull on them.

I mean, he's having a pull on me and I know exactly what I'm dealing with. And I realize this too late, because as I'm about to take my seat, as I'm about to avert my eyes, he looks up at me directly and his eyes meet mine.

In that second I am defenseless, pinned in place, and it's only when he looks back down at his desk that I feel I can breathe again. He had me there. He really had me for that one second and I couldn't do a damn thing about it. I stared directly into his dark eyes and I felt like giving everything up for him, I wanted to lie down on his desk, expose my neck, and offer myself to him.

In that second, I was no longer a witch with magic at her disposal. No longer the slayer I was trained to be. No longer the hunter. I was the hunted and I was his prey and I was *happy* about it.

But then all sense came back to me, followed by panic. He

didn't see past my glamor, did he? Does he know that I'm a witch, does he know who I truly am?

How the fuck am I going to do my job when he has me wanting to bend over for him the very first time we make eye contact?

I swallow those thoughts down and try my best to disappear into my role. Luckily if he's paying attention to me, which I am sure he is, I could easily chalk up my fast heart rate and flushed cheeks to being nervous on my first day of school.

I take out the history textbook and my notebook and pencil from my bag (I take notes better by hand than laptop) and stare at him while waiting for the class to start, like every student seems to be.

"Ah," he says, standing up straight and glancing over his shoulder at the clock on the wall. "I guess we shall begin our class then. My name is Professor Valtu Aminoff, but please call me Valtu." He says this in Italian, his accent fluent. I have no doubt he can speak countless languages fluently. While I learned German and French growing up and in university, it takes a spell or two to really master another language. As a result, I learned Italian quickly but writing it can be hard for me, and I definitely don't sound Italian when I speak. He, on the other hand, looks and sounds as if he was born in Venice. Perhaps he was. The history books of the witches have Dracula born in Russia, but they might be wrong.

The thought of Russia slams a memory into my head, one of me on the ground, looking up at a man speaking to me in Russian. But I realize this isn't a memory at all but a fragment from a dream, from the nightmare I had last night. In all those dreams I could never understand the language spoken, but suddenly now I do.

Why was I dreaming in Russian?

"Now I know you are all students of music," he goes on,

his deep, slightly melodic voice bringing my attention back to him, "and you probably don't give a rat's ass about history. You know your stuff, so you say. You can tell me all about Mozart, right? You know Verdi, of course you do, this is Italy. But what about Mendelssohn? Do you know that he was subjected to anti-semitism, brought on by Wagner who was actually jealous of his success? How about Barber, who composed Sadness, a 23-bar piece in C minor at the age of *seven*." He pauses, a crooked smile on his lips, as if smiling to himself. I swear I hear the internal swooning of the girl in the seat beside me. "I know you are all here because you want to perfect your skills, whether in strings, percussion, keys, whatever it is. You are musicians ascending to the next level. But in order to really play music, you have to understand where it comes from. There's no way around it."

And with that speech, Professor Aminoff launches into what we will be learning over the semester, and I do my best to listen and take notes, like a normal student would do. Only my notes are written down as if I'm on autopilot, because what I'm really doing is trying to understand him. What excites this vampire? What is he passionate about? How will I stand out in this classroom amongst other students who are far prettier or handsomer? How will I endear him to me, enough to get him alone, to infiltrate his life so I can do the job I was sent here to do?

"And *you*," Valtu's voice penetrates my thoughts and I realize he's turned his attention to me. In fact, I'm only now cluing in that he's been asking everyone in the class to divulge a little bit about themselves.

Everyone's eyes are on me and Valtu gives me a slight smirk, his dark eyes glimmering like he knows he's caught me not paying attention (the irony, when he's all I've been thinking about).

"And what about me?" I say to him, looking him dead in the eyes.

He holds my gaze, his right brow arching slightly. "If you care to follow suit and introduce yourself to the class."

"As if we are in kindergarten?" I ask, then look around at my classmates who are staring at me, some smiling at what I said, a few looking far-too serious. "All right then. My name is Dahlia Abernathy. I was born in Victoria, British Columbia, Canada. My musical instrument of choice is the organ."

"Ah," the professor muses and I bring my attention back to him. He's in front of the desk now, leaning against it with practiced ease, arms folded across his chest. A lock of his dark hair falls across his forehead, giving him the brooding, wild look of Heathcliff wandering the moors, or so I've imagined. "One of the four organists I am teaching this year. You're a dying breed. You'll have to tell me why you took up the instrument."

I straighten my shoulders, belied by some inner confidence that slides upon me like stage makeup when I'm playing a role. "I'd rather show you why," I tell him.

He tilts his head, as if taken aback, staring at me like I've totally thrown him off course. "Very well," he says, then clears his throat, moving onto the next student.

I don't know what I'm doing. I'm trying to endear myself to him, not challenge him and piss him off. I've had easier times playing nice with vampires in the past—many of my kills started because I appealed to them in one way or another. I can only hope that the one they call Dracula finds it alluring that I'm not fawning all over him.

But only time will tell.

CHAPTER 4

VALTU

THE WHORE GETS DOWN on her knees, staring up at me with big eyes, which would be alluring if she didn't have one false eyelash hanging off, making her look like she'd just had a stroke.

"Want me to suck it?" she asks sweetly.

I bristle with impatience. "Is there some other reason you're on your knees, dollface?"

She gives me a lazy grin. She's trying to come across as sly, but I know the look of drugs intimately. While drugs barely do anything for me, the majority of the humans that frequent the Red Room are on them. I suppose that as much as they put on this bravado that they're edgy, boundary-pushing, open-minded, brave, whatever the fuck they call themselves, the most nihilistic of humans quiver in the presence of vampires. They want to give up their blood, they want to be compelled, they want to be used by us, but in order to get through any of it, they have to be as a high as a fucking kite.

It shouldn't bother me. It's no different from the opium dens we used to run at the turn of the last century. And yet here I am, sitting naked on my throne with some lazy-eyed chick eyeing my dick like it's candy. Can't say I blame her—it's hard not to be turned on with all the sex and feeding going on around us—yet I hate to think I might be bored. We vampires avoid boredom like the plague.

"I'll do anything you want," she says, coming forward between my legs and pressing her hands against my thighs. Despite my better judgment, my cock twitches in anticipation.

"Anything?" I ask, my voice careful not to get too cynical.

"Anything," she repeats, looking up at me with her big brown eyes. She lets go of my thighs and reaches for my cock, bending forward and sucking the head in her mouth like a lollipop. I shiver and reach down to undo the braids in her hair. She reaches for my knees with her hands, bracing herself, ready for me to pin her down. But I don't. I let her run her hand up my inner thigh, suck on my cock, and play with herself.

"Every time I get on my knees for you, you take my breath away," she says, looking up at me with those big brown eyes and such a dreamy expression on her face, drugged as hell. It's hard to believe that a woman who looks this good could be found in this place, but humans still surprise me sometimes. The way they think they're at our level but in the end they're just slumming it.

"Enough with the platitudes, dollface," I tell her. "Be a good little whore and get me off."

Her cheeks go pink at that and I know she likes the degradation kink. Good, because I've a lot of that to dish out. "Then I want your ass up here." I press my hand into my chest. "And you're going to get me off again."

She nods, not questioning. "Anything you say, Count Dracula."

Not just Dracula, but *Count* Dracula. I like that title. But it's not my favorite. "In here I am your dark lord and you will address me as such," I tell her.

"Yes, my dark lord," she says.

I can't help but let out a laugh. "How about just *my lord?*"

"Yes, my lord."

I smirk and lean back in the chair, letting her continue to suck on my cock. She takes me deep into her mouth, her lips sliding up and down my shaft, her tongue swirling around the head. I groan and reach down to run my fingers through her hair again, guiding her movements as she sucks me off.

"That's it," I murmur. "Take my cock deep into your throat. I want you to choke on it."

She moans and does as I say, taking me deep and gagging on my dick as she goes. I grit my teeth and thrust my hips forward, fucking her mouth slowly, wanting to savor every second of her talented mouth.

"Mmm, that's good," I growl, my fingers tightening in her hair as she sucks harder. "I love how you take my cock, such a good little whore."

I keep fucking her mouth, groaning as she sucks me off, deeper and harder with every thrust. I can feel my balls tightening and my release getting closer, and I grit my teeth against the rush.

"Just like that," I growl, slamming my cock deep into her throat as I come, groaning as she swallows every drop of my hot cum.

She continues to suck me off, milking my cock until I'm completely spent, and then I reach down and pull her up to my lap. She makes a motion to kiss me but I move my head away. I like the taste of myself, but I'm not about to kiss a human on the mouth.

"Turn around," I tell her. "Take me in your mouth again while I feed from your ass."

Her eyes widen for a moment and there's a glint of clarity

before it fades away. I can hear her pulse, her heart beating faster now, and the air spikes with a tinge of adrenaline. She's afraid. Even the drugs can't bury that feeling. The smell of her fear makes me so fucking wild.

She swallows. "Whatever you wish," she says, and there's a waver to her voice.

I decide to cut her some slack. "If you don't wish for me to feed from you, I will pick someone else," I tell her. "Regardless, I will have someone watch over me to make sure I don't lose control."

She looks around the expansive room draped in red velvet and black leather. In this hidden world, accessed only by a door in a school library, she's very much alone. Everyone is fucking. Humans with humans, humans with vampires, vampires with vampires. Some vampires are feeding, blood freely flowing into their mouths, watched over carefully by the few vampires that are on duty tonight, their job to make sure that others, like me, don't end up killing the humans by accident. The old days are no more and human life is to be preserved at all costs, even if not every vampire agrees with that.

I make a motion for Bitrus, who happens to be my dearest friend, to come over to me. He's just finished fucking a human and looks sated and amiable enough to volunteer.

"Bitrus," I tell him. "Can you watch?"

He nods, wiping his lips as he saunters on over, his dark skin gleaming with crimson highlights under the red lights.

"And do you still want me to feed from you?" I say to the girl, feeling the power of my teeth as they yearn to sharpen into fangs, my hunger building. "It's your choice."

She takes a deep breath, and then she nods. "Yes, take me. Feed from me."

Then she straddles me. I slide down against the chair so that her ass is in my face, her head at my cock again, a 69.

I grin, savoring the moment. My blood is strong, my power undeniable, and I can feel my fangs pressing against my tongue. She's mine.

With her ass in my face, I spread her cheeks, every hidden part of her pink and wet and waiting. I press my thumb into her cunt, watching as her back arches and she lets out a low moan.

"Get to it," Bitrus says to her, baring his teeth in a threatening manner.

It works. She obeys and takes my cock in her mouth. I bring my thumb up from her cunt to her ass and push it inside. She tightens around my thumb and I know all the blood is coming toward me.

While she sucks at my dick again, I lean forward enough to sink my fangs into the soft flesh of her ass. I groan as the blood rushes into my mouth, her taste and scent and power enveloping me. There is so much I can know about this girl by tasting her, so much that she doesn't even know herself. The blood is a record of history, her history. All that she's eaten, seen, done, lived—and I can feel it all flow through me as if I'm living it too, albeit in a superficial way, like watching something on TV. I know for a fact that this is the most excitement she's ever had.

She moans as I suck at her, then the noises turn into a gasp, a whimper, as my teeth are tearing through her flesh and drawing her blood into my mouth. I bring her pain, there's no way around it, but at least the pain is mixed with pleasure.

I work my thumb into her ass, my fingers sliding through her cunt and scissoring her. The blood is rushing into my mouth and down my throat, a rush of sensation, a burning desire for more. More blood, more flesh, more girl. I want to make her come; the blood tastes so much sweeter that way.

Bitrus meets my eyes. He's standing by her head, watching my cock pump inside of her mouth. He's naked, though not quite hard, his focus is on me and making sure I don't get carried away. After decades of friendship, he knows me enough to pick up on the signs and always stops me before I become too uncontrollable. I don't like to lose control at any rate, it's beneath me, so when he starts to edge toward me, his look turning to a warning, I know that my feeding time is close to finishing.

Speaking of finishing, the whore is coming now. I can taste it as I suck on her, the surge of flavor in her blood as she comes undone. My thumb is buried in her ass, my fingers knuckle deep inside of her cunt, and I feel her spasms around me. I pull out and slide back into her wetness, fucking her a few more times, and then I'm pumping her harder now, my hips meeting her face, my cock plunging deep into her throat. I feel myself start to get close, the pleasure building in my loins, my balls tightening up.

Bitrus dips his chin toward me, which means I'm being savage with my bite and hurting her, her orgasm mixing with her cries of pain as the warm blood spills over her skin and down my chin.

I nod and with a growl I come, filling the girl's mouth, while Bitrus goes beside me with a thick metal chain in hand. We use a lot of ropes and leather straps in here—bondage is my speciality—but the chains are reserved for unruly vampires. I could snap a leather strap with just the flick of my wrist, but the chains mean business.

Bitrus brandishes it between his hands, the silver chains glinting red, his way of telling me that he's going to tie me down and get the others to help if I don't stop feeding. He doesn't have to tell me though, the girl has already collapsed on me in a pool of her own blood that has gathered on my chest and stomach. She's barely breathing and I don't think it's because I made her come to high heavens.

With a deeper roar that comes from the bottom of my

chest, I close my eyes and unhook my fangs. The air in the room feels so cold against them compared to the warmth of her blood and flesh.

Bitrus reaches over and picks the girl off me like she weighs nothing.

I want to ask if she'll be alright, but I don't have the ability to speak words at the moment, only communicate through sounds. I watch as he takes her over to the baths at the corner of the room where two female volunteers take her. They'll wash off her blood, clean her up, and on rare occasions they can give blood if too much was taken. We keep a blood bank for emergencies, if a vampire needs to feed and can't find anyone, but we all prefer fresh blood, so sometimes we use our stores on humans who have been too depleted.

Bitrus comes back over to me. "You're in a mood," he mutters.

I slowly straighten up in the throne, staring down at all the blood on my body. I raise my hand to my mouth and lick the remainder off. It's already losing vitality.

"I'm fine," I tell him.

"You're unsettled," he comments.

He picked up that word from my mind without me even realizing it. "What's unsettling is you accessing my thoughts," I admit carefully. Vampires often have the ability to pick up on each other's thoughts, if not emotions, but I have learned over the centuries to put walls and guards up to shield myself from intrusion. The only problem is that the walls tend to falter when I'm around people I trust.

"I take it you don't want to discuss it here?" he asks, lowering his voice. Normally there would be no point to acting secretive since my brethren have a supernatural sense of hearing but right now, with all the moaning and groaning and sounds of skin slapping and fucking that's happening in this room, no one is paying us any attention.

"Another time. Drinks at my place soon," I tell him, getting to my feet. "I have to get to class."

He smirks at that. "It's a dangerous habit, *Professor*," he says, mocking my title. "Feeding before class..."

"Means I'm better at my job," I tell him with a wink.

I walk across the room past the writhing bodies to the private bathroom at the back, the dark hallway flanked by two vampire guards. I nod at one of them, Dessoude, who was my personal bodyguard when I was going through a period of upheaval after I was involved with the death of the king and father of all vampires, Skarde. I had become a wanted man, an enemy for too many, all of whom lurked in the dark with veiled threats.

But some time has passed and it turns out the vampire world was grateful that Skarde had fallen. He was too powerful and too linked to our past, when all vampires want to do is keep moving forward into the future. For many of us, the past can be a tomb.

I step into the bathroom and take a shower, washing the blood off, going over every inch of my body with scented soap. Even though humans' sense of smell isn't as good as ours, I take no chances. When I step into my professor role at the conservatory, I step into the role of a man, a human, and keep my vampire nature behind a mask.

Which might be one reason why I'm feeling unsettled. It started a couple of weeks ago, just this buzzy undercurrent that seems to be flowing through the murky canals of this fair city. I can't quite put my finger on it, it's just a feeling that there's a change in the air, and that something is coming or is already here, hiding in the shadows. And considering *I'm* what's hiding in the shadows, that makes it rather disconcerting.

I rub my hands over my head, hoping to eradicate the feeling of tension, but it's there. The fresh blood from that girl should have put a spring in my step, dissolved my headache, but it hasn't. I turn off the water and step out of the shower. I dry off and dress quickly in black jeans and a black dress shirt. I push my dark hair back, a scruffy five o'clock shadow on my face, then take a hard look at myself. I should look the same as I always have, ever since that terrible day when I changed at thirty-five. Even my hair is the same as it was. And yet, even though I don't have any grays, or any new lines, there's age in my eyes. I look into my eyes and I see the eyes of an old man who has done too much and seen too much and who, deep down, just needs some fucking rest, a deep and uneventful sleep, but can't stand to admit it to himself. A man who is also a monster, and that monster is losing its edge.

I stare at myself, wondering what it must feel like to be human and see the rest of your face change over the years. Or is the change so gradual that it feels a lot like this? Is their face always familiar to them no matter who they become or how many years have passed? Do they look at old photos and think of the past them as another person entirely? I try not to have many photographs of myself around, but I wonder if film had existed in the 1700s if I'd see myself as someone else.

I inhale deeply and shake out my shoulders. No point brooding over this when I've got a job to do.

I have class with the organists next. Aside from my history of music class, I'm teaching only two practical classes this semester. One is piano, which is jam-packed full of students, as always. And the other is the organ. Last year we didn't have any organists for either semester, so the fact that there are four this year is like a surprise.

The biggest surprise is one of the organists herself.

I'm not usually one to be all that taken with humans. I have learned in the past that they only bring you tragedy and heartache. They're only good for fucking and feeding, if

44

I wanted some sort of companionship or relationship I would look to a vampire. But the truth is, in all these years, neither companionship nor a relationship have appealed to me. It's too much complication in an already complicated life.

But while all that stands, there is something about the organist in my class that has me looking twice. She's not the most beautiful woman in the world by conventional beauty standards. She has a strong chin and nose, eyes on the smaller side. But there's something about her that stirs something inside me. A hunger, of course, it's hard to look at an attractive woman and not want to taste their blood. Same goes for wanting to fuck them. But there was something else about her that had me on my toes. I felt like I knew her from somewhere before, or had at least seen her. With her ancient features, pale skin, scattering of freckles, and long red hair, I feel like she could have been anyone I've crossed paths with and yet I can't bring up anyone specific. It's just a feeling in my gut that she's someone I need to keep an eye on, for better or worse.

Just then the air fills with the scent of jasmine and my hackles raise.

"Valtu," Saara says as she steps into the bathroom. "I thought I smelled you."

Her reflection comes behind me in the mirror. Saara is a vampire, all long limbs, honey-colored hair, built like a Russian supermodel turned influencer. She and her brother Aleksi have a stronghold over the vampires of Venice. Actually, it goes beyond just vampires at this point. They have influence over all the lawmakers, businessmen and socialites as well. They have lived here for a long time, though they moved elsewhere for a while and recently came back. Regardless, this fabled city is in the palm of their hands.

But they aren't in the palm of mine.

"I was just leaving," I tell her, turning around and she's just inches away, smiling through red shiny lip gloss.

"Where are you going at two in the afternoon?" she asks, her blue eyes sharp. "To teach a class? When are you going to give up this charade, Professor Aminoff?"

"And what might this charade be, hmmm?" I ask, folding my arms across my chest. "I am a professor. Qualified by numerous universities. I get paid an acceptable wage. My students graduate and go on to do either wonderous or mundane things, but they do earn a degree that I, in part, taught them. There is no charade with me."

She rolls her eyes and twists a long piece of amber hair between her fingers. "The charade that you're a human."

"No different than your charade," I tell her.

The corner of her lip curls into a snarl, making her look most ugly. "It's very different, Valtu. I don't pretend to be anything I'm not. You're getting paid to be a teacher when you don't need the money. It's gross."

Saara knows that all the money I make from my job, even though it's not much by old-money standards, is donated to various charities.

"Then perhaps I'm doing it for kicks," I tell her. "Impressionable young men and women walking through my doors every day. Blood can't get any fresher than that."

She lets out an acidic laugh. "If I didn't know you, I'd believe you. And to think they call you Dracula."

I raise my hands in protest. "I didn't ask for the title. I can't help if Mr. Stoker was besotted with me."

"You think the whole world is besotted with you, Valtu."

I shrug. "And it's not my fault if it's true." I flash her a mirthless smile. "Now, if you're done badgering me, I need to be off."

I move past her and she doesn't move out of the way, causing my shoulder to brush against hers. For a moment I see her for who she really is. Not some leggy Slavic model, but something made of bones, crepey skin, and red eyes.

A monster.

All vampires are monsters, but some are...extra special. Some have been created by Skarde himself. Not through breeding with humans, which has resulted in ninety-nine percent of the current vampire population, but by the "old-fashioned" way—bringing them close to death, then bringing them back to life with vampire blood. The only problem with creating vampires that way is that they turn into raging monsters, debased to primal animals with insatiable blood-lust. It's against vampiric code to create any this way, but that didn't stop Skarde. He was above the law until the moment of his death.

Some, over the centuries, learned to control their hunger and rage, suppressing their monstrous forms until they were hidden under the human skin. But sometimes the creature is hard to hide.

I look back over my shoulder at Saara to see her baring her fangs at me before her teeth slide back to normal. "Have a good day, Professor," she says to me, a sly gleam in her eyes.

She knows what I saw, what I felt back there.

And she likes that I saw it.

The truth.

That she's a daughter of Skarde.

This is going to make things complicated for me, isn't it? Considering most of the vampire world believes I played some role in his death.

I quickly leave the washroom, hurry through the club, and then out through the main door at the top of the spiral stair-case until I'm stepping into a small, narrow hallway. There are no lights in here, on purpose, but I can see in the dark. Once the door to the Red Room shuts, I walk to the door in front of me and push it open.

I'm met with fluorescent lighting. One of the most impressive libraries in Italy, and the books are still treated with the horrid aesthetic of fluorescent light. Luckily the lights are dim where I am, but even so it's enough to make me wince.

My eyes adjust and I make my way from the back of the library through the aisles, passing the section that is set aside as a museum, with rare books, music sheets, and musical artifacts under display, then past the stacks that have eager beaver students already flipping through books to study.

No matter what Saara says, or how it looks to the rest of the vampires, I really do love working here. I've always flitted from place to place throughout my life, and while I'm not setting down roots here in Venice, it does give me a sense of purpose to be a teacher, a way to pass on all that I have learned over the centuries. It makes me feel relatively normal, even though I'm not.

And most importantly, because the Red Room is accessed through the library, I'm in charge of it. It doesn't matter what city I find myself settled in, I usually create a feeding club for vampires if there wasn't one before. I like to be the one who unites the vampires together. The reason Saara thinks everyone is besotted with me is because they are—I provide them with fresh human blood to drink, and fresh human bodies to fuck. Every vampire knows who Valtu is, even without the Dracula notoriety, because they need me. That's why I'm popular.

Well, perhaps not in my class. As I make my way through the storied halls of the grand school and down to the concert room, I'm already picturing the look of disdain on the one person that doesn't seem all that enthralled with me.

Dahlia.

And when I enter the concert room and see her on the stage, sitting at one of the pipe organs, her fingers and feet poised to play, I feel that animosity again. It surrounds her like this dark cloud that I don't know how to read.

"I assume you know well enough to not let your feet touch those pedals," I say loudly to her as I shut the door behind me and walk through the rows of chairs toward the stage.

She freezes, her red hair falling over her shoulder in such a way that it reminds me of a sunset hitting a waterfall. It does something to my gut, that feeling again of knowing her, coupled with a surge of adrenaline that seems to go straight to my dick.

Christ on a bike. You'd think I got it all out of my system.

"I know well enough," she says, twisting on the bench to face me. She's already wearing her own organ shoes, her slim Adidas sneakers resting beside the bench.

A throat is cleared and I realize that the three other students in our class are staring at me expectantly. I've completely ignored them so far, and unlike Dahlia, they're all sitting in the front row of the chairs like most students should be.

I gesture to the students and give Dahlia a steady look. "Well? Perhaps it would be best if you sat with your classmates instead of jumping right into things. As you can see, there are four students and only two organs."

She gives me a small smile but doesn't look reprimanded at all. She slowly takes off her organ shoes and puts her sneakers on, then walks off the stage, taking a seat beside the others.

I give my head a small shake and then paste a smile on my face when addressing the others. "Welcome to your first practical class."

I run over the curriculum with them. Unlike the history class, which students of all instruments attend, everything in this class is focused on having the best training on the pipe organ. Everyone here can play, but today it's a matter of finding out how well, and that in turn will affect things down the line, such as the winter recital and other small concerts they'll be involved in.

Then we proceed to the demonstrations. On the concert hall stage, beneath the molded ceilings and alfresco paintings, are two organs, one on each side of the stage. There are two grand pianos situated closer to the middle, as well as cello, a percussion set, and a few other instruments.

One by one the students take their place at the organ that Dahlia was originally sitting at, playing a piece of music.

The first student, Leo, an Italian boy who can't be any older than twenty, played a very lively and vibrant rendition of "A Whiter Shade of Pale." The next student, a bespeckled girl from Bristol in her thirties called Margaret, who I switched to English with since her Italian was so atrocious, played a noisy version of a Jehan Alain piece. A quiet and brooding-looking German boy named Johann played a surprisingly jolly piece of something he said he wrote himself.

And then finally, Dahlia slips her organist shoes back on and takes her seat on the bench.

She glances at me over her shoulder, waiting for my cue, and I'm momentarily distracted by the smoothness of her pale skin, a couple of freckles that appear under the thin strap of her burgundy camisole.

I clear my throat, bringing my eyes to meet her. "Go on then, Dahlia."

She nods, closing her eyes as her fingers pause in the air above the keys.

Then she starts to play.

Toccata and Fugue in D minor.

You have got to be kidding me.

It's arguably the most famous piece of organ music in the world, and most people don't know that it was Bach who wrote it. All they know is that this is Dracula's music. This is the music for vampires and haunted houses, and whatever version of me that Hollywood wants to throw at the world.

And here is Dahlia, playing it and playing it extremely well.

It's like she knows, I think to myself. But of course she doesn't. She can't. Humans will never believe in vampires unless the vampire explicitly shows themselves. After that, there is no turning back, but until then, the human mind won't allow it. They truly believe we are as made up as Santa Claus.

She's continuing to play the song too, which makes me realize she'll play the whole long damn thing unless I stop her. It's hard to, though, as I watch the skill in her fingers and feet, how effortless it is. She's almost as good as I am. Yet another thing for me to puzzle over.

"Thank you, Dahlia," I say loudly and she abruptly stops, giving me a loaded look over her shoulder, as if I'm being rude. "I'm afraid I have to cut you off or we'll be here all day."

She shifts around on the bench, her brows raised. "And what do you think?"

"About the song? It happens to be one of my favorites."

"One of your favorites?" The corner of her mouth lifts. "Well that's pretty cliché."

I frown, feeling my body go still. "Cliché?" I repeat.

Well, fuck. Maybe she does know the truth.

"Yeah," she says, her smile turning to a smirk. "As an organist."

I swallow. "Right."

As an organist.

Not a vampire.

An alarm chimes on Leo's phone, signaling end of class. It can be easy to lose track of time in here.

"Well then, that's the end of your first class. I'll see you all tomorrow."

Everyone gets up from their chairs and leaves the classroom and I am acutely aware that Dahlia is still sitting on the bench, not moving.

I give her a quick smile. "I know you probably want to play some more but I'm afraid another class is coming in here."

"Are students allowed to practice after class otherwise?" she asks me in English.

I make the switch. "Not without permission."

"From you?"

I nod, folding my arms across my chest. "Yes."

"Can I get your permission?" she asks, her voice taking on a sweet tone that causes a rush of blood to my cock. For a moment I see her in the Red Room, on all fours, asking for permission to come.

Bloody hell.

"Not today," I tell her, shifting my stance.

"Then another day?"

"We'll see," I say hoarsely gesturing with my chin to the door. "We better get a move on. I believe strings are up next and they can be a moody bunch when they don't get their way."

She breaks eye contact with me and I feel a strange sense of relief, like she had been looking too far inside me, past all my walls. She quickly slips on her sneakers and gets to her feet, sweeping her hair over her shoulder as she walks over to me, stopping a couple of feet away. I can smell her clearly, a meadow of wildflowers on a summer's day. The scent triggers a memory but it's too fast and fleeting to catch.

"Can I ask your permission for something else?" she asks, her eyes staring right into mine. I can't get a read on them.

There's a boldness there, a desire, and yet underneath it all I still get the feeling that she despises me.

It's confusing as hell.

"What?" I ask, my voice dropping.

"If I may take you out for a drink?"

I blink at her. She's serious? I laugh. "You're asking me out for a drink?"

She nods, her mouth in a firm line.

I give her a half-smile, unsure how to handle this. "I can't...I don't do that. Date students, that is."

"Who said it was a date?" she asks. Then she shrugs. "Okay. I'll see you tomorrow."

She hops off the stage and walks past the rows of the chairs to the doors, leaving just before students for the next class start walking in with their violins.

Did she just ask me out for a drink?

And I said no?

The violin students are giving me a funny look, so I get off the stage and make my way past them to the halls, trying to mull over what just happened.

I wasn't lying. It's in the rulebook that teachers can't have relationships or sexual encounters with their students. People do get fired for it and I wouldn't be an exception. The last thing I want is to lose my job here.

I'm just surprised that my first instinct was to turn her down.

I'm also surprised she asked me in the first place.

If it wasn't a date—and perhaps I was being a bit presumptuous there—then even her just wanting to be around me has me perplexed. I thought she didn't like me? In fact, I swear she still doesn't, which has me even more curious about her.

And that's a problem in itself.

Because curiosity almost always gets me in trouble.

CHAPTER 5

DAHLIA

"Ciao bella," Livia says to me as she gets out of her chair to give me a kiss on each cheek. "You look beautiful."

"Glamor still holding up?" I ask, patting my head as if I have an invisible shield over me, which I suppose I do, in some ways.

"You tell me," she says, gesturing for me to sit.

It's Friday afternoon, a few days after our meeting here for coffee. I tried not to be a nervous wreck all week, and if I was, I tried to play it off as if I was just nervous about my first week of school. It was hard not to worry that at any moment my glamor might slip and that Professor Aminoff would see me for the witch that I am.

"So far so good," I tell her. "I think."

"It's tiring though, isn't it?" she says, studying my face in such a way that I wonder if I look haggard. "Having to keep up the façade. Not just in the sense of all your energy making sure the spell stays on, but the energy it takes to truly hide who you are." She grins at me, her teeth stark white against her brown skin. "But I know what helps. I'll get you a coffee. Another espresso, or do you want something else?"

"A macchiato would be nice," I tell her. "I drink those espressos too fast."

Livia gives me an understanding nod and gets up to go into the café.

I bring out my mirror from my leather messenger bag and check my face to see just how tired I look. There are some dark circles under my eyes that even my concealer couldn't diminish. So much for looking like a femme fatale who's about to seduce her teacher. No wonder I've been having zero luck with the professor.

It hasn't been for lack of trying, either. Vampires are good at compelling you, but it doesn't mean they are easily compelled. I was bold that first day, even bolder the next when I invited him out for a drink. I thought since he seemed so impressed by my playing that I could further charm him, but he turned me down. He did it so easily too, like he thought it was amusing that I'd even try.

Can't say my ego didn't take a hit. But I'm obviously in this for the long haul now.

"So," Livia says, coming back with two coffees. She places them on the table and sits back down, folding her hands under her chin, the morning sun peeking over the building behind us and lighting up all the silver rings on her fingers. "Have you made any progress with Valtu?"

I take a sip off the coffee, my eyes shutting briefly as I swallow. The coffee here is strong enough to put hair on your back. "Not yet," I admit. "These things take time."

Her smile tightens. "I agree with you. However, I'm starting to think we don't have as much time as we thought."

A chill runs down my back, despite the warm and sunny September weather. "What do you mean?" I ask carefully.

"Can't you feel it?" she asks, her voice dropping. "The change in the air?"

I stare at her for a moment before shaking my head. "The weather?"

"Not quite. I guess you're still so new to Venice," she says with a note of disappointment. "Perhaps the glamor is dulling your senses, as well."

She's not wrong about that. My senses aren't as heightened as they usually are and my instincts feel a bit muddled. Honestly, I hate the feeling but there isn't anything I can do about it. All my energy is going toward my façade: keeping the glamor on and my true self concealed, keeping my Italian flowing at a higher degree, and allowing myself to play the organ at a professional level.

"But let me tell you," she goes on, "that things are getting worse. I can feel it. A few other witches here can feel it too and Bellamy..."

I stare at her expectantly, my heart rate increasing.

"Well, you know how he is," she says with a knowing half-smile. "He's aware of everything at all times. He senses it too. Which is why you need to try harder."

"I'm doing the best I can," I tell her sharply. "I get that the vampires have a book that opens portals and that we need to get it from them, but if the professor was such a threat, why wasn't he dealt with before? From what I understand, Bellamy originally wanted me to dispose of Valtu. Why now? I may have been off my game for the last two years, but I've had my ears open. After what happened in Northern Scandinavia, the destruction of both Skarde and Jeremias, Dracula hasn't done any harm. If I have been sent here to kill him, why now? Why not years before? What has Valtu done recently, and more than that, why couldn't *you* have dealt with him?"

Her eyes widen for a moment. "Are you sticking up for a vampire?"

I glare at her for that. "I'd kill all of them if I could."

"Well, I suppose that's the answer, isn't it? You'd kill them all because you can. I'm just a witch, Dahlia. A sea witch if you want my specifics. I'm not a slayer. I wasn't trained to kill vampires. I didn't go to school for it. I wasn't hand-picked by Bellamy at a young age. You know very well I can't do what you do. Vampires can't be killed by anyone but a slayer and with the blade of *mordernes*."

"That's not true," I point out for argument's sake. "I've heard of non-slayer witches killing vampires before. Hell, I've heard of normal humans killing vampires before."

"By luck or accident. Believe me, if Bellamy or anyone in the guild thought that I could be the one to take out Dracula, I would have already done it. I can't glamor myself as well as you can and I don't know how to get close enough to kill him, let alone actually have it stick. In the end, you're the one with the blade." She pauses, taking a sip of her coffee. "There's not many of you out there."

"I know," I say tiredly. "I keep getting reminded of it." When Bellamy showed up at my aunt's house, days after my parents were killed, he told me I was needed because there were so few of me left in the world. If I didn't take vengeance on the vampires who did this to my parents, who would?

"Then you understand how important you are and that we're all relying on you."

I sigh heavily and tear open a sugar packet, pouring it in my cup to soften the blow of the coffee. "Gee, no pressure."

"Listen," Livia says, placing her hand across the table and leaning forward, her expression softening. "I don't want to scare you. It's just that when I talked to Bellamy on the phone, well, he scared me. The longer that portal is open, the more that...things will come out. I've *seen* them, Dahlia."

I frown at her, that chill returning. She looks scared for once. "What?"

She presses her lips together tightly, until her mouth

resembles a line of chalk. "The monsters," she whispers. "I've seen them come out of the canals."

Her eyes dart to the canal beside us and my eyes follow. A gondola has just finished passing through, the gondolier singing in Italian to the selfie-taking couple on the boat, the dark, murky water filled with small whirlpools from the gondolier's oar. Though the sun sparkles off the surface, I get these uneasy feelings, as if I'm sensing the depth beneath the water. I'm seeing the limestone walls that form the foundations for the buildings, sunken boats, tires, thick clay at the bottom, and this sense of something hiding in the muck.

"What did the monster look like?" I ask her.

She just shakes her head and looks back to me. "I didn't want to say anything in case it turned out to be nothing."

"In the event that it is something...what did it look like?"

"I don't know. It was dark out and I was walking back to my apartment at night and it...at first I thought it was a black garbage bag floating in the water. I was ready to head over to it and pull it out, I thought it was some garbage from tourists, you know? But then it *moved*. It reached out of the water with long black fingers," she holds her hand out, fingers stiff in exaggeration, "and I...I froze. And then it pulled itself up into the shadow until I couldn't see it anymore but I could hear it. I could hear it walking, this wet, dripping...slithering sound. It was big, Dahlia. It was very big."

I'm no stranger to the supernatural. My parents were witches and my mother was big on holding séances in the attic, but it was to contact our relatives and nothing scary or bad ever happened during those times, usually just my grandmother turning the lights on and off or my grandfather's disembodied voice coming through the spirit box, telling us he was fine. Later, when I was at university, my dorm room was haunted by a ghost called Mary, but again, she was harmless. Annoying, when she was trying to talk to me in the middle of the night and I had an exam the next day, but still harmless. What Livia is talking about though, that's something else entirely. Monsters. The only monsters I knew of were vampires. They were the only ones I'd seen with my own eyes. Everything else was just myth.

"It's probably a vampire," I say, trying to reassure her. "You know that some vampires have other forms. Their original selves. The mad ones."

"And if it's not? If it's one of the creatures that has come out of the portal? Then what?"

"Then…" I say, exhaling as the weight on my shoulders gets heavier, "I guess I need to try harder."

She straightens up, putting on a brave face. "Good. I'll let Bellamy know."

"Is there a reason he's not contacting me about any of this?" I ask carefully.

"He seems to think that if you talk to him, it will make your glamor fade. Better not to take the chance."

Hmmm. I only talked to Bellamy briefly when he called me up to tell me the guild was giving me a second chance. That's all I needed. I'd be happy if I never talked to him again. We didn't end things on good terms. He went from being my substitute father to being a stranger faster than I could blink.

Somewhere nearby a church bell rings, the sound solemn, and I glance at my phone. Time for my music theory class, sadly it's not one with Professor Vampire.

"I have to run," I tell Livia, finishing the rest of my coffee.

"Okay," she says. "Next week this time?"

I get out of my chair and nod, pulling my purse onto my shoulder. "I'll text you if I have any problems," I tell her.

"Hopefully you won't," she says, her face going grim. "Be safe, okay? I mean it."

I give her a shaky smile. "I'll do my best. On all accounts."

I head off toward the school, wishing that the sun felt warmer on my skin. The shadows of the buildings are long, the canals dark, and even though it's still crowded with tourists, the spooky feeling follows me all the way to my class. Even during class I have a hard time paying attention. Doesn't help that music theory is incredibly boring.

When the class is finally over, I don't really feel like going to my apartment. It's too small and isolated and feels like a hotbox at this time of day. It's rare that I actually want to be around people—I crave solitude above all else—but after the talk with Livia, I don't want to be alone.

I decide to head to the library. I'd only been in there twice this week, both just to take a peek, but now that I have some exams and projects coming up I figure it's good to get a head start in studying.

The library is located on the top floor at the back of the school. With its high arched ceilings, alfresco paints and moldings, it would rival the concert room in grandeur if it didn't have a haphazard way about it. It's darker than it should be, as if the light doesn't travel very far, and the rows are stacked in an awkward manner. That usual smell of old books, the vanilla-ish lignin, is absent.

At the back of the library is a small museum of sorts with rare manuscripts and music sheets on display, a room that's portioned off by glass. It's there that I find Professor Aminoff, standing behind a large table in the center and opening an envelope, his hands encased in plastic gloves.

For a moment I think I should just go through the stacks and find the books I need for my courses, but knowing that every second I waste not getting to know the vampire is a second longer that this so-called portal is open.

And it doesn't matter because I watch as Valtu smiles to himself and then gazes up at me without raising his head, making him look both sexy and sinister, a deadly combination.

The hair raises at the back of my neck, the urge to flee tugging at me.

"Dahlia," he says quietly, straightening up. "And to what do I owe your presence this evening?"

He's speaking English and his tone is amused yet dry, as if I'm someone he could do without seeing. The feeling is mutual.

"I was going to check out some books," I tell him. I walk toward him and stop just outside the entrance to the glass room. "What are you doing?"

He raises up an old book in his hands. "Just received a donation of a rare manuscript from the 1700s. Cover is worn off but the inside is intact."

I peer at it from where I am. "Who is it from?"

He shrugs. "I don't know. We get donations here all the time. I'm sorting through some of them now." He eyes me. "Come on in."

I hesitate. "I'm sure you don't need me breathing all over your rare books."

"Too much garlic?" he asks, another quirk of his lips. "You're in Italy now, *rossa*. Garlic is coming out of all of our pores."

For a moment I ignore his new nickname for me and wish that the Hollywood ways of killing or repelling vampires actually worked. Garlic? Nope. As you can see, Valtu eats it. Silver? He's got a few silver rings on his slender fingers. Sunlight? The vampire lives in Italy. I know that vampires in general don't like the sun because their eyes and skin are extra sensitive, but it certainly doesn't kill them. A cross? Some vampires go to church. A stake through the heart? Unless it's the blade of *mordernes*, the special slayer's blade I have, then their heart will continue to beat around it. Only decapitation and sometimes fire can actually end their lives.

At the thought of my blade, my fingers start to twitch, something Valtu picks up on.

"Are you alright?" he asks, eyeing my flexing hand.

"I'm mentally playing the organ," I lie. "Just something I do sometimes."

He meets my eyes and I have to suck in my breath, the intensity in his dark gaze seeming to steal the oxygen from the room. He knows I'm lying, doesn't he? He knows that I'm the one to wield the blade that can kill him, that the metal handle fits perfectly in my palm like we were once fused together.

"Ah," he eventually says before turning his attention back to the book. "Then don't let me keep you."

I want to take the exit. I want to turn and disappear into the stacks or maybe just go straight back to the apartment after all. My pulse is quicksilver, the ends of my hair still standing up, and fuck it, can't he tell that I'm scared?

And yet I stay. And it's not because I am stubborn or that I really want to get this job done (though both are true), but because I am compelled to be by his side. The kicker is I can't tell if it's because he's using his power to compel me or if it's something else, like hormones gone wild.

So I step inside the room beside him, and one brow lifts as he eyes me. "Do you need any help?" I ask him, my gaze going to the stack of envelopes beside him, ripped open, and the books displayed beside them. "Are those all donations?"

He stares at me for a long moment—long enough to make my cheeks feel hot—then nods. "They are."

"All anonymous?"

"All anonymous."

"Don't you think that's weird?" I ask.

He pulls out a drawer from the edge of the table and

removes a box of latex gloves, handing it to me. "Rich people are eccentric," he says as I take the box. "Not all of them want to be associated with handing over relics, especially if they came across them in some, shall we say *unscrupulous* way. Besides, it wasn't long ago that the tidal surge of the *acqua alta* flooded the library, ruining a lot of our most prized books, which led to a surge in donations. Who thought it was a good idea to have them housed on the ground floor in Venice is beyond me."

"That explains why the library feels so new," I tell him, slipping on the gloves. I stay on the end of the table, not wanting to get too close to him.

"Yes, they could have done a better job in moving it," he comments dryly. "The lighting in here is atrocious. But at least the books are safe."

He reaches over and hands a book to me, then puts a pen and a library card beside it. "I haven't checked this one over. Just try to make some sense of it and write down the key characteristics on the card. It will help with cataloging it."

I carefully flip the book open and I'm hit with the smell that's been missing from here. I close my eyes for a moment and when I open them, Valtu is staring at me again and I'm suddenly aware I've been smiling.

"Do you know what causes the smell of old books?" he asks me.

I give him a smile that borders on triumphant. "Lignin. The breakdown of the wood in paper, plus the glue, ink and other chemicals."

"So then you know," he says, flipping through the book he's holding before glancing at me again. "Are you able to read that?"

I peer at the musty pages. The ink has faded a bit but it's in Italian and clear enough. I nod. "I read Italian better than I speak it."

"I think you speak it just fine."

I refuse to let him compliment me. "I sound terrible and you know it."

He tries to hide a smile but his eyes are dancing. Good lord. He has a way of making me forget what he really is. "For an American, your accent is superb."

"I'm Canadian."

"Oh right. Then you're really doing well. But your writing? Well, that remains to be seen."

I don't bother telling him my writing is even worse. Learning a language through witchcraft only does so much, especially on a short amount of time.

Don't even think about that, I remind myself. *What if he hears your thoughts?*

But even though vampires can do that with some humans, my glamor is preventing him from doing that with me. At least I assume so. Otherwise he would have known my intentions from day one.

"Tell me," he says thoughtfully, "why did you decide to come to school here?"

"I've always been charmed by Venice," I tell him.

"But in class the other day, you said it was your first time here."

"I mean, I've always been charmed by the *idea* of Venice."

"I see. And has it charmed you yet?"

No, but its vampire is giving it a run for its money.

"I'm not easy to win over," I tell him with a teasing smile.

"I can tell," he says.

"Neither are you," I add.

He frowns, looking me over curiously. "What makes you say that?"

"I invited you for a drink and you said no," I say bluntly.

His brows shoot up. "And you think that didn't win me over?"

"You said no," I repeat.

"I had to say no," he says with a scoff. "What kind of gentleman do you think I am?"

"I don't think you're much of one at all," I say plainly.

He bursts out laughing at that, his smile giving the dim room all the light it needs. The hair on my neck stands up again but this time not in a frightened way. In a pleasurable way. Which I suppose is frightening in itself.

I clear my throat, trying to ignore the floaty sensation in my stomach. "Why are *you* in Venice?" I ask him.

"Me?" he asks when he stops laughing. "Why not?" Then his features harden slightly, his mouth turning down. "I suppose I want to see Venice, experience it, while it's still here."

"Still here?"

"This city won't be here forever," he says as he picks up a pencil and begins scribbling something down on a library card. "With the way the waters are rising each year, they say it will all be underwater by 2100."

I purse my lips in puzzlement. "But you'll be long dead by then," I say without even realizing what I'm saying. It's what a normal person would say, of course, they wouldn't know the truth, that he wouldn't be dead by 2100, because he's immortal.

Though technically he could be dead next week, I think to myself. *By my own hand. But he doesn't know that.*

"Are we to only care about things that happen in our life-time?" he asks, his eyes solemn, brows lowering so that it casts dark shadows. "There's no harm in caring about things that happen after you're gone. Someone has to inherit the earth, don't they?"

Yeah, you, I think. I remember in one of my classes at university, a fellow witch she found sympathy for vampires for being immortal, for being the ones who would

65

truly have to deal with the effects of climate change because they would be the last ones on earth. She then went on to mention how vampires were behind a lot of the clean earth initiatives, but she was ignored for that. Witches don't like to hear about vampires doing any good. It goes against all our beliefs, all that we've been indoctrinated to.

"Tell me something, Dahlia," he says, his voice going lower, rougher, enough that it causes my scalp to prickle, like I'm getting a head massage. He leans forward, his hands splayed on the table. Strong, large, and capable, with two silver rings, one a bird skull signet, the other a candle. "This might sound strange but...do I know you from somewhere?"

I stare at him in surprise. "No..."

He tilts his head and I feel his eyes starting to probe me, feel myself tipping forward slightly, as if I'm standing on the edge of his irises, the shades of brown, black, and gold spreading out before me like a pond in the night, inviting me for a dip.

"Because," he says, and now his voice is inside my head, moving around like a snake, "I feel like I've met you before." He practically hisses the words.

My eyes flutter, wanting to close, wanting to fall into the pool of his gaze, to sink, not swim, and I have to fight against the pull, like a fish on a line.

"Have you ever been to San Francisco? Where did you go to university?" he says abruptly and suddenly I regain my balance again. I felt like I was about to fall over, but I'm standing straight, the book still in my hands.

I manage to swallow. "Uh. Um. I went to university in Scotland. And no, I haven't been to San Francisco. Why?"

"Just a place I frequent. As is Scotland. Where?"

"Aberdeen." I feel breathless.

"No kidding," he says. "I spent a lot of time there. I had a very good friend who lived in Cruden Bay for some time."

"Oh?" I manage to say. "When? Maybe you were there while I was studying. Perhaps you saw me on the street, or maybe we met briefly at a party."

He chuckles, looking back to his library card. "I'm much older than you think. No, I don't think I was there when you were at school. Guess you just have one of those faces."

"Maybe I remind you of another girl you turned down for a drink," I muse.

He pauses, glancing at me for a moment. "You would think I wouldn't make that same mistake twice, then."

Okay. Is that a sign that I should ask him for drinks again? Or is he going to rectify it? But the professor doesn't say anything, just hums a little tune to himself and continues writing on the library card. I do detect a playful smile just teasing the corners of his full lips.

So close. I feel like I'm so close. But perhaps I'm doing this wrong. He's a hunter through and through. A blood-sucker. An animal. A predator. And I'm the prey. I shouldn't be going after him guns a' blazing, so shameless, putting myself on a platter for him. He's used to pursuing, not being the one pursued. It probably gets him hard just the thought of hunting down a woman.

At the thought of him getting hard, my body immediately tenses, heat pooling between my legs in a sudden burst of need.

Jesus. I can't be thinking about that.

But of course, I need to be. How the hell else am I supposed to get close enough to Valtu in order to kill him, let alone learn the whereabouts of the book? That's part of my job. Sometimes in order to vanquish vampires from this world, you need to do things you don't want to do. I've done it before. Done things that people would view as shameful, degrading. Hell, even some witches outside of the slayer's guild pity us for the things we sometimes have to do.

I guess the difference is, now I find myself *wanting* to do it.

I decide to take a step back. To let him be. I'll never get anywhere if I keep coming on so strong.

"I really should go study," I tell him, rolling off my gloves.

He looks up, his brows together in puzzlement. "Already?"

"It's why I came here," I say, placing them in the trash can under the table and adjusting the purse on my shoulder.

"If it's for my class, the essay isn't due for a few weeks," he says.

"I like to get a head start," I tell him. "I'll see you Monday." Then I'm turning around and walking out of the glass room of rare books and artifacts and into the darkened stacks of the library. I half-expect him to come after me and feel a twinge of disappointment when he doesn't.

I sigh, blowing a strand of hair out of my face and wishing I had brought a cardigan with me. It's been so hot and muggy here, even at night, but in the depths of the library there's a deep chill that makes my bare arms erupt in gooseflesh.

I spend some time going through the stacks, pulling out a few books, then work my way to the tables. There are students occupying most chairs, so I go to the back of the room, where the light gets dimmer, until I spot a long empty table, thankfully with a couple of desk lamps to illuminate the work area.

I sit down, my eyes drifting over to a metal door at the wall, complete with a keypad, then the arched stain-glass windows above it. Where could that door possibly go? Perhaps that's where they keep the really valuable stuff. After all, it wouldn't be too hard to smash the glass cases that house the books the professor was working on.

After flipping open a book, I bring out my pen and notepad and attempt to make notes. We were given free range for our essays and I don't really know where to start except that I think I'm most intrigued by Modest Mussorgsky, a Russian composer who was suspected of being involved with witchcraft and the occult back in the day. I start going through the books I have that feature him, trying to find something that speaks to me. Though I'd only graduated from university six years ago, it feels like a lifetime ago and the idea of constructing an essay feels foreign to me.

But I love research at heart. I could spend hours doing it and it seems I've done so, by the time I've breezed through two books, made a heap of notes, and my phone is telling me it's nearing closing time.

"You're still here," Valtu's voice comes from behind me, his words rough and elegant at the same time. I suppress a shiver and twist in my seat to glance at him over my shoulder. He shouldn't have been able to sneak up on me like that, but I was hyper-focusing on my work, my senses are dulled, and he is a vampire after all. They can be as silent as snow.

"I must have lost track of time," I tell him. I quickly get up and start slamming the books shut and suddenly Valtu is at my back, peering over me at the table. His scent overwhelms me and my knees threaten to buckle.

"Mussorgsky," he says quietly as he notes the books. "He's an interesting man."

"Was," I correct him, since he died in the 1800s.

"Of course. *Was*."

I swallow hard. For the first time since I met this vampire, I feel afraid. Not terrified, but the prickle of fear is distinct. If he knows who I am truly am and what I have been sent here to do, he could kill me right here in the back of this dark, emptied library and I wouldn't be able to stop him. The blade of *modernes* is tucked away in my closet. I am completely defenseless.

"How about I walk you home," he goes on. "It's late."

I blink at him and then turn away, gathering my books. Perhaps I wasn't wrong. The moment I put distance between us and back off, the more he feels compelled to chase.

Careful, I remind myself. *That might not be a good thing.*

"What makes you think I need you to walk me home?" I ask, turning to face him, the books clutched to my chest.

He gives me a sly, crooked smile. "You don't know the city, *rossa*. It can be full of dangers." His voice lowers softly over that last word, the desk lamp casting his face in shadows.

"Such as?"

"One wrong step and you're," he makes a diving motion with his hands, "right into the canal."

"I think I can manage," I tell him. "And you don't know where I live, I could live around the corner."

Actually, I wonder if he does know where I live. I suppose it could be on the school records. I'm not sure how strict the privacy laws are here and if teachers can access that.

"Do you?"

I shake my head. "Cannaregio. By the Chiesa della Madonna dell 'Orto."

"Interesting," he notes. "Did you know that area is haunted?"

A wash of cold air comes over me. "I didn't. Too bad I don't believe in ghosts."

"You don't have to believe in ghosts for them to exist. They just need to believe in you." He gestures behind him with his chin. "Come on. We're the last ones in here. I need to close up."

"You're the librarian here too?"

"When I need to be," he says mysteriously.

I step away from the table and then nod at the metal door at the back. "Where does that go?"

"Headquarters for the Secret Society of Undervalued Librarians," he says, walking off to the main door. I watch him for a moment, then follow behind. He's wearing black jeans, black moto boots, and a slim-cut black sweater which makes him look like a creature of the night, but there's no denying he also looks like a sexy piece of ass at the same time.

"Not much of a secret now," I say to him when I catch up. I know he's being facetious, but it does pique my curiosity even more.

He opens the front doors and then waits till I'm close enough before flicking off the main lights. The library goes dark, putting him into silhouette and for a flash his eyes seem to glow red, shots of crimson in the void where his face should be.

I suck in a shaky breath and step out into the hall, feeling relief at the light.

He gives me a quick smile and then locks the door behind him. "Now where were we?"

"You were trying to walk me home," I say. "Think I need protection from ghosts and stuff."

"Men, mostly," he says as we head down the hall to the stairs.

"Oh is that so?"

"I'm sure you have a flock of Italian men following you down the streets."

"And you're supposed to protect me from them?"

"I just want to make sure you don't offer them a drink as well," he says, which makes me laugh. I'm not used to vampires being funny. I'm not used to being relaxed enough around them to actually laugh, but somehow with Valtu he lets me put my guard down.

He's compelling you, that's why, I remind myself. *None of this is real. He's making you feel what he wants you to feel.*

I keep that in mind as we step out into the night, the scent of brine, exposed tide, and seawater combining with fried garlic from nearby restaurants flowing over us. Even in

September, Venice is busy and tourists walk past, German, English, and Mandarin filling the air as people dressed in carnival costumes try to entice them into schmaltzy gift shops.

I turn and walk up the street, Valtu walking beside me. He has such a way about his movements that makes me jealous, like he's barely here at all, just moving with silky ease. He could be part of a dream for all I know.

"So, Dahlia Abernathy," he says, shoving his hands into his pockets. "Tell me more about yourself."

Here it goes. Time to keep my lies straight by telling as much truth as possible.

"What do you want to know?"

"What made you go to university in Aberdeen?"

"My dad was Scottish," I tell him, which isn't a lie. "So I wanted to go to school there. In the end it was between there and Glasgow, but I wanted to be by the ocean. Grew up in the Pacific Northwest and all."

"And what did you take?"

"Don't you know all this?"

He gives me a quick smile. "I don't research every student that steps into my class."

"Maybe you should. What if they turn out to be a psycho?"

He laughs lightly. "I have a way of figuring that out."

"And?" I ask him as we pause at a bridge to let a swarm of drunk backpackers stumble through. "What do you think of me?"

"You know," he muses, putting his hand at the small of my back as he guides me onto the bridge, "I haven't made up my mind yet."

Even though the pressure of his hand is light, this is the first time he's touched me. I feel his skin against me as if I'm wearing nothing at all. It shoots down into my veins, turning them warm, thick, like honey, and that peculiar knee-buckling feeling is back.

I manage to keep it together and walk onto the bridge with him guiding me, even though I feel like I'm unraveling on the inside. All the vampires that touched me (and then some) before, none of them made me feel like *this*.

While I'm pondering this feeling, we pass by a nun who shoots us a frightened side eye and does the sign of the cross.

"She seemed to think you're a heathen," Valtu says, leaning in conspiratorially.

"Me?" I say. For a moment I'm aghast, because he's the heathen here. But of course, that's not true. Witches are just as blasphemed as vampires are. The only time I'd ever group our species as the same is the only time we're met with the same prejudices. I guess the difference is that people know witches exist, they merely suspect that it might be true for vampires.

"Nuns don't lie," he says. "But it's okay. I prefer my company on the sacrilegious side of things."

If you only knew, I think. But since he's implying he enjoys my company, I'm taking it.

"So the University of Aberdeen," he goes on. "That's an interesting school."

"Is it? Honestly I don't remember much. More partying than studying." The thing that both of us know is that there is a secret department within the university. It's like Hogwarts but without the capers and whimsy. I studied history on the outside and walked away with my degree, but on the inside I was learning how to murder vampires along with the rest of the slayers. The other witches called us The Buffys, for obvious reasons. There were only six of them in my class. Each year there are fewer and fewer.

But, of course, Valtu doesn't know this about me since my glamor is working.

"So you graduated with a hangover. Then where did you go?"

"Back to Canada," I tell him, while the truth is I was living outside of Boston, ready to be dispatched to wherever Bellamy and the guild wanted to send me. Some years I'd have a vampire to kill every month or so. Other times things were slower. "I did some odd jobs, tried to find myself, that sort of thing, until I finally decided I wanted to take my music further. Which of course led me here."

He nods, seeming to believe that. "And do you know what you plan to do when you leave here? If you don't mind me saying, you have a great natural talent."

Supernatural talent, you mean.

"I don't mind you saying," I tell him, playing the role of being bashful. "But I don't believe it."

"You should," he says. "I've seen countless musicians throughout my life and none of them have impressed me the way that you have so far."

Okay, now I feel my cheeks going hot for real. I guess I do have my own talent—I honed that at university too—it's just in order to get to his level, magic helped me the rest of the way.

We talk about music and musicians for the rest of the walk and I have to admit I'm enjoying listening to him wax poetic about the greats, as well as some underrated ones that I hadn't heard of. The thing about listening to vampires talk about the past, other than them being natural storytellers that make you grab on to every word, is that they've experienced so much of history firsthand. I could easily tell which musicians Valtu knew or at least saw perform in person, and which he hadn't. Explained why he knew of so many that never made it big.

Pretty soon, we've made it to the last bridge before we get to my apartment. We're just crossing over it when I suddenly feel an acidic twist in my stomach that nearly makes me sick. I pause and Valtu stops right beside me, frowning. He opens his mouth to talk but then shuts it abruptly when a loud splash sounds from underneath the bridge.

We exchange an uneasy look. There's no one else around us and only a few lights from the surrounding buildings. They don't seem to reach far into the canal and there are no boats passing by. The silence, the stillness, is beyond eerie.

The splash sounds again and we both peer over the edge of the bridge, his hand going to my lower back again and I grip the stone railing. Something is in the water just below us, swimming beneath the surface, causing ripples. It's big and it's long and then suddenly the ripples stop.

"What the hell was that?" Valtu asks.

I glance at him. "Do you have river otters in Venice?"

He shakes his head. "No."

"But you do have dolphins. Maybe seals?"

He seems to think that over, then looks up and around us, as if gauging something in the air, his nostrils flaring. "Perhaps."

He looks on edge, which makes me further on edge. All I can think about is what Livia thought she saw come out of the water. It also makes me think about what I thought I saw earlier in the week, this shape on the dock below my window. If these are in fact monsters that have come from an opened portal, why would Valtu look so concerned?

Unless he has no idea.

"We should get going," he says uneasily, his hand guiding me again over the bridge and then I'm heading right toward the apartments. We walk past a few buildings and crumbling old walls that seem to hide trees and gardens behind them, their autumn-kissed leaves looking pale in the moonlight, and then we're in front of my building.

"I can't believe you live here," he says looking the building over.

"It's all I can afford," I tell him, feeling defensive, even though I shouldn't be because the guild is paying for it after all.

"I don't mean that," he says. "This is one of the most haunted spots in the city."

"As I said, I don't believe in ghosts," I tell him.

"Or creatures in the water, it seems. So very pragmatic."

I give him a bit of a shrug. It's dimly lit in this corner and most of the windows in the building are dark, giving it a feeling of being abandoned. The lone light above the front door is weak and flickers like crazy, no doubt affected by the vampire's presence. It casts moving shadows across his face, his eyes seeming to glow, his cheekbones more pronounced.

Remember what he is and what you are, I remind myself. *He is your enemy. This is only a play.*

"Well, I better get inside," I tell him, and this thick cord of tension suddenly wraps around me. I can almost see a silver line of electricity flowing from his body to mine. We're a couple of feet apart and yet I feel a tug, as if it wants us to be closer.

He gives me a soft smile, something dark and dangerous glimmering in his eyes as they flicker in and out of shadow. "Thank you for letting me walk you home. I enjoyed getting to know you better, Dahlia Abernathy."

"Thanks for volunteering," I tell him, though my words come out in a whisper.

He takes a step forward and I instinctively want to take one back, feeling his predator instincts taking over. For a panicked moment I fear he may try and bite me...or kiss me. I can't make heads or tails of his energy.

But then he reaches down for my hand, raises it to his mouth, and kisses the back of it, his eyes never leaving mine.

And just like that, the world flashes and brightens and changes and suddenly...

I'm inside what looks like a museum.

There are people around me dressed like they're from the Victorian age, and Valtu is standing in front of me, holding my hand in this same way. He too is wearing a dapper waistcoat, a top hat upon his head.

"Pleasure to meet you, Lucille," he says in an English accent, staring at me with what can only be described as love.

And then suddenly the image fades and we're back in the dark outside my building.

What the fuck?

"I'll see you on Monday," Valtu says to me. "Good night."

Then he drops my hand and turns, walking off into the night.

And I'm left wondering what the hell just happened.

CHAPTER 6

VALTU

IT HAS BEEN years since I have last attempted to write in this journal. It keeps disappearing on me for years at a time, then popping up on a bookshelf or at the bottom of a chest I swore was empty. Perhaps this book is cursed just as my memories are. Perhaps it's controlled by a demon who enjoys fucking with me, letting me live my life with all the pain behind me before making me face it all over again.

I've read *the* book. *The Un-Dead*, which Mr. Stoker decided to call *Dracula* in the end. A silly name. He told me he thinks it means "the Devil" in Romanian, but having lived in Romania for years, he is completely wrong. Not that he ever sought my opinion after he published the book. He met with me but once, this time when I happened to be in Dublin. We had a night together and then parted ways. He didn't ask me any more questions about being a vampire, and I didn't ask him about the book. It was better that way. I never saw him again.

But the book, my god, the fucking book. He took Mina and Lucy's names and put them in the book but attributed them to the wrong people, none of them my lovers. Dracula was given no love story whatsoever. I was still a count, but the name Valtu Aminoff was nowhere to be found. He took my tales of living in Eastern Europe in various castles and turned them into pure schlock. Doctor Van Helsing became a fucking vampire slayer, can you believe it? At least his name was correct. And who the devil was this Renfield fellow? I guess the mind of a writer can only do so much with reality. Stoker never set about to write *my* story, he wanted to write his own, one in which he was in total control. He liked to be in control, that Bram, which I abhorred. It never would have worked between us.

But while this journal is in my possession again, I might as well settle down with a brandy and remember what was real and true, before I become Dracula, and Dracula's story becomes my own.

THE VICTORIAN AGE
London – 1888

"DREADFUL DAY," VAN HELSING SAID, PUTTING DOWN HIS newspaper for a moment to glower at the rain on the window, the streets outside filled with the sound of hoofbeats and carriage wheels splashing through dirty puddles.

I reached over for the sugar and dolloped a large amount into my coffee, giving it a stir. "I have a hard time believing you're not used to this weather."

He glared at me over his newspaper. "You would think that the rain would agree with me, but I can't stand it. Can't stand the sun either."

"Not many of us can," I mused, the scent of the coffee overwhelmed me for a moment before I instinctively compartmentalized it. If we didn't do that on a minute-by-minute basis, we would go insane, the world too rich with sights, sounds and smells.

"Aside from you," Van Helsing said.

I shrugged. "Sunglasses go a long way."

"You look ridiculous in those things," he pointed out.

I shrugged again. "I've never cared about looking ridiculous or not. Humans find a way to stare at me at any rate, I might as well give them a reason they understand."

"The ladies stare at you for reasons I'm sure you understand," he said grumpily.

"The men do too," I said with a smile.

He ignored me. "I can only compel them, you seem to have a natural talent, Val."

That brought out another smile from me. "We can't all be this handsome, Doctor."

He grumbled and went back to reading. It was a rather dreadful day, but it seemed to suit his mood just fine. It was true that I didn't have an aversion to the sun the way that Helsing and the other vampires did, but I think they didn't know to ignore it. The sun didn't bother our skin much, just our eyes because they were so sensitive, so sunglasses, even though they were a relatively rare thing to see about town, were helpful.

I found something invigorating about the sun, like it gave me energy. Too much of it for too long and I would become drained, but bursts of it here and there were like a tonic to my soul. It even helped stave off the hunger and in times that I was trying to be good, I could go for months at a time without feeding if I escaped to the sunny climates of Southern Spain, Italy, Greece, Morocco.

But in London, I had to feed much more often. I felt a pang of hunger just thinking about it and drank down the rest of my coffee to help quell it. It helped for the most part.

"You are looking rather wan," the doctor said, putting his newspaper down and peering at me. "When was the last time you fed?"

"I'm fine," I told him dismissively. I didn't want to think too much about that last time. I was haunting Whitechapel, the same place that Doctor Helsing often sourced, looking for someone the world wouldn't miss. There was a lot of them there, people that could disappear and no one would bat an eye. It was a sad place, but I told myself that I had to feed in order to survive, that it wasn't my fault I was born this animal any more than it was probably their fault they were born into poverty. I told myself that I was doing them a favor and putting them out of their misery. It helped squash the guilt. Better to be dead than to sell your body on the streets, or so I told myself.

But the last time I fed, my prey fought back. She was drunk, and old, but still she fought. She even had a name, Mary Ann, which I cared not to know. It always made things harder to know their names. It was why farmers should never name their cattle. I had to slash her throat and drain her blood that way. It felt so violent, not in the style of a vampire. I much preferred to bite and feed, it was the way beasts were meant to.

It was the middle of the night, and after I killed her and fed, I left her body right there on the street in Buck's Row, disappearing in a flash before anyone could see. I often got carried away during feeding, violence taking over, and if I wasn't careful, I could become lost in time.

I saw the inquest days later into her death and I could have kicked myself for not being more careful. I should have hidden the body. I shouldn't have done it on the street.

Not that anyone would ever suspect a Finnish Count of murder, not when I resided in a grand house in Marylebone, when I donated so much of my wealth to the poor and other charities. Vampires aren't all bad, not when the money we have invested and saved for a century helps us improve the lives of others—even when we take away those very lives in the end.

But there were no solutions yet. How were we supposed to live without taking human life? While I have admitted my truth to some humans in the past, the majority became afraid of me, and even if some of them volunteered to be fed on, who would control me? When a vampire feeds, they lose all control, the bloodlust always getting the better of them. The only way I think I would be able to feed without killing anyone is to have someone with me who could make me stop. But would Van Helsing do that? Or would he join in too?

Of course, Van Helsing came up with the best solution—he became a doctor. Now he had access to all the blood he needed, even though he did enjoy the hunt.

"I would be happy to share some vials with you, Val," he said, picking up on my thoughts as we sometimes do with each other.

"I'm fine," I said again. Old blood wasn't the same anyway. I finished the dregs of my coffee and sighed, feeling both weary and restless. "How about we make the most of the weather and go to the British Museum? They have a new exhibit I hear."

Van Helsing never cared much for going out in public, preferring to spend his days studying medicine or relaxing with a boring book, but he would often accompany me on my outings even when he didn't feel like it. While he liked to study the body, I liked to study how people worked. What made them tick, what made them different from one another. A museum was a great place to do that. Even when so many people were putting on airs, pretending to be smarter than they were or interested in history and art, I liked to see how they were beneath the masks.

"A new exhibit," Van Helsing mused, getting to his feet. "New to most humans perhaps. It's never new to us." A slight exaggeration, considering there was a lot of history that even us vampires weren't witness to, but since the doctor was born in the 1400s, I let that slide.

We called for my carriage and trundled off toward the museum, an easy walk most days but I didn't want to listen to the doctor grumble about the rain ruining his fine clothing. He acted like he didn't have more wealth than anyone in the city.

The new exhibition turned out to be paintings from the Far East, China and Japan to be specific, located in the white wing. We stepped on through and joined the hordes—seemed everyone in London had the same idea to escape the weather.

As usual, we took our time looking at the Ancient Egyptian artifacts. Since neither of us were alive back then, their whole society fascinated us. We often stared at the hieroglyphs and mummies and tombs and wondered who we could have been had we been vampires then. But with vampires only having come into existence via Skarde, the so-called king of us all, in the twelfth century, our lineages don't stretch back that far.

Eventually we made our way over to the white wing to see the exhibit. There was a crowd gathered so we took our time waiting to view the paintings, recognizing many people from various parties I've either thrown or been to as they milled about.

That's when I heard her.

This melodic song of a laugh.

It seemed to soar right through the museum and hit me straight in the heart.

I immediately stiffened, the blood whooshing loudly through my veins like a drum.

It couldn't be.

It was impossible.

And yet I knew it was her all the same.

"What is it?" Van Helsing asked, noting the strange expression on my face, the way I froze.

I could not even answer him. All the air from my lungs and words from my tongue were stolen when I laid eyes on her.

Across the exhibit, talking to a couple of other women, was Mina.

Mina, my true love. My long-lost love.

Mina, whom I have spent a century trying to forget, for remembering her brought too much pain.

And yet here she was. A proper lady, wearing a burgundy dress with velvet accents, her red hair curled and pinned up under a ruffled hat. Though her waist was small, no doubt from the constraints of her corset, she looked like she had put on weight since I last saw her. It looked ravishing on her —we were both too thin back in the early days—but that was the only difference between the Mina that I loved and the Mina who stood before me.

I found myself walking toward her, as if in a wonderful, strange dream, until I stopped in front of her. Behind me I heard Van Helsing's footsteps, heard him asking what I was doing, but I paid him no mind.

Two of the ladies that Mina was talking to abruptly stopped when they saw me, their mouths snapping shut. They felt interrupted by my appearance and seemed ready to rebuke me, as if protective of their friend, but I merely glanced at them.

You want me here, I told them inside my mind, compelling them. *You will give us privacy*.

I watched carefully as their eyes dimmed, a change unde-tectable by an ordinary human, and they both nodded in unison, stepping away from Mina.

Mina was looking at them in confusion then her gaze was brought to mine.

I expected a look of recognition in her eyes, something that told her that she was looking upon the face of her old lover, from another life.

But there was no recognition there. No spark. There was bewilderment, then intrigue as she studied my face and decided she liked my face, but she didn't know who I was.

Just a stranger.

"Can I help you?" she asked and there was no mistaking that voice, though her accent was refined British now, nor the directness in her gaze.

"I am sorry to interrupt," I said to her, bowing slightly. "I had to come and say hello. Seems you look like someone I once knew."

She frowned at that, discernment in her eyes. "Let me guess, some long-lost love?"

My, she still had all the fire.

This really was her. From the strong curve of her jaw, to her perfect pale skin, to the slight hump in the middle of her nose, to the constellation of freckles across both cheeks, and the starburst of blue and gold at the middle of her green eyes.

The color of unfurled spring leaves.

I gave her a hint of a smile. It was all I could do to keep from grinning with joy. "You could say that." I paused, holding out my hand. "My name is Valtu. Valtu Aminoff."

"*Count* Valtu Aminoff," Van Helsing said from behind me and I bristled at that.

Mina gave us both a dry look. "Oh, a count. That's too bad. You were more interesting when you didn't have prestige." She took my hand in hers and even though she was wearing satin gloves, I could feel the pulse of her underneath. "Lucille Rollins."

I brought her hand to my lips, kissing the back of it while

never taking my eyes off her. Oh, how I wanted to compel her. I wanted her to see me for who I was. But I couldn't do it, not to her.

"Pleasure to meet you, Lucille," I told her, my lips lingering on her hand for too long. She even smelled the same, just beneath the scent of her soap and flowery perfume. My eyes fluttered closed for a moment while I remembered us together by the pond, that hit of pure happiness before her life came to an end and mine came to its beginning.

It's been too long, I thought.

"I am Doctor Van Helsing," the doctor said, butting in. He took Mina—sorry, Lucille's—hand and shook it.

She seemed bemused by the both of us and I was frantically trying to figure how to keep her in my life. After this, she would not be rid of me. She would fall in love with me again, that much I knew.

"Do you come to the museum often?" she asked, looking from him to me and back, and I knew she was playing the game of niceties and politeness, not saying what she really wanted to say. I could sense it, the way her heart was starting to beat rapidly, her pulse fluttering in her neck, the way her skin was growing warm, her natural scent which was growing stronger. All of this pointed to signs that she was aroused by me, and the more I picked up on it, the more aroused I became, though it was hardly the place for it.

Easy there, the Doctor's voice slipped into my head. No doubt he could sense what was going on between the both of us.

Did I ever tell you about Mina? I asked him back. A dumb question because I had told him a million times over.

Every vampire has a sad love story to tell.

He blinked at me, then looked back at Lucille, who was now frowning at us.

This is her? he said. *How can it be?*

Do you believe in fate, Doctor? What if humans have more lives than one?

Lucille looked over at her friends, perhaps for support as we continued to converse in our heads, but they were still compelled to ignore us.

"We do come to the museum often," I said to her, clearing my throat and flashing her a smile I hoped would help put her at ease. "I came today so I could check out the Far East exhibit here. Have you managed to get close yet?"

She shook her head, giving me a smile of relief. "No, not yet. I don't do well in crowds."

"Ah," I said. "Well, if you wish, I can accompany you. I have an uncanny ability to make most people stay away from me."

She seemed to consider that for a moment, then gave me a shy smile. "All right," she said, then scanned the crowd. "Appears my friends have gone off to see it on their own."

"Then you shant miss out," I said, putting my arm out.

She nodded and stepped into me so that my hand went to the small of her back.

I hope you know what you're doing, Van Helsing said in my mind. *You never knew her when you were a vampire. You must be careful.*

I wanted to ignore that but he was right.

I had never been a vampire around Mina.

Her death coincided with my rebirth, the transition into a vampire.

I had never loved her when she could have been prey.

I'd never loved anyone while I was a predator.

And yet, I kept my hand at Lucille's back, smiling down at her, and led her toward the paintings, determined to create a future with her once more, one without so much bloodshed.

CHAPTER 7

VALTU

"I AM A PREDATOR," I say to Bitrus, leaning back in my chair and tilting my head to the sun. This is my favorite time of year in Italy, when the sun doesn't hurt so much but fills my body with warmth and energy. A damp breeze runs through my garden, making the blood oranges on the branches sway, the silver leaves of the olive trees rustling like feathers. The boats tied up on the canal beside us knock against the wood of the docks like a melody.

"Tell me something I don't know," Bitrus muses. I look over at him as he has a sip of his orange-tinted wine, his eyes covered by shades that would have made Blade proud. "I've never seen you interested in a woman until they don't seem interested in you. That goes for humans and vampires alike."

"This one is different though," I tell him. "And I can't put my finger on it. It feels like I know her from somewhere, but no matter how hard I try to place her, my brain puts up a brick wall."

"Honestly, Valtu, I'm surprised you turned her down," he says.

"So am I," I admit. "It was instinctual. Obviously I'm not

supposed to date students. The last professor that did that was fired. But it also came from some other level of my subconscious."

"Perhaps you're not attracted to her. You fuck anything that walks but I'm sure you have your limits."

"Funny." I give him a withering glance. "I do wish that was the case. Would be easier. No, Bitrus, she's beautiful. Young, supple, and beautiful. The scent of her blood..."

I pinch my eyes shut. The way she smelled the other night, the scent of her blood and lifeforce...it made me want to do some very, very bad things to her.

"Then perhaps you know you'd lose control with her. You have been trying to turn over a new leaf, and yet I've seen you lately..."

He doesn't need to remind me of the Red Room the other day.

"Maybe that's it," I say, staring back up at the blue sky above. "She's just so hot and cold. One minute she's coming onto me and I feel this urge to back up, to run, and it's ludicrous because she's just this girl. The next she acts like she doesn't care for me, and then I want to stalk her and run her down, pin her to the ground and feast on her." Though the urge to pin her down and fuck her is even stronger than my bloodthirst. Like I said, I want to do very bad things.

"How old is she?" Bitrus asks.

"Twenty-eight," I tell him. "But she seems older somehow. Not in her looks but...in her eyes. It's not all the time, but sometimes I get this glance at her, like I'm seeing the real her and not some front she's put up, and I see an old soul."

"You know what they say about old souls," he says. "If they aren't vampires, it generally means they've gone through a lot of trauma. Any child who is told they're an old soul, or seem old for their age, is no doubt because they had to grow up fast, that they had to experience more than most adults ever will."

"And how are you making that conclusion?" I ask. "Was that you in your youth?"

Bitrus shrugs, having another sip of his wine as he glances at me over his sunglasses. I don't talk about my beginnings any more than he does. There's an understanding with vampires that generally the further back you go into their past, the unhappier it gets, so it tends to be a topic of avoidance.

"Perhaps," he says. "I was told I was an old soul, but only when I left Nigeria, in my twenties. When people weren't used to seeing those who had been displaced by war. But when I was younger, as the British took over Sokoto, every child looked like me. Every child was an old soul. Every child had to grow up fast, had seen things most others wouldn't."

"When was this war again?" I ask, trying to remember my history of the area.

"Early 1900s," he says. "You know I am young compared to you." He gives me a bright smile. Then his smile fades and he has another sip of his wine. "It wasn't until I moved away and went through my transition that I felt I moved past it all. Sometimes I wonder how much easier it would have been to have gone through all of that as a vampire. I knew what I was, the people we lived and traveled with were vampires too, but when you're still human and young...I think you feel everything more."

I don't say anything to that. Just close my eyes and let the warm breeze wash over me. He really is still young. Only been on this planet for just over a hundred years. The first hundred years after I lost Mina were the hardest. I had lost my mind and gained a terrible reputation.

"But anyway," he says, sitting up straighter. "We are not here to discuss the sad stories of my youth. We were discussing this girl, who may or may not have a sad story of her own."

"Well, she's human," I say to him, picking up my wine glass and swirling the burgundy liquid around, "and humans are born into suffering. They spend their short lives either trying to run from it or rise from it. As for Dahlia, she's got her baggage, but what it is I don't know. I can't figure her out."

"You'll go mad trying to," he says. "I know you, Val. You have that look in your eyes, when you start getting possessive and obsessed and can't let something go."

"Have you ever seen me that way around a person? I don't think so."

"Not a person, no. Not a vampire either. But when you get an idea, like the idea you had to open the Red Room right inside the very school you got a job at, well you didn't let go of that idea until it was done. You get possessed."

"I'm not possessed, I'm merely curious."

Bitrus grunts as if he doesn't believe me and finishes the rest of his wine.

"Want some more?" I ask him.

"I better not," he says with a dismissive wave. "Need to think clearly tonight."

"Oh? Do tell..."

"I met someone," he says hesitantly.

"Well, look at that. You're giving me grief over Dahlia and you're the one who has met someone...are they vampire or human?"

"Vampire," he says.

"So then I've seen them at the Red Room."

"You have," he says. "They're quiet though. You probably wouldn't have noticed."

"I notice *everything*, Bitrus. What do they look like?"

"Tall. Handsome. White dreads. Like a male version of Storm."

There aren't many black vampires with white dreads frequenting the Red Room. I know who he is right away. "Sebastian?"

"Yeah. But he goes by Bash. Anyway, it's nothing, just wanted some company and he's up for the same. Doesn't know many people, you know."

"Bitrus and Bash," I muse. "You sound like a sitcom. Or a clothing label. Either way, you sound good together."

"Oh, come off it. It isn't serious. I just want a bit of fun."

"And you deserve it," I remind him. Bitrus was married to a woman, a *human*, for quite a long time, until she died in a car accident. It was sudden and tragic and though it happened about ten years ago, I haven't seen him get involved with many others since.

"So, where are you planning on taking Bash for your date?"

"It's not a date," he says. "And I don't know. He's new in town so I figured we can do the touristy things."

Just like Dahlia. I can't help but think of where I would take her if I ever did take her up on her offer. Lead her by a collar right into my bedroom, I guess.

"I've never been in a gondola," he adds with a laugh. "Can't get more touristy than that."

"Well, be careful with that. Strange things are lurking in the water these days."

"What are you talking about?"

I shrug and finish the rest of my wine. "It's probably nothing. But last night when I was walking Dahlia to her apartment, there was something in the water. Something very large with a very peculiar smell."

"Big fish?"

"Not a fish. I couldn't quite see it, but you could tell it was very long. It's the smell that gets me. It smelled familiar but in an awful way. Like it was bringing...death."

Bitrus lowers his sunglasses and frowns. "You okay there, Val? You forget that death can't come for us?"

"It can and you know it," I say rather sharply. I clear my throat. "Anyway, it made me uneasy. There's been something in the air lately."

"So you've been saying."

I eye him. "You don't feel it?"

He rubs his lips together, pondering something over. Then turns his head to me, lowering his voice. "I do sense something. Like a shift of some kind. I think it all started when Saara and Aleksi came back into town."

He might be right. That uneasy feeling has been here ever since they reappeared in the Red Room weeks ago, saying they were staying for a while.

"I think she's a daughter of Skarde," I tell him quietly. I don't know where they live in the city but since a vampire's hearing is second to none, better not to take my chances. They know I don't like them but hearing it firsthand would hamper the peace in this city.

Bitrus shivers, his lip curling with disgust. "I wouldn't be surprised. She's not like the rest of us. Aleksi is supposed to be her brother though, and I don't get that feeling from him."

"Brother can mean many things," I remind him. I also don't get the sibling vibe between them either, but that doesn't mean anything. Vampires, especially very old ones, are a little more, shall we say, *lax* about familial relationships.

"Why do you think they came back?" he asks.

"I don't know. I don't even know where they went."

"It's possible they brought something back with them," he says.

"Something like what?"

He shrugs and adjusts himself on his chair. "I don't know.

Maybe another vampire or two we haven't met yet. Maybe some cursed artifact. Black magic..." he trails off, his brows furrowing. "Come to think of it, something strange did happen the other night."

"What?"

"I had woken up in the night, like something had woken me up. Like a bang of a door. I got out of bed and saw the bathroom door slowly inch open. By itself."

I stare at him to go on. "And?"

"It was dark in there but I swear I saw a shadow moving. Shouldn't have been possible but all the same it was like there was something physically in the bathroom, like in the bathtub. Suddenly I was cold. Like arctic cold. You know it's cold when we feel it. I almost chickened out. Then I told myself I was being silly. Walked into the bathroom, turned on the lights. Nothing there, of course." He pauses. "The weirdest thing was I couldn't look at the mirror after. I was afraid to. I can't explain it. You know they say vampires don't have reflections? Well this time, I swear to god, it was like if I looked in the mirror I would see someone else staring back at me."

I can pick up on Bitrus's fear like he's put on new cologne. Until this moment, he wasn't really scared. Now, though, he's got adrenaline in his veins.

"I'm sure you were just spooked," I tell him.

"I know I fucking was," he says. "But you're saying there are monsters in the canals and I'm thinking there's something in my mirror, ready to steal my soul, so..."

"Technically I never said it was a monster," I remind him.

"Well, it's enough that whatever my plans tonight, I'm going to avoid my reflection and the water. Tell you what, if you're still offering some of that wine, I'll take it."

I chuckle and get up, heading into my house to get him another bottle of wine.

MONDAY ROLLED AROUND QUICKLY. WHEN YOU HAVE AN infinite amount of weekends in your life, holding onto them is never a big deal, even when you're working a steady job. For me, I was glad the time passed swiftly, and for all the wrong reasons.

It meant I got to see Dahlia.

Not that I have a lot of time to talk to her during history class. I'm there to teach everyone, not just her, and when I finally did talk to her for a moment after class, asking her how her weekend went, if perhaps she saw any ghosts, she was standoffish with me. Again, with the hot and cold.

Today though, we have more one-on-one time together. I have to give my students their piece for the winter recital, something they will play accompanied by a few string or wind instruments. Each student gets something different, something I have selected based on their style and skill level.

Dahlia is up first.

With the four students watching, I get up and open my folder, handing each student their piece.

Dahlia is looking especially ravishing today. A romantic mint-green dress that reminds me of another time, paired with Doc Martens for contrast. Her long red hair spills over her bare shoulders as she stares at the sheet music I've handed her.

"Do you want me to demonstrate first?" I ask her.

She stares up at me, her eyes matching her dress, a fiery determination in them. "No. I can figure it out as I go."

I figured she would say that. The woman seems to abhor help.

I smile at her and nod my head to the organ. "All right, Ms. Abernathy. Have at her."

She gets up and, with her chin held high, walks to the

organ. She delicately places the paper on the stand, slips off her sandals, slides on socks and her organ shoes, then assumes the position.

I watch her carefully as her eyes flick over the sheet of music, taking it all in, trying to make sense of it. It's like I can see the way she slots it in her head, like doing a mathematical equation, playing it there first before she tries to bring it to her life with her hands and feet.

She clears her throat and gives me an impatient look over her shoulder, as if she's been waiting for my cue.

I just nod slightly.

Then she's playing. Jumps right into it with more confidence than I've seen from her. The piece starts off purely with the organ and it starts off with a bang. It's composed not by a famous musician, but by an artist I know personally, Sigmund Krahe. It's a fast and furious haunting piece that I think fits Dahlia well, for all her moodiness, her timelessness, her mystery.

And how she plays it well. There's something magical about the way the organ responds to her, how fast her feet and fingers fly. She's in her element, becoming one with the notes, and it makes me hard as fuck. I have sit down to watch the rest of her performance because all the blood in my body is rushing straight to my cock, the music, *her* music, overwhelming my cells. It's the music of God, of a church that opens to both heaven and hell, filled with sinners and saints, all of it swirling around to make us the fallen creatures that we are.

I watch, holding my breath, drawn into a warm stupor of sorts, like I'm being spun in a web, caught in a spell, until she finally finishes playing.

I find myself clapping, coming back to reality. The rest of her classmates applaud too. It wasn't a perfect performance—

that's what practicing will accomplish—but it was brave and it was bold and utterly captivating.

She twists around on the bench, her cheeks flushed, her smile bright, and it's been such a painfully long time since I ever saw someone so beautiful.

"That was a gorgeous piece of music," she says, breathless. "Who is Sigmund Krahe?"

I clear my throat, trying to calm my heart. "A musician who I knew you would do justice to."

"Never heard of him," she says, but from the twinkle in her eyes, I know that she's proud of how she played. She seems to enjoy impressing me right now. Wanting to please me. That's good to know. That makes me fucking harder.

"That may change after the recital," I tell her, trying to act like her professor again and not some blubbering fool. "You may yet make him famous."

Unfortunately having an erection during class is frowned upon, so I have to move onto the other students and forget about Dahlia for now. Luckily I'm dealing with the Bristol woman, Margaret, who has an uncanny way of sucking the life out of what she plays, and I feel myself calm down accordingly.

It isn't until class is over and Dahlia is walking off, that I catch up with her and stop her, my fingers pressing lightly against her elbow.

She stares at me curiously, waiting for me to say something.

Normally this is the part where I would compel her. I would ask her for a drink and make her do it.

But I can't seem to bring myself to do it with her, especially since there's a chance she's going to want to go for that drink.

Instead, I don't say that at all.

"Are you happy with the piece I chose for you?" I ask her.

"Very," she says. "Though you seem to have more confidence in me than you should. That wasn't the easiest thing to learn off the bat."

"I guess I like testing you. I am your teacher, after all."

She gives me a quick smile. "You don't have to keep reminding me, Professor Aminoff," she says before walking off.

CHAPTER 8

DAHLIA

"Can I borrow this?" a guy from my history class asks, gesturing to one of my textbooks. We're one of the few people in the library this late, sitting at the table near the front of the room where the most light is.

"Go ahead," I say, handing it to him. We have our first exam the day after tomorrow and I need to do well on it. I can't afford to use any memorization or focus spells since it will detract energy from my glamor, so it's old-fashioned cramming for me.

It doesn't help that I haven't been sleeping much lately. I don't know if it's the glamor itself, the magic working over-time keeping me both wired and tired, or something else, but my dreams have been fitful. I can't really remember them, but they feel so real, so vivid. Every time I try and grab hold of it and keep it still, the images float away. At night I pray that I don't dream at all because it feels like my brain isn't getting any rest, and I wake up more exhausted than ever.

I haven't really felt right since two Fridays ago, when Valtu walked me home from this very library. When I was spooked by the thing in the water, and later when he kissed my hand goodnight and suddenly I was transported to another place.

I still can't make sense of it. He did say that the area was haunted. Did a ghost's wires get crossed with mine? I've heard of that happening, when you step into the leftover energy of another life. Could that be what I saw?

But why was Valtu there? Why was he dressed like a count of the 1800s? Is that what I wanted to see? Is that what *he* wanted me to see, like a shared memory?

Normally I'd pass it off as being overtired, being afraid of this whole portal business, worried about the job ahead, plus the stress of dealing with living a lie. Yet there was something about the experience that makes me think it was important. Trying to tell me something? Perhaps my subconscious? I don't know.

And I really can't spend a lot of time wondering about it either. I have an exam to study for and a vampire to charm and I'm only making headway on one of them.

The thing with Valtu is that I know I'm probably coming across as moody—and in general, I am—but I'm learning that the more I back off, the more he comes forward. It's like a dance where we're trying to avoid each other's feet. The only problem is that something keeps stopping him from making a move or taking the next step. I can see he likes me. That I amuse him. That I confuse him. And maybe my glamor is actually compelling him, much the way that a vampire can. But for whatever reason, he manages to keep his distance. Maybe it's too big of a risk for a teacher to go out with a student, but he is a vampire and I know they can do Jedi mind tricks with people. He could easily convince the faculty of any lie.

Which then makes me step forward, for him to step back, and we keep going round and round. Right now he's in the library too, back in the artifact section, going through new donations. I wanted to go over to him when I first got here and see if he needed help but I made myself sit down at this table with a few other students and study instead.

I check my phone. Ten minutes to ten. Library should be closing soon. I'm just about get up and put a few books back on the shelf when suddenly the air inside the library turns ice cold and I feel a sickly prickle at the back of my neck.

Vampires.

The door to the library swings open and two very tall, very beautiful people step inside. They're both dressed to the nines, a man in a slick navy suit and a woman in a simple black dress that she manages to wear like she's on a runway. They're long-limbed and skinny with sky-high cheekbones, full pouty lips, bright blue eyes, and honey-blonde hair against tanned skin.

The other students notice them too, looking up from their books with interest, probably because of the way they're dressed and not because they are vampires.

Then I hear a female voice rasp inside my head.

You don't see us.

The other students automatically look down at their books and laptops, reading and typing away.

The female vampire is compelling us, and if I want to keep up the ruse, I have to do the same and act like it affects me.

I put my attention on my own book and I can feel the female's gaze on my head. It's hot, like a laser is trying to burn a hole in my skull, and I realize she's trying to pry inside, perhaps read my thoughts.

Why me? That's the last thing I need.

Then the pressure stops.

"What are you doing here so early?" I hear Valtu's tense voice as he comes over now and I know they're standing behind me.

"I didn't think anyone would be studying so late," the female says. "Bunch of nerds."

I almost laugh at that.

"They can hear you," Valtu hisses.

"I compelled them," she says. "They aren't paying attention. Now, take us to the room. We cut our previous dinner short for this. Mayor of the city, you know."

So this vampire, whoever she is, just had dinner with the mayor of Venice? Interesting.

Valtu sighs. Though I can't see them behind me, I can tell from his energy that he doesn't like this woman. Good. I don't like her either.

I hear them walking off and once I'm sure they're far enough down the aisle, I get out of my chair and grab my books, heading into the stacks to put them away while also keeping an eye on them. I make sure to stick to the opposite side of the shelves so I'm not too close.

I keep still, holding my breath, and spot them through the spaces in the shelves. Valtu leads them to the door at the very back of the room, punches in a code on the keypad, and then the three of them step inside total darkness, the door closing behind them.

What the hell?

Then it hits me.

The two vampires.

I know who they are.

Saara and Aleksi. No wonder they creeped me out so much. They're the ones with the book. Which means there's a chance the book could be behind that door. Maybe that's where they keep it.

Forget the book, a voice in my head says. *Go home and get your blade and kill them all. They're sitting ducks right now. Those two killed a witch to get that book, killing them is your top priority.*

It's hard to ignore my instincts. This is what I was trained to do. This is why I'm here. I need to get the blade, come back here, and kill them.

But then how am I supposed to get inside? I suppose I could charm Valtu to let me in, but that's highly unlikely.

All I know is I have to take some kind of action. I won't have many chances like this.

I shove the books back on a shelf where they don't belong, then hurry back through the aisles over to my table, put my belongings in my purse and take off. No matter what, I need to get back home to figure out what I'm going to do. I should probably text Livia and let her know, but I feel like that might just complicate things. Better to just do the thing and then report in when I see her face to face for drinks tomorrow night.

The question is, what is the thing am I doing? Getting the blade, heading back to school and somehow getting back in the library—which will be closed by then?

No. As much as I feel the vengeful need to kill the two vampires, I need to be smart about this. If I fuck up now, all of this is over.

I hurry through the darkened streets of Venice, and even though I'm heating up from the exertion, the air has a chill to it and fog is wafting through the canals, just hovering above the murky surface. It feels like autumn has truly arrived and I wish I'd brought my cardigan to school, but those thoughts take a backseat to the pressing matter at hand.

It isn't until I step foot inside my apartment that I know what I have to do. It's going to take everything out of me, I may not even make it to class tomorrow if I feel the way I've felt before, but it will at least give me answers.

I need to put aside my glamor for a moment.

I need to astral project.

Astral projection isn't an easy thing to do, but neither is putting on a glamor spell. While we were taught both at the academy, astral projection was always harder for me. I can do it, but I can't do it for as long as others, and it leaves me absolutely wiped the next day. But right now it's the only chance I have to figure out where the book is, especially if Valtu and the leggy vampires are together in that mysterious room.

I lock the door behind me and start clearing the floor, picking up my scattered pieces of clothing that have overflowed from my suitcase. Even though I've been here a few weeks now, part of me doesn't want to unpack and start hanging up my clothes for fear it would mean I'll be here longer. Also, I'm lazy.

Once I've made space, I take chalk from the small wooden chest where I keep my supplies and draw a large pentacle on the old wood floor, a circle big enough for me to lie down in. I take out my candles and light them up around the edge of the circle, murmuring incantations as I light each one, getting my mind to focus on manifesting my astral travel, thinking of Valtu, of the vampires, of the book. Beside each candle I place a chunk of clear quartz for amplification.

Then I turn out the lights and open the window a little bit, enough that the wind forms a stream for my consciousness to leave my body. The flames flicker in the damp breeze but don't go out.

Next, I take four other crystals from my collection and carefully step over the candles and into the circle, taking my time to lie down so I don't disrupt anything. I go on my back, my eyes open to the ceiling, and place a small ametrine generator on my solar plexus to bring me comfort and confidence. In one hand I make a fist around a tumble of black tourmaline for protection from the vampires, in my other I do so with angelite for opening my mind. Finally, I place a very rare piece of moldavite on my forehead to open my third eye. Immediately I feel the moldavite vibrate, generating heat into my skin. I've had a tricky relationship with moldavite since its energy is so intense, but that's exactly the help I need to do this.

With everything ready, I do my best to relax. I meditate for a bit, clearing my mind, bringing forth the image of myself leaving my body. Every time I attempt to do it though, I lose focus and feel pulled to the ground again.

Knowing that time is of the essence doesn't help, but I have to act like I have all the time in the world. I have to let it happen, it can't be forced.

Mind awake, body asleep, I start to chant.

All my focus goes to the burning moldavite between my eyes, a shimmery green crystal that's not a crystal at all, but glass, the result of a meteor slamming into the earth fifteen million years ago. When I use it, it's as if I can feel the origins of the universe inside it.

It isn't until I finally feel calm and at peace, the ametrine helping me feel buoyant and clear, that I feel myself enter the vibrational stage, where it feels like waves of energy are rolling up and down my body. Eventually there's a kick, and I lift away from my body and enter the spirit realm. I'm now floating in the air and I head for the window, letting the breeze take me away. I don't look back at my body lying on the floor, the sight would be too shocking and I would be pulled back. Instead I find myself floating just above my apartment building, the lagoon spreading before me, its dark waters seeming to swallow up the lights of the city.

I try not to marvel at what I'm doing—doing so seems to break the spell—instead I accept it and use it while I can. On the astral plane, you are free to create whatever you want (within reason) or do whatever you want, but I have no intentions of having fun while I'm here, I just need to get a job done.

Of course, being on the spirit plane means that I'm drawn to places of spiritual significance, such as San Michelle, the

Island of the Dead, that sits across from my building. The call there is strong, an island comprised only of tombs since you can't bury the dead in Venice, but I make my way down to the conservatory. I get there so quickly, it's like teleporting, and suddenly I'm inside the library.

The lights are all off save for a few desk lamps here and there, and it's definitely closed and empty. I focus on the metal door and move through it, then through a black space that feels like a hallway, then through another door.

And then...

I'm there.

At first I don't know where I could possibly be or what the hell is going on. Though I don't have a body, my senses are all still there, and I'm hit with the musky scent of sex and the metallic tinge of blood. I realize I'm at the top of a spiral staircase looking down over a vast windowless room. The walls are red velvet, the furniture black leather, candles lit in sconces casting dark shadows. There are straps and chains and other contraptions you'd find at a BDSM club, if it was held in a gothic cloister.

There are also people fucking all over the place, and a lot of the straps and ropes and chains are in use, which makes me think it *is* an actual BDSM club.

Until I notice why it smells like blood.

It's everywhere.

The feeding.

For every couple or throuple or orgy that's engaging in enthusiastic sex, there are vampires feeding, drinking blood with equal abandon, some of them fucking and drinking at the same time. Deep gasps and moans come from all around the room below me, and I know I need to leave this place. Even in my astral form, it feels unsafe, and like I shouldn't be seeing any of this at all. It's too dangerous for me to stay.

But I can't stop myself. I'm too curious about what's

happening here, and there's still a chance that the book is somewhere amongst all these vampires.

I slowly descend down to the main floor, looking for Valtu or the leggy vampires, but it's hard to find them in this sea of naked writhing bodies. There's just too much going on at once, too much to focus on.

Eventually I make myself look at the people closest to me. There's a woman, a human woman, tied to an iron-post bed with silky ribbons, her legs spread wide open and her wrists tied to the headboard. She's a pretty blonde, early twenties maybe, and her eyes are wide, her jaw slack with pleasure. She's moaning and crying out as a vampire is fucking her and another man is sucking on her breasts with ravenous hunger. His lips leave bloody marks as they work at her but he doesn't seem to be drawing blood.

I watch as a tall, naked, lean man approaches the bed, grinning. His cock thick and hard, a drop of precum glistening at the tip, and I recognise him as Aleksi. A chill runs down my spine despite the warmth of the room.

The woman gasps when she sees him, and starts to struggle against her restraints, but it's no use.

The man currently fucking her pulls out with a groan, giving Aleksi room to slide in, and the other man steps away from her breasts.

"Not him," she cries out but Aleksi only grins, his fangs sharpening before my eyes. He lets out a malicious laugh and thrusts deep into her, her body bucking under the strain.

"She's afraid you're going to feed," the vampire who fucked her says, laughing, running his hand over his cock. He's hard again, always ready to go, like vampires usually are. "We've already had our fill of her earlier. She might not have much left to give."

"I can wring water from a stone," Aleksi muses in an Eastern European accent, thrusting harder and faster. "I'll fuck her properly for a change. Get her blood really pumping. That will make all the difference."

I watch as the woman cries out again, her body tensing and releasing in orgasm, her pussy clenching hard around Aleksi. She went from being afraid to coming hard in seconds flat. As much as I hate vampires, no humans can ever compare when it comes to sex with them. This is giving me flashbacks. It's hot and sexy and deliciously depraved, and despite not having a body, I can't help but feel myself getting wet between my legs.

My eyes are still focused on the couple, watching as the man who was fucking her goes to stand by the bed, his cock hard and ready, trying to put it in her mouth.

"Don't even think of it," Aleksi snarls at him. "She's mine now. She'll be useless when I'm done with her."

"A woman is never useless," the other vampire says, "even if she's dead."

Aleksi bares his teeth at the other vampire until he walks away, then Aleksi's pupils go red and he bites down on the girl's neck. I can actually hear his fangs puncture the skin in a sickening pop.

I turn away just in time to see Valtu striding out of a black lacquered door at the end of the room, guards stationed on either side. For a moment I am totally shocked to see him here in this setting, then I chide myself for thinking that way. Of course he's here. He's a vampire like the rest of them. He's the one who let Aleksi in here, like he's the doorman of this place.

Unfortunately my professor isn't naked at the moment. He's wearing black pants, bare feet, but he's shirtless and that has my attention. His upper body is perfectly sculpted, smooth skin with broad shoulders, a wide firm chest with a light dusting of chest hair, and washboard abs complete with a treasure trail. He looks beyond powerful, manly, and commanding. I'm so grateful he can't tell that I'm here right now watching him, or he'd totally catch me staring at him with drool on my chin.

Valtu looks annoyed, his dark brows furrowed, and he marches toward Aleksi and the girl.

"Who is watching you right now?" Valtu practically barks at him.

Aleksi pays him no attention. He's completely given over to bloodlust, draining the girl as he fucks her.

"Hey!" Valtu says, pressing his hand against Aleksi's shoulder, hard enough that it dislodges his bite, nearly knocking him off the bed. Blood gushes down the woman's neck, pooling in her collarbones, and she lets out a soft cry, her eyes looking empty.

Aleksi roars at Valtu, baring his fangs, blood spraying as he speaks. "What the fuck!?"

"You're killing her!" Valtu yells. "You know the rules."

"Rules?!"

Quicker than my eyes can follow, Aleksi leaps over the bed and pushes Valtu back, a hand wrapped around his throat until they float backwards through the air and Valtu is smashed into the velvet walls.

"Rules!" Aleksi sneers in Valtu's face. "I don't follow any rules you've attempted to throw down. I own this city. My city. You have nothing. You think you're a god for creating this place? Most vampires were happiest when they could kill for their dinner, not eating while on a leash."

Valtu doesn't back down. He takes a moment to stare right into Aleksi's blue eyes, breathing hard through his nose, then with a growl he pushes Aleksi off and whirls him around so that Aleksi is pinned against the wall, his forearm against his windpipe. To my shock, Valtu reaches down with his other hand and grabs Aleksi by the literal balls.

"If you don't like it here, then don't come here," Valtu

rasps, his eyes piercing. "Until then, you're going to listen to the rules. These aren't just my rules, these are the rules agreed upon by the council and by the vampires in this city. You want to break them, go ahead, but if you do it while you're in here, then I'm twisting your tiny balls off, one by one."

"My dear brother," Saara appears from out of the crowd that has slowly gathered around. Like her brother, she's naked too, and she saunters up to Valtu, running her slender hands over his shoulders. A spike of jealousy gets me in the gut, and I'm surprised at how visceral my reaction to her touching him is. With relief I notice the contemptuous look on Valtu's face, his lip sneered in discomfort at her touch.

She rests her chin on Valtu's shoulder, easy to do since she's nearly as tall as he is and he's already well over six feet. "Aleksi," she coos, staring at her brother who squirms under Valtu's firm grip. "We didn't come back to make enemies. Only friends." She leans in and puts her lips on Valtu's outer ear, causing his eyes to flutter closed, his throat to move as he swallows hard.

Oh shit. Maybe he does like this after all.

"I promise he'll behave," she whispers to Valtu. "I promise I'll behave too. For tonight, I'll do anything you want me to do."

Another twist of jealousy comes through me and I have to push it away to stay focused on the matter at hand.

With a grunt, Valtu lets go of Aleksi's balls and brushes Saara off of him. He walks a few feet away, running his hands through his hair, then turns to face the brother and sister.

Only now I'm starting to wonder if they really are brother and sister because she has her arms all over Aleksi, stroking his skin much the same way she did to Valtu. Aleksi doesn't seem to mind either. Though he looks furious at Valtu, and in a bit of pain as well, he leans back into Saara's touch. She seems to calm him.

This keeps being all kinds of fucked up heaped on more kinds of fucked up.

"I don't want to be inhospitable," Valtu says to them in a deep voice. "But this is sacred ground and a safe place. The humans that come here," he gestures to the crowd behind him, "that volunteer to be our dinner, they are promised safety. They don't want to die. If you can't honor that, then you can't be in here. You'll compromise everything for all of us."

Damn. I had no idea this is what Valtu was really doing. I suspected that a feeding club existed, I know there are many throughout the world, but I never thought Valtu would run one. If he's so against killing humans that he regulates other vampires' feeding, then how is he someone worthy of being killed by a slayer? Why did the guild send me here to kill him for his past injustices (whatever they are) if he's more than making up for them now?

Something isn't sitting right with all of this. It never did. I'm starting to think that maybe Valtu was never my original target. Maybe Bellamy lied to me—it wouldn't have been the first time—and giving me such a high-profile target such as Dracula himself was enough to get me interested, to make me believe I could handle it after so much time away. And maybe if Saara and Aleksi and this damn book were the *real* targets in all of this, maybe he thought I would get too scared or not have the confidence to go through with it.

He's probably right. If I had known originally that my assignment was to kill Saara and Aleksi and get the book, maybe I wouldn't have accepted it at all.

Though who am I kidding? I was low enough to have accepted anything, just to be given a purpose in life again.

At the thought of having purpose, I snap my attention

back to Valtu. Music starts pumping from unseen speakers, a slow, sexy industrial beat that reminds me of my NIN phase in my college years. A handsome black man with a shaved head appears beside Valtu, holding the elbow of another man. I can tell the other man, with his dark looks, is probably a local and most definitely human. The black man stares at Valtu and Valtu stares back and I think they're having a telepathic conversation like vampires often have.

The black man places his hand on Valtu's shoulder and whispers something to him, something that makes Valtu bite his lip. Then the man walks away and the Italian human drops to his knees in front of Valtu.

Everyone else goes back to what they were doing before. Saara leads Aleksi somewhere, the vampires resume feeding and fucking the humans, and then there's this guy on his knees in front of Professor Aminoff, reaching up and unzipping his fly.

Holy shit.

Is this actually happening?

I shouldn't stay and watch this. I should resume my search for the book. But I know deep down the book isn't here. Aleksi and Saara wouldn't leave it with Valtu, they both seem to have disdain for the vampire, which means this room behind the door is just for feeding and fucking.

I should go.

But I can't.

I stare as the Italian man pulls Valtu's cock out of his fly. He's hard and thick and long and holy hell, he is beautiful, every inch of him. His eyes close as the man wraps his fist around him. Valtu's mouth opens in a hiss and the man's hand works up and down his cock before he brings his lips to it.

Heat flows through me and I try to ignore the fact that I'm turned on but it's impossible. This is the hottest thing I've seen, watching my professor get sucked off by another man in front of me. For a second I think that maybe Valtu is actually gay and that's why he's brushed off most of my clumsy advances, but then I know I've seen hunger in his eyes when I've caught him looking at me, and a sexual hunger, not just for my blood. Valtu is probably like most of the vampires, without a label, not wanting or needing to be defined by their fluid sexuality.

Even so, I shouldn't be watching this. But I can't look away. I can't stop staring at Valtu's dick and the man's mouth on him as he sucks him off. I want to trade places with that man, I want to be on my knees and making my teacher's eyes roll back in his head.

My god, Dahlia. Get a hold of yourself.

But I can't. Valtu moans deep and low and the heat inside me starts building and building, a fire that's growing out of control. God I would do anything to get myself off, to come, and yet I can't unless, unless...

Suddenly Valtu's head snaps up as if he heard my thoughts.

He looks right at me.

Like he actually sees me.

Then his eyes close again and he's coming, his groans filling the room.

And suddenly I'm being pulled out of the room like I'm caught in a backdraft, sucked through the walls, through the city, nothing but hot wind and then I'm falling into my body again.

I jerk, my limbs rising off the floor of my apartment, that feeling you get when you're falling asleep and you suddenly flail as if you've been dropped.

Gasping for air, I sit straight up in shock, crystals clattering to the floor. The candles are still all lit around me, the window open a crack and letting in the sea breeze. Everything as before I left it.

I press my hands all over my body, taking quick stock of my feelings and sensations and the knowledge that I'm here. I'm no longer there in the feeding room, the library, no longer on the astral plane, I'm back in my body, back on the floor of my apartment.

And I feel like I have a massive case of blue balls, a relentless throbbing between my legs.

But before I can even think about it, I feel myself drifting away, my body falling back toward the floor. My head hits the ground and everything else goes dark.

CHAPTER 9

DAHLIA

I'M GOING TO DIE.

I'm in the dream again. I know it's a dream, I'm lucid, and I can control it. Or I should be able to. But no matter what I do, I can't seem to get away.

The man above me, the man I know is my father, has his boot on my stomach, pressing down hard and I'm squirming, trying to escape but I can't. I try to control him, to get him to take his boot off, to change the game that I often can when I'm lucid dreaming, and yet he won't move.

The look in his eyes is pure hatred. It crushes me to think, to know that this man is my father and yet he hates me so much that he would rather have me dead than give birth to a bastard child, a child that belongs to one of his serfs.

And he's over there, I tell myself. *Your lover is over there.*

I turn my head to see the scene that always follows these moments. The one where there is a man that I can't see covered by soldiers that are holding him back, fighting him. I hear his cries now, and they're so painfully familiar, they kick me in the gut. He cries for me, he's screaming for me, he wants to save me.

I know my father is going to bring his sword down, slice my head clean off, and there's nothing I can do to stop my fate. But I keep my eyes focused on the man I love, because I love him, I feel it deep in the marrow of my bones, a feeling that seems go beyond this dream, into the universe.

Because is this even a dream?

I watch as the man fights and I start to see more of him, the top of his head, his black, thick wavy long hair and just from that, just from that little glimpse, I know who it is.

It makes me scream.

But the scream dies in my throat.

And the world goes still as the blade slices me in two.

Instead of going black as it always does, the world glows white.

Brighter and brighter than I've ever seen it and then I'm hurtling through space, flung amongst the stars, in the most beautiful light show, and then I'm falling, falling back down.

I wake up.

Eyes open.

Staring at my ceiling in the apartment.

It's pitch black. There's only a faint light coming in through the window and I can barely see.

I push myself up so that I'm on my elbows, my head feeling like it's full of lead. My eyes adjust enough for me to make out some shapes in the dimness. I'm lying on the floor in the middle of the chalk circle. All the candles have completely melted down, which would take longer than twelve hours to do, and it's night time so...have I been out for twenty-four hours?

I wince and lay my head back on the floor, trying to think. This happened the last time I used astral projection, all the energy was sucked from me and I slept for a day straight. Which means that right now it's the next night, and fuck, I don't know what time it is, but not only did I miss a full day of school, including organ practice with Valtu, I'm supposed to meet Livia for drinks.

I sigh and reach into the pocket of my jeans for my phone. I pull it out and tap the screen. It says it's nine, which means Livia is already on her way here to meet me. I also see a few texts from Livia as well as several missed calls but when it attempts to face ID me, the phone goes dead.

Fuck.

I put the phone back down and stare up at the ceiling, trying to gather the strength to get up since I have to piss like a race horse. Then I have to charge my phone, quickly get changed and—

Oh my god.

Something just moved.

On the ceiling.

Something just moved *on my ceiling.*

I stare at it, trying to focus, my heart stuttering in my chest. My eyes still see the white impression the phone's light left behind but I blink it away until, until...

I see it.

I see all of it.

A creature, black as sin, the size of a crocodile, on the ceiling. Long spindly limbs with crooked narrow fingers and claws hooked into the drywall, a leathery black tail at one end, a bulbous head at the other. Teeth. Open gnashing teeth and red dots for eyes.

The bad thing, a voice whispers in my ear.

Then it yells in my head: *It's the bad thing!*

The bad thing on the ceiling twitches, hisses like a broken machine, ruby red eyes focusing on me.

I scream.

I scream bloody murder and get up, running to the door.

At first it won't open, then I remember I locked it, and I can hear the thing on the ceiling moving.

And then I hear a *thump*, the floor shaking beneath my feet and I know it's right behind me, reaching for me with its claws and the door it won't open fast enough, I can't get out fast enough, it's going to drag me to hell with it and—

The door unlocks. I yank it open and run out, shutting it behind me just as I see a whirl of black. It hits the door, making it thump, and now the doorknob is fucking turning.

I fumble for my keys, searching each pocket of my jeans, trying to hold the doorknob straight while the creature on the other side starts to twist it. Someone down the other end of the hall comes out and asks if I'm okay, having heard my scream, but I can't even answer.

Finally I find my keys in my back pocket of my jeans, pull them out and quickly lock the door.

I start running down the hall, going past the guy who is staring at me perplexed.

"Rabid animal," I mutter as I go down the stairs, trying to seem like it's just some lost raccoon and not a literal fucking demon. "Going to get pest control."

I run outside the building and into the dark and I keep running, not sure where I'm going, only I have to get away and—

I turn the corner and run right into someone solid, tall and dark.

I scream again and then strong hands grip my biceps and I hear Valtu say "Dahlia? What happened? What's wrong?"

Valtu? What the fuck? Why is he here?

I don't know what to say to him either. If I mention the bad thing in my room, he's probably going to want to play hero and go investigate. He knows nothing can hurt him. And yet that's the worst thing that could possibly happen, even worse than a demon on the ceiling, because he'll see the pentacle and the crystals and the candles and he's going to know I'm a witch.

And fuck, does he even know right now? Did all the energy I used toward astral projection drain me of my glamor?

But from the way he's staring at me, dark brows furrowed, deep eyes full of worry, I don't think he suspects. My glamor must be holding.

"I..." I say, trying to explain in the most plausible way. "I had a bad dream."

His frown deepens and he looks me over. "A bad dream?"

I nod, swallowing quickly, then turn the tables over to him. "What are you doing over here?"

He lets go of my shoulders, looking the tiniest bit chagrined. "I was worried," he admits, placing his hand at the back of his neck. "You didn't show up to class today..."

Oh. Right. "I was sick," I say weakly.

"I actually called you..."

I stare at him for a moment. He called me? I guess those were the missed calls on my phone. "I was worried when you didn't show up. Are you okay? You look a little pale. What is it?"

I have to say, I'm liking Valtu doting on me like this. The fact that he genuinely seems worried is a foreign feeling to me. I can't remember the last time anyone enquired after me and meant it. Maybe my parents...

I give him a quick smile before I can dwell on that too much. "I'm fine. Just stomach flu. I, uh, couldn't bothered to charge my phone. I just kept sleeping for most of the day."

"And you just woke up," he notes, looking me over while pursing his lips. "You're wearing the same clothes as you were in class yesterday."

I glance down at my tank top and wide-leg jeans, suddenly

aware of how chilled the night air is. "I was just too tired to change," I say dumbly.

"So you had a bad dream and...?"

I shrug. "Thought a walk would clear my head."

"It's getting cold out," he cautions.

"The cold feels good after all that heat."

He studies me for a moment. "Well, I'm glad you're up and about," he says. He gestures toward the square in front of us. "Mind if I accompany you on your walk?"

I give him a shaky smile. "Not at all," I find myself saying. But of course, it is kind of a problem since Livia is going to make her way here any minute. What if she runs into us? What if she acts like she knows me before she realizes I'm with Valtu.

"Must have been some dream," he comments as we head toward the bridge. "I can practically hear your heart racing."

I shoot him a sidelong glance. "You must have good hearing."

A small smile tugs at his lips. "What was the dream about?"

I take in a deep breath and decide to be bold. "You were in it."

His brows raise. "And it was a bad dream?"

I nod. "It was."

"May I ask what I was doing in your dream?"

"I think you were trying to save me," I admit, not wanting to tell him the rest.

"Save you?" He looks surprised. "From what?"

I shake my head, gnawing on my lower lip for a moment as we cross the bridge. "I'm not sure."

"And did I?" he asks, his voice growing fainter. "Save you, that is?"

"I don't know. I woke up."

"And decided to run for your life?"

I give him a weak smile. "I'm not always the most rational person."

He nods slowly, seeming to think that over. "Being rational is overrated, in my opinion. There's less surprises that way. I think surprises are what make life fun, don't you?"

I glance at him, the way the streetlights cast shadows in the hollows of his face. To think I saw him last night getting his dick sucked by some human. To think that this is the sort of lifestyle he leads when he's not lecturing about Bach or teaching us proper hand placement on the keys. The sexy yet respectable Professor Aminoff on the outside. A depraved bloodsucking vampire ho on the inside.

I feel it again. The pressure between my legs, the blood pumping thicker through my veins, my nipples getting harder against my bra, all at just the image of him last night, all the things I wanted to do to him, the things I wanted him to do to me.

He breathes in deeply through his nose and fuck, I know he can tell. The only thing I can hide from him it seems is who I truly am.

"If you feel like going for a longer walk," he says, his voice now taking on a silken quality, like a warm bath, "maybe I could persuade you to help me with the donations at the library."

Normally I would said yes, but after the dream, the demon, and the vampire sex dungeon of last night, I feel like I need to stay in public. I may find my guard lowering around Valtu, but I also don't fully trust being alone with him either, no matter how concerned he seemed to be about me. I mean, he actually called me on the phone. Found out my number because he was so distraught that I wasn't at class, and when he couldn't get a hold of me, he actually showed up almost outside my front door. I know vampires are known for stalking their prey, so this does have me a little on edge.

Remember what he is and what he's capable of, I remind myself. *He may seem to have morals, but he is still the predator and you are still the prey.*

For now.

"Or," he says, seeming to read me, "since you look like you should take it easy and relax a little, how about I finally take you up on that drink?" He flashes me a wicked smile that makes me weak at the knees. "I promise I won't bite."

Oh, if you only knew what I knew.

"Sure," I tell him. "But I'm afraid I don't have my wallet on me, so I'll have to owe you."

"I'm sure I can manage."

"And I also request it be one nearby because I have to pee like crazy." His brows go up. "I guess that was information you didn't need to know."

He laughs. "I plan on getting a lot more information out of you. I find you beguiling, you know. I can't quite make heads or tails of you."

Good, I think to myself. *Keep it that way.*

"Depends on how many drinks I have," I tell him.

"Duly noted," he says. "I know of a good bar that makes some gorgeous negronis. Just up here."

I look up the narrow street and at that moment I spot Livia walking toward us in a hurry, like she's running late to meet me.

Oh *fuck*.

Please don't say anything, please don't say anything, I think. My eyes are trained to her and I can tell when she spots me, her eyes brightening for a moment, then they go to Valtu and she quickly looks straight ahead, her face impassive, like she never saw us at all. Luckily he wasn't looking at Livia at the moment she was looking at me or he would have seen the recognition.

However, as she does pass us, along with the rest of the

people on the street, Valtu's head practically snaps around, his nostrils flaring.

I stare at him and hold my breath as he zeroes in on Livia, nothing but pure hatred distorting his face.

Holy shit.

He knows a witch just by smelling her.

CHAPTER 10

DAHLIA

I WATCH as Valtu keeps craning his neck to follow Livia as she hurries along the narrow street and eventually gets lost in the crowd.

"You okay?" I ask him, because that's what a normal person would do.

"Hmmph?" he practically grunts and looks back at me. Quicker than a flash his face morphs from something terrifying and enraged to blank and passive. "What was that?"

"I said, are you okay?" I press, wanting to see what he comes up with. "You look like you saw a ghost. But like a ghost you wish you could kill all over again."

He blinks at me, seemingly taken aback. "You got all that? No, no, I thought I saw someone I knew. Someone I don't like, but someone all the same."

Would a normal person press him at this point? Or would they let it go?

I decide to let it go and just give him an understanding smile, while he tries to compose himself back into the assured creature he is most of the time.

"Anyway," he says, clearing his throat. "Here we are."

We've ended up at a bar that has small tables lined up along the canal. Even though I don't feel a hundred percent secure considering the weird thing we saw in the water, plus the demon on my ceiling, which are probably the same thing, it's pretty romantic.

I quickly use the washroom inside the restaurant's main building and when I come out, Valtu has procured a shawl from the restaurant and slips it over my shoulders like a gentleman as he pulls out my chair for me. The negronis are already on the table and the waiter comes out and takes our order, Valtu getting us a plate of fried squash blossoms stuffed with goat cheese.

"Really, you don't have to buy me food," I tell him, gathering the shawl closer to my body. Now that the adrenaline of earlier is wearing off, the cold damp air is more noticeable.

"What if I'm hungry?" he asks. "Besides, I'm sure you haven't eaten anything if you've been feeling sick and sleeping in your clothes. How is the shawl?"

"It's warm, thank you," I tell him. I look around us, at the mist coming over the canal. It's spooky and ominous, despite a teenager cruising past on his boat, playing hip hop from the speakers. "Fall came on pretty quickly," I add, taking a sip of my drink. It's sweet, bitter and strong, hitting my taste buds in a way that makes me feel bold. I've needed this badly.

When he doesn't say anything to that, I look at him. He's sitting back in his chair and quietly observing me as I drink. In his navy Henley shirt that shows off his shoulders and muscular arms, and with the slightly seductive look in his dark eyes, I can pretend for a moment that I actually am on a date with a guy. Like a normal guy. Not a vampire I'm eventually supposed to kill, but some hot as fuck guy on vacation in Italy and I'm just a fellow traveler, looking for a night of romance and sex.

"Yes," Valtu says in a low voice, clearing his throat.

"Autumn falls quickly here. Like a guillotine, overnight." He pauses, licking his lips and I find myself staring at his mouth. "What is it like back at home for you? I imagine it must feel the same in the Pacific Northwest."

"It happens a lot earlier. Usually the Labour Day weekend is the signal of the end of summer and start of fall. The rains come and they don't stop."

"Do your parents still live there?"

"My parents are dead," I say too bluntly.

He blinks. "Oh. Fuck. I'm so sorry to hear that."

Must be strange to be someone who will never die, to hear about the dead. They must feel a type of pity for us mortals.

I lift my shoulder in a weak shrug. I never know what to say. "It's fine. It was a long time ago."

"How old were you when they died?" he asks.

"Ten," I say, looking away. I don't want to talk about this. I don't want to feel it, not the anger and rage that comes so quickly, sweeps through me like a brushfire. The fact that it was vampires, like himself, that murdered them, makes this all the more complicated.

"Jesus," he swears under his breath. "I can't imagine how hard that must have been." I can tell by the look on his face that he wants to ask me how they died. People always want to ask and often do.

But he doesn't. Instead he says, "That must have changed you in so many ways."

It's a surprising thing to say because it definitely did change me. It just feels like no one has ever noticed or acknowledged that. The only people who ever would have noticed, who would have paid attention, were my parents. I nod and take a bigger sip of my drink. "I think I'm going to need another one after this." I tap the side of my glass as I put it back down.

"I don't blame you. I'm sorry for the conversation going

into an unhappy topic," he says. He looks to the kitchen which seems very busy yet somehow the waiter comes straight out and over to us. No doubt I just watched Valtu compel him.

"How are we doing?" the waiter asks in English, suddenly extra attentive. "Need another drink? Your food is coming shortly, so sorry for the wait."

Valtu nods and gets us another order of negronis. I guess I'm on a mission to get drunk tonight and I think he's on that same mission.

He watches me curiously as I have another large sip of my drink.

"For what it's worth, Dahlia, I think you've changed into an incredible woman."

I would have laughed at that cheesy line if only he didn't look so sincere. "You didn't know what I was like as a child," I tell him. "Most people only change for the worst when horrible things happen to them."

"Most people get stronger," he says quietly. "Most, but not all. So which one were you? Did you get stronger? Or did you change for the worse?"

I tap my fingernails along the glass, noticing the chipped black tips of my shoddy manicure. "Both."

Because before my parents died, I at least had love in my life, from them. I had love and I was innocent. After they died, all love for me was gone, and my innocence was lost.

I became a killer.

"Who took care of you after they died? Where did you go?" he asks.

I suck on my lip for a moment, wishing I could tell him the truth, so that he could really see why I'd changed. "I went with an uncle."

A lie. Bellamy came from nowhere. I'd only known him for a couple of weeks before my parents died. He came to visit, stayed nearby. He had a lot of interest in me and my parents humored him but it came from a place of unease. Looking back, I wonder if my mother had feared him. My father definitely didn't like him. But they explained that he would be hanging around because of the guild. They didn't tell me why at the time, nor did they seem to want me to have anything to do with him.

Then they were murdered.

I found them in the kitchen after school one day.

The blood...there was so much blood. That's what I remember the most. It was broad daylight and the blood was everywhere and later I would scream because these fucking vampires didn't even bother to feed from them. They just killed them and left the blood, like it wasn't worth tasting.

"I take it things weren't so happy under your uncle's care," he says carefully, and I can feel his eyes on me, studying me. I don't want to give anything away but I feel this need to let it out.

I shake my head, not wanting to meet his gaze. I stare at the dark waters of the canal instead. "I didn't know him well. I was in shock, obviously. He took me to this small town, on a cove, in the middle of nowhere, northern end of the island. New school and new everything. I had money, you know he had money. But he..." I try to find the right words, "he was fake. He never really cared about me. I found that out later. I thought that because he took me in, you know, that it meant he would be a parent. But I don't think he ever saw me as a human being. We had a falling out a couple of years ago and I learned how counterfeit our relationship was. I had always been...disposable to him."

"Do you still talk to him?"

I'm about to shake my head but I stop. I tell the truth. "I wish I didn't. He has this...hold on me that I can't explain. It's like even though I know he doesn't value me as a person, I still want his attention. Pretty pathetic if you ask me."

"That's not pathetic, Dahlia. That's just...human."

"Then sometimes I wish I wasn't human."

His eyes glimmer darkly. "You don't want that."

I know he's speaking from experience but sometimes I wonder what it would be like to be a vampire. To have that edge, to not have to play by society's rules. Maybe if I had known how I was different, why I was different from everyone else, I wouldn't have become what I am. Vampires seem to own that, they revel in it, in being different. I barely feel human most days, barely feel like I exist here at all, and it kills me deep inside how not normal I am. Even sitting with someone else, having drinks and a conversation and taking part in society like everyone else feels utterly fucking foreign to me.

"What are you thinking about?" he asks quietly after I've stewed in my head for far too long.

I don't know why I keep feeling this need to be honest with him. I guess it's because I have been honest to a fault with people, opening up to people who don't even deserve it, people who aren't safe, and yet I'll never be totally open to the core of who I am. I live a lie no matter where I go. Most humans in this world don't know I'm a witch, don't know what I've been indoctrinated to do, don't even know vampires exist. Back at home, I have a friend or two that will hang out with me, but they don't know what I am, and only seem to like me when I'm wearing a mask, pretending to be whatever they want me to be, whatever role they think I fit for the evening. And if I were to be in a real relationship with someone, I would have to hide my true nature from them. No matter where I go, I can never truly reveal myself.

"You know, I can't remember the last time I was on a date."

He tilts his head as he gives me a soft smile. "I thought this wasn't a date."

I open my mouth to clarify, but nothing comes out. Instead I take a sip of my drink and the waiter arrives with the plate of fried squash blossoms, right on time to quell the awkwardness.

We dig into our food and I can't help but steal a glance at Valtu. He eats with patience, handling his fork delicately, no doubt centuries of fine manners bestowed upon him. I know that vampires are born human, have human bodies until they transform at the age of thirty-five (females at twenty-one), and that until that happens they eat food like the rest of us. I also know that when they are vampires, they do require blood to survive, and they hunger for it like nothing else, but they will occasionally eat food as well. It seems that Valtu has no problems indulging in it, though I'm not sure how much he enjoys it or how much is for a show of normalcy.

"I have a hard time believing that, Ms. Abernathy," he says between bites, his voice gentle. "That you can't remember the last date you were on."

"It's true," I tell him. "I honestly can't remember. I don't date, I've never even been in a relationship. Never been in love."

Now he's really surprised, but not as much as I am for just telling him all that. I quickly shove the fried flower in my mouth so I don't say anything else stupid.

"I don't need to tell you how beautiful you are," he says. "You must already know it. So I know it's not a matter of people not being attracted to you, rather—"

"But it is," I interrupt him, quickly swallowing my food. "It is. And it's not my looks, I know I'm pretty enough, it's just the moment people get to know me, they..." I look away, feeling like an idiot. Why am I telling him this?

I take in a deep breath. "You know about the whole uncanny valley thing right?"

His brows come together. "How something looks almost human but there's something off about it, which in turn makes them repulsive to others?"

I bite my lip, my eyes focused on my hands as I slowly turn my glass around on the table. "Yeah. That. Sometimes I think that people get that feeling from me. Like I look like them, like I'm almost like them, but then there's just something about me that tells them I'm different. That I'm not the same as them. And so they stay away."

He's quiet and I'm almost scared to look up at him. I've never admitted that to anyone before, I think I've barely admitted it to myself.

But when I meet his eyes, he's looking at me like he's recognizing something in me, maybe putting two and two together.

"Have you ever felt that way about anyone?" he asks. "Have you looked at someone and thought that something doesn't feel right?"

I know the irony in a vampire asking me this question, and I suddenly realize just how similar the two of us are. The difference is, humans are naturally drawn to vampires, they have that inner charm that makes them so alluring—and deadly. And even if they didn't, they certainly have the power to compel them.

"I have," I say slowly. "But it hasn't scared me off. It doesn't scare me like I seem to scare everyone else."

He leans forward slightly, a piece of black hair falling across his forehead, and I find myself reaching forward, brushing it back behind his ear, his skin cold against my touch, his hair silky soft. His eyes meet mine, an intense mahogany storm, and we're so close now...

I quickly take my hand back, putting distance back between us.

He swallows thickly, watching me as I quickly take a gulp of my drink. I feel so fucking insane right now, I'm vibrating. "What if I were to tell you that I feel the same way as you," he says softly, pressing his fingers into the table. "That I know exactly what you're speaking about?"

A normal person would brush him off. They'd tell him, don't be silly, you're this accomplished handsome professor at a prestigious music school. I should say all that to keep up the ruse, but I can't. I don't want to. I want someone to relate to for once in my damn life.

"Do you really?" I whisper.

He nods gravely and I find myself wondering about his real story, his real past, all the things I would normally be asking him but I can't because he's only going to hide who he is, much the way I have to hide who I really am.

"As a child, I had no friends," I say after a moment. "I really didn't. And I didn't understand why, you know? I tried so hard to be good, to be nice to everyone, I really did. I tried so hard it was sad. And yet I was always the last to get picked for anything. When there were assignments we had to pair up for in school, no one ever chose me. The teacher then had to put me with someone and I always saw the resentment in the one I was paired with. The teachers didn't like me either for some reason, even when I never spoke out of turn and I always did my homework. And whenever there was a team for like soccer, baseball, or something, I was always picked last, even though I was pretty athletic. I was the one never invited to birthday parties even though I would always get them a gift. I always sat alone in the back of the school bus. I never had a best friend, and if I did they only lasted a short while before they realized there was something wrong with me. Every time I opened my mouth kids would tune me out, and adults did the same. It's like they didn't want the weird quiet kid hanging out with their child. And I still don't know what it is about me. I don't know what's wrong with me. I didn't understand...I don't..."

Tears sting at my eyes and I know I should shut up, that I'm ruining everything, that I'm saying too much and to the absolute worst person, but I can't help it. I always thought it was because I was a witch, and that's what people saw in me, that they saw I was different because of the magic in my veins and it scared them. And if that was true, well that I could understand. But then I was raised around other witches when I went to live with Bellamy, and then went to the academy for slayers, and it was the same thing. It was the same damn thing. It had nothing to do with being a witch at all, people just didn't want anything to do with me no matter how hard I tried to be nice or to be funny or smart or relatable.

So I just stopped trying.

I chose to shun the world and be alone. Spent my days with only good books for company.

And I became the only person I could rely on.

But I still don't know why it has to be this way. What is it about me that makes me so unlikeable? Am I really that awful, really that broken inside?

"I was a good kid," I go on, tears now flowing down my face, and I can't stop them, can't stop talking, "before my parents died, I was a good kid. I could never understand why me? Like why...you know once, when I was like eight, I was so lonely and just so desperate, I took out the phone book and called every single kid in my class and asked them if they would play with me. And every single one of them said *no*. They all said no."

Oh god. Now I'm really crying. What the fuck is wrong with me?

I look at Valtu through my tears and shake my head. "I'm

so sorry. I don't know why the fuck I'm telling you this." I glance around, trying to see if people are paying attention to us, and there are a few curious looks thrown my way to see why this girl is crying on her date. I'm making a fool of myself for no reason. I could be enjoying a drink on a night out in Venice, but instead I'm crying over shit from my childhood in front of my teacher, who happens to be a fucking vampire, who I was originally sent here to kill.

Everything is just such a damn mess.

"Don't be sorry," Valtu says, reaching forward and placing his hand on mine, his skin cold but electric. "You're telling me this because you need to tell me. You want to. And you know you can trust me. You know that I am the same as you."

As much as vampires are different from the average human, there's no way he can relate to all that I've just spilled my guts over, I don't care who he was in his past.

I shake my head, wiping my tears.

"Can I kiss you?"

I go still, staring at him in surprise. "What?"

Did he just ask to kiss me?

"I would like to kiss you," he repeats, intensity burning in his eyes.

"Now?" I practically sputter, blinking at him. "While I'm crying?"

He doesn't answer. He just moves, leaning across the table in a flash of black.

His hands go to either side of my face, fingertips pressing against my cheekbones, going into my hair, and his lips come to mine, soft and sweet. I can taste the salt of my tears as our mouths open against each other. His kiss is gentle, delicate, and yet there's something foreign and primal about it, something dark and rough swirling at the edges of his lips, eliciting a strange response from deep inside me.

I feel my body weaken at his touch, melting into him, and

I moan softly into his mouth as our tongues meet, the sweet bitter taste of negroni mixing with the salt of my tears, and it's unlike any kiss I've had before. It's as if something inside me is opening up, my body reacting to every touch, every movement of his tongue against mine.

And then he gently pulls away, leaving me breathless, like I might just slide down my seat and under the table into a puddle.

I open my eyes and blink at him, discovering my fingers are clenching the edge of the table as if to hold on.

I can't believe he just kissed me.

He's sitting back in his chair, running the tip of his tongue over the edge of his lips, his eyes so deep in thought as he stares at me, I feel like I'm on fire.

"Do you know what I tasted in your tears?" he says in such a low, rough voice that the skin on the back of my neck prickles.

My lips open and close weakly before I manage to say, "What?"

"Darkness."

My body goes stiff and I stare at him.

"I felt the darkness inside of you." He's whispering now, his words enveloping me like a cloak.

He can't know. He can't ever know about my darkness. Why it's there. How it accumulates with each life that I've taken, each awful thing that I've done.

I clear my throat. "You got that from my tears?"

His gaze doesn't lighten. "I wanted to feel it for myself. To know you. To know why I've been so drawn to you. And now I know. The darkness in me calls to the darkness in you."

I don't know what to say to that. Anyone else would have told them he was being a fucking weirdo, but I have no doubt he really can taste the darkness inside of me. I'm just glad that's all he's able to see. If he were to get into the specifics...

"I'm going to go pay," he says, suddenly getting to his feet and disappearing into the restaurant. I wonder if now he feels he said too much.

I finish the rest of my drink and then get up, feeling a little lightheaded from the drinks and emotional vomit, folding up the shawl and putting it on the chair.

"Do you want to take that with you?" Valtu asks as he approaches me, nodding at the shawl.

I give him a look. "I'm not stealing a shawl from a restaurant."

"I could persuade them to give it to you."

I bet you can. "I'll be fine."

"Then I'll walk you home. Keep you warm." He smiles. It's almost bashful, with just a bit of cunning.

"I'd like that," I tell him, feeling shy all of a sudden.

Then he holds his hand out for me. His hand. And not only do I feel shy, but my heart is fizzing, as if someone poured champagne in my chest. It's just his hand, and he's already kissed me, and yet it feels so much bigger than that. Like to hold onto him is to step into something I may not be able to get out of.

But I place my hand in his and he grasps it tight, his skin both hot and cold at the same time. His grip is strong and I feel butterflies fly up through my veins, spurred on by his contact, a sense of electricity whirling around us.

He leads me back to the street and we continue our walk, side by side, his hand in mine, and I know this might be a vampire thing that he's doing to me and that's why he wanted to hold my hand, or maybe it's just the alcohol and my nerves, but I feel warm, inside and out.

"You know, what I told you back there," he says, his voice low and thoughtful as we walk, "that I could feel you, know you through your tears...any other woman would have run the other way. What I told you was not normal. And yet I told you all the same. And you haven't run. Why is that?"

I swallow hard, aware of the quickening pulse in my throat. "I don't know. Perhaps it's the same reason why I suddenly unloaded all of my deepest, saddest emotional damage onto you. Any other man would have called me nuts and left. Indeed they have, and for much less. But not you..."

He stops suddenly, pulling me up to him just as we're on the crest of a small bridge. With his other hand he puts his palm against my cheek, studying my face like I'm some code he's trying to solve.

"I swear we have met before. I don't know where and," he licks his lips, "I don't know when. I just know that everything you told me, somehow I already knew. Like I know you without...knowing you. Like one day I'll wake up and all will be revealed."

It is strange that he thinks he knows me. Maybe I remind him of a past lover. Sometimes I think I get that same feeling about him. But the last thing I want is for everything to be revealed.

He leans in closer, his eyes searching mine, the faint lights from the city looking like fireflies in the darkness. "I am drawn to you Dahlia, like a bat to a flame."

"You mean moth to a flame," I correct him, trying not to smile.

He gives me a wicked grin. "I prefer bats. Moths don't have teeth. I like things to have a little bite to them."

Then his smile fades and he suddenly kisses me again. There are no tears to taste this time, instead it is a deep and searing kiss that I feel in my bones, a kiss that rewrites both the past and future, and the only thing certain is the present. His lips are soft but firm like the ripest fruit, and there is a kind of soft desperation in him that touches something raw and aching inside me.

I pull back to catch my breath. "You'll get in trouble—" but the words are torn from my mouth when he grabs the back of my neck and kisses me again, harder this time. My head spins from the kiss, from the raze of his teeth, from the way he licks my bottom lip. I can't help but think about his fangs, how it takes nothing for his canines to transform, that I am making out with a creature that could murder me on the spot. Then again, that's not a new fear for most women.

And I don't feel afraid of Valtu, my professor. I'm only afraid that there might be consequences for this. From the faculty if we're caught, and also from myself. Because while seducing Dracula was always part of the plan, I was never supposed to enjoy it. I was never supposed to *want* this.

But I do.

And that scares the life out of me.

Enough that I pull back, and already the smallest bit of distance feels like I'm leaving part of me behind.

"Aren't you worried someone will see?" I whisper, trying to breathe as he presses his lips against my forehead.

"They won't."

He has his ways. No doubt every person who has passed us on this bridge hasn't really seen us at all. We're hiding in plain sight.

My body wants to bring him to my apartment. I'm craving his touch like nothing else. But I can't. Not in the state I left it and not with a possible demon still inside. I can only hope it left through the open window; I assume that's how it got in. But my knowledge of demons doesn't go very far. I never thought I would have to deal with any of this.

"I have an exam tomorrow," I suddenly blurt out.

He widens his eyes and nods, taking a step back, though his hand is still firmly holding onto mine. "So you do." He clears his throat loudly. "I'm guessing you need to study."

I'd rather study you, I think, but I nod. "Yeah. Thank god I didn't leave it all to the last minute like I usually do."

He sucks on his lower lip for a moment and I want nothing more than to kiss him again. "I'm sure you'll pass," he says.

"It's not enough to pass," I tell him. "I want to get a good grade."

"I'm sure you'll get a good grade," he says in a knowing tone.

"Don't you dare try to do me any favors," I warn. "I need to get good grades on my own accord."

"Help you? Wouldn't dream of it." He gives me a convincing smile. "Still, let me finish walking you home. I promise I'll be out of your hair."

So we walk hand-in-hand the rest of the way, until we're standing outside my building.

"I'm going to go upstairs now," I tell him.

He slides his hand around my lower back, holding me in place, while his other hand cups my jaw. "And I'm going to kiss you again."

This time the press of his lips is so faint, so light, and yet it makes my knees tremble, my stomach to do summersaults. "Dahlia," he says, murmuring against my mouth. "I don't want you to be ashamed of your darkness. I don't want you to be afraid of it. I am not a delicate man. I am brash, volatile, controlling and demanding and I always, always get what I want. What I want is your darkness to play with mine. I want to make it come so beautifully alive, so that we can revel in it together."

He presses his lips to mine firmly then pulls away and I feel like I can't breathe at all as he stares inches from my eyes. "I am choosing you. And if you accept me, there is no turning back."

I try to swallow. "And what do I get out of it?" I whisper, my voice shaking slightly.

The corner of his mouth lifts in a smirk while his eyes narrow. "You get to feel things you'd only dreamed of feeling. You get to do things you were too afraid of doing. To live in the very darkness you run from. Isn't that you want most of all? To be so pushed past the point of terror that you no longer fear anything at all?"

Holy shit.

"As I said," he says gruffly, running his thumb over my lips, "I am not a delicate man. I can be rough. I can cause pain. I may make you hate me sometimes. But I will always be on your side. I will always make you feel chosen."

I don't know what the hell I'm agreeing to here but I'm nodding.

Because I have to.

Because I want you.

"Then choose me," I say softly.

He leans in and kisses me on the cheek. "I already did. First day I laid eyes on you." He pulls back and then gestures to the building. "Speaking of, we better part ways before I end up interfering in that studying of yours, though I know you'll pass with flying colors."

And just like that, Valtu turns into my professor again, charming and cordial and not at all telling me he's going to push me past the point of terror.

I turn to put my keys in the main doors and pause, glancing at him over my shoulder. "This might sound silly, but do you mind waiting around until I'm in my room. I'm just on the end there by the water."

"Of course not," he says. "I would have done it anyway."

"You wouldn't have known which room I was in."

"I would have figured it out." His smile flashes in the night.

Somehow I'm comforted. I go inside the building, then up the stairs to my apartment. I wait outside the door and take in a deep breath. If there's still a demon on the other side, I'm going to be very, very upset.

I quickly put in the keys and push the door open, hard enough that it does so with a bang.

The lights are on.

The lights are on and my floor is clean. No candles, no chalk, no crystals.

And the window is shut.

"What the fuck?" I walk inside carefully, looking around.

On the kitchen counter is a note.

I pick it up.

Don't mind me but I let myself in. I hadn't heard from you but then I saw you with the target. I'm not sure what happened but judging by the state of your place, I have an idea. BTW I did a cleansing in here and put up a protective spell and some wards because I'm pretty sure that there was a demon in here when I first got in. Charge your phone and call me in the morning. Livia.

What's funny is that with all that she wrote, the thing that sticks out is that she referred to Valtu as a target. Though I know it's true, it's not sitting right with me.

Speaking of Valtu, I quickly put the note away and run to the window, looking outside. I see Valtu standing below and to the side, a shadow in the night. I raise my hand to let him know I'm okay. He raises his, gives me a nod, then stalks off into the darkness of the city.

CHAPTER 11

VALTU

IT HAS BEEN painful to remember those days, to keep writing them down in this journal. There was so much joy in them at the time, so much hope for the future. In so many ways I was young, because we are all younger before love shapes us and changes us. I was naïve in thinking that finding Mina again would make all my problems go away. All it did was make things worse.

But at the time it was heaven. I didn't think that far ahead, about the fact that she didn't know I was a vampire, and that if I were to marry her, that she would be doomed to live a mortal life. That she would one day die and I would keep on living. I didn't let myself think that far because the present tasted far too sweet.

Now, though, all these memories taste like death.

THE VICTORIAN AGE
London – 1888

"I PROBABLY SHOULDN'T COME IN," LUCY SAID TO ME IN A small, apprehensive voice as we approached my front door in Marylebone, the gas lamps outside my house flickering.

"And why is that?" I asked, letting go of her elbow.

She dipped her chin, staring at me demurely. "Because I've never been alone with you. Not in your house."

"And?" I wanted to hear her say it, for her to tell me my intentions.

"And I know what you want, Count Aminoff." I stared at her to go on. She took in a deep breath. "A lady never gives her body to a man before marriage."

"And who told you that?" I asked, taking off my hat and holding it under my arm as I peered at her, trying to hide a smile. "Your parents? Your friends? God himself?"

I had been courting Lucy for about two months. Back in those days, you took your time in getting to know one another, and in this case, it was all for her benefit. After all, I already knew Lucy. I knew her as Mina. And even though she seemed to have zero recollection about her past life, at that moment in time it didn't really matter. I knew that one day she would have to remember. One day I would make her remember.

I figured sex would be the way to do it. That does seem to be my solution for all things. I thought that the moment I came inside her would be the moment she'd really recognize me. All of me. But ravishing Mina in the fields of seventeenth century Finland proved to be a lot easier than trying to get Lucy naked in my bed in Victorian England.

That said, tonight I could tell she was waning. Months of innocent dates to museum exhibits and plays and walks in the many gardens and parks of London, and she was starting to bend to my whim. I did my best not to compel her, as I wanted her to want me on her own accord, but I admit there were a few times I managed to push the logic out of her head and let her sensual nature come forward.

Unfortunately even when logic was gone, there was good old fashioned guilt over being a lady and what society and God would think and all of that baggage that was thrust upon women the moment they were born.

Tonight, though, I was going to show her the stars. I was going to show her who the God was in her life, not some unseen creator, but me, an immortal being with far more mercy. When she came so hard that she yelled my name, that's when she'd discover the real religion, the religion of sex.

Van Helsing thought I was nuts, though. He had met Lucy often after that first time in the British Museum; the three of us would often go to the opera together. He liked Lucy a lot but the whole idea of her being my past love reincarnated didn't sit right with him. Despite being a vampire, the doctor was another person who was awfully fond of science and logic. To him, it didn't make sense and so it couldn't be true. Reincarnation just wasn't believable.

But none of that really mattered to me. Van Helsing may have looked at Lucy and saw a beautiful young girl and assumed I was just projecting the trauma of losing Mina onto her. "After all," he had said once, "there is no photographic evidence from those days. You never had a painting of Mina. I am sure you just think they are the same person when they aren't. If you could pull up Mina from the grave right now, I am sure you'd see that they merely look the same. She reminds you of her, that's all, and you want it to be her so badly that you'll believe anything."

I humored the doctor. I let him believe that if it made him feel better.

But I knew. I knew this was Mina, my long-lost love, and I was going to do whatever it took to make her remember who I am and what we were to each other. I knew I was no slouch in the looks department, I knew I had status as a count, lots of money at my disposal, a gorgeous house in the city, rare artifacts and art I'd collected over the years. I knew there were many reasons why Lucy would be interested in me anyway, but I chose to believe that the main reason was because she felt something for me that she couldn't explain.

She felt something for me that would make her trust me because deep down in her subconscious she knew who I was. She knew what we had lost.

But that night, I was yearning to take the next step. I needed her trust in order to do the things I had been dying to do with her, to bring my body together with hers in an unholy union.

To make her finally see.

At the time, Lucy lived with her parents at an estate on the outskirts of the city. Though her family was wealthy and they had drivers themselves, I always had my driver bring her home and at a reasonable hour. Tonight's play, however, had been cancelled just as we got to the theatre, so I thought it was the perfect time to bring her back to my place and, well, deflower her, for lack of a better word. I guess, fuck her like a dog in heat would also get the point across.

"What makes you think that stepping inside my house would lead to your defilement?" I asked her.

She giggled coyly, playing the game. "My intuition, I suppose," she said. "I am a woman after all, Count Aminoff."

"I can always take you home if you'd like," I say, gesturing to the carriage that was out of view. "I am at your disposal. The choice is yours."

I could see a real war waging behind those pretty green eyes of hers.

"I think I'd like to come inside," she eventually said.

God, those words made me hard immediately. She would be coming all right.

"Good choice," I told her. I unlocked the door and we stepped inside. It was barely lit, a few paraffin lamps in the grand hall and the sitting room that my servants had kept going while I was out, while the gas lights on the ceiling had been turned off.

Lucy looked around, impressed. It wasn't as large as her parents' house in the country, but my wealth was displayed in different ways. I took her by the hand and led her to the velvet sofa in the sitting room, then quickly went into the back of the house where the servants' quarters were. One of them was a German named Han who was a vampire who was down on his luck and dealing with depression. At the time I just saw him as a poor soul who needed help. In those days vampires didn't even think they could get depressed as they believed they were immune to physical impairments, aging and disease, and though that's the case, the mind doesn't work that way.

I saw Han and told him that I was home for the evening and I had company and wasn't to be disturbed. He was used to the women I would bring home into this house, the things I would do to them, so I knew he wouldn't dare interrupt.

Then I went back into the kitchen, grabbed a bottle of red wine I had gotten from this small but mighty vineyard in Bordeaux a few years back, and joined Lucy in the sitting room.

She was standing up, marvelling over the instruments I had in the corner beside the fireplace: a violin, a cello, and a piano.

"Do you play?" she asked.

I nodded. "I do."

Her eyes sparkled. She loved music. "I didn't know this about you."

"You should have come into my home sooner then," I said. I strolled over to the bar and set down the bottle, opening it with a corkscrew and pouring us both a glass. "To us," I said to her, staring deep into her eyes.

"To us," she said. She had a sip of wine, her gaze growing intense, and it was that moment that I could smell her. A gorgeous scent that signalled she was ready for me. Fuck, I had missed that.

"To tonight," she added, having a larger gulp this time.

I slammed back the glass, perhaps a waste for a wine so rare and as she said, "Maybe you could play me some music," I was grabbing her by her face, my hand behind her back and her wine glass dropped to the floor, bouncing on the soft rugs, wine spilling like a bloodstain.

She let out a faint cry and I kissed her roughly. Until that moment our physical contact was on the chaste side, which was torture considering how deeply and intimately I knew Mina's body. With Lucy I had to behave, I had to hold back, and even though I knew she was a virgin and had never been with a man like this before, I knew I couldn't be too delicate with her. I could only hope she liked it rough.

"Valtu," she whispered as my mouth went to her neck and I inhaled the scent of her, tasted her skin, heard the singing of her blood in her veins, begging for me to bite. In that moment I remembered what Van Helsing had said about how I had never been a vampire around Mina, I had only been a guileless human.

It was enough to stop me from sinking my teeth in, from finally tasting her blood. All these centuries and I only dreamed of what her blood would taste like, if it would taste as sweet as her cunt.

Now, though, her cunt would have to do.

I brought her down to the rugs, pushing the glass to the side, and tried feverishly to undo her dress. There were so many hooks and buttons I didn't think I could get through at all. I ended up tearing at her clothes, I think I may have told her I'd buy her new ones. She protested at first, the thought of her dress being ruined, but I ripped the bodice open and her breasts bobbed free. The sight of her creamy pale skin, her heavy tits, those nipples hardening in the air, I felt like I was going to come right there and then.

Kissing her again, I cupped one of those perfectly full breasts in my hand, squeezing it and teasing the nipple with my thumb. She moaned, her back arching as I stroked her, licking the other rosy tip while she writhed beneath me.

"Oh God," she hissed through gritted teeth. "Oh Valtu. Please don't stop."

But I had to take my time.

Grinning, I ran my tongue over her nipple, teasing it with just the tip of my tongue, tasting her skin and hearing her moan in pleasure. My hands moved down to her hips, pulling up the layers and bustle of her skirt, my fingers curling over the waistband of her drawers ready to yank them down until I discovered hers had an open crotch. I loved how convenient that style was back in the day.

"Be gentle," she whispered to me.

I could only smile wickedly. I would be gentle at first, and then she was going to want it wild. I knew my love. I knew what she liked, even if she didn't know it yet.

I put my hands between her thighs until her legs were spread wide apart, begging for me to taste every inch of her. I felt my fangs threatening to come out, but I used the tip of my tongue to push them back in. I was going to feed in a different way.

I lowered my face into that delicious cunt, the smell and taste of her bringing me back in time. Mina. My Mina.

She cried out in a loud gasp that nearly made the chandelier shake and I licked along it slowly at first and then faster, harder, until she was bucking against my mouth so hard I thought she would choke me with those soft thighs of hers.

Then I plunged two fingers deep into her wetness and drove them in and out rapidly, prepping her. "Oh God," she said through a sharp gasp, her hands clutched at my hair as I sucked and licked at her clit, my tongue devouring it and sending tingles of electricity through her body. She was a goddess. A goddess sent through time for me. She was my destiny.

"I like this," she whispered, her words ragged, and she grabbed my hair, pushed my head harder into her cunt. "I like you down there," she went on, gasping for air as she bucked against my face. She was so new to this, so innocent, I loved how she didn't know she could have this pleasure from a man. Or from a vampire, as it was.

What she did know is that she wanted it, wanted me, and she was ready for it.

"Oh Valtu!" she cried out, and I felt her grow tighter and wetter around my fingers, getting close.

I gladly continued to eat her out, inhaling her scent deeper into my body and when she came, her cum on my tongue, I felt the satisfaction of lifetimes of waiting. Of dreaming. Of wishing.

I moved up along her body to stare at her.

She was trembling, her beautiful hair all over the place, her cheeks flushed but she was smiling, beaming up at me.

"I want you," she said, breathing hard. "I want to be with you. Fully."

"I know," I said. "I want you too. More than you can imagine."

I have waited centuries for you.

"Now," she begged as she reached out, her fingertips grazing over my face, my lips. "Now, please. I ache for you so much. I didn't know it could be like this."

I understood her completely.

But she didn't understand all I wanted.

"Get on all fours," I told her. "Your ass toward me like a bitch in heat."

Her eyes went wide, mouth as round as the moon.

I gave her the softest, most non-threatening smile I could muster. "I'm well endowed. You're tight as a fist. This is going to hurt you, do you understand? It's going to hurt, you're probably going to bleed..."

I trailed off because the idea of her bleeding fresh blood made me even harder than I was before. I would need to hold that part of me off.

I cleared my throat. "You might bleed. There's nothing we can do about it, except to turn that pain into pleasure. Let me show you how."

I gestured with my hand for her to turn around. "Turn around and get on your knees or I'll pick you up and do it for you."

She blinked at me, fearful and curious at once, the same combination that Mina was. I knew how to handle her.

Lucy did as she was told. I pushed up the bustle and layers of her dress, then yanked her bloomers down to her knees, leaving her perfect ass bare. It looked like a creamy peach and I was just dying to take a bite.

Instead I got up and went over to the violin, picking up the bow from the stand.

"What are you doing?" she asked, staring at me in confusion over her shoulder.

"This," I said, brandishing the violin bow between my hands, showing her. Then, with a grin, I brought the violin bow down hard against her ass. She shrieked with surprise, jerking violently.

"Valtu!" she managed to say.

"Feel the pain," I told her. "Feel it. Know that you control it."

I did it again, whipping her. She cried out again, her white skin turning pink.

"Don't let it control you," I told her. "Don't run from it."

I spanked her again, then after I ran my tongue over her raw pink flesh that the bow left behind, my fingers going over her clit. The moan of relief from her was so deep I could feel it rattling in my bones.

"Do you see now, my love? The pleasure and the pain? How we need one to make the other one sweeter?"

She made a breathless noise that sounded like a yes.

So I spanked her over and over again with the wooden implement, breaking the strings, hearing it smack loudly against her soft skin and she cried out every time, her voice getting lower, driven by desire. The sound of the bow slapping against her flesh echoed throughout the room, sending waves of pleasure straight to my cock.

She writhed in ecstasy as I continued to spank her, taking time to impart pleasure, to make her close to coming. All the while my throbbing cock strained against my trousers. Finally I could take it no more; I needed to feel her tight and wet and wrapped around my aching shaft.

I tore at my clothing, shoving my trousers and drawers down my hips. My cock sprang free, hard and pulsing. Lucy stared at it over her shoulder, her eyes wide, biting her lip.

"This is going to hurt," I warned her again as I positioned myself behind her. "But I promise you, the pleasure will be worth it."

She nodded, her face tight with anticipation.

Slowly, inch by inch, I pushed inside her. It was even tighter than I thought it would be and she cried out as I forced my way in further. The squeeze was sharp but quickly turned to pleasure as I began thrusting in and out of her tight heat, my eyes already rolling in the back of my head as my fingers gripped her hips.

"Oh, Lucy," I whispered, staring down at her ass as I fucked her. "You feel so good. So good."

Her breathing was fast and hard, her head fallen forward, clutching the bunched-up rug beneath her. I grabbed a handful of her hair and used it to pull her head back, making her look at me over her shoulder as I fucked her. I know this was all so rough for her first time, but she was giving herself to it, like on some innate level she remembered what it was like to be fucked by me before.

I stared into her eyes, my hand going down to rub her sweet clit as I fucked her, wanting all the pain to slip away, for her to see the fucking stars. The sight of her in front of me, staring at me with heavy-lidded desire, my cock inside her, fucking her hard, was enough to drive me out of my mind. I felt my balls tightening, but I held off, wanting this to last.

"I could come right now, Lucy dove," I told her. "But you're going to come first."

She nodded and I rubbed her clit harder as I drove my cock in and out of her, feeling her tighten against me, feeling her cunt squeeze my shaft even tighter.

"I'm going to...I'm..." she cried out, her breath catching in her throat, her body breaking out in a sweat and the wetness dripping out of her, the scent of her filling the room.

With a loud cry she came, her body writhing against me, my cock deep inside her, spasming and clenching. I fucked her hard enough to give her rugburn, driving in and out, in and out of her tight pink cunt.

"Yes, my dove. Yes, that's it. Come for me."

She collapsed against the rug, tears and sweat beading her face as she panted for air.

And I came. I came hard, my cock pulsing through her, my entire body shaking with the strength of the orgasm. I fucked her through it and when I was empty and exhausted, I leaned on top of her, completely spent.

Lucy wept quietly then, her face against the rug, her skin damp with sweat. I pulled out, trying not to look at the sight of her blood mixed with my cum, and lay there next to her, not sure what to say. I was so happy, all I wanted was for her to be happy too.

"I'm sorry," I whispered to her. "I didn't mean to hurt you."

She turned to me and smiled, her eyes brimming with tears. A few escaped, running down her face.

"I'm not sorry. I'm not sorry at all," she said, smiling through it. "I'm just so overwhelmed. I never knew...I never knew it could be like that."

I kissed her then, the taste of her salty tears on her lips.

"You are the most beautiful thing I've ever experienced," I murmured against her lips. "And I'm never letting you go. Not in this lifetime, not in the next."

And that was the beginning of our union together.

The next day I asked for her hand in marriage.

She accepted.

We were both so fucking happy.

But trouble was just around the corner. Life would never let us be happy for long. Looking back, I should have told her then what I really was. That I was a vampire. I should have spent my remaining years with her living in the honest truth. At the very least I should have told her who we were to each other, helped her uncover her memories of her past life as Mina.

When I would finally do so, it would be too late.

CHAPTER 12

DAHLIA

"Finally!" Livia says loudly as I move the phone away from my ear, her voice too much for this time of morning.

"Sorry, I fell asleep just as my phone was charging," I tell her, gathering my jean jacket closer as I make my way over the Rio Madonna dell'Orto. It's misty this morning and damp and though I'm glad I'm wearing Docs, I immediately regret wearing a dress. Summer really is gone.

"Thank you for everything you did," I quickly add so she doesn't think I'm ungrateful. "I was fully expecting to come home and find that demon waiting for me."

"So there was a demon," she muses coldly. "I sensed as much. When you weren't answering, I feared the worst. That you got found out, that you had to leave or...they killed you. But then I saw you with Valtu and you looked fine, but I couldn't be sure. I went to your apartment and let myself in—"

"How?"

A pause. "I didn't use magic. I have an extra set of keys."

"You have an extra set of keys to my apartment?" I ask.

Nope, I don't like that.

"It's not your apartment, Dahlia. It belongs to the guild. And right now, you belong to the guild too."

I frown, lowering my voice as I walk through a crowd of tourists. "What does that mean?"

"It means that you are here under their control, until they deem you worthy enough to come back fully."

I stop, stepping out of the way of the pedestrians, leaning against a shadowed wall. "What? That's not what we agreed on, me and Bellamy. He said that I could come back to the guild if I did this one thing."

She chuckles dryly. "You never leave the guild once you enter it. You're in it for life. You know this. After your, you know, after your *last* mission, Bellamy thought it best if you were retired. You had your sabbatical, sure, but you were still bound to your duty to us. You knew what you were getting into when you decided to be one."

"I was thirteen years old!" I yell into the phone. "I didn't know what I was agreeing to do! My parents had been *murdered* and Bellamy told me if I wanted revenge, then I would have to join!"

"And you did get your revenge, didn't you?" she says, her voice aggravatingly calm. "How many vampires have you killed over the years, Dahlia? How many?"

I don't want to answer that. "I never killed the ones that killed my parents."

"How do you know? You don't. All you know is that you are doing what you were born and bred to do—"

"I wasn't *bred* to do this," I cry out. "I wasn't born to do this either."

"That's not what the guild has decided. You know what they believe with natural born killers. You were chosen, Dahlia. And with every vampire you take out, you are preventing another child out there, another kid like yourself, from losing their own parents to vampires. Or their spouses.

Or their own children. You're saving people by doing what you do, and that's why you need to keep on doing it." She sighs heavily and I'm clutching the phone so hard I'm afraid I might break it. "You made an oath. You're back on the job. Finish the job or the next time there will be something worse than that demon in your room."

"Are you threatening me?"

Her sigh deepens. "*No.* I mean, the longer you take, the more time that Saara and Aleksi have to keep opening the portals or doing whatever the hell they are doing. You need to find that book, and fast. The last thing you want is for Bellamy to go there and finish your job for you. Believe me. You don't want that."

Then she hangs up.

Fuck. This is not the conversation I wanted to have this morning, not when my first class is the exam that I didn't have a chance to study for last night because I fell asleep. Not to mention that my brain had been absolutely stewing over the events from last night.

Everything that happened between me and Valtu.

I mean, really, what the fuck was going on with my head yesterday? What made me think that I could just open myself up to him, when I've never been able to do that with anyone? As Livia reminded me, I am a slayer. My purpose is to kill vampires like him, and kill *him* specifically.

And yet I wanted to lay my soul bare to him and I don't know why.

Is it because I knew, on some level, that he would understand me?

Is it because I feel I understand him?

He is a killer, sure. But so am I. How are we any different?

That darkness inside of me is the result of taking life after life.

Perhaps that darkness inside of him is the same.

Both of us are bad fucking people. At least he has the excuse that he's just trying to feed, trying to survive.

What's my excuse?

I try to push that out of my head. I need to stay focused. I step back onto the street and hurry along to class, running late now. The funny thing is, it doesn't even matter if I fail my exam or not because this is all a ruse anyway. None of this matters, and yet I'm making it matter. I'm making it important because a large part of me wishes this was all real. I want to be just a music student falling for her professor. I want the simplicity of it all.

And you're not falling for him, I tell myself as I enter the school. *You're not falling for your target. You're not going to compromise your mission yet again.*

But the last time was different. I befriended a vampire, Ottilie. There was nothing sexual about it. I just got too close to her. She was able to use that to manipulate me before I could manipulate her.

I learned my lesson. I almost lost my life doing so.

I enter the classroom, the last one in. Valtu looks up from his desk and his hardened expression softens with relief when he sees me. I can tell that he probably thought I wouldn't show because I was avoiding him after everything he told me last night.

After the way he touched me.

After the way he kissed me.

Even now, with his dark gaze locked on mine, I feel my body starting to come alive again, a fire building deep inside.

There he is.

So damn beautiful.

I sit down at my desk, averting my eyes now because I think if we keep staring at each other, the other students are going to suspect something.

And Valtu swiftly turns into Professor Aminoff, a man

with charm and authority that has everyone hanging on his every word as he preps us for how the exam is going to take place.

My whole life I've left things to the last minute. Tomorrow has always been a preferable day to do something. Though I didn't study as much as I would have liked, I'm glad I at least got some done at the library the other night, because as I'm doing the exam, I realize I know most of the answers. I suppose I could have used a memorization spell to help me through, but honestly that astral projection completely wrecked me and I'm too afraid to use any magic now for fear of losing my grip on my glamor.

When the exam is over, class is dismissed and even though I want to approach Valtu at his desk, another teacher walks into the room to talk to him. For a moment I fear that maybe someone saw us kissing on the bridge last night and he's about to be reprimanded, but that doesn't seem to be the vibe since they're joking around.

So I leave the room and decide to head out into the city for a bit, grab an early lunch somewhere. I pick a taverna across the Ponte dell'Accademia that I heard Valtu mention once, hoping that maybe he'll show up here when he's done.

But he doesn't. I have some bruschetta since the food is fairly expensive and a couple of Aperol Spritzes, taking my time to linger like the locals do since my next class isn't for a while. Then it's time to head back into the school for my music theory class, then my composition class—I take both with a bit of a buzz going. Finally I have the chance to see Valtu again in the concert hall for my practical, last class of the day.

He is different with me this time. When he meets my eyes, he smiles, but he doesn't let his gaze linger on me for too long. He addresses everyone else in the class more than he does me, even this British chick with the coke-bottle glasses that he normally seems to dislike.

I have to wonder if he's doing this on purpose, maybe the teacher he was talking to earlier really was warning him. Or maybe he came on too strong last night and he spooked himself. Could easily be either one. I mean, he *was* coming on strong, it's just that I happened to like it.

So I keep my expression as sweet as possible (which is a challenge when you have resting bitch face), I smile at him when I can. But when it comes time for me to play some pieces on the organ, even his compliments come up short. Instead he thinks I need some work with my ankles to play on the inside of my feet, which is the first time I've heard that.

But maybe it's not that he was coming on strong. Maybe I'm the one who scared him off. I'm the one who basically told him I was a loner child with dead parents and no friends and no dates and I'm inherently unlikeable.

Yeah, that's what it was all right.

I'm the fucking problem.

As usual.

When class ends, everyone goes and it's just me and Professor Aminoff left.

I go up to him, feeling extremely awkward.

"Hey," I say to him, just as new students are filling the room, dragging their instrument cases with them.

"Hey," he says back, giving me a quick smile. As if we're just teacher and student. And maybe that's all we are. Maybe I'm an idiot.

"Listen," I say. "I thought about what you said, with my ankles and all that and well, you did say I needed permission to use the concert hall after hours to practice. So...can I?"

He clears his throat and frowns, folding his arms across

his chest and I do what I can not to stare at the way his biceps look under his black shirt. "When?"

"Tonight," I say. I gesture to the students taking out their clarinets. "When they're done."

He thinks that over, looking away as he rubs his lips together.

My god, were those lips really on mine last night?

"Okay," he says. "Come back here when this class is done and I'll make sure to keep it open for you."

"Thanks," I tell him, about to walk away but then I pause. "Hey...are you okay?"

His face is totally impassive. "Why wouldn't I be?"

I blink at him, quickly pasting on a stiff smile. "No reason. You just seem a bit off today."

"I'm fine," he says, tone a bit sharper now.

Well good for you, I think.

I turn and quickly leave the room before he does, deciding to head to the library for a bit. I haven't been back since the other night and I'm looking at it with new eyes. Part of me hopes the professor doesn't show up so I don't have to pretend to be normal and fine all over again. Part of me hopes he does.

I find a chair in the corner and just spend most of the time flipping through encyclopedias and reading in earnest about everything I come across, much like I did as a child when I needed to destress and hyperfocus on something. The time flies and when I look at my phone, the last music class has been over for a while.

Gathering my stuff I head down into the building, going to the concert hall. As classes are done for the day, a stillness has descended on the school and as I pass through the dim hallways, the statues of famous composers and musicians seem to watch me as I walk past, as do the eyes from various portraits.

True to his word, Valtu left the concert hall door open a crack. I push it the rest of the way and step inside. I've never been in here alone before and it's a completely different experience. It's lit like there's a concert in progress, with all the chairs and the balcony above in the dark, with only a single light on stage.

Aimed right at the pipe organ.

"Hello?" I call out softly as I step inside the hall. I glance around at the shadows, expecting to see shapes and eyes staring at me but I really seem to be alone.

I close the door behind me and make my way down the aisle, then up the stairs to the stage.

I look around again anxiously, feeling apprehensive, like this room was lively and breathing before and now that I'm here, it's holding its breath.

I sit down on the bench, take off my jean jacket and my boots, and I'm about to put on my organ shoes I have in my bag but I stop. There's no one here. How much better would it feel to play the organ in my bare feet? He did say that I needed to work on my foot position, maybe it's better achieved at first by playing without shoes.

Besides, I carry antibacterial wipes and hand sanitizer wherever I go. I'll just clean the pedals before and after.

I fish them out of my bag, wipe it down just in case a less hygienic person did that before, then take my position on the bench, smoothing out my dress. When I asked Valtu if the room was available, I did so with the hopes that maybe he would show up and we could talk...or do something more than talking. But now that he's not here and I have the place to myself, I'm compelled to really master the piece he gave me for the recital.

I start playing it from memory, not needing a sheet. It's a song that gets off to a galloping start with only a few quiet slow sections where strings would kick in. I'm excited to hear it with the string students once we start rehearsing with them before the recital.

As I play, it's much easier with bare feet to master what Valtu was teaching me about my ankles, how I have to turn them to play more from the inside of my feet, but when I finally finish the song, my ankles are sore from the new position.

I reach down to rub them and hear slow applause erupting from the balcony. I gasp, quickly twisting around to see a dark figure on the balcony clapping. I swear I see red eyes too, but I'm thinking that's just my imagination.

"Who is there?" I call out, my voice shaking slightly.

Oh god, please don't tell me it's the demon again. This time patronizing my musical performance.

But then I see the figure stand up and the room grows cold and from his silhouette I can tell it's Valtu. I would recognize that wild hair and height and those broad shoulders anywhere.

I watch as he walks gracefully up the aisle and disappears, my eyes drawn to the back of the room where the staircase is until he appears.

My heart jumps and skips in my chest and I'm holding my breath as he approaches, sauntering down the aisle, out of the darkness and into the light. His eyes are glued to mine, his shadowed gaze intense under those low brows.

I feel buoyant. So light that I might just float away. Just seeing him here, knowing he's come for me, knowing that he was watching me in secret...I hate how many butterflies he's let loose inside my chest.

"You really took my critique to heart," he says in a low smooth voice as he approaches the stage, staring up at me. He nods at my feet. "Don't know the last time I saw someone play with bare feet."

I raise my chin, feeling on the spot. "I didn't think anyone was here."

A sly grin twists his mouth. "I know you didn't. Which is why I was so keen to see how you'd perform on your own. Without me, your classmates, or any audience at all watching. I wanted to see how you play when you're just playing for yourself."

Well, thank fuck he didn't see me trying to use a spell to play better.

"And?" I goad him. "What did you think?"

He walks along the stage then up the stairs, the closer he gets to me the louder my heart beats against my rib cage. He stops right beside me, peering down at me and I feel so small next to him.

"I think you have a real talent, Dahlia," he says in a low voice. "And you take a real joy in music. And that is so nice to see."

I can't help but feel a bit proud about that. Despite being helped along by a spell, I really do like what I play, I really do escape in the music I create. It clears my head better than anything.

"It's the only time I can quiet the thoughts in my mind," I admit.

His eyes are kind when he says, "I know. I'm the same way." Then he gestures to the organ. "Do you mind if I give you some pointers though? It's not often I get to have one-on-one classes with my students."

I gulp. The tension in the air immediately gets thicker, making it harder to breathe.

I manage to nod, about to get off the bench but he places a firm hand on my shoulder, sending a jolt of electricity through me. "No, you stay where you are."

There is an authoritative quality to his voice, quietly commanding.

He comes behind me now, his other hand on my other shoulder and positions me so I'm facing the organ.

"Put your fingers on the keys like you're about to start," he says.

I obey, placing my fingers in position.

He leans forward so that his lips are at my ear and I shiver as I feel his cool breath. "Let me guide you," he whispers. "Let everything go."

He reaches forward, his large cool palms sliding down over my bare arms, leaving a trail of goosebumps in their wake, going all the way to my hands, his own hands encompassing mine, fingers pressed down over fingers.

"Now don't look at your hands," he says in my ear, his voice rich, making the hair rise on my neck. "Close your eyes."

My eyes fall closed and he continues. "You work the keys in groups of three and four, like we practiced earlier."

I try to remember and when I do, I tense up, almost bringing my hands off the keys.

"Relax, Dahlia," he says quietly, his lips grazing lightly over the shell of my ear. "I've got you. Submit to me." He pauses, bringing his lips down to my earlobe where he brushes it with his nose. "Let me be in control from now on."

It feels like hot lightning is shooting straight down my spine into my core.

Fuck me.

I swallow thickly and try to nod, try to make a sound, but I already feel like I'm handing myself over to him.

He lets out a faint grunt and then brings my fingers down on the keys. I keep my eyes closed and let him take over, let the music flow from the organ as he makes me play like a puppet on a string.

"Just concentrate on the pedals," he whispers to me. "Yes. That's it. Inside of the foot. Yes. Trap the note."

I do as he says, the notes rising louder and clearer than before, filling the room with drama that I feel vibrating in my bones. I can't help but smile to myself, loving what he's coaxing out of me.

"Yes," he hisses. "That's a good girl."

My cheeks flush at that praise. How good it feels to hear it from him.

"Now I'm going to take my hands off yours," he murmurs, his mouth going to my neck now. "And you keep playing. And I'll play you."

I want to ask him what he means by playing me but then he kisses the crook of my neck, a long, soft, wet kiss that makes my toes want to curl on the pedals.

I gasp, my head going back until it rests against his shoulder, and he brings his hands down over my breasts, fingers brushing gently over my nipples.

Oh my god.

I suck in a breath, almost stopping the song but he sucks at my neck lightly and says, "Keep playing. Unless you want me to stop."

I don't want him to stop. I keep playing the song, my fingers moving over the keys as his fingers pinch my nipples, squeeze my breasts, and I'm arching even more now, molten heat between my legs.

"Your body is an instrument itself," he rasps to me, licking up to my ear until I'm moaning, and he's cupping my breasts now over my bodice. "Rewarding those who learn how to play it properly."

He gives my nipples another sharp tug and I cry out. It takes everything in me to keep playing the music and I'm surprised I haven't majorly fucked up the song by now. I can barely concentrate, all I can think about is how fucking turned on I am right now, and how damn sexy this is.

Then Valtu brings his hands down my sides and with slow

deliberation he starts hiking up the hem of my dress. Higher and higher and higher until it's around my waist. I'm wearing underwear, thankfully forest green and lacy, and I look over at the door to make sure it's still closed.

"Submit," he warns me, his voice rough now as he brings his lips to the edge of my jaw and I close my eyes again. "Let yourself be mine and give yourself over to me."

I make a tiny noise of want, trying to agree, and his fingers slide underneath my panties, going down until they reach where I'm completely soaked.

"Fuck," he hisses against my neck. "How drenched you are for me. Your smell is intoxicating."

I'm about to freak out over that since he shouldn't be able to smell me, but I'm swiftly reminded that he's a vampire and he can smell everything, including the blood in my veins.

Damn. It didn't take long for me to forget what he is and what I am. How quickly that was thrown away once he started to touch me like this.

"Keep playing," he says, stroking my clit with his finger now, spreading me. "Keep playing while I play you."

My breath is coming in short and shallow as I try to do as he says but the more his fingers rub and tease me, the harder it is to continue.

"Don't make me stop," he says and then thrusts a finger inside me.

"Oh god!" I cry out softly, my back arched, my hips rising, and my feet slide off the pedals.

"Be a good girl and keep going," he murmurs roughly, inserting another finger, plunging them in deep and I'm squeezing around him, starting to buck as he fucks me with his hand, his thumb rubbing my clit in swift, wet circles.

I try to continue with my fingers but it's so hard to concentrate when all I can think about are his. The song starts to fade, the notes skipping as I miss the keys.

"The sound of you is gorgeous," he murmurs as he moves his fingers in and out of me, the wet noise lewd and audible even above the sound of the organ. "I bet you sound even better when you come."

With a grunt he bites my earlobe and shoves his fingers in deeper, dragging over my G-spot and then I'm coming, my hands now gripping the keys so the organ cries out with an ungodly sound that matches the ragged cries of my own.

"Oh my god, oh god," I eke out, my heart beating in my words. "*Valtu*."

He continues to fuck me with his fingers until I've come all over his hand and I'm jerking from the spasms, nearly falling off the bench.

Holy shit.

Did that just happen?

My head is swimming, my insides feeling lit up like a million fireworks have just tore through me, and I don't know which way is up. Valtu holds me in place, his fingers still inside me as my pulsing slows and I feel myself coming back into my body again.

"Fuck," I whisper, my head going back and resting against his shoulder. I stare up at the frescoed ceiling and I'm suddenly reminded of where I am. Oh Jesus, my professor just fingered me while giving me music lessons.

I roll my head to look at the door, thankfully still shut.

"You're a very apt pupil," he says to me, kissing the back of my head. "But I'm not done with you yet."

He gets up behind me and I'm in a daze as he grabs me by the elbows and brings me up to my feet, grabbing me by the waist and spinning me around so that my ass is up on the organ, pushing down on all the keys. The instrument cries out in a cacophony of notes that surround us, making my teeth rattle, and before I can figure out what's happening, he spreads my legs and crouches down, burying his head under my dress and pulling off my underwear, discarding it on the floor.

The contact of his mouth on where I'm already sensitive and swollen sends a fiery jolt through my body and I gasp loudly, my hands automatically going into his hair, my fingers curling around his soft strands.

I feel him smile against my clit before he gives it a long, slow lick then trails his tongue down until it's pushing up inside me. I moan, feeling like a live wire, crackling and burning, soon to burst into flames.

His hand slides up and down my thighs as he continues to lick and suck me and I shudder at the sensation of his wet, hot tongue gliding against my clit. His tongue laps at me and my fingers make a tight fist in his hair and I can feel myself getting wetter by the second. I'm practically dripping into his mouth.

My eyes roll back into my head and I moan loudly, the organ crying out again as if competing with me as I shift on the keys. His hands slide under my ass, holding me against his mouth as he sucks and licks, the heat of his tongue hitting every inch of me.

I feel like I'm going to explode. I can't take it anymore. So close, so fucking close.

I dig my hand into his hair, tugging hard as I rock my hips forward, grinding my pussy against his mouth, needing everything he's offering me. Needing to come so badly that it hurts.

Suddenly his tongue is flicking up and down in fast, hard strokes and I feel myself falling over that edge I've been teetering on for several minutes. It feels like a tidal wave crashing over me and I yelp out his name, my body shaking as I almost slide off the organ, his firm grip the only thing holding me in place.

"Stay there and hold on," he commands, getting up and

my mind is spinning as he starts to unzip his pants, the shape of his cock outlined in the shadows. Despite having just come twice, I'm practically drooling for it and—

KNOCK KNOCK.

Our eyes go wide and we look over to the door to see the handle jiggle.

Oh shit.

I quickly slide off the organ and straighten my dress while Valtu zips back up and turns to the door.

It opens and a professor I sort of recognize pokes his head in.

"Oh, I'm sorry, I heard the organ playing this god awful..." he trails off, frowning at us. "My apologies...is this a lesson?"

Valtu hops off the stage and lands on his feet with supernatural ease, movement that makes the professor's frown deepen.

"You didn't see us here," he says quietly to the professor as he gets closer to him. "There's no one here at all."

The professor stares at Valtu for a moment and then looks around the room in confusion. "Hmmmphf," he says, then shakes his head and closes the door behind him.

My eyes are wide. I can't believe Valtu just compelled that man, and right in front of me. Talk about Jedi mind tricks.

"What was that?" I ask, wondering if he realizes he just did two very vampiric things in front of me, or if his erection has taken all the blood from his head and he can't think clearly.

"Don't worry, he didn't see anything," Valtu says, his eyes glinting. "Though we should probably go."

I nod and quickly shove my socks and boots back on, grabbing my bag and jacket, hurrying off the stage toward him.

But where we are going, that remains to be seen.

CHAPTER 13

VALTU

I WALK SILENTLY beside Dahlia as we make it out of the conservatory and into Campo Santo Stefano. Night has fallen like a blade, and the tables from the various cafes across the square are filled with patrons having their dinner, tourists who are braving the chill to sit alfresco. The locals are wisely inside. No one is paying us any attention and I know that Professor Fratelli won't even remember seeing us in the concert hall. If things are to continue with Dahlia in one way or another, there will be more people I'll have to compel to get them to look the other way.

"This way," I say softly to Dahlia, wanting to reach out and guide her with my hand, but I'm not taking chances being so close to my work and having us being noticed without me realizing it.

We go over the Ponte dell'Accademia, the high wooden bridge crowded with people taking pictures of the bustling Grand Canal. It would be a photogenic scene, the arms of fog stretching across, the dim lights of the city dancing on the dark waters of the canal which is constantly moving, busy with passing boats, gondolas and vaporettos, but I only have one thing on my mind at the moment and I can still taste her on my tongue.

She's been on my mind ever since we parted ways last night. I don't even think I slept last night, instead I just jerked off through the darkened hours, thinking of all the things I wanted to do to her. That kiss opened up something inside me last night, but it wasn't just the kiss, wasn't just knowing what her sweet lips finally tasted like. It was how she opened up to me. How after these weeks of puzzling over her, I finally got a look at who she truly was. It wasn't just some glimpse I managed to spy through a crack, no. She put her heart and soul on the table, served it up on a silver platter and I knew she'd never done that with anyone before.

She chose me. She trusted me. She knew that I would hold her secrets safe, that I wouldn't judge, that I would understand.

And like Bitrus had warned, this has opened up a new obsession in me. It's made her my obsession. It's made me want to make her mine in every way possible, a feeling so deep and solid that it surprises me, but it's true all the same.

There's only one thing left to figure out.

Can I trust her?

Can I do the things I want to do, reveal the person I truly am without her getting scared and running away? The fear is normal when you deal with a vampire, but I need to know how malleable her fear is.

Can she embrace her fear, and in the end, embrace my darkness?

Once we're deep on the other side of the city in Dorso-duro, heading north toward my house, I finally put my hand on the small of her back. Her skin burns me through her dress, a heat that spreads up my arm and makes my head feel hot and muddled. Forget her being afraid, the effect she has on me is terrifying.

"Where are we going?" she asks as we walk up a narrow street and she peers curiously at the bars and cafes we pass.

"You're coming home with me," I tell her, keeping my voice low.

She glances at me, her expression unreadable. Then her lips give way to a smile. "Okay," she says quietly.

I suppose I could have asked her instead of told her but I didn't want her answer to be no. I didn't think it would be no, at any rate, not after she came all over my hands and mouth. She wants more of it, just as much as I do, and I will bring her so much more than she bargained for.

We don't talk during the walk. It feels pointless when I want to use my tongue and mouth in other ways. It isn't until we get to my house that she says, "Holy shit. This is where you live?"

I can't help but feel a bit of pride as I look it over. "It used to be a hotel, the Oltre il Giardino, until I bought it. Before then it belonged to a storied woman called Alma Mahler who lived in it at the turn of the century." Of course I don't mention that I not only knew Alma but was one of her lovers.

We walk through the small square leading to the front door, bushes of black roses surrounding us and cloaking us in their sweet scent, and step inside. The hotel itself was white and bright to be welcoming to guests, but I painted the interior a dark grey, with lots of red and black accents and walnut floors. It's dark and moody, which makes it much easier on the eyes, and on the soul.

Dahlia's attention immediately goes to the grand living area where I keep all my prized possessions that I've collected over the years.

"And this is all on a teacher's salary?" she asks in a hush as she looks over all the rare paintings on the wall, the sculptures throughout the room, all the books placed artfully on the shelves, the collection of antique musical instruments by the fireplace. For a moment I get slammed with déjà vu, as if I've seen this all before, seen Dahlia standing by the instruments in her burgundy dress, marveling over them, with her hair up just as it is.

Then before I can grasp the image, the sense of acute familiarity, it fades like sand through my fingers.

"I'm not just a teacher," I admit, slowly walking toward her, trying to ignore how painfully hard I already am, my cock pressing against my jeans. I don't even think I'll make it to the bedroom. It's fine. The rug in front of the fireplace will do.

And then I'm hit again with another image, this time I'm fucking her on the floor, taking her hard from behind, a violin bow beside me and for a moment I think I'm back in London. With Lucy. But when I look at Dahlia, running her slender fingertips with the chipped black polish over the edge of my harp, I know it's not Lucy. They aren't the same person. They don't look a thing alike.

Besides, I gave up on ever seeing her again a long time ago.

"So..." Dahlia says, looking at me curiously. "If you're not just a teacher, what else do you do? Raid museums?" She pauses by a stack of old music books beside the mantle and then gives me a bright smile, realization dawning on her face. "Wait a minute. All those donations you get at the library. They aren't from anonymous donors. They're all from you. *You* bring them in."

She's got me there. I shrug lightly and come over to her, reaching for her hand and grasping it in mine. "I want them to be someplace safe," I admit. "They'll get the proper treatment at the school, and those who need to see them can see them. No point in having such things if you can't share them with the world. Besides, I'm not the only one who donated. Richard Wagner donated his fair share."

"Can I ask why you have all these rare artifacts and shit, or does that have something to do with you also not being just a teacher?" She pauses. "You're not the real-life Indiana Jones, are you?"

How about the real-life Dracula?

I shake my head gently, giving her hand a squeeze. "I wish I were. No, I just happen to be a count."

"A count?" she says measuredly. "Like, Count Chocula?"

Interesting that's where her brain went. "Sure. Like Count Chocula."

Honestly if she said Dracula, if she asked if I was a vampire, I don't think I could lie to her. I think I would tell her the truth and she would believe it and the darkness in her veins would call to the darkness in mine.

What is it about this woman that I want to drag her down to hell with me?

"A count for what country?" she asks. "Where are you really from?"

"Perhaps that is an outdated word. I am a lord."

Or perhaps that's outdated too.

"So I can call you my lord?" she asks in an overly sweet voice, a heated look coming into her eyes.

Oh, this precious girl.

"I fucking insist that you do," I tell her, grabbing her by the back of her neck and bringing her mouth to mine in a hard, bruising kiss. Her lips feel like they're made of the softest velvet, her tongue deceptively innocent of the havoc it's causing in my body as she kisses me back, a beautiful whimper escaping from her throat.

I had warned her I could be rough but from the way she is grabbing my shoulders, my back, her nails digging in through the fabric of my shirt, I know rough is how she likes it.

I place my lips at her neck and she stiffens for a second, a pulse of adrenaline spiking the air, the scent spicy. It's like she's afraid I'll bite her...

Then it fades, replaced by the heady scent of her arousal and her hands are all over me, reaching down for a hard squeeze at my cock, making my toes curl and my hips buck forward.

"Fuck," I growl against her neck, nipping at her skin for a moment, relishing the taste of her before licking up toward her ear.

My hands roughly skirt down her sides and I want to tear off her dress. I want to fuck her on the floor with her just this way, her legs wrapped around my waist, my hands gripping her hair. I want to see her tits bounce as I pound into her, but then I don't want to stop. I want to fuck her until she can't even walk. Until I pass out from exhaustion and then I have to have her again.

She's a drug and I'm an addict on his first hit and this strange chemical reaction between us is only beginning.

I kiss her again, deeper this time, my hands gathering up the hem of her dress, sliding over her bare hips and I pause.

"What is it?" she asks as she pulls back slightly, already breathless.

"I think we left your underwear on the floor of the concert hall," I tell her.

Her eyes go wide and I laugh. "Don't worry. I'll go early and retrieve it," I assure her, trailing my lips back to her neck. I nip at her earlobe, going lower, right to the hollow above her collar bone, and breathe in deeply through my nose so it goes straight to my head. That sweet, sweet scent of her blood. I distract myself by slipping my fingers between her thighs. She's so warm and gratuitously wet, achingly ready for me, and I slide my forefinger down over her clit. "Open for me," I say and she does, her stance widening, and I slip two fingers inside her. She moans, her back arching, bearing down.

But I pull my fingers out and she lets out a soft whimper of disappointment at their absence.

"What?" she asks, staring at me with need. "You can touch me."

I will do more than touch you, I think.

"You know you're mine now," I whisper, licking at the shell of her ear as I caress her with my fingers again. "I told you last night that there was no turning back and I meant it."

"Yes, my lord," she purrs.

Fuck, I love that. I didn't think my dick could get any harder.

"That's my good girl," I praise her, plunging my fingers back inside her. "And what else will you do for your lord?"

"Oh god," she whispers, eyes falling closed, mouth open. "Anything."

"Beg me for it, love," I say as I reach up and yank down the neckline of her dress, her chest heaving, her nipples hardening as the air cools them. I nudge them with my nose, lighting them on fire. "Beg me to fuck you."

"Please," she whispers.

"Please, what?" I ask, sucking and licking at her breasts. Her skin tastes salty and sweet, a flavor I cannot live without. Every inch of her tastes like heaven.

"Please," she says again, her voice shaking. "Fuck me, my lord, I beg you."

I groan, my cock so fucking hard now I feel I might break right through the fly of my jeans. She is so, so good at this.

I nip at her earlobe, trailing kisses down her neck as I run my fingers over her clit again. She's wet, so wet and ready and I can't get enough of the slick feel of her. I can smell her lust for me and I need it coated around my dick. I need to taste it, taste her. "Touch me like the obedient girl you are," I tell her.

"Yes, my lord," she hisses, her eyes glazed as she pulls back to meet my gaze. "I'm yours." Her hands drop to my fly, undoing it, taking my cock out into her hands where she gives it a hard squeeze.

Jesus.

I need her.

I need to ravage her.

Let the darkness envelope us.

She cries out as I spin her around and toss her to the ground, the lush rug cushioning her fall. I quickly shove up her dress around her waist as she rolls over to face me and tries to push herself up on her elbows.

"Stay like that," I command.

"Yes, my lord," she says, her eyes heavy with lust as she lies back down, swallowing hard.

I stand there and let my eyes roam over her like I'm inspecting her, making a hard fist around my cock. She's so fucking beautiful, her skin flushed, her chest heaving, a rosy blush across her cheeks, her lips parted and her eyes full of desire. My body is on fire, my blood pounding in my veins like I'm going to explode at any moment, and I stroke my cock harder.

She shudders as I trail my gaze over her breasts, full and exposed over the neckline, then down beneath where the skirt of her dress is gathered, acting as if she can literally feel my eyes on her body.

"Let me see," I say, giving my dick another near painful squeeze. "Let me see that pretty cunt of yours."

Her fingers curl at her sides as she spreads her legs even further apart, her hips rising.

"Good girl," I say and I drop to my knees in front of her. I trail my fingers over her soft skin, over everything slick and pink, and she squirms, the muscles in her thighs quivering from my light touch.

My dark gaze meets hers and I watch her, my fingers sliding up to stroke her clit. She gasps as her hips roll toward me, her mouth slightly open.

"You're a bad girl, aren't you?" I say, my voice a low growl.

"I'm a good girl for my lord," she pants.

"Will you be a bad girl for me now?" I ask, rubbing her clit and she arches her back. "Will you succumb to your darkness?"

I push my fingers inside her and she moans, her hips jerking forward, wanting more as she pushes down on my hand. I pump my fingers inside her as she writhes on the rug, so fucking hot and tight and wet, I can barely stand it.

The damn skirt is falling in the way and I need those hips bucking against me. I push it up even further, yanking it up until it's around her waist again. I smooth my hand down her thigh and then slide it under her knee and up her legs again. She shudders, her back arching, wanting more. I want to give her more, but not like this.

I slip my hand under the small of her back and like she weighs nothing more than a feather, I flip her over until she's on her stomach.

I push my hands against her ass, spreading them, opening her up to me. She's so fucking beautiful, her ass perfectly smooth, pale and plump.

"So good, so fucking good," I growl, lunging forward to lick at her wet pussy.

I kiss it, spreading her open with my fingers, my lips pressed against her clit. Her fingers dig into the rug by her head as she arches her back, her ass pressed toward me.

I can't hold back any longer. I'm surprised I lasted this long.

I quickly shove down my jeans until my cock is totally

free, then with a vice like grip I push it into her soaking wet cunt, grabbing her ass.

I'm not gentle. I shove myself inside her, my hand going to her hair. I pull her head back, arching her neck, and she lets out a gasp of shock.

Then she starts to moan, her body trembling as I hold her in place and thrust inside of her. It's so good, this feeling of being completely enveloped by her, the wet depths of her heat, but I want more. I want to claim her completely.

I let go of her hair, leaving a few strands in my hand and I quicken my pace, my cock burying deep inside her, again and again, my fingers gripping her hips.

She whimpers and moans. "Yes, oh god."

She's close to the edge, I can tell from the way her breath is coming in gasps, and I pull out of her. She looks back at me with confusion, almost pained anger for having stopped it.

I grab her by the hair with my left hand, yanking her back to me. Her eyes are wide and her breath ragged. "I'll be your darkest secret," I whisper, my lips pressed against the her ear. "Is that what you want?"

"Yes, my lord," she moans.

Suddenly I'm compelled to raise my hand. I bring it down hard across her ass, the slap echoing throughout the room. She yelps, jumping and before she can say anything I spank her again on the other cheek.

Fuck, there is something else about this that is damn familiar.

"Did you like that?" I murmur and lean down, running my lips over the blooming pink patches on her skin.

"Yes," she says shakily.

"Well, you've been a very good girl so far. I'll give you what you really want."

I guide my cock back to her entrance and she wriggles

beneath me with need, her eyes filled with lust, her mouth open and panting.

I hold her there for a moment and then I drive my cock deep inside her, so deep it feels like I'm nailing her to the floor.

She lets out a cry that is music to my ears, a cry of the sweetest agony.

She takes my breath away.

I pull her hands behind her, pinning them at the small of her back and, holding her in place, I fuck her like a fucking animal, thrust after thrust, her ass rocking back against me, taking it all. Her moans, loud and full of need, fill the room, as does the slap of my balls against her skin.

She's so close. I can feel it. I can feel her legs quiver as she tries to stay on her knees. I jerk her head back by her hair, my cock throbbing as I feel her tighten around me. This is what I need. This is what I crave. It's the deepest part of her, her darkest desire and this is it.

"Oh god!" she cries out as she comes. "Fuck, fuck, fuck."

I bury myself to the hilt inside her and I groan as I feel it. The fire, the heat, the sweet pain, the hunger, they all come flooding over me. Her release grips my cock and pulsates through me, and I come violently hard. I spill deep inside her, marking her for all time. She's mine now, whether she likes it or not, she's mine.

I pull back and look down at her, our gazes meeting. She's breathing heavily, her head bowed. I run my fingers through her hair and I lift her head up and look her in the eye. "Look at me," I say.

She looks up, looking into my eyes, her face flushed, her lips parted.

"I'm yours, my lord," she whispers.

"Good girl," I tell her, kissing her cheek.

Then I pull out of her. Watch as my cum drips down her

thighs and to the rug and I have time to save it before it creates a mess.

I run my hand up over her thigh, gathering my cum on my fingers, and push it back inside her cunt. She jerks a little, no doubt surprised at what I'm doing. Much tidier this way.

And luckily for the both of us, I got a vasectomy a very long time ago. Vampire sperm is known for blasting through any birth control pills or methods available, probably a way to ensure the survival of my species. I couldn't stand to have a child now, and I'm pretty sure Dahlia doesn't want a vampire baby messing up her life either.

"Don't worry," I tell her, sliding the rest of my cum back inside her, my fingers sliding in deep. "I'll let you rest for a little bit before I fuck you again."

But from the way she's already moving her hips, I can tell she doesn't need any rest at all.

CHAPTER 14

DAHLIA

THE NEXT MORNING I awake in a tomb.

At least, it feels like a tomb, it is so fucking dark.

I figure I'm in Valtu's bedroom because I vaguely remember that's where we ended up and I can tell it's morning because of the birdsong from somewhere outside, but I didn't think his room would be this dark, vampire or not.

Then I blink and my eyelashes press against something and I realize that the room isn't dark—I have something over my eyes.

I gasp, trying to move, to bring it off my face, but my arms are above my head, my wrists tied to each other.

I open my mouth to yell but suddenly a rush of cold comes at my face and a large, cool palm is placed over my lips.

"Shhh," Valtu says quietly, his voice rich and soothing. "It's just me. Professor Aminoff."

I breathe heavily through my nose, trying not to panic as he presses his hand over my mouth harder.

Oh my god.

He found out, didn't he?

He knows what I am. The glamor slipped during sex last night and he knows I'm a witch, he knows I was sent to kill him.

Oh my god, oh my god, oh my god.

He's going to kill me.

"You're trembling," he remarks in surprise.

He pulls his hand off my mouth and I gulp for air as his fingers go to the side of my face, lightly touching my cheek-bones. "Have you forgotten last night already? Have you forgotten what I am to you?" he whispers.

I swallow hard, trying to regain my breathing. "Why...why am I tied up?"

"Because," he says.

That's all he's got?

"Because what?"

You're a psycho?

"Because I wanted to see your fear," he says, dragging the last word out. "I told you that I would push you beyond what you were comfortable with."

"I believe you used the word terror, actually."

Does my fear turn you on? I want to ask. But I know the answer. Of course it does. Perhaps this is the only way he can be with me without feeding on me, to elicit fear in some other way. Maybe he feeds on my fear just like he does on blood.

"Terror is subjective."

I try to move my arms over my head again but find them attached to something, maybe the headboard, and I struggle a little. I can practically hear him smile.

"When did you do this?" I ask, trying not to panic. "I would have woken up."

"You were out like a light," he says. "And I would have

done your ankles next. Kept your legs spread. Then I would have ensured you woke up while you were coming on my tongue."

It doesn't sit right that I didn't wake up while he both slipped a blindfold over my eyes and tied my wrists together and to the bed, but I have no choice but to accept it. Either he did something to me, compelled me to stay asleep, or I was just that exhausted from all the sex last night.

Okay, considering how it went last night, getting completely fucked downstairs on his rug, then against his piano, then on the table in the kitchen, then giving him a blowjob in the shower, it could totally be the latter.

I just hate that I can't see him. What if I'm not alone in this room? What if there are other vampires in here with him? I've seen what they do in their vampire sex dungeon, how they share humans like a piece of meat. Is that what they're going to do with me here? Sure I was aroused when I was watching it, but being an unwilling participant is something else entirely.

I mean, it's one thing to be willingly blindfolded when you know what the room looks like around you. It's another to literally wake up that way. I don't even remember getting into his room last night, we were too busy smashing our bodies and faces together in a hurricane of deviant lust.

Because that's what last night was. I'd never been treated so roughly during sex before, never felt so debased and primal. Valtu was determined to call up my darkness, but more than anything I felt like I wanted to drown in his. I would have done anything he said, because in those moments he was my lord. The words felt good to say—*my lord*—like I've said them before, like I've let him take control some other time.

And now that darkness has come for me again.

He's brought it.

Literally.

"Relax, my dove," he says to me softly and the phrase makes my brain jolt.

Why did that sound so familiar?

Has he called me that before?

Last night he called me *love* but this...this is jogging my memory and bringing up nothing except the most intense feeling of déjà vu.

I hear him take in a shaking breath and my skin leaps as he brushes his fingers over my breasts, my nipples growing tighter.

I'm naked. Of course I am.

"I love to see you like this, Dahlia," he says. "Do you know that you bloom, just like your namesake? Makes me want to bury myself in your petals. There isn't a more beautiful sight than seeing you open for me."

His head dips down so I feel the stubble of his chin and he brushes it over my breasts, my skin tingling and on fire, my heart leapfrogging in my chest. He blows gently, his breath cold and I gasp.

"That's it," he says. "Let go of the fear. Let me take you to some place better."

His smooth cool palms skim over my ribcage, the dip of my waist, the curve of my hips, then across my belly and down. He slides a hand between my thighs and I'm shockingly wet already. My body has lapped up the fear, using it as fuel.

God, I can't believe how turned on I am, like my body has been wanting this for a long time but has never bothered to tell my brain.

"Do you want to come for me, Dahlia?" he murmurs, a thumb sliding over my clit.

I swallow hard, nodding.

"Let me hear you say the words," he says.

"Yes, my lord," I say, ready to play for him, to live in this role. "I want to come for you."

A low groan leaves his lips. "That's my good girl."

He pulls his thumb across my clit and I cry out, jerking against my bonds.

"You like that, hmm?"

"Yes, my lord," I breathe.

"You want me to lick you, don't you?"

"Anything you want," I say, raising my hips to try and get purchase against his hand.

"But what do you want, my dove?" he asks, using that moniker again. There's something so unnervingly affectionate about the way he says it, something that tickles a pleasure spot in the back of my brain.

"What do you want?" he repeats, pulling his hand away, leaving me feeling empty, greedy for more.

"I want you to make me come, my lord," I tell him. "I want to make you come inside me."

"Do you want me to hurt you?" he asks.

I go still at that question. What does he have in mind? I know he spanked me last night and I liked it. I could take more of that. He tore some of my hair out. I could take that, too.

"You're afraid," he muses, his hand spreading across my thigh. "You're afraid of what I might do to you. And I thought you trusted me, Dahlia."

I never said I trusted you. I almost say it, but bite my tongue instead.

"Let me ask you again," he says. "Do you want me to hurt you before I make you come? Do you want the sweetest kiss of pain, pain that melts into you like snow under sunshine? If I tell you it pleases me to see you overcome that pain, that it gets me harder than anything in my life, will you let me hurt you?"

Oh god. I feel so fucking insane right now, like I already can't breathe properly, like my heart might burst right out of my ribcage. I'm scared, I really am, but I no longer have the same fear as I did earlier. I don't have that real fear, the fear for my life.

No, right now it's pure curiosity.

It's fear and anticipation.

It's a combination I could get drunk on.

"Yes," I say, my mouth feeling so dry.

"Yes, what, love?" he asks me as he spreads my legs and I feel him adjust himself between them, the bed sinking under his weight. God, I want him.

"Yes, my lord," I say, squirming with need, my nerves dancing with the unknown, unsure what he's going to do next. "You can hurt me."

He chuckles warmly, a sound that brings a hit of relief, sounding like the man I know. It's hard to reconcile the fact that this is Professor Aminoff, my teacher at school, and he's also Dracula, the vampire I'm supposed to kill, and now he's this...I don't know what he is but all I know is that I want him so bad it scares me.

I feel his bare arms press against my thighs, his head lowering. "I'm going to lick you now," he whispers, his breath over my cunt, making me gasp. "And I'm going to make you as wet as I can, make you come as hard as I can. And then I'm going to fuck you until you break, even if that takes the rest of the day."

The day. Somewhere in my head I remember that I have school at some point in the day, as does he, and yet none of that seems to matter now. If he doesn't seem worried, I'm not either.

His tongue slides over my clit, wet and hot, sending a

bright wave of pleasure through my body. I let out a little cry and jerk against the confines of my ropes.

"You're so responsive," he says, his voice guttural, his words vibrating over my clit. "So greedy. I can feel how close you are and I can smell how much you want it. I can smell how much you want me," he growls, his tongue flicking out, his teeth scraping over my most sensitive skin.

Oh god!

I tense, waiting to feel the pinch of his fangs but his teeth are gentle and he doesn't draw blood.

Holy shit. For a moment I really thought he was going to feed.

And yet somewhere in the back of my mind...it's almost like I wanted that.

He intensifies his licks, his tongue sliding lower, lapping at the wetness gathering between my thighs, making me writhe with quick flicks of his tongue, making me want to moan. He's fucking me with his mouth, eating me with deliberation, the hungry growls, making me hotter and wetter and more desperate for him. It's like none of last night happened and he's doing this for the first time, like I've spent my whole life waiting for it.

"Please," I breathe, twisting around, wishing my hands were free so I could grab his head and push his mouth into me harder, wishing I could watch. It's painful.

"So polite," he says pulling away for a moment, then dropping his mouth to my cunt again and I'm not expecting the long slow lick he gives me, the sensation making me cry out, the pleasure so intense. I feel like I might come just from that one hard pass of his tongue.

"Oh God," I moan. I'm going insane.

It takes a few more minutes of torturously soft licks and kisses before he finally adds his fingers, sliding deep inside me, the burn and stretch more delicious than I remembered.

He presses his fingers against the wall of my G-spot, his mouth coming back to my clit. He sucks on the sensitive flesh and pulls at it with his teeth, the sharp pinch of pain making me whine. I can feel a wave of pleasure building inside me and it's so intense that I don't know how I'll make it without going insane

"Please," I whisper again, feeling wild and lost, so beyond my control. "I'm so close. Keep doing that, please."

"Don't come until I tell you," he says, sliding his mouth away and adding a third finger. "You don't want to be a bad girl, do you?"

I don't fucking know at this point, I'm not sure what the hell kind of punishment he would dole out to a bad girl if he does this to a good one.

"Oh fuck," I cry out, feeling myself stretch to accommodate him, my hips trying to thrust up, my feet curling against the bed. "Please. Please, more, I'm so close."

"Not yet, my dove," he murmurs, slowing his pace, his fingers circling slowly inside me. "Not until I let you."

"But I can't hold on," I cry out, feeling tears of frustration as I approach the edge again and again.

"I want you to come on my lips and then I want you to come on my cock," he says and then sucks at my clit until I'm bursting, my orgasm pulling me apart.

"Fuck!" I come hard, the world going white—white heat, white explosions, white waterfalls, white stars and I feel him move, his body shifting, and then he's on top of me and it's his cock that fills me instead of his fingers, shoving his hard, stiff length deep inside me while I'm writhing.

His weight is heavy, pushing me into the bed and I'm coming around his cock now, pulsing around his shaft. I feel his cheek slide against mine and his mouth on my ear, smell his breath of peppermint and espresso, feel it on my face. He's doing this slowly, fucking me with careful deliberation, and igniting my inner fire, keeping it smoldering so I can't go out. Every slow thrust of his cock inside me makes me more desperately crave the next, I feel like I'm getting fucked by a phantom, all this darkness around me.

"You want to keep going until you're raw and you can't feel a thing anymore?" he whispers against my ear. "You want to keep fucking me until you won't be able to walk straight? Until you'll think about my cock between your legs every time you sit down?"

I'm close again, so close it's agony.

"Yes," I moan, my hips lifting to meet his every thrust. He's smirking against my ear, his breath warm and wet. "I want you to come inside me."

"I am going to come inside you," he says, his voice like warm honey. "My first load will be in your cunt and then the next will be in your ass and then the rest will be coming out of your mouth."

Dear lord. What did he say? My eyes spring open against the blindfold, but of course I see nothing.

"But first, I'm going to make you see the universe," he says, and I feel him shift over me, his hand going to my throat. "You know I could damage your windpipe if I press right here," he says as he presses his palm down on my trachea.

I instantly panic, starting to squirm, pulling at the restraints above my head, my fight-or-flight instantly triggered.

"I could cause some serious damage," he goes on and I'm gasping, freaking out at the pressure, knowing he could easily kill me right now with just one wrong slip, there's so much power in his hands. I start to kick now, wanting him off of me, but he just continues to drive his cock deep inside, in and out, in and out.

He takes his hand off and I'm gulping for air, my throat

throbbing just from that bit of pressure. "The best place is here," he says, bringing his hand back, but this time he puts the pressure on his thumb and fingers, his palm resting lightly against my trachea. "On the two arteries. The squeezing causes the reduction of oxygen to your brain. Not a lot, just a little. Like so."

His fingers and thumb press into my neck as he continues to fuck me, the pace picking up. I shudder, and I can hear my breath coming in short panting noises, but I feel like it's from somewhere else, like I'm someone else, watching.

"First you start trembling," he says, his cock slowly fucking me, driving me crazy as he sinks in so damn deep, his thumb and fingers lightly pressing in until he's full on choking me. "You're not sure why you have the shakes, but then you realize it's because you can't catch a breath. The shock of it makes your body seize, like a strong electric current."

The pressure is starting to make my head feel foggy and I'm struggling to breathe through my nose. My throat is closing and I can't seem to control it. Oh god, I might pass out.

"You start shaking," he says through a ragged breath, thrusting into me deeper, faster, and the pressure on my throat intensifies. "Maybe you'll tap me on the shoulder to get me to stop, but you can't because your hands are tied to the bed. So then I let go for a moment."

He lets go of my throat and I gasp for air, filling my lungs as much as I can as adrenaline and endorphins start to flood my body, making me feel alive.

"Yes," he hisses. "You feel that. The oxytocin. That wave of pleasure," he reaches down and rubs his finger along my clit and the pleasure is so intense I feel like I'm going to suffocate.

There's no warning this time. I come hard and then he's choking me again, pushing up so deep inside me I feel like

I'm filled to the brim with his cock, his weight pushing me into the bed. I can't think, I'm just gasping for breath and then I'm coming again somehow, the muscles in my pussy going tight, squeezing his shaft.

He slides his hand from my throat up to my mouth and pushes two fingers between my lips and over my tongue, pressing down. I can taste the salt and musk of our bodies, the orgasm still rolling through me as I suck at his fingers, pulling them deep into my mouth, my body shuddering, convulsing. "That's it," he growls. "Sucking like a good girl... oh God..."

His voice trails off, growing thick with lust and his breath gets shorter and raspier as he pounds into me, the bed jostling from the frenzied strength of his fucking.

Suddenly his hips slam once, twice and he stills and I wish I could see him as he comes. The way his head goes back, his throat exposed, the way his mouth falls open. He lets out a long, deep groan that makes my body shiver, a primal sound that makes up for the fact that I can't watch.

Then he pulls out, his cum splashing hot on my thighs, and then I'm being flipped over, my hands pulled tighter to the bed now as the rope twists. He shoves his hand under my stomach and yanks my ass up so I'm on all fours.

"I'm not done with you yet," he rasps, his fingers digging into the tender flesh of my hips. "Do you want me to be done with you?"

"No, my lord," I say, and it hurts to speak, my throat feeling raw.

"I promise to take my time," he says, voice dipping, growing rougher, and he brings his hands to my ass. He runs his fingers over my cheeks, down where his cock was just inside me, tracing the line of my slit and I squirm under his touch, moaning as he spreads me with one hand. "Is that what you want?"

"Yes, my lord."

He chuckles, sounding satisfied and then there's a pause before...

WHACK.

He spanks me hard, his hand like a whip.

I cry out, I can't help it.

My skin feels like it's on fire as he strikes me, his hand coming down on my ass again and again, each slap harder than the last, growing hotter and hotter. My whole body jerks at each blow, the rough rope biting into my wrists, making my chest ache, my breasts jiggling.

Then I feel him get off the bed, the sound of him walking across the room, and a drawer opening and I hold my breath to focus better. Is he getting a condom? We hadn't been using one. But then I hear the click of a cap, then a loud squirt and I know he's probably grabbed a bottle of lube.

Which means he wasn't kidding about what he said earlier.

The bed dips down again and he's right behind me. I can feel him over my body, his breath on my back, and then he's pressing against me, the tip of his cock right against my ass. I feel his slick hand slide between his cock and my skin, making himself wet, then he pulls back just a little, adjusting himself behind me.

I gasp when I feel it, the thick head slipping inside and I make a soft noise as he pushes, inch by slow inch, filling me up in a way that I hadn't even imagined. I'm so slick from the lube but it still takes a minute for him to get all the way into my ass, and I'm stretched wide around his thick shaft, the head of his cock hitting deep inside me.

"Oh my god," I moan. I can't even describe it.

And I can feel him watching. He says nothing, lets me feel his eyes on me instead, no doubt drawn to where his cock disappears inside me. I just hear his heavy breathing, his breath ragged and slow.

And then he starts fucking me, pulling out slowly and pushing back in just as leisurely and his hands return to my ass, one hand on each cheek and he spreads me, my body growing even tighter around his shaft as he pulls me open with his hands, my ass cheeks spreading wide and I feel the roughness of the rope on my wrists as I try to pull my arms back down. My pussy is wet and my clit is throbbing as he pushes into me from behind.

I can feel how long his cock is, how thick, and as he fucks me, I can feel every inch of it.

"Does that feel good?" he asks through a shuddering breath. He's trying to take his time, trying to hold back and I know he wants to let loose. "Can I make you feel better?"

"Yes," I manage to say, the word shaky. "Yes, my lord."

He brings his hand to my cunt and slides his fingers inside, fucking me with them, in an expert motion that grazes over my clit, and *fuck*! I'm immediately coming, a tsunami that rolls over me and pulls me down until I don't know which way is up. I'm screaming his name, I'm convulsing, jerking on the bed like a rabid animal, and the waves of pleasure just don't stop as they pound me again and again.

"I can't hold back," he says through a groan and then he grunts loudly, his cock driving in deep and I feel the sudden heat of cum shooting deep inside me, filling up my ass as he holds me wide, shooting again and again, his length pulsing inside me.

When he's emptied himself in me, he pulls back and I feel his cum leaking from my ass and down my thighs, sliding down my legs and onto the bed.

"Had enough?" he says and for once he's sounding breathless. Does this man never tire? Even vampires have their limits, despite being able to come again and again without a pause.

I try to speak but I'm so exhausted and spent and my body doesn't even feel like it belongs to me anymore, like I've been shot up into space and left there among the galaxies.

"I know I said I was going to put my cock in your mouth," he adds with a chuckle, "but I think we can save that for later."

Thank god, because as much as I've discovered some dark and dirty kink side of me, I'm not kinky enough to put a cock in my mouth that's also just been up my ass.

"Here," he says softly. "Let me clean you up." I feel him get off the bed, coming back with a soft warm washcloth that he gently rubs all over my body. His actions are so precise and delicate and caring that it conflicts with how rough he likes his sex.

"There," he says. He leans over me and places a gentle kiss on my forehead, then his hands go to mine and I feel him undoing the ropes.

Suddenly my hands drop away, flooded with a rush of pins and needles.

"Ow," I say quietly.

"Did that hurt?" he asks and then I feel his fingers gently brushing over the raw grooves the rope left in my wrists. "They will heal," he says, then leans over to place kisses on them.

Then he pulls back and his hands go to the blindfold.

He undoes it and lifts it off.

I wince at the light, as dim as it is, until my eyes come into focus.

Valtu is staring at me, his face inches away. His gaze is light, almost adoring as he studies my face, his mouth quirked up in the corner, smiling softly.

My god, there's never been anyone so handsome.

"There you are," he says quietly, reaching forward to brush a strand of hair off my head.

I take a moment and look around the room. It's dimly lit in here, the walls a charcoal grey, faint light coming in from the windows, but otherwise a very cozy space with old paintings on the walls, no doubt originals, in gilded frames, and antique lacquered dressers and armoires, candles stacked on top of them along with vases of black roses. I feel like I'm waking up in the house of a man from the 1800s and I guess that's not too far off.

We're also alone. Now that I can move, now that I can see, nothing seems so scary anymore.

"Thank you," he says, picking up my hand and kissing the marks on my wrist.

"For what?"

"For trusting me," he says gravely. "I know you didn't want to but...it was really important to me." He lowers my hand and licks his lips, his eyes growing darker as he stares at me. "You see, I have trust issues. I...I have gotten close to people before and when they've discovered who I really am, what I'm really made of, they run away. That darkness you have? I wanted to make sure you wouldn't run away from mine. I wanted to know if you would freely submit yourself to me, through pleasure and through pain. I wanted to know if I could trust you as much as you could trust me."

The funny thing is, I do trust him. I shouldn't. He doesn't know that I know he's a vampire, that he's killed people, that he could easily do the same to me, especially if he finds out who I truly am. But after all I just went through here in his bed, I do trust him.

There's no one else I want to give my body over to like him.

I nod, my heart pounding in my chest. "I want you to," I

tell him softly. "I want you to trust me as much as I trust you."

He smiles, leaning in and kissing me on the lips again. I taste our sex on the light swipe of his tongue.

"Good." He pulls back and bites his lip for a moment before asking, "Can I ask you something?"

"Anything."

His brow raises expectantly.

I punch his arm weakly. "Don't you dare think I'm going to call you my lord outside of the bedroom."

He laughs, briefly looking up to the ceiling. "Okay, well it was worth a shot." Then his smile turns wistful. "But seriously. I know I have a class to teach today and you have classes to go to but...is there any chance you'll play hooky with me?"

My eyes widen in surprise. "You're skipping school? Professor Aminoff!" I cry out, admonishing him.

He leans in closer to me, cupping my chin between his fingers. "How can you blame me? Look at you, Dahlia. You beautiful, wicked creature. An angel in disguise. I have you naked in my bed. You just let me defile you in the most deviant ways. There's no way in hell I can go to work today and not be thinking about the taste of your cunt."

My cheeks immediately flush with heat at that. Such a dirty mouth on him, my god.

"Stay in bed with me," he goes on persistently, running his thumb over my lower lip before pushing it inside so it rests on my lower teeth. "Let me play with you all day."

Luckily the classes I have today aren't with Valtu, so the both of us won't be noticeably absent from the same class.

I'm not a real student anyway.

A smile slowly spreads across my face as I give in. "Okay."

He grins, his eyes squinting with delight, and my god I think I'm falling for this man.

Enough so that I'm staying here with him because I want to. Not because I should, or that I'm on the right track with him, and this is what the guild would want me to do to reach our goals, but because I *want* to.

And I know this is going to be a huge fucking problem for me down the line.

CHAPTER 15

VALTU

THERE'S nothing I like more than Venice on the cusp of winter. That sweet spot near November, when the rains haven't started yet in earnest, so there's no worry about flooding or *acqua alta*, but the tourists are gone and the fog settles in with the early darkness. It makes me feel at peace, like everything in life is just a little bit easier.

But despite winter just around the corner, and the quiet-ness that has befallen this beautiful moody city, my life has only gotten more complicated.

I've been having my dalliances with Dahlia over the last couple of weeks and I've grown closer to her than I ever thought I would be with anyone ever again. She's brought me her darkness, but in doing so has made my world so much brighter. There's this perverse understanding between us, this rare and precious way that we give ourselves to each other, not just in our bodies but with something deeper. I often question if I have a soul, as vampires will proudly claim they do not, but she does have one and I feel as if when I'm with her, she lets me borrow her soul and wear it for a while.

She feels good on me.

But as it is in my life, everything good that happens is swiftly followed by something bad. In this case, it's nothing to do with Dahlia, but with Aleksi and Saara, who seem to be complications in my life ever since they arrived.

Seems I've made enemies of them since Aleksi's stupid stint in the Red Room. Normally it wouldn't matter if a vampire got kicked out because everyone knows that it only exists for them as long as they follow the rules. But because those siblings have such a strange hold on this town, I'm in a position where I have to make nice with them.

As such, tonight me and Bitrus have to take a boat out to the island of Poveglia to have a meeting with Saara and Aleksi. They asked me specifically to go so that we could settle our differences. I may be a vampire, but I'm no fool. They may be wanting to kill me, I wouldn't put it past them. So I asked Bitrus to come with me, just in case. It doesn't hurt to have another witness.

"Could they have picked a spookier night?" Bitrus says.

I turn to see him coming toward me out of the mist, the collar of his black coat spiked up high, his hands in his pockets. All he needs is a fedora covering his bald head and he'd be straight out of a film noir.

"You know how dramatic vampires are," I say.

I'm standing on a dock along the south side of the city, just behind the famous silhouette of the Basilica di Santa Maria della Salute. The siblings said they would send a boat for me at eleven p.m. and even though it's late, many boats and vaporettos are still cruising through the canal that separates us from the island of Giudecca, their lights barely visible through the fog.

"So they live on Poveglia, huh," Bitrus muses as he stands beside me. "That's all sorts of fucked up."

I sigh. "Yeah, well, if it looks like a duck and walks like a duck..."

Poveglia is a small island that's grand with infamy, reported to be the most haunted place in the world and for good reason, too. During the plague it was used as a lazaretto to confine the dying. Rumors have it that there were so many plague-ridden bodies burned on the island that the soil is comprised mostly of human ash. I don't think that's a rumor though, I've been there once just passing through on a boat, and I didn't even have to step on the island to smell how deep the stench of death goes.

After the plague, it was used as a quarantine station for those entering Venice, then it was turned into an insane asylum, naturally, then a hospital and care home for the elderly to spend their last days, until it was finally closed in the 1960s. Now it's completely abandoned, though the hospital and watchtower remain.

And apparently not fully abandoned since the siblings have taken up residence there. I'm assuming they've converted some secret part of the hospital into their dwelling, since the last I heard everything was left to rot.

"So, how is it going with Dahlia?" Bitrus asks as I search the fog for any boats that might be ours. "Are you any closer to introducing me to her?"

I give him a wry look. "Not yet."

I've wanted her to meet Bitrus but I'm worried that introducing her to other vampires might trigger her fight-or-flight instincts. Humans are pretty good at ignoring vampires for what we are, but only one at a time. If she met Bitrus she might start picking up on the fact that there is something very wrong with me.

Though who am I kidding?

She already thinks there's something wrong with me.

And she likes it.

"I've introduced you to Bash," Bitrus goes on, running his fingers over his clean-shaven jaw.

"Yes. The Bash that you're still just casually fucking," I comment with a laugh. "How about I'll let you meet Dahlia when you vamp-up and realize that you're in a god damn relationship with him?"

He just grunts dismissively at that, pulling his collar up higher as if he's cold and faces the sea. Then he frowns. "This must be for us."

I follow his gaze to see a small motorboat coming our way, a man in black at the back piloting the prop. At least I think it's a man, the closer he gets the more that I can't make heads or tails of his face. It's like he's the Elephant Man come to life.

"What the...?" Bitrus whispers as the boat comes to the dock.

The man at the helm is disarmingly tall, cloaked with such dark and chaotic energy that it feels repellant, and on his head is a plague doctor mask.

I exchange a wide-eyed look with Bitrus. He raises his brows.

They can't be serious? he says inside my head. *This is our ride?*

I look back to the plague doctor, seeing only black fathomless holes for eyes, the long beak for a nose. "Did Saara and Aleksi send you for us?" I ask, as if there's some other explanation.

The man in the mask just stares at us.

I guess that's our answer.

"Guess we should be on our way, then," I say with a weary sigh, heading toward the boat, which the plague doctor holds to the dock with one very large leather gloved hand, a hand far too large to be human.

"Boy am I regretting coming along with you," Bitrus says under his breath, following me as we step onto the boat.

The minute we sit down, the boat pulls away from the dock and we head into the mist. I keep looking over my shoulder at the plague doctor piloting the boat, wondering who could be under that mask. If it's a vampire I can't tell, and usually my vampire radar would be going off. If it's a human, well, he's a giant, and I don't know what the hell that weird energy around them is since that's akin to witchcraft.

Maybe it's a witch. I think back to when I saw one recently. I was walking with Dahlia, that night we first had drinks and I kissed her. The witch looked of Middle-Eastern blood, fairly young and pretty, and she didn't seem to notice me but I sure as hell noticed her. I could smell her. Venice is said to have more than a few witches hanging around but for whatever reason I don't run into them very often. If this masked person driving the boat is a witch though, I should be able to smell them and I'm getting nothing.

Do you ever wonder if there are more ways to kill a vampire than what we've been told? Bitrus asks in my head. *Maybe it's not just fire, decapitation, or being stabbed in the heart by a witch's blade. Maybe it's being scared to death by ghosts of plague doctors?*

Not helpful, I tell him.

Especially not helpful as the boat goes deeper into the mist, the lights of the city and Giudecca being swallowed up. All sound is swallowed up too, leaving only the whir of the motor and the beating of my own heart inside my head. I don't spook easily but I'm feeling more and more unsettled the longer the boat ride is. I'm thinking back to the creature in the water, to what Bitrus had told me about something being in his room, I'm thinking about how these last few weeks I could have sworn something was following me in the dark, something insidious and rancid that never appeared to my eye, forever in shadows.

And now, as the island appears before us, the belltower rising above the mist which is clearing just enough to show the dilapidated hospital, the crumbling bricks and overgrown weeds, I have that feeling again, the one of being watched by something that doesn't belong in this world. As someone who doesn't belong in this world myself, it's a most unsettling feeling.

There isn't a single light on the island and I only now just realize the boat must have turned off its light too. Because we can see quite well in the dark, it makes it easy to live undetected in the shadows.

"Shit!" Bitrus suddenly cries out, pulling back from the edge of the boat where he was staring down into the surface. "I just saw faces in the water."

Completely fucking normal.

I look over my shoulder at the plague doctor, as if the man in the mask has a rational explanation for Bitrus seeing faces under the surface, but the doctor is pointing straight ahead with a rigid arm.

I turn around to see Saara and Aleksi standing on the end of the dock. They sure as hell weren't there a second ago. As usual, the two of them are dressed to the nines, Saara in a long white slinky gown, Aleksi in a white suit. They look like they're going to some vampire prom, except they both have bare feet.

"Welcome, Professor Aminoff," Saara says. She smiles sweetly at Bitrus as the boat bumps the dock. "I see you've brought a friend."

"Can't be too careful," I tell her, getting to my feet. "Saara, Aleksi, I'm sure you've met Bitrus before."

"I don't think we've formally met," Saara says, "but I'm very familiar with him. I trust you had a pleasant journey over here."

I get out of the boat, Bitrus right behind me, muttering under his breath about seeing crazy shit. "It was more peculiar than pleasant," I say, gesturing to the plague doctor sitting in the boat. "Can I ask what the deal is with, uh, that?"

"You'll find out soon enough," Saara says quietly, running her tongue over her teeth. "Come along now."

"Welcome to our island," Aleksi says, gesturing to the crumbling building, "our humble abode. The perfect place for a vampire, wouldn't you say?" He grins at me showing too much teeth.

"I don't know," I sniff, the stench of death permeating the air, "I think I prefer my house in the city."

"Aleksi is so very proud of its history," Saara says, coming over to me and taking my arm. "Did you know over one hundred thousand people died on this island? The plague pits were just bursting with people. Too bad they were all rotted, their blood poisoned by the disease, otherwise we would have had quite a feast."

I raise my brow and look between both the siblings as we walk along a narrow path to the building, broken iron gates swung open to one side. "Don't tell me you were around back then."

The siblings exchange a smug look. "There's a reason why this city is so dear to us," Saara explains. "It's been our home for a *very* long time. Back when the locals referred to us as shroud-eaters. Before your friend Mr. Bram Stoker had to sully our names."

Ah. So maybe that's part of the reason she hates me. Notoriety. Vampires can get awfully territorial, and especially entitled. A lot of vampires don't like me purely because I am the one the whole world knows by name, as if I'm the Prince of Darkness himself. When humans think vampire, they think Dracula and no one else.

Vampires are prone to jealousy like anyone else.

"My apologies," I say to her as we continue to the building. "Bram took a lot of liberties with my life story." I clear my throat. "May I ask why you invited me here?"

"We have a surprise for you," Aleksi speaks up. "A gift."

I look at Bitrus and he just shakes his head slightly.

"Don't worry," Saara says, noting our exchange. "You can partake too. Bitrus. It's a way of saying we're sorry for the way we've come across. As I'm sure you now understand, we're used to the city being a certain way. Your influence with the Red Room, well, it complicates things."

"So then why did you leave Venice to begin with?" Bitrus asks.

"You know vampires, we need to keep moving or we get bored," she says with a shrug, flipping her stick straight blonde hair over her shoulder. I pick up the scent of human blood when she does that. Fresh blood.

"And we had good reason," Aleksi says, "which will become clear soon."

I grumble to myself. Things only get murkier, not clearer.

"Watch your step," Saara says as we head through a broken path toward the building covered with rusted scaffolding. "They were going to do some work here but it got abandoned. It's just enough to keep the building from collapsing."

We go past a faded sign that reads *Psychiatric Department* in Italian and then enter through the main doors. The building feels entirely unsafe and rotted.

"And so where do you really live?" I ask them, looking around at the vines growing inside, the stacks of broken beds, the crumbling walls, and the shattered windows covered in bars, while that unsettling feeling continues to seep into my bones.

"Downstairs," she says. "Underground. We'll give you a tour later, but first let's eat."

My stomach growls at the mention of eating. It has been awhile since I last fed. I find that when I'm spending nights with Dahlia in my bed, it's hard to make time for the Red Room. Besides, she's been distracting enough.

"Eat?" Bitrus says, knowing that we never feed outside of the Red Room.

Saara just nods and we follow her and Aleksi down a damp, narrow hall until it widens at the end. There is a large wooden door with two seven-foot-tall plague doctors standing in front, guarding it. For a moment I think they're statues, but they move to the side to let us in.

"The fuck is this now?" Bitrus grumbles quietly.

"This is the chapel," Saara says, coming to a stop in the middle of the room. "And here's your dinner."

The chapel walls are white, molding with green fungus, and there are only a few pews standing, the rest broken. At the front of the chapel, in front of an altar lit with burning candles, are two people, a young man and a young woman, no more than twenty years old. They are naked and sitting on the floor, duct tape over their mouths, their wrists and feet bound together. They stare at us with wide eyes, trying to move closer to each other, their anguished sounds muffled against the duct tape that flexes against their mouths with each breath.

There's no blood anywhere but I spy two holes on their necks, most likely sampled by Saara. It's then that I notice their legs. Both their ankles are smashed in, flattened, so they can't walk or escape. If it wasn't for the heavy stench of death and decay in this place, I would have noticed the adrenaline and horror flowing from them.

"Who are they?" I ask Saara, trying not to meet their fearful eyes.

"They are your gift," Aleksi says. "An apology dinner from us. Come now, feast." He gives me an eerie grin, breathing in deep. "I can smell how hungry you are."

I shake my head. "No. No, this isn't right. You won't hold me back if I get carried away."

"You have your friend here to mind you," Saara says,

placing her hand on my shoulder and leaning into my ear. "I already had a taste of them," she whispers. "Their fear is the sweetest I've ever had. You should be so honored to get your fill from them."

I close my eyes. "But who are they?"

She pauses for a moment, her nails digging sharply into my leather jacket for a moment. "It doesn't matter who they are. Young adults separated from their church group. I don't know. They're here now. No one will ever find them here, probably no one will notice them being gone." She pulls back and frowns at me. "I'm starting to think you aren't appreciating my gesture."

Remember to play nice, I remind myself, though this is making it quite hard.

"Brother," she snaps at Aleksi, while still looking at me. "Bring me the girl. She at least has nice tits he can eat."

"Saara," I warn her, but Aleksi picks the girl up by her throat and lifts her with his supernatural strength so that her broken ankles are dangling above the floor, then brings her over to me.

The girl pleads with her eyes, bright blue eyes, for me not to hurt her. She knows now we are vampires, she knows what's going to happen to her. Even if I refuse to feed from her, she won't be getting out of here alive.

"Valtu," Bitrus says from behind me. "You don't have to do this. I know you're hungry, man, but we can go back to the Red Room."

I open my mouth to agree, I get ready to turn away, but suddenly Saara takes a knife and slices the woman's throat wide open, right below the jaw.

Her scream gurgles as the blood rushes out like a waterfall. The sight of the crimson river, the sharp scent of horror-filled blood, combined with the deep hunger inside me, flips a switch.

"Drink her before she goes to waste," Saara says. "Suck her dry."

I watch as it splashes all over her tits, over her belly, down to the floor where it splatters and for a moment I think of Dahlia and I think about all the times I wanted to feed from her, wanted to taste her blood and didn't, and I guess there's only so much restraint a vampire can stand.

I let the monster inside me take over.

I grab the girl, my mouth at her neck, and I drink and drink, losing myself to the pure frenzy of it, letting myself be the creature of darkness that I am. For once I don't have to hold back. She's already dead and dying and I can just let myself go.

But the hunger only spurs on more hunger. When she's bled out, all her blood coursing through my system, I set my sights on the man. I don't see that tears are streaming down his face, I don't see the pain in his eyes, I just see another meal.

I'll put him out of his misery.

I lunge for him, leaping on top of him like a panther and then I'm tearing into his jugular, ripping out flesh and muscles and arteries, and I am just gnashing teeth and claws and everything bad and dangerous in this world. Humans foolishly pride themselves on thinking they are the deadliest predators on earth, but if they knew at all that vampires exist, they'd be quickly put in their place.

Soon I'm as satiated as I've ever been. I can't remember being so full of blood, it would have been the last time I enjoyed murdering someone. And while I don't want to say I enjoyed what I just did, it does feel good to feel satisfied for once. It feels part of my nature.

I look up, dazed. I'm sitting on the ground, my clothes drenched in blood, beside the body of the dead man, barely recognizable now from what I did to him. The woman is a few feet away where I left her as a molted heap on the ground. Saara and Aleksi are standing behind her, Saara with a book in her hands, and Bitrus is nowhere to be seen.

I clear my throat. "Where is Bitrus?"

"He's waiting by the boat," Aleksi says. "He didn't want to intrude on your feast. It was for you, after all, not him."

I nod at the book she's holding. "And what's that? Turning to the Bible now?"

Saara gives me a sharp look. "It's why we left. It's our prized possession. And thanks to you, we've unlocked another door."

"What do you mean?" I frown, getting an uneasy feeling in my chest.

"There was a witch in Wales who had a certain book we wanted, that we had been searching the world over. A book of spells and magic that was not only accessible to us but had great power. Had you ever heard of such a thing? As someone who collects rare books, we thought this would be right up your alley."

I try to think. Books of magic and spells were nothing new. Many witches around the world had them and often-times they fell into the hands of vampires. Some vampires, like my friend Solon, were able to procure the magic with ease, but the spells for the most part were fairly benign. Sure, you could create flames with your fingertips (a spell Solon actually taught me) but there wasn't usually anything that was very black magic or dark arts about them, and if there was, vampires just didn't have that natural access to them that witches had.

But there were rumors about one book in particular, the *Book of Verimagiaa* that was created by both a witch and a vampire that had gone rogue and worked together in the dark arts. That book was reported to open doors to other dimensions, worlds, even the past and future. The spells were bound in the book in such a way that any witch, vampire, or even human could use them to conjure everything dark and evil.

"So you do know," Aleksi muses slowly, reading my face. "The Book of Verimagiaa is real, Valtu. And it's in our hands. We've been having such a fun time accessing the Red World of Skarde's, but we've struggled to get to the next level. To open that next door. You just helped us do it."

My throat feels tight. "What do you mean?"

"Spill the virgin blood by an altar," Saara says in a deeply inhuman voice, reading from the book, "let the Prince of Darkness drink. Sacrifice two innocent humans, open the portal to the brink."

I can't believe what I'm hearing.

Did they actually try to use me for black magic?

"Listen," I say, getting to my feet, feeling a little unsteady. "I'm sure you think you have some magic book, but no portal is going to open because of me. I'm not the Prince of Darkness, that was something that Bram made up for the book. Or hell, Milton did for Paradise Lost."

"But you were called that," Aleksi says, his eyes looking feverish in the light of the candles. "Before Stoker, you were called that. Do you even remember the vampire you used to be, Valtu? How you raged throughout Europe, killing everything in your path? Why are you trying to dilute your own history, water down the darkness? Own it, for fuck's sake."

I try to swallow, the taste of their blood now tasting like pennies in my mouth.

"I put all of that behind me," I manage to say.

He gestures to the dead bodies. "Clearly you didn't. No matter how hard you try to find your humanity, opening up fucking feeding rooms, you're just running from who you really are."

I let out a huff. "Is this where you tell me to join you?"

"Frankly no," Saara says, snapping the book shut. "You're not trustworthy. Your humanity has taken too much of a hold of you that I don't think you'll ever fully go dark again. And if you're not careful, other vampires will start feeling the same way."

"Are you threatening me?"

"I'm warning you. About yourself."

I shake my head and throw out my arms. "Okay, fine. So you just did a spell. I don't see a portal to Hell, do you?"

She looks around. "It doesn't always happen like that. It can take time to appear. Last time it appeared in the plague pits out back. I thought all the skeletons were coming alive for a moment."

"Maybe we should go check," Aleksi says to her.

"Wait, you've been successful before?" I ask, feeling a stab of dread.

Her eyes narrow. "Did you not listen to a word we've been saying? We opened a door to a level of the Red World. We pulled out ghosts and creatures we've never seen before. We let demons crawl out. One of them, they call it *the bad thing*, is roaming the city looking for witches."

"Witches?"

She rolls her eyes like I'm an idiot. "We killed a witch and stole a book that gives us unlimited dark magic. You don't think their guild has dispatched vampire slayers? They've probably figured out it was us, they might already be here in the city. But this demon can sniff them out even when we can't. Think of it as a pet you should never let off the leash... even though we do."

No wonder I saw that witch the other day. But I don't want to bring that up around them. I don't want to give them anything. For some reason, I'm extremely worried about Dahlia now. It feels far too dangerous with demon-hunting witches on the loose, let alone the other things that will crawl out of hell. Let alone me, a relapsed monster that just killed an innocent man.

And while Dahlia isn't a witch, slayers do use glamor to disguise themselves so that they seem like any other human. What if Saara and Aleksi discover her and think that she's a witch? They'll kill her without remorse.

She isn't a witch, right?

"Well, I'm sorry that the party is over so soon," Saara says in a tired voice. "I was hoping after the meal, you could at least see the portal, the result of your efforts. But hey, if it ever pops open and you want a look, you're welcome to come back."

I am never coming back here.

I give her a tight smile. "It's getting late. I trust the boat will take us back."

"Of course," Aleksi says, putting his arm around Saara's waist and kissing her shoulder, his eyes on me as he does so. "Thanks again for your service, Valtu. Remember what we talked about. We don't have to be your enemy, not anymore, and especially not now. It just wouldn't be wise."

I grumble and turn on my heel, eager to leave this creepshow of a place, heading out into the cold night air.

Bitrus is standing on the dock by the boat. He looks as relieved to see me as I am to see him, but we just nod at each other, and I step into the boat.

I stare at the plague doctor and I wonder if under the mask I'd find a creature from the Red World, a creature no one had ever seen before.

I try not to think about it.

Bitrus takes the seat beside me and we fall into silence for a few moments. There's no point speaking about what happened. He knows.

"I don't think I can see Dahlia anymore," I say in a weak voice as the boat pulls away from the island and starts heading back to Venice. I swallow hard, too many emotions competing inside me, the worst one of all is how damn good I feel for drinking as much as I did. "I don't think it's safe for her."

Bitrus just puts his hand on my shoulder and squeezes. "Vampires and humans never work out, Valtu. You know this yourself."

I squeeze my eyes shut and nod.

I know it far too well.

CHAPTER 16

DAHLIA

"Did you hear about that woman who was found last night?"

"Yes, such a tragedy. I always say that people drink too much and go out on the boats. The police should be more vigilant!"

"Imagine that, falling over onto the propeller and having it do that to your body. I just didn't think a prop was strong enough to do that sort of damage."

"I agree, something very odd about it all. Perhaps keep an eye on your Enzo tonight, huh? There's a strange feeling in the air. I may have to wear my cornetto."

I'm standing at the corner of the espresso bar half-way between my apartment and the school, listening to a couple of elderly local women talking. It's been a strange couple of days here in the city. First, a couple of nights ago, a pair of nineteen-year-olds who were visiting with a church group went missing, now last night a woman had been found washed up on the steps into the water in San Marco, her body completely mutilated. Officials are saying it looked like damage from falling overboard and onto an engine, but no one seems to believe it.

I want to ask Valtu about it but he's been completely unavailable all week. We don't act any different in class with each other, lest we make people suspicious, but even so I feel like he's giving me the cold shoulder. Like his eyes are cagey when he talks to me. And I haven't seen him after class at all the last few days because suddenly he has some friend over who came in from out of town. A doctor from England, who I assume is a vampire too.

Everything had been going so well. I told Livia about my progress, which she relayed to Bellamy, so they've been off my back lately. I've come far in my playing and now that we've been rehearsing with the string section a few times, I'm confident for the recital.

And then there's the fact that I've been getting railed by Professor Aminoff nearly every single night. For obvious reasons I haven't brought him back to my apartment. I'm afraid that he'll be able to sense the blade of *mordernes* in my closet, and there's all my other witchy stuff, but he seems more than content to keep our nights at his place. Besides, his house is a gorgeous gothic dream with everything you could want, including a lush garden out back overlooking a canal, that has oranges, lemons, limes, olives, and rows of dark roses, plus red and orange dahlias (obviously my favorite) which are still blooming despite the fact we are heading into frosty mornings soon.

If I felt myself falling before, now I'm in the freefall where I know it'll hurt soon. Every waking minute I'm thinking about him, about the way he looks at me, the things he says, the more profane the better, I'm thinking about how he makes me feel more myself and more present than I ever have in my life, especially when he's fucking my brains out. I swear his dick is borderline addicting and the minute we're alone together I can't seem to keep my hands off of him.

This feeling I have for him is consuming me.

And I want nothing more than to be consumed by him.

Somewhere in the back of my lust-addled brain I know the only reason I'm with him at all is because I'm supposed to kill him and the others. But the longer this goes on, the more I realize how impossible that all is. I know my duties—I will get that book out of Saara and Aleksi's hands, especially with the dangers that are roaming this city now, and I will kill the siblings as well—but I'm not going to let any harm come to Valtu, even by my own hand.

Last week, when we were laying in bed in the wee hours of the morning, he was asleep and I was running my hand over his chest, right over his steadily beating heart, and I couldn't in a million years ever picture having the blade in my hands and stabbing it through him. Maybe that makes me weak or a bad witch, or maybe it's foolish because I'm falling for him while wearing a disguise, so how far can this relationship between us really go? But it's the truth.

I am his now and that also makes him mine.

Which is why it's been painful these last few days not being able to be with him.

I finish my espresso, which was probably a bad idea this late in the afternoon, and I head to school. It's my music history class with Valtu and the last one of the day for both of us. I'm hoping that if I linger after class, he'll reach out and invite me over to his house.

But when class is over and I'm slow to get my things together, he doesn't even look my way. I take a deep breath and approach his desk, wishing I didn't have this hard knot in my stomach.

"Is your doctor friend gone?" I ask, trailing my finger along the edge of his desk.

"Hmmm?" he says distractedly, gathering up his stuff before looking up at me with a blank expression. "Oh, yes. He left yesterday."

I stare at him expectantly, my brows up. "So if he's gone... shouldn't I be coming over?"

I feel a little foolish when I say it, feel even more so when he doesn't say anything right away. Instead he gives me the kind of unsure smile that tells me I'm not going to like what he's about to say.

"I don't think that's a good idea," he says to me and that hard knot in my stomach turns to one of dread.

I have a hard time swallowing, my throat feeling thick. "What do you mean? Your friend is gone right? And we haven't seen each other in a few days..."

His eyes dart to the door and back and I turn to look but there's no one there.

"It's just not a good idea, Dahlia," he says, lowering his voice. "None of this is."

I shake my head. "I don't understand," I whisper. "You mean..."

"I mean the two of us together," he snaps at me, his dark eyes looking wild. "It's too dangerous."

My heart feels like it stops beating. I don't understand. "Dangerous? For who? Your job? We've been careful, we can be even more careful, I—"

"Stop," he growls at me, his nostrils flaring. "Just stop. Look at me. Listen to me because I'm not going to tell you again." He leans in close so I can see the red and gold in his brown eyes, their intensity paralyzing me and pinning me in place. "It's over between us. We had a good run. We had some good fucks. But this shit doesn't last forever. I'm done with you now, okay? So get that in your head and leave me the fuck alone."

Then he strides off through the room and out the door, leaving me behind, feeling like I've been shot close-range with a shotgun.

I open my mouth to speak but only a ragged whine comes

out and I press my hands to my stomach as if to stop the bleeding. I've lost it all in a second.

What the hell has gotten into him? He's just...he just decided he's done with me now? Just like that?

No. No, that can't be. I don't care if he told me to leave him the fuck alone, that can't be.

And the book, a voice inside me says. *Now you'll never learn about Saara and Aleksi. Now Bellamy will have to come and finish the job and he might just finish you.*

No. No, no, no.

I place my hands over my eyes, whimpering like I might explode at any moment, wishing I could just go back in time and—

"*Stai bene?*" someone asks in Italian.

I lift up my head to see one of my classmates by the door. I'm terrible with names so I don't remember what his is, but he seems nice enough.

I paste on a smile. "I'm fine."

I walk toward him and he moves to the side as I go through the door.

"*Stai attento,*" he says, and I stop. *Be careful.*

"What?" I ask, looking over my shoulder at him.

"Be careful out there," he says, switching to English. "It's not safe in the city."

I nod. I'm sure the guy is just being helpful or protective but the whole thing plucks another chord of unease inside me. "I will."

I leave the school, the sun having just set and dark clouds cover the sky painting the city in this hazy grey glow. It's windy and it has a bite to it and I should probably go home but I can't bear the idea of being in that apartment right now. I don't feel afraid despite what's been happening in the city, in fact, after the way Valtu just decimated my heart, I don't really care what happens to me. But if I go to my apartment I'm just going to cry and I don't feel like doing that.

So I go to the nearest bar, right across from the school. I'm hoping to see a familiar face or two, or maybe that guy who just talked to me will pop by. By my second glass of prosecco, I wish I actually struck up more of a conversation with him. Hell, I wish I talked more with anyone. I've been so wrapped up with Valtu that I've forgotten about everyone else in my school.

But who am I kidding? It would have been the same patterns I've known all my life. I never would have become anyone's friend, not when they really got to know me. They'd stay away like the plague. That's how everyone treats me.

Except for Valtu.

With him I felt he honestly understood me, even if he only saw parts of me. But the parts he saw, he accepted them.

Until he didn't.

I sigh and order another glass of prosecco, drowning my sorrows in the bubbles, trying to understand where I went wrong and what happened. Did I say something that scared him? I tend to blabber a lot after I've come, but I never said anything nuts like I love him or want to be with him forever or anything like that. The two of us have been keeping things very physical for the most part.

Or maybe he spooked himself. He may be a vampire, but he's also a man and men get scared easily when it comes to feelings and whatnot. Though from the way he talks, how he doesn't hold back with me, how forthright he is (about everything except being a vampire), I'm not sure if that's the case. He seems too secure to worry about that.

I just can't figure it out and the more drunk I get, the less I want to cry and scream and the more I want an answer. This isn't fair. You can't just cut someone off like this with barely an explanation.

With newfound determination, fueled by liquid courage, I pound back the rest of my drink and head out into the night. The clouds are lower now and the air smells like rain, feels like mist. I head over the bridge, following the route I know by heart now all the way to Valtu's house.

When I finally get there, it starts to rain, and I'm wondering what my plan is after all. I guess knock on his door and see if he's home. There are no lights on that I can see from the front view but he is a vampire so that doesn't mean anything.

But when I knock on it, there's no answer.

I start pounding on it. "Valtu!" I yell.

No answer.

I ring the doorbell.

Nothing.

And yet I swear he's there. My witchy sense can tell.

I go to the sides of the house but there's no way I can scale the huge stone walls.

The rain is coming down hard now. My sweater is keeping me warm, and my leather jacket provides some protection against the rain, as does my long skirt and boots. I decide to try to access his place from another angle.

I go back on the street and walk for a bit until I see a small bridge going over the narrow canal behind his house. Then I cross over it and loop around through a small tree-filled square outside someone's residence. From there I can see straight into Valtu's house.

I stand there in the rain, stare at his windows. In the breeze, the orange trees sway back and forth, some oranges falling to the ground below. There's only a narrow canal between me and his backyard and if I wanted to I could step onto the boat below and then step out onto his side which is unprotected.

But I don't want to do that. I feel this is as close as I

should get. I'm starting to feel like a stalker, which is ironic since vampires are usually the ones who stalk people, not the other way around.

You're nuts, I tell myself as the rain continues to pour, fat droplets bouncing off the water of the dark canal. Get over it and go back to your place.

But I can't. I can only stare, hoping for a sign of him. All the lights in the house are off and—

Suddenly the light in the bathroom on the second floor comes on. I watch as Valtu walks past the window, naked from the waist up, and I suck in my breath, feeling like a creep watching him but feeling so angry at the same time.

Why did you do it? I think.

As if he heard my thought, his head swivels and he looks to the window.

Then he comes right over to it and peers out.

He sees me.

He disappears. I stand there, wondering what I should do. I feel stupid, foolish. The rain keeps coming down and I'm soaked.

"Dahlia," he cries out as he crosses his garden, nearly slipping on a fallen orange. He's shirtless still but has a towel around his waist. I thought he was ignoring me but I guess he was in the shower. "What are you doing?" he hisses.

I shake my head, feeling tears building behind my eyes.

"Jesus," he swears, and then steps down onto the bow of the small boat, one hand still gripping his towel as it rocks back and forth. He walks toward me and holds out his hand. "Come here." He sounds cross.

I sniff, wishing I could disappear, but he's insistent. I put my hand in his and he carefully guides me into the boat, across and then a big step onto his garden on the other side.

We take a few steps away from the edge of the water and

he turns to me, looking me over with wild eyes. "What is wrong with you? Have you gone mad?"

I press my lips together and nod, trying to hold it together. "I think I might be."

"Dahlia," he says, shaking his head. Then he pulls at my hand. "Come on, let's get you dry."

"No," I cry out, rooting my legs in place. "No, I want to know why you said what you did. Back there at school you told me it was over, that you were done with me. You told me to leave you the fuck alone," I sputter, throwing my arms out, the rain flinging off of me. "Why did you say all that?"

"I told you," he says, stepping toward me so he's towering above. "It's dangerous."

"But for who?"

"For you!" he hisses, grabbing my shoulders, his fingers digging into my jacket. "It's dangerous for you."

I blink at him, droplets gathered in my lashes falling and mixing with the tears on my cheeks. "Please explain to me how. I deserve to know the truth, Valtu. If you don't tell me the truth, then I've given you my all for nothing. I trusted you."

"I can't explain," he says through gritted teeth, his jaw tense as his eyes search mine. "Please keep on trusting me when I say this is for your benefit."

I raise my chin. "It's a cop-out. You got scared."

"I did get scared! Scared of losing you." He releases my shoulders and runs his hand over his face, looking away.

"You're not going to lose me," I tell him quietly, reaching out for his arm. I run my fingers down it, grasping his fingers. "We're okay. Right now, the two of us, we have a good thing and we're okay. We're safe."

"You don't know who I am, my dove," he says to me with a grimace, his words sounding pained. "You don't know what kind of man I am."

"I know you have darkness in you, the same I have in me."

"No, no, it's not the same. I'm dangerous. It's me. I'm the one that's dangerous. If you really knew me..."

"Then I would love you just the same."

Shit.

The words come out of my mouth without any warning, without any thought, they just sit there in the air between us and not even the rain can wash them away.

"What?" Valtu whispers harshly.

I stare at him, blinking, because what the hell. I didn't think I was going to say that. I didn't even think I felt that way but now that I said it, I know it's the truth.

I'm in fucking love with him.

The worst person I could ever fall in love with.

"I—I'm sorry," I say, fumbling for words, looking at the shock on Valtu's face. Now I've really gone and fucked shit up. First, stalking him outside his house in the damn rain, next telling him I love him, and doing both after he told me to leave him the hell alone.

I shake my head. "I know you didn't need to hear that, I certainly didn't mean to say it, I—"

He lunges for me, the towel dropping to the grass, and he grabs my face between his hands, kissing me hard, so hard it knocks the air from my lungs. I immediately wrap my arms around him, pulling him as close to me as possible as the rain beats down around us, wanting more, more, and he gives me this, pressing his body against mine, completely naked now, his cock hard and pressing into my hip, his lips moving hungrily against mine.

I can feel the passion coursing through me, building, playing with my emotions, mixing them with need, and I melt into him as our tongues dance together in the rain.

He pulls back slightly, looking deep into my eyes with a

look of raw desire, one I've seen plenty of times, and yet this one seems different. It's almost the look of a mad man.

Without warning, he lifts me up off the ground and spins me around so that my back is pressed up against a nearby trunk of an orange tree, scattering more oranges to the ground.

He urgently removes my jacket, throwing it to the side, hikes up my skirt to my waist, then slides his hand up my thigh, grabbing the seam of soaking wet panties and ripping them off of me. I cry out in surprise, the rain is coming down harder now, and the cold air makes my body shiver, goose-bumps forming on my flesh even though my skin feels like fire.

He reaches around and cups my ass, lifting me up slightly, and I wrap my legs around him and pull him close to me as he pushes me against the tree, the bark abrasive against my sweater.

He kisses me hard again, so damn deeply it's like he's fucking my mouth, and his cock twitches, hard and expectant against my inner thigh. I groan and he presses it against me, rubbing it along my wetness, his cock sliding along my clit, and I cry out with desire, my whole body throbbing with painful need for him.

He suddenly thrusts hard inside me, filling me up until I feel I might break. I throw my head back against the tree and moan, the rain washing away all of my inhibitions. I wrap my arms around him and press my body against him, wanting him to never, ever leave me.

He starts to move inside of me, rocking his hips, his cock sliding in and out of me, my pussy quivering and shaking with need for him. He's a machine now, thrusting into me hard, his hips rocking against me, his rock-hard length shoving deeper and deeper. His mouth finds mine again and he kisses me, our lips aching for one another, and it's raw and messy and I can't get enough of him.

With his cock stiff and throbbing inside me, I push my hips back against him, needing him deeper inside of me, wanting to feel all of him, all at once.

He thrusts harder, faster, and I moan loudly, the sound of the rain drowning out my voice. His hands grip my ass tightly and he pushes me against the tree harder, pinning me against the trunk.

He moves his hips faster now, grunting in pure determination and desire like he wants to fuck me to death, his cock thrusting deeper inside me, my moans growing louder, and I feel like I'm going to explode with this wild greed for him.

"My love," he whispers to me, his voice ragged, his eyes feverish as he meets my gaze. "Oh, fuck. Your cunt is heaven."

His cock slides easily in and out and I'm so wet that he's starting to slip when he goes faster and I can feel my whole body tense, a hot coil of need inside me tightening and tightening. His hand is under my sweater, squeezing at my breast, while his other is at my mouth, his thumb pushing between my lips. I suck at him for a moment and then gasp he drives in so deep it feels like I'm being nailed to the tree.

"Fuck!" I cry out, not caring if the neighbors hear us. Not caring about anything right now but that urgent need to come on his cock.

I wrap my arms around his neck and bury my face in his shoulder, my hips grinding against his, our bodies completely in tune with one another.

He thrusts hard, and I can feel his cock deep inside me, his whole body tightens and he moans loudly, his length twitching and throbbing, and I'm ready to come. Suddenly, my body explodes with waves of pleasure. I cry out loudly and he wraps his arms around me, his cock still thrusting inside me as I ride them, nonsensical words falling out of my mouth as I yelp into the night.

He pulls back slightly and then before I know it he's picking me up and pushing me to the ground. I land on top of the oranges on my hands and knees, the fruit spilling open and coating my skin red. Blood oranges.

Then he flips me around so I'm on my back, rain in my face, and he's right on top of me, covering me with the large mass of his body. He pulls my legs apart and thrusts deep inside me, moving his hips against mine to the rhythm of the rain.

I moan loudly, my body completely overcome with pleasure and yet here I am, ready to be fucked again and again. He pounds deeper and harder into me, the rain glistening on his skin as he fucks me wildly.

And in that moment, I know that nothing could ever feel this good. I'm his for now and forever, lost in the throes of ecstasy under the wet leaves and falling fruit with him, our bodies made for each other.

Fucking hell, I *love* him.

How and when did this happen?

When did my heart decide to finally pipe up and take control, take hostage of my mind and body without telling me? How fucking *dare* it?

But my thoughts are whisked away as his mouth goes to my neck, biting lightly, sucking, licking as his hips continue to slam against me, driving himself in deeper and deeper. I let my head fall back, no longer able to contain the sounds of ecstasy that escape my lips.

I'm lost in the moment, in the feel of him, in the sound of his breathing and the way his cock slides in and out of me, sending molten hot lightning through my body.

His teeth graze my neck and I cry out, my pussy clenching tightly around him. He groans against me, his thrusts becoming faster and harder still, our bodies slapping together, wet in every single way. He's pure animal when he fucks me like this, operating on basic instincts, rutting me into the earth under a violent sky.

I moan and cry out beneath him, feeling my orgasm quickly building and building. And then it hits me, a sudden rush of pleasure that consumes every part of me. I cry out desperately as my pussy spasms around his cock and he shudders against me, coming hard in my depths, a low, guttural moan filling the air. He's such a beast when he fucks and he's even more so when he comes. With the muscles of his thick neck corded as his head is thrown back, his shoulders straining as he spills inside me, how every muscle in his body is tight and hard, he looks like the ultimate predator, born to kill and fuck and maybe, just maybe, break your heart.

Oh damn.

That's where I'm headed, isn't it?

As he pulls out of me and collapses on the ground beside me, I realize that I'm in deep. Too deep to ever get out. And as I look up at the storm clouds overhead, I know it's too late to try.

CHAPTER 17

DAHLIA

"Amazing what a hot cup of tea can do for you on a night like tonight," Valtu says, puttering around his kitchen. I've just walked in dressed in one of his fluffy white robes, like the ones that a luxury spa would have. After having sex in the rain and getting stained with the red juice of blood oranges, both of us needed a shower badly. Naturally that led to sexy times in said shower, but I feel a lot better being all clean and warm now, wrapped in the robe, my hair in a towel.

"Tea?" I ask him, leaning against the kitchen island in his gourmet kitchen. "You don't strike me as a tea type of person."

He gives me a crooked smile, his eyes softly affectionate. "Oh yeah? What do I strike you as?"

A blood-drinker, I think.

I smile, watching as he grabs a box of tea from the cupboard, taking a moment to admire his ass in his grey sweatpants. They fit him like a glove and there's only one reason why a man owns grey sweatpants that fit like that. He wants me to stare.

"Well, most nights you aren't grabbing tea, that's for sure. You're either reaching for red wine or a stiff drink."

"Mmmm most nights I don't find you outside in the rain like you've lost your damn mind," he says.

I look down at the tiled floor. "I'm sorry."

"No," he says quickly, coming over to me. He takes my hand in his, puts his fingers under my chin and raises it to look at him. "I'm sorry, my dove. I..." He closes his eyes and sighs, licking his lips. Gives his head a shake. "I'm really sorry. What I said to you was uncalled for and undeserved, I just don't know what to do."

I honestly don't know what he's talking about. I know that part of it must stem from the fact that he's a vampire and he thinks I'm a human and that there's danger in our relationship because of it. And that might be true. But there's something else there. Something else that happened recently that made him pull away like this.

I'm scared to find out it has something to do with the book.

With the demons.

With the murders and disappearances in the city.

"Then why don't you try telling me the truth," I tell him. "I told you my truth. I told you I loved you."

His expression crumbles at that. "And I'm completely undeserving of it," he says, raising my hand to his lips and gently kissing my knuckles.

Well, he hasn't said it back to me. But I didn't even know I was in love with him until like an hour ago. How the hell that snuck up on me I don't know. It's fast, I know it's fast. Too fast. But I haven't been in love before so I have nothing to compare it to. All I know is that it comes from some place deep inside of me, like it was always there, just waiting and biding its time, like a once-dormant volcano that's been holding back for too long.

Now that it's been unleashed, I just want to revel in it, dance in it, say it all the time. Even if he doesn't quite feel the same way about me.

"Valtu," I say, reaching up and placing my hand at his cheek. "You are deserving of it."

He gives his head a sharp shake, eyes pleading. "Not if you knew who I really was."

"Then you're going to have to take the risk and tell me, because if you don't I'm going to start jumping to some crazy conclusions."

His eyes darken. "Sometimes there's nothing crazier than the truth."

Then he leans in and kisses me softly on the lips, sweet and tender.

"Okay," he whispers, leaning his forehead against mine. "How about we have some tea and I'll tell you something you won't believe. I'll bring some whisky too, in case you need it."

He moves over to the kettle, pours the hot water over the teabags in the mugs and then brings it over to the living room. The fire is roaring—he must have put it on while I was taking my time freshening up after the shower, though it is strange that it got so hot and big so fast.

We sit down on a dark green velvet couch, an odd choice of furniture but it suits him just fine. Vampires can be eclectic and Valtu is no different.

I cup the tea in my hands, the steam rising from the mug, and patiently wait for him to talk. Outside, the rain continues to patter against the windows, making the room feel extra cozy, even though I know what he's going to tell me will be anything but.

"You know, the city feels different lately," he comments, sipping his tea and not seeming to be affected at all by its scalding hot temperature. He has to tell me, his vampire mask is slipping every day.

"I've noticed. First those people go missing, then that woman gets killed by a boat, but boat engines don't mutilate like that."

He nods grimly. "Yes, there's that. For sure. But there's also a change in the air. Can you feel it? A darkness. Something more than what resides in you and me. A darkness that wants to eat and consume and spit out the bones after. I feel my city is changing and that the people here are at risk..."

I lean forward slightly. "At risk of what?"

His eyes flick to mine. "People like me."

We stare at each other for a moment. He's gauging my reaction and I'm trying to react how a normal person would. "What do you mean, people like you?"

He sighs heavily and adjusts his position on the couch, a long leg tucked under the other, and I do my best not to stare at his package, because hello, a big dick and gray sweatpants are as subtle as flashing neon lights that say "Get Your Cock Here!"

"There are things you don't know. An underbelly to this city. A dark one. A grim one. There are secret societies here that operate under everyone's noses, going completely unnoticed except by a select few. And while those societies operate in peace, there are some people who don't care for peace. Who want chaos and violence and power. And those people, those are the ones that are dangerous."

Pretty sure he's talking about Saara, Aleksi, and the Red Room. "If these people are dangerous, can't you report them to the police?"

"Not if the police are in on it," he says with a loaded look.

Oh shit. I never thought of that. The cops are vampires too?

"So, uh, what is this society about?"

He worries his lip between his teeth, his dark eyes drifting across the room. He focuses on his reflection in the mirror above the fireplace. "You told me you don't believe in ghosts. Does that still hold true?"

I have to remember what this non-witch version of myself told him. "That's true."

"Do you believe in the supernatural at all?"

And here we go.

Of course, I want to say yes, but I have to say, "No."

"Not even a little?"

"I've never seen proof of the supernatural existing," I tell him, which is a great segue for him to tell me he's a vampire and give me proof about it.

"So you need proof, you can't just take people at their word?" He eyes me curiously, taking a sip of his tea.

"Depends on who was doing the talking and what they were saying," I tell him.

He nods slowly. "Okay. Yup. I figured that with you."

He puts his mug on the coffee table and walks over to the mantle, picking up a dagger that was lying on top of a cigar box. It's short, sharp and gold with a black stone star at the base.

He brings it over to me, displaying it on his palm. The dagger looks ancient.

"What is this?" I ask.

"Proof," he says.

I expect him to go on and say the dagger belonged to some king he personally knew in the 1600s or something. But instead he hands it to me.

"I want you to stab me with it."

My mouth drops. "I'm sorry. Stab you with it?"

He nods. "Stick it right in my heart."

I let out a dry laugh and get to my feet, trying to give the knife back to him. "Okay, now you're the one who is acting nuts here. I'm not going to *stab* you. What the hell?"

The fact that he said that surprises me so much that for

one sweet moment I'd forgotten that I actually know what it's like to stab a vampire in the heart. I've done it a dozen times.

The muscle memory makes me sick.

"Okay, then I'll do it myself," he says, swiping the knife from me and pressing the tip against his chest, the sharp end already piercing a hole through his t-shirt.

"Wait! Stop!" I scream, trying to wrap my fingers around his wrist and pull his hands off but he's an immovable rock and I'm only a feather. "Stop, Valtu!"

He grunts and I watch as he pushes the dagger straight into his heart, driven in with inhuman strength, the sound of his sternum cracking under the pressure.

I've stopped screaming. I'm just watching in horror as blood begins to spill from his chest in waterfalls of red as he drives the gold dagger deeper and deeper into his heart.

I know what it feels like to do that.

I know what it's like to drive a knife through that bone, to find the heart, to plunge it in. It's some kind of sick joke, a twist of fate that has me reliving all my past kills right now, all the vampires I murdered with my glowing blue blade.

I'm staring at this blade sticking out from his chest, and I'm hit with such sadness, such regret for everything I've done. What if the vampires I killed were just like Valtu? What if they had done nothing wrong but try to survive for centuries? What if killing so many of them, just like this, robbing them of their immortal lives, just meant that real ones who deserved my vengeance, the ones that killed my parents, ones like Saara and Aleksi, were running around free?

Tears burn at the corners of my eyes and I look up at Valtu, wishing I could tell him my truth and ask for forgiveness, but I can't do that now, not ever.

"Don't cry," he says through a grunt, his face distorted. "I'm okay," he wheezes.

Suddenly he removes the blade from his chest and flings it to the floor. Then with pained gasp, he pulls his shirt off over his head so I can see the wound.

We both stare at it, at the blood as it flows, coating his chest, stomach, pants, and then the blood starts to slow to a trickle. I watch it actually congeal in real time. Now this is what's different from the kills I've done. Valtu isn't dropping dead like the rest of them because it wasn't a slayer with the blade of *mordernes* that stabbed him. Instead his wound is healing before my eyes.

"What the fuck," I whisper, forgetting for a moment that I'm supposed to be more shocked than this. Instead I'm finding it strangely beautiful, watching his body repair itself. "I don't understand." I glance up at him. "How did you do that? *Why* did you do that?"

"I had to show you that I can't die."

"Can't die?" I snort. "What are you, a vampire?"

His gaze is sharp and steady on me. "Yes."

This is the moment. When a vampire tells a human that they're a vampire, there generally isn't a lot of fanfare. The minute a vampire speaks its name, speaks the truth, is the moment that the veil is lifted from the human's eyes. They finally see what they've only subconsciously known all along. There might be some pushback, some refusal to believe, but they come around quickly.

Or so I've been told. I've always believed in them from day one.

Which begs the question: "Why did you just stab yourself?" I ask. "You could have just told me."

He tilts his head at me, frowning. "Because you were very adamant you didn't believe in the supernatural. I thought you'd need more of a push."

I shrug and look down at the floor where his blood has spilled. "You could have not and saved your rug."

He gives me a half-smile, blinking in confusion. "So that's it? You believe me?"

"Now that you've told me, yeah I believe it. You've been doing a few things that I've tried to make sense of. Doing Jedi mind tricks on the teacher. Having superhuman strength. Being able to come a million times and still be hard."

"Hey, that last one isn't a vampire thing, that's all me."

Whatever you say.

"Anyway," he goes on, waving his arm around. "I suppose I like a dramatic reveal. I am the one they call Dracula, anyway."

Oh I was wondering when he was going to drop that one. Straight off the bat it seems. I wonder how badly he's been waiting to tell me that.

I fold my arms across my chest. "Oh really?"

He nods, a sly smile lifting his lips. He wiggles his brows. "Oh yes. The one and only."

"So you really are a count," I muse.

"I really am a lord," he says. "Your lord."

I grin at him, elated that we're finally on the same page. Or at least a partial page. I run my hand over his chest, tracing the wound which is in the midst almost being healed over, though it's still red and raw. "Tell me, Count Dracula, did it hurt when you stabbed yourself in the heart?"

He winces. "Yes. A lot."

I shake my head. "So I suppose you want me to do something to make it better?"

Now he's full-on grinning. "I mean, I wouldn't say no."

I run my hands down over his taut stomach, sliding down beneath the waistband of his sweatpants, wrapping my hand around the thick hot length of his cock. The man gets hard in less than a second.

"So," he says to me, a heated look washing over his eyes as he stares down at me, "you don't have any questions for me?"

Right. I guess I should be asking him a million things about being a vampire, acting like I don't already know. What I really want to talk about is Saara and Aleksi, but that will come later.

He's the one who's coming now.

"I do," I tell him, batting my eyes at him as I stroke him. "I just find myself compelled to suck your dick. Are you compelling me to do that? Put your big fat cock in my hot little mouth? Want me to be a good little slut for my vampire lord?"

"Christ on a bike," he says through a gasp, eyes going wide at my dirty talk. "I should have told you this *much* earlier."

I grin and quickly yank down his pants, his cock bobbing free, then drop to my knees. I wrap my hands around it again, slowly working them along his shaft, squeezing as I go. "Tell me what you want me to do," I whisper, teasing the tip of his dick with my tongue, tasting the salty hit of his precum.

"Call me your lord again and gag on it," he growls, grabbing my hair and pushing my head forward onto his cock, my mouth taking him in.

Fuck, I love it when he's bossy like this. A switch gets turned on in my brain that makes me become so obedient, like he could do anything he wants. Part of me wonders if that really is about being compelled. Maybe it's not so much something vampires do but that people naturally want to be compelled by them.

And, fuck, do I want to be compelled by him.

I swallow him all the way to the hilt and then slowly ease back, sucking hard as I go. "Harder," he tells me, and I suck him deeper, until he's hitting the back of my throat. "Take my cock like a little slut."

His hips start thrusting, fucking my mouth slowly, his tight balls slapping against my chin as he holds me in place. I'm not going anywhere, not that I want to. I'm all too happy in my place on my knees, sucking on my vampire lord. It feels so much more freeing now that the truth is out in the open.

"You're such a good little whore, aren't you?" he asks me, his fingers tightening in my hair, pulling on it until I feel a kiss of pain.

"Yes, my lord," I moan around his rigid length, staring up at him through my lashes.

"Dirty, filthy whore, isn't that right?" he asks me, and I know I'm doing something right from the way his eyes are rolling back in his head.

"Yes," I say, the word muffled with his cock in my mouth, "I'm your dirty little whore."

"And what are you going to do for me, slut?" he taunts me.

I groan around his thick length and slide my hands to his balls, gently squeezing them until he lets out a deep groan.

"Anything you want, my lord."

"What do you want, little whore?"

"Your cum."

"Then beg me for it."

He gives me a couple of slow, hard pumps, working his thick cock against my tongue.

"Please, my lord," I whimper. "Please, let me taste your cum."

This is so fucking wild. I'm so turned on that I'm tempted to start playing with myself, to give myself some relief, but right now I want it to be all about him. I want him to know that his truth didn't scare me, that my feelings didn't change, and that I'm still completely his, even if he's a vampire.

He leans forward, his cock pushing deep into my throat, and I know that my only option is to suck him and swallow him completely.

"That's it," he says, his words turning into a groan. "Take it all."

He thrusts into me a few more times and then he's

coming, hot and thick and salty, straight down my throat. I swallow him greedily, not letting a drop go to waste, and then when I'm done, I pull my face back and stare up at him.

He smirks at me, a look of total satisfaction on his face.

"I think you enjoyed that," he muses, breathing hard. "More than you usually do."

"Maybe a secret fantasy of mine has always been to suck Dracula's dick," I say, getting to my feet, feeling off-balance. I'm about to wipe my mouth and chin but Valtu quickly leans in, grabs my jaw and licks his cum off my face like I'm an ice cream cone.

My eyes go wide. This guy is full of surprises.

"What did I ever do to deserve you?" he asks, his eyes heavy-lidded. After the night we've had, I think the best course of action is to head to bed.

"You must have done something right in your life," I tell him.

The dazed smile on his face fades. I've said the wrong thing.

"What?" I ask.

He swallows hard, his expression grave. "You do realize what this all means, don't you? I'm a vampire, Dahlia. I'm not a good person. I'm barely a human. I'm a predator."

"I know what it means," I begin. "And I have so many questions. I just don't want to be overloaded with information right now."

He nods slowly, seeming to buy that. "You're different, you know that? Different than any human I've ever told."

Oh shit. "Oh? What do they normally do when you tell them?"

"Well, they don't suck my dick," he says with a chuckle. "And they bombard me with questions, for sure. But they're afraid. No matter what or how quickly they believe me, they're all afraid. A few lose the fear over time, and with some we formed good relationships in the process, but almost everyone is afraid of me."

"But I'm not afraid."

"No, you're not. And I can tell you're not. I could smell if you were. There was only one other person I knew who..." he trails, looking confused for a moment, like he was trying to recall a memory but lost it.

"I'm not afraid because I know you. I don't know how I do, but it's true. All those things you said about how familiar I seem? It's the same with you, except it's not about how familiar you are rather..." I bite my lip, not wanting to go on.

"What?" he whispers, grabbing my hand, his eyes imploring. "What?"

"Rather I feel like I've loved you before," I say, looking away, not wanting to make eye contact. I already feel too vulnerable as it is.

"That's the most beautiful thing anyone has ever said to me," he says softly. "Hey, look at me." He raises my chin so I look at him. "I mean that." He leans in and kisses my forehead. "I'm glad you're not afraid. I was so worried that when I one day told you, you would run. That was my fear. But you didn't run, instead you've dug in your heels. It's why I feel we are one and the same. I know what it's like to feel you don't belong in this time. In this world."

He pauses, his lips moving to my mouth, leaving a ghost of a kiss. "I will make you feel like you belong with me."

CHAPTER 18

VALTU

THIS IS where writing in my journal gets harder. Throughout my years, I've learned more about the human mind than most, and a curious thing I learned was selective memory bias. This is where the human mind (and for all intents and purposes, the vampiric mind) has a tendency to not remember things as they are but how they want to remember them. It's why people may look back at an awful period of their life and only remember the good times peppered through, such as when looking back at a relationship and thinking it was better than it actually was.

Being aware of this doesn't change my feelings about this part of my life. There is nothing happy about this part. Yes there was joy and love, but my mind won't rewrite the truth, it won't hide the sorrow, and so it's easiest just not to think of this at all. But by writing down the pain I am forced to remember what really happened.

The memories flood my brain and leave as tears.

THE VICTORIAN AGE
London – 1890

"HOW IS SHE?" I ASKED DOCTOR VAN HELSING FOR THE umpteenth time that day, my cyclical pacing in the sitting room coming to a stop.

He gave me a faint smile as he came into the room and took off his glasses, rubbing them along his handkerchief. With perfect vampiric eyesight, he never needed glasses, the lenses were clear and he wore them because "It makes me look smarter." But he never needed any help in that department either.

He didn't have to say much. I could feel it off him, the dread of having to tell the truth. I braced my heart, my hand pressed against it as if to keep it in place, but I already knew.

"It doesn't look good, Val," he said to me with a shake of his head.

"Is the baby..." I couldn't even finish the sentence.

He swallowed thickly, taking a measured pause. "There's nothing I can do. I'm sorry."

I closed my eyes and sat down on the couch, like the weight was too heavy for my chest. "I don't understand. The baby would be a vampire." My eyes darted to the ceiling, to the bedroom above where Lucy was with the midwife and the nurse but they couldn't hear me from down below. "Vampires can't just die."

"You're only a vampire when you turn thirty-five," he pointed out. "Until then, yes we can and do die. In this case, I'm sorry Val but the baby didn't make it. There is no heartbeat from it. It died in the womb. Stillbirth. And..."

"And?" There's more? How can there be more? What can be worse than losing my child before it's even born?

"We're going to need to do an operation if she doesn't go

into labor. She should have at least had the signs already. We will try to induce but..."

"But?"

"If we can't, we will have to take it out via caesarean."

I nodded, biting my lip. "Okay..."

He gave me a grave look. "Lucy is weak, Valtu. She was never in great health to begin with. There is a chance she might not survive the operation, and if she does, she may succumb to puerperal fever."

I stared at him. Just stared. I couldn't come to terms with it. I couldn't go from losing the baby to losing her. Not when I felt our lives were just getting started, not when I just got her fucking back.

"She will survive," I growled at him. "You will do all in your power to make sure she does."

He promised he would try.

After that, I went up to the room to be alone with my wife. I told the nurse and midwife to leave. I had some things I had been dying to say and I needed to say them before it was too late.

Lucy lay on top of the bed, a thin sheet covering her large belly. The sight of her, knowing that our child inside was dead, nearly brought me to my knees right there and then but I managed to keep going, to hold it together for the sake of her.

I walked to her side of the bed and sat on the chair across from her. Lucy's head was to the side, her hair a wild storm of red. She opened her eyes and looked at me, tears dried on her pale cheeks. "Val?" she whispered.

"I'm here, my dove," I told her, taking her hand in mine and kissing it. Her hand was so small, so frail and cold. She was almost a vampire herself.

"The doctor told me the news," she managed to say weakly.

"I know," I said to her, trying to sound brave. "He told me the same."

"I'm sorry," she said, closing her eyes. "I know how badly you wanted a child."

It's true that I did. We had been married for two beautiful years. Two years of having my Mina back, though now she was Lucy with her own interests and personality. The same, but different. I had been meaning to tell her who she was in her past life but I was waiting for the right time. I had also been wanting to tell her that I was a vampire. It had been a real pain in the ass to keep hiding my feeding sessions.

The problem with vampires is that they know they have all the time in the world, so they assume everyone else does too. But with Lucy, that time suddenly became very narrow and very clear.

I wasn't running out of it, but she was.

And I had wanted a child, maybe more than she did, because even when Lucy would have to inevitably go one day, her legacy would live on in our offspring. I would have them with me for life, a way of keeping her alive.

But now it looked like I was not only going to lose the child, but I could lose her as well.

So it was time for the truth.

"Don't be sorry," I plead, kissing her hand. "This isn't your fault."

"The doctors, they warned me when I was younger," she said. "My sister died during childbirth. The same thing almost happened to my mother when she had me. They say we're cursed."

"You're not cursed," I told her, but those words rang false. It was enough that she looked at me sharply, as if she knew.

Then she surprised me. "I remember you."

I could only stare at her in response.

She nods, squinting slightly as she licked her dry lips. "I know you remember too. I remember who I was. I loved you so, as I love you now. But my name isn't Mina anymore. I died. I remember so clearly how I died. But you...you never died, did you?" She coughed, pink going to her cheeks. "You are still Valtu. How?"

I couldn't help the smile on my face, the way her words opened up a whole new world for me. I wouldn't have to get her to remember, she already did. She already knew who we were to each other.

"When did you start to remember?" I asked, unable to hide my excitement. "Why didn't you tell me?"

She gave me a look, like she was aware that I just skirted over her question with more questions. But she answered. "I think on some level I always knew. When I first met you in the museum, I thought that I knew you from before. I told my friends that but they thought I was just silly. When we first made love, I submitted myself to you in a way I thought I never would, because deep down I knew how to be with you. There are so many examples that I would brush away, thinking I had no explanation."

She paused and gave me a weak smile before taking in a few shallow breaths. "And then the day I found out I was pregnant, I remembered being Mina. I remember how I felt when I learned I was going to have a baby, that it was going to be yours. It brought it all together." Her eyes closed and a tear spilled out. "Oh, and that's when I knew this baby wouldn't live. I am cursed, Valtu, don't you see?"

Tears pricked at my own eyes and I managed to hold them back. "No, no," I said adamantly, reaching forward and brushing her tear away. "No, you are not cursed. We will be okay. We will have another."

The truth is, I was the one who was cursed.

And deep down I knew there would be no other.

And she knew this too.

"Valtu," she whispered to me. "Please tell me the truth. Why are you still you? I know you didn't wake up one day and remember, I know you've known all this time. How is this possible?"

Back then, the concept of a vampire wasn't as known as it was today. *The Vampyre* and *Carmilla* were two books about vampires that had come out before *Dracula*, that naturally I had already read, but I wasn't sure how much Lucy knew other than it being Eastern European folklore.

"What if I were to tell you that I can't die," I said, "would you believe me?"

She nodded. "Yes. I can see that you haven't yet. You are the same man I knew back then. Perhaps a better dresser now."

"Well that certainly makes this easier." I gave her a warm smile, suddenly enveloped by how much I loved her. "Lucy. I am a vampire. Do you know what that is?"

She stared at me for a moment, processing it. Then she said, "You are a vampire. Of course you are." She sat up a little in the bed as if having a sudden burst of strength, and looked me over, her long red hair falling over her shoulder. "The undead."

"In my case, I never died," I explained, a little shocked that she was taking this so well. "I was born a human but turned into a vampire the day I turned thirty-five, which happened to be the day you died as Mina. I never knew, of course, and I often wonder why God couldn't have had me turn just moments earlier. I could have saved you from your death. You and the baby."

She frowned. "You are a vampire and you still believe in God?"

I shot her a puzzled look. "Who else is there to believe in?"

She gave her head a weak shake and gently rested her hands on her belly, the motion making my heart wince at all the loss. "Could you turn me into one? Is that not how it works? I read a story in a woman's digest and they said vampires can turn humans into vampires too."

She sounded so hopeful it broke my heart to tell her no.

"I can't do that," I told her. "But our child would have been a vampire, or at least would have turned into one at the age of thirty-five, if a boy, or twenty-one, if a girl, when they would become immortal, living solely on human blood."

Her upper lip curled. "So that part is true."

"Yes. I have to drink blood to survive. But if I were to bite you, drain you of your blood and fill you with my own, you would become a vampire but you wouldn't be like me. You would be damaged."

"Would I live forever?"

I mulled that over before I answered. "Yes. But you would live forever as a monster. It takes years, decades, probably even centuries for the monster to be buried, for the madness to stop and for the humanity to take over. It might not even happen at all. You wouldn't know who you are or who I am. You would be this dangerous beast who would kill for the sake of killing. No one wants to live like that. And as much as I hate this world sometimes, the people of this world don't deserve to have monsters like that roaming all over it. They are better kept in the other world."

"Other world?" Her blood-shot eyes widened.

"The Red World," I told her. "Where vampires originally came from. A place way up north, accessed through a veil, to where the king of vampires resides."

She sighed heavily—it was obviously a lot to take and all too much for her at that moment—and I immediately put my hand on hers on top of her belly. "Now is not the time for me to be telling you this," I added. "You need to rest. The doctor says he's going to induce labor soon."

"And if that doesn't work?" she said in a bone-weary voice.

"Then he will perform surgery to take the child out," I told her.

"Take the corpse out," she said, giving me a dull look. "That's what you mean."

"Oh Lucy," I cried out suddenly in a rush of emotion. I leaned in and I held her as tight as I could without hurting her, my heart breaking into a million pieces.

She fell asleep shortly after that and the nurse and midwife came back in to take over. I went back downstairs and talked to the doctor for a bit. I told him that she remembered she was Mina and Van Helsing was impressed that I had been right all along. It would have felt good to have that win over him, if the rest of my world wasn't falling apart.

The next two days were precarious and Van Helsing was growing impatient. All the natural methods to induce labor, such as special herbs, weren't working. There was a moment when I thought the doctor was going to call over a witch to see her through, but he had the good sense not to. Even witches that were said to be helpful to vampires could never be trusted, which was a shame because their herbs and spells and potions worked.

"We need to get the fetus out," the doctor said. "Today."

He brought out a de Ribes bag which he inserted inside of Lucy with a pair of forceps, pumping it full of water to induce labor. I am sure a lot of men wouldn't have been in the same room with their wife for this, but being a vampire there was a lot I could handle. The ways vampires viewed the human body were a lot different from everyone else, and I wasn't about to let my wife go through all of this torture alone.

Except when the doctor brought out the formidably

pronged cervical dilator, a nightmarish steel tool. When that didn't do anything except make my poor Lucy scream, I was starting to feel sick to my stomach.

Which then got worse when he brought out something called a decapitating hook, and I don't have to tell you how that thing worked.

"Stop," I told him, pushing the serrated hook away from her. "No. You're not using that."

The doctor gave me a steady look. "It is dead, Val," he said in a harsh whisper so that Lucy wouldn't hear, but she was pretty much passed out from the pain as it was. I had given her some morphine to make the process easier.

"It doesn't matter," I told him. "Get it out another way, not in pieces."

I remember the panicked look that came across my friend's face. I hated that look. He knew somehow she wouldn't survive an operation, and I think Lucy and I knew it too. But if I was going to have to bury my child with her, at least I wanted it whole.

"All right. You're the father," he conceded. Then he took in a deep breath. "Are you sure you want to be here for this? There will be a lot more blood. When was the last time you fed?"

"I'll be fine. Focus on her. And do whatever you fucking can to make sure she lives."

To Van Helsing's credit, he did everything he could to save Lucy.

But the blood didn't stop and her body had already gone through too much.

My wife lay there in a sea of crimson, thankfully so drugged out of her mind that she didn't feel much pain. But there was nothing anyone could do to stop the bleeding. It came and it came, and it didn't stop.

Van Helsing carefully took the baby's body away, and gave

me my last minutes alone with Lucy, the love of my life who I had already lost and was losing once again.

"Lucy," I whispered to her, staring down at the bed. She was so pale, like snow, all the blood drained from her, and even though I had seen so many people like that in my life, because of what I had done to them, it had never looked beautiful until now. Because she really was that beautiful. It transcended death.

"Val," she managed to say, her eyes fluttering open for a moment.

I got into bed with her, lying in her blood, holding her gently. "My dove," I told her, kissing the top of her head. "I'm so sorry, my dove. I have failed you again."

"No," she croaked. "You didn't...I loved you, Val. I lost you..." she trailed off and I heard her heartbeat slow, death approaching. "I lost you and I found you again." She let out a shuddering breath, a single tear rolling down her cheek. "I will find you again. I will find you in another lifetime. My heart will always find yours."

And then she died.

Her heart stopped and my entire world went still.

My Mina, my Lucy, was gone, and I was left with nothing but an empty hole where my heart should have been.

Lucy and the baby were buried the next day in the same grave.

I still haven't been back to see it.

After I lost Mina the first time, when I first learned what I was, I gave myself over to violence too easily. I became a monster who killed without morals or thought. I spent a century as a walking plague, bringing death to all I encountered. I was darkness personified until eventually I found a way to live through my rage. Until I was able to find my humanity again.

But my foothold wasn't very strong.

Losing Lucy knocked me right off and into that darkness again, letting it consume me, until the only thing I knew was death, the death that I brought.

I may have believed in God, but people were wrong about Hell.

Hell isn't a place. It's inside you.

CHAPTER 19

DAHLIA

AFTER VAL TOLD me he was a vampire, everything became easier between us. Not that things didn't feel easy before but that was always confined to sex. Sex with him felt as natural as breathing, our bodies were so in tune with each other that it felt like I had been with him before somehow, like my hands and my lips and my tongue knew all the perfect places on his body. I knew that he liked to be kissed right behind the ear, I knew he liked his balls tugged and played with, I knew that he was ticklish on his inner thigh, to the point of him exploding into a panicked laughing fit (and I also knew when to use that to my advantage).

But I digress. With the truth out, our relationship sifted into one of comfort, a feeling of ease that was able to coexist alongside the unstoppable swarm of butterflies that filled my stomach with each aching second. Valtu excited me like nothing else in this world had. I was starting to prefer love over death.

We ended up talking all night. I had to play the role of a human who knew nothing of real vampires, so I asked all the right questions and he gave me all the right answers. This was all stuff I knew, but after the basics were done ("Can you create other vampires? Do you need blood to live? Does it need to be human blood?") we started delving into the personal stuff. This is what I was here for.

"You said you were born in Finland," I muse, tracing my fingertips over the scar that his knife had left in his chest. The mark was almost gone now. By the time the sun comes up, I'm pretty sure there will be no trace of it. "What year was that?"

"Technically it was the Kingdom of Sweden at the time. Early 1700s. When the Russians took over."

"And...who were you?"

He cranes his head to look down at me and smiles, holding me closer to him. "I was me. Valtu Aminoff."

"You weren't a count then."

"No, I was a peasant," he says. "Far less glamorous."

I try to picture him as a peasant and suddenly I have a vision so clear it's like I'd seen it with my own eyes. There's something so damn familiar about him too, seeing him in breeches, a white shirt, surrounded by a wheat field that it takes me a moment to realize I'm not actually in the past.

I blink and bring myself back around. "So...what was it like back then?"

He exhales, his fingers playing with strands of my hair. "It was hard. Punishing. There was some room for pleasure and beauty but in general, life was not meant to be enjoyed, only endured."

"Some today would argue that hasn't changed."

"Unlucky ones, I suppose," he muses. "Not that I didn't have my fair share of endurance. A lot of my life was...less than favorable."

"Were you married?"

"I was," he says. "Only twice, though."

"Vampires or human?"

"Humans," he says. "At first I didn't know any better. I was adopted, back in the day. I didn't know I was a vampire. I wasn't raised as one."

That's news to me. "You're kidding..."

He gives his head a shake. "Nope. So I got married to a woman in my small village. Ana."

"What did she do when she discovered you were a vampire?"

"She never got a chance to. She died during childbirth."

"Oh," I say to him, feeling awful. "I'm so sorry."

"Don't be. It was a long time ago. I cared for her, but I didn't love her. Back then you didn't marry for love, not most of the time. You did it because the woman was pretty or had good genes and the man had money or land. There was always an excuse, always a reason for it. Love was an afterthought. And anyway, for me it was the first loss of many."

"So if that was your first wife..."

What happened to your second?

"I was in love with a woman I met shortly after Ana died. I never got a chance to marry her though. She also died. And my wife after that, a century later? She died too." I feel his eyes on me and I glance up at him. He gives me a soft, melancholy smile. "When you're in love with a human, it always ends in death. It's a hard thing to accept but it's the way our lives are."

Meaning, there might be a reason why he hasn't told me he loves me. He won't let himself love me. And why would he? Why let love in if you know it's going to end in death and heartache, something you'll have to live with for a literal eternity?

"Oh," I say softly. "So I suppose it's better you stay with vampires. They aren't going anywhere."

"True." He makes a huff of amusement. "But vampires are

still difficult people to be with. If I ever met a vampire I could love, things might be different, but I haven't."

"You're picky," I tease him.

"Yeah. I am," he says, giving me a squeeze. "And I'm glad. Because you're here."

"A human," I point out.

"I know," he says, his eyes taking on a sad sheen.

I need to change the subject. Talking about death and lost loves doesn't feel right. Even though I'm curious to know more, I don't want Valtu to have to dwell on the sorrows of the past.

"So do you not hang out with other vampires, or...?"

"They are the only ones I hang out with," he says. "Believe it or not, but you're the exception."

I suspected that but didn't know for sure. I can't help but feel flattered. "So where do you hang out? Where do you meet them?" I ask, trying to get him to give up more info. If I can get him to start talking about Saara and Aleksi, that would be a good start.

"We always find each other it seems," he says. "Helps that we have a club."

"Vampires Only Club?"

"No, humans can join too...but there's a, how shall we call it, a fee?"

"Okay, tell me about it..."

"I could show you."

"Really?" I honestly didn't think he'd want to bring me to the Red Room, though I suppose it's only fair if other humans are able to go. "Wait, what's the fee?"

He clears his throat. "If you don't mind paying the fee."

"What's the fee?" I repeat.

"Blood. You pay in blood."

My brows go up. "And you think I want to..."

"The club is called the Red Room. It's a safe place for

vampires to feed on willing participants. The humans there want to be of service. They get off on it. They like the kink of it. Whatever their deal is, it's like donating blood at a blood bank, just a little sexier and edgier than that."

That's putting it mildly.

"But blood is the price," he goes on. "You can't just go and observe. And everyone who enters is vetted, signs a contract, everything."

"That's impressive. Who started it?"

He pauses. "Me."

"You? The one they call Dracula?"

He sighs. "Yes. Let's just say I used to be a lot worse than I am now. Maybe this is me making amends for it, I don't know. But it's better this way. We have a steady supply of blood, and we don't have to kill innocent people." His expression darkens at the end, so much so that he looks haunted. Maybe he's reliving all the people he did have to kill, but I don't want to think about that either. It will only remind me of why I was sent here, and how I'm not different than he is.

"Where is this club?"

"You'll never guess," he says teasingly.

Since I already know, I don't bother playing the game.

"So when can we go?"

He blinks. "Really? You still want to go?"

"It depends. Who am I giving my blood to? You?"

His nostrils flare and the sheet that half-covers our naked bodies jerks and I know he's got an instant hard-on. "Yes," he rasps. "Only me. You're mine, Dahlia. No one else gets to feed on you but me." He swallows hard and I feel the heat in his eyes. "I have to tell you...I've been dying for a taste."

Holy fuck. Shit just got real.

"All this time," he goes on, his voice low and raspy, "I've sampled the rest of you. Your tongue, your ass, your cunt. The taste of you is exquisite. But your blood, Dahlia. Your blood is something I've been craving more than anything else."

Jesus. I thought the idea of him drinking my blood would have scared me but it just turns me on instead.

"All this talk about craving," I say with a sly grin, kissing his chest and making my way down his body to put his cock to good use.

"Are you nervous?" Valtu asks me as we walk down the aisles toward the door at the back of the library.

I give him a look, like, *what do you think?*

It's past midnight and everything is dark. He let us into the school using his key card and the library is especially eerie tonight, probably because I know what I'm here to do. This morning I told him I wanted to go to the Red Room and for him to feed on me there. I didn't agree to public sex or anything like that, but I did say he could have my blood. Only him, of course. It's Saturday, so we didn't have to go to school, we just stayed at his house, and all I could think of was tonight, what was going to happen while trying not to psych myself out. Now that I'm here and on the menu, I'm having second thoughts.

He chuckles. "You'll be fine. I've got you. I won't let anything bad happen to you."

"Except the fact that you're going to suck my blood," I mumble.

He stops in front of the door, hand to my shoulder, a grave expression in his dark eyes. "Listen, we don't have to do this. I get my blood from other people, that's how this has always worked. I don't have to drink from the woman I'm with."

I nod, rubbing my lips together. "Yeah. I know but, I

don't know, I guess I feel territorial about you." For some reason, the act of feeding seems just as intimate as sex. The idea of him drinking from another person burns a hole in my stomach.

He gives me a soft smile as he squeezes my shoulder. "And that's how I feel about you. Which is why, if you still do want to do this, it will cement you as mine in front of the other vampires."

"Can't you just tell them I'm yours?"

"You'd think, wouldn't you? Vampires are strange. I can't pretend to understand my brethren half the time. We tend to go by oaths and codes, things that have ceremony to them. I can tell everyone you're mine and they'll probably stay away, but unless I claim you publicly, I suppose some don't think it counts. Lots of partners have been stolen that way."

The way he says that makes me think he's leaving some part out.

"Did that happen to you?"

He just grins at me, the shadows making his smile look extra macabre, and I have my answer. Somewhere along the line he stole someone else's girl. He probably thinks karma is out to get him now.

"Shall we?" he asks, gesturing to the door.

I nod and with flourish he punches in the code and the door swings open.

He grabs my hand, his palm cool as he holds me tight, and leads me through the narrow black corridor. It feels like walking through a coffin. Even though I already did all of this during my astral projection, it feels different now. Corporeal. It has consequences whereas it didn't before.

Valtu then brings me to the other door, opening it so that we're standing on the iron landing at the top of the red-walled room.

"Welcome to the Red Room," he says to me, gesturing with a swoop of his arm to the scene of mayhem below.

Like last time, the metallic scent of blood and the musky smell of sex hits my nose, and also like the last time, no one seems to notice my entrance. Everyone below us is deep into their fucking and feeding sessions, though there seems to be even more participants than last time.

Valtu closes his eyes and breathes in deep, nostrils flaring, and when he opens his eyes again, his pupils are bright red. This is the first time I've really seen that with him and from personal experience, I know he's feeling bloodlust. The question remains. How long will he remain in control until it totally takes over?

He looks down at me and smiles, and I watch in real time as his canines sharpen into fangs. "Don't look so alarmed," he says, and even his voice has changed. It's become smoother, like it's been dunked in silky fine wine. "This is something you'll have to get used to. You don't think me more handsome now?"

He runs the tip of his tongue over his fangs.

"I don't think it's possible for you to get any handsomer, if we're being honest here."

His grin widens just as the bass of the music downstairs rattles on. Even in bloodlust, his ego is the thing that needs to be fed the most.

"Come with me, my *colomba rossa*," he says, holding out his arm. I'm his red dove now. "Let me introduce you to my world."

We go down the steps until we're at the main floor and still no one is paying us attention. The music is loud, hypnotic, drowning out most of the moans, and slaps, and groans, there's blood and naked bodies everywhere.

"You hardly seem fazed," he notes, looking over at me. "I would have thought walking into a vampire feeding frenzy and orgy would have spun your head around...then again, why am I surprised, when you've proven to have quite the appetite yourself."

I clear my throat, my pulse starting to quicken as the sounds and smells start to get to me. "Yeah, well, guess I've watched too much porn."

He laughs. "What kind of porn are you watching? And why aren't we watching it together?"

Then his face grows serious and he steps further into the middle of the room, cupping his hand over his mouth. "Attention everyone!" he bellows.

Only a few people look up from their activities with mild interest, the rest carry on as usual.

"Don't make me compel you!" he adds, his voice booming and I can feel it enter my head like I'm hearing it from inside my brain. This is certainly a loud way to compel people but it seems to work because finally he has their attention. Not everyone stops entirely, but a lot of the thrusting has slowed and the moans have grown quieter.

"I have a new human I wanted to introduce you to," he says, rather proudly I might add. "Her name is Dahlia Abernathy and I have chosen her as my own. I wanted to bring her here to make sure you all know that she is a part of my life and will be treated with only the highest regard. To do otherwise is to face very grave consequences. She is mine and mine alone. Do you understand?"

A few murmurs sound from the crowd and I find myself looking for people I recognize, or Saara and Aleksi, but I don't. I guess that's kind of a relief that no one from my local coffee shop or my school is here. That will avoid future awkward conversations in class (though Valtu did say it was forbidden for humans to talk to other humans about vampires outside of these walls).

"Okay then," Valtu says to them with a wave. "Go about your business."

But they don't. They stand there, watching us.

Waiting now.

We have their attention.

Great.

"Come here," Valtu says, holding out his hand. I take a deep breath and put my hand in his, feeling like I'm sealing some deal as I do so, like all of this is now binding.

I'm led to a circular bed in the middle of the room, covered with black leather, with four metal poles around it and chains attached, the shackles dangling at the sides.

"Who are the shackles for?" I whisper, my heart now beating so fast. Everyone in the room continues to stare at me, and I know they can hear my pulse.

And smell my fear.

"Sometimes it's for the human when they really want to submit," he says with a wicked gleam to his red eyes. "Often it's so the vampires don't get out of control. Sometimes there aren't enough, uh, *sober* vampires to watch over you."

"And what about you? Now?"

"I got us covered." He waves at the crowd and the tall, handsome black man I had seen earlier in my astral projection comes over to us. "This is Bitrus," Valtu says, introducing us. "He's been wanting to meet you for a long time."

"I've only heard good things," Bitrus says with a light African accent, his smile bright. He puts his hand out and I shake it. Like most vampires, his grip is strong, skin cool and disarmingly soft.

"Nice to meet you," I say to him. "I'm sure if Val had been able to talk about you, I would have only heard good things too."

Bitrus snorts and gives Valtu an amused glance. "Him? I highly doubt that."

"So you're, like, the spotter?" I ask.

He laughs. "Something like that."

We make our way over to the bed and I've never felt so odd in my life, the fact that there are at least a dozen people, humans and vampires, standing around in a circle and watching me. The fact that most of them want to eat me like I'm cake is especially unnerving.

"Have a seat," Valtu says, gesturing to the bed. "Let me take your jacket."

I plop down on the bed, the leather squeaking beneath me, and Valtu lifts up my arms, taking my jacket off before handing it to Bitrus. Then he glances down at my outfit. "You sure you want to keep that on?" he asks, fingering the strap on my shoulder.

I look at my black dress. "I don't want to be naked in front of strangers," I hiss at him. "I don't care if it gets ruined." I had some clothes stashed away in his house from when I was spending most of my nights there, and this dress was the only thing I didn't mind ruining with blood.

"Suit yourself," he says.

"What, you wouldn't care if anyone saw me naked?" I ask him.

He just grins again, showing off his fangs. They look so sharp now that the alarm bells are going off in my head.

Go! Run! Get away! Save yourself!

And it takes everything in me to not just make a run for the stairs. But that would probably invoke his chasing instincts.

Part of me thinks I might actually like that.

"You humans are so very uptight about nudity," he says to me with a tired sigh. "If you want to remain fully clothed, be my guest. I don't wish to bloody my clothes, so..." he finishes with a shrug and starts undressing.

I look around, wide-eyed. Everyone is watching him get

naked, but they don't seem particularly interested in it. Then I realize it's because it's nothing they haven't seen before. Last I was here I watched his dick get sucked by some guy and I'm pretty sure that guy is somewhere in the crowd.

But my attention is drawn to Valtu as he hands his dress shirt to Bitrus, then starts unzipping his pants. He's not even wearing underwear today, I guess because he knew what he had planned for this evening. He's hard as hell, his cock sticking right up and he looks downright menacing as he stands there amongst the leather and red, the way his pupils glow with hunger, how he's slowly dragging a loose fist over his dick, his muscles popping, his hair wild.

He's a fucking beast.

His gaze is locked to mine and for once I really feel like his prey, like I'm his food, I'm just not sure if he's going to fuck me first or feed from me, or maybe even both.

"Get on the bed, on your hands and knees," he commands. His voice is totally different now. Sinister and inhumanly deep, like it's coming from somewhere ancient inside of him.

I have to admit, I'm terrified. And he can smell it too, he keeps closing his eyes and breathing in deep and I think we're getting close to the point of no return now.

I look at Bitrus because he seems to be more in control and normal and he gives me a short nod to reassure me that this is okay.

I give him the nod back. *Take care of me*, I tell him in my head.

I don't expect him to hear me but he does.

And he looks surprised by it, staring at me curiously. I take it that most can't do what I just did and I really hope I didn't fuck things up by doing that. The last thing I need is to be outed as a witch.

I take in a deep breath for courage, and look back to

Valtu. It's nuts that despite how feral and dangerous he looks right now, I'm also finding him sexy as hell. Not sure what that says about me.

I twist in my seat and start to crawl on the bed but then he holds out his hand.

"Stop," he commands and I obey.

Then he goes to the other side of the bed and gets on his knees, still stroking that magnificent cock between his legs as his gaze intensifies.

"Crawl to me."

I think I'm supposed to find this humiliating but for some reason I don't. I crawl to him across the bed, moving slowly, feeling animal-like myself, like a sleek cat in heat. I know people are watching and I figure that no matter what happens here, if I at least look like I'm enjoying it then that gives me some control.

Because honestly, unless Valtu goes in those shackles, I'm at the mercy of him and Birtus and the other vampires here. What would stop them from just tearing me apart if the bloodlust were to get hold of all of them? What would the humans do? They couldn't save me. They're as powerless as I am.

"Look at you," he says in that inhuman voice, his red eyes skirting over my body, leaving flames like a blowtorch. "Such a willing participant."

He makes an elegant gesture with his finger for me to turn around.

I do so hesitantly because I don't like the idea of my back being turned to him. Where I grew up on Vancouver Island, when we're hiking in an area with cougars and bears, we're taught to never turn our backs on the predators, and right now it's going against all my instincts.

But I obey and I'm facing the crowd. I could fixate on the fact that they're all butt naked, with their dicks hanging out and I'm fully dressed, but it doesn't really matter when you're on all fours, your ass to a vampire with a raging hard-on.

I feel him behind me, feel his dark, focused energy at my back, and he comes closer and I think I might just hyperventilate, I'm that scared, that excited.

The hard, thick length of his dick presses against my ass, but he hasn't raised up my dress, so there's still a thin layer of fabric between us. He brings his body over top of me, looming like a storm cloud, his chest brushing over my back and I hold my breath. I can feel myself growing wet between my thighs.

He reaches out for my hair and to my surprise starts braiding it loosely behind me so it's gathered down the middle of my spine. His finger trails along the jugular in my neck, delicate but probing, and he lets out a quiet gasp of desperation.

His head lowers with teasing deliberation until his whole upper body is pressed against my back, hot and cold and tight, and I can feel his heartbeat, how loud and steady it is, like a tribal drum that shoots right through me.

His lips go to my ear.

"I'm going to feed from your neck," he says softly, voice raspy and rough, making my thighs squeeze together. "It will hurt at first, but then it will turn to pleasure. I'll probably end up fucking you while I'm at it." He pauses. "If that's okay."

I try to nod, feeling like there's no breath left in me.

"No matter what happens, my dove," he says, running his lips over the shell of my ear, "I won't be the man you know. I might do things you won't agree with. Please know that I would never purposely hurt you on my own accord, it's just that once I taste your blood, I will be lost to it. I will become the hunter and you will be hunted until I get my fill."

Then he takes in a deep shaking breath and I brace myself.

It happens so suddenly.

He plunges his mouth against my neck and fangs stab into my skin, a sharp pain that travels down my spine, shattering through the rest of my nerves.

I try to scream but it gets choked in my throat as Valtu's grip on my neck is so strong it feels like his mouth has been fused to my body. The pain starts to subside, almost like I've been given numbing cream, and now I just feel the way he feeds from me, consuming me, and there's something so innately sexual about it that when he roughly shoves up the skirt of my dress so it's bunched on my hips, I find myself pushing back into him, wanting him to fuck me at the same time.

I hear him swallow my blood down, so much blood, and he growls, the sounds vibrating in my bones, and he's starting to move his mouth more, tearing into my flesh, enough so that it's starting to hurt again.

Crying out, I try to signal to Bitrus that maybe he's getting a little carried away, because I was okay with the neat little holes vampires leave in your neck, but not a gaping wound. I won't heal like he does.

And that's when the real worry comes in.

What if he gets close enough to killing me that I lose hold of my glamor? What if he feeds so much that I can no longer hide who I truly am?

In this state, finding out I'm a witch, he'll kill me. And the other vampires will cheer him on.

You need to run, a voice inside my head says. *You need to get out of there now!*

Only his fangs are in me and he's a powerhouse, supernatural, unstoppable, and I don't know how the hell to make a run for it.

Then he reaches back a bit to grab his dick to position it against me, ready to thrust inside, and while I want nothing more than that right now, the audience be damned, my instincts are telling me to take advantage of the distraction and run while I can.

I quickly make my move, pulling my neck away from his teeth, rolling out from under him, and then I'm stumbling off the leather bed and onto the floor, making a staggering run for the stairs.

I'm screaming as I go, the adrenaline taking over now, and while no one is stopping me, I'm worried I still won't make it out of here.

Valtu roars behind me like some kind of hellish creature, and then I feel the rush of him at my back and I'm at the stairs now, scrambling up them, hoping I can get up them to the door in time.

But of course I can't.

When vampires want to use their speed, they're quicker than the blink of an eye.

I make it up one step before Valtu grabs me, hands at the back of my dress, ripping it in half, his nails scratching down my back, and I scream. I'm struggling, half-naked, trying to escape, crawling up one more step before he drags me back down. I try to hold onto the steps, to move, but I know it's no use. This is what I signed up for, isn't it?

"You're mine," he says, guttural and mad, and he pushes aside the remains of my dress. "I've claimed you."

He flips me over so that my back is on the edge of the stairs and I'm staring up at his face, red eyes, wild hair, those fangs, those fucking bloody fangs, and I fear that he's going to bite my face clean off.

But instead he kisses me.

It's passionate and deep and when his tongue slips into my mouth I can taste the blood on him. My blood.

Then he shoves his hand between my legs and parts them roughly, leaving bruises. I'm wet and I'm succumbing to him, only trying to put up a little bit of a fight because I know that's what makes him excited.

Turns out it's what makes me excited too.

He pins my hands down above me with one hand and then drives his cock inside me with one deep, tight thrust, the air knocked out of my lungs.

I gasp into his mouth as he fucks me, captive, locked together and no way out, right there on the steps of the Red Room, with everyone watching. He grabs my jaw, my hair, he's lost in a frenzy and I can tell he's trying not to hurt me, trying to regain control. He wants so badly to feed on me it's making him insane.

I can barely breathe as Valtu slams into me again and again, his passion and his lust overpowering me, making me dizzy and wild. I am his to do with as he pleases, and there is nothing that I can do about it.

Finally he gives in and bites my neck again, this time the other side, a groan of relief escaping him, like an addict finally getting their hit. It hurts like fuck but the fact that he has his dick in me helps. And the more blood he seems to take from me, the bigger he feels.

Enough that I think I'm imagining it. It's like my blood in his body is going straight to his cock, doubling in size until I feel full and stretched in the most delicious way, my body adjusting to his new mammoth size and melting around him.

Holy. Shit.

Now this is something I didn't know about vampires. I'd been with them before, but never while they were feeding, and oh my god, no wonder all the humans are lining up around the door to donate here.

But soon my thoughts aren't coming easy to me anymore and I don't know if it's because I'm losing blood or that I'm lost to the feel of his supersized cock as it squeezes into me. I let myself be swept away in a haze of pleasure and pain as

Valtu takes what he wants from me, my blood, my body, my breath. I cry out in euphoria as he plunges into me again and again, taking what he needs while bringing me to the edge.

I finally come with a scream, my body quaking, my world spinning and falling apart around me, feeling like I've been born again, and then...

Valtu releases his fangs from my neck and roars as he joins me, his body rigid and taut as he spills himself inside me, his back arched, every muscle corded and tight from strain.

I'm still so out of it when suddenly a thick metal chain appears, sliding around Valtu's neck and he's tugged off of me like he's a rabid dog.

I gasp and watch as Bitrus pulls Valtu back, Valtu on his knees, breathing heavily, the chain around his neck. I'm on the steps, my dress torn, pretty much naked, covered in cum and blood, and the bystanders are no longer watching us, instead they've gone back to their usual activities, though a little more enthusiastically than before. I guess we gave them a good show.

I press my fingers to my neck, the blood flowing at a disturbing rate and then a beautiful Asian woman with platinum hair, dressed in nothing but a lacey red thong comes over with a towel and a vial of clear liquid.

"I'm Adora," she says to me, moving my hand out of the way and pressing the towel there. "Hold that there for a minute, then we're going to put this on it." She waves the vial at me. "It will seal up the bleeding. It's like glue. A witch gave it to me."

I stare at her, wondering where the hell she came from, but I guess this whole club has a lot of people waiting in the wings.

"A witch?" I repeat, my voice shaking from all the exertion.

"It's okay, she's cool," she says. She looks over at Valtu and Bitrus. "She's lost a bit of blood, I'll take her to the bank."

Bitrus nods and Valtu doesn't say anything, he just stares at me with a mix of desire and pain. He's pulling at the metal chain, as if to get close to me, but not hard enough to be a problem. At least I hope not.

Adora helps me to my feet and I do my best to keep the towel on my neck, walk without falling, *and* keep my dress together, but I can't do all three.

"It's okay," Adora says as my dress falls to the ground and I'm completely naked now. "It's actually weird if you are dressed."

She leads me to the back area of the room, behind a Japanese-style partition, where there are a few black leather stretchers laid out. She helps me onto one of them, then opens a restaurant-style freezer and looks in it. "Do you know your blood type?"

"No," I say. My parents would, I almost say, and for a moment I feel a hit of shame because what the hell would my parents say if they could see me now? Vampires killed them and now I'm not only getting willingly fucked by one, but giving them blood as well?

"That's fine, we'll give you a universal donor." Adora takes out a bag of blood, hooking it onto a stand, sorting through the tubes.

"Have you given blood before?" she asks me, grabbing a needle and attaching it to the end of a tube.

"Given blood? Once, in school," I tell her. When I first joined the academy and we were told our blood might be helpful in a registry for spells and certain magic.

"Well this is like that. But in reverse. You'll feel better in no time."

I frown at her. "Are you a nurse?"

She smiles. "I am actually. Don't worry, this happens all

the time. It's why Valtu has this blood bank, in case vampires get carried away. It's in their nature to get carried away, so it's always best to be prepared."

I'm about to ask her if she's just a really beautiful human or a vampire because I can't seem to tell when I see Valtu poke his head around the partition. He's wearing his pants, his shirt unbuttoned showcasing patches of dried blood on his chest, his hair messy.

He looks most apologetic.

"How are you?" he asks quietly, cautiously stepping toward me.

Adora gives him a passing nod as she leaves the area so the two of us are alone.

I give my head a shake. "Honestly I'm too dazed to figure that out."

He comes over to the blood bag and picks up the needle. "May I?"

"If you know what you're doing."

He gives me a look like, *of course I know what I'm doing, I'm a vampire.*

He sticks the needle in my arm and starts the transfusion.

"I'm sorry," he says with a heavy sigh.

"About what?"

"For trying to...eat you."

I manage a smile. "Isn't that what I agreed to?"

He gives his head a shake, a strand of black wavy hair falling across his forehead and he pushes it back. "I didn't think you'd run."

"I didn't either."

"I think I hurt you."

I exhale loudly. "Yeah. I'm going to feel it tomorrow." I know my spine is going to be bruised from being fucked so hard on those steps, not to mention how rough his hands were with my thighs and wrists, and of course the wounds on my neck.

"She said to put that on it," I say, pointing at the vial on the freezer top.

"Ah, yes," Valtu says. He takes it and then removes the towel, wincing at my wounds as he does so. "Again. I am *so* sorry."

"I know you are," I tell him. It's plain to see. "Maybe next time we—"

"There won't be a next time," he says sharply as he drips the liquid onto the wounds. It immediately numbs it. "I can't lose control with you."

"Well, I don't want you to feed from anyone but me. Also, you never told me that your cock gets bigger when you're feeding."

He shrugs lightly. "Just makes sense, doesn't it?" He finishes the sentence with a grin. "How about we take this one step at a time? I can't just tell you I'm a vampire and then throw you in the Red Room for some public feasting a day later. Baby steps."

"Baby steps sound fine with me."

He leans in and kisses me softly on the lips, brushing my hair off my face. "Can I tell you though, I feel the most whole I've felt in a long time? Years. Decades." He peers deep into my eyes and there's an affection inside his depths so poignant it feels a lot like love. "It's like I tasted a universe inside your blood. A universe just meant for the two of us." He chuckles and looks away. "That sounds cheesy, I know it does, but it's true."

I can't help but smile. "I think you need to be a little cheesy sometimes, Val. Helps to balance all of *this*." I gesture to the blood all over myself and everything else in this room.

"You called me Val," he says, blinking at me.

"Is that okay?"

"It's what those who are closest to me call me," he says fondly. "I'd be honored if you did too."

"Okay." I smile shyly. "Val."

He kisses me again. "My dove," he whispers against my lips.

CHAPTER 20

VALTU

My favorite night of the year has arrived; the night of the winter recital.

Never mind the fact that it's late November and technically not winter yet. It's cold, foggy, raining most days, and Venice already dove headfirst into Christmas decorations. It's winter enough for me.

The best part of the night, however, isn't just that I can watch my students display their talents that they've been developing over the last few months, but that after the recital there's a black-tie cocktail party in the inner courtyard. The school strings a canopy across the roof to keep the rain off and they go all out with the food, drinks, and decorations.

Of course, tonight is more significant than ever.

Tonight, Dahlia is playing.

I just know she's going to be spectacular.

"Val, you're blushing," Doctor Van Helsing says.

I glance at him as he appears behind me in my mirror. He's wearing a black suit and looking dapper as always, and other than the hipster-ish glasses on his face, he looks exactly the same as he did back in the day.

I give him a withering look and finish adjusting my bowtie. "Remind me why I said you could come, Abe?"

He raises his martini glass to his lips. "Always good to have a doctor in the house, I say."

"Yeah, that's what you say." I finish with the tie and then attempt to put some sculpting paste in my hair so that it's not a wavy mess. I put too much and with a sigh of frustration, end up slicking my hair back off my head. Thank god I stopped aging before my widow's peak expanded.

"Oh, a new look on you," he says. "You are definitely trying to look like a count tonight. Have you ever thought about blending in? You Venetian vampires are something else."

I turn around and notice he's actually holding two martini glasses. He hands one to me.

"Cheers, by the way," he says with a wink and we clink our glasses together.

I have a sip. Gin with a twist and it's stronger than it should be. I cough. "Did you put ether in here or what?"

He shrugs. "Nothing wrong with a little hair on your chest, Val. Might stop you from blushing." He walks out of the bedroom.

I go back to inspecting myself in the mirror, vanity taking complete control over me. He's right, of course. My cheeks are a little pink and the whole reason I'm fussing is that I want to look good for Dahlia tonight. The recital is a big deal for the both of us, of course, and it will be the first time we'll be in public together outside of class. Not that I plan on revealing our relationship to anyone, that would be stupid, but it will feel good to be with her in that setting. I just hope I can hold myself together when I'm near her, I have a bad habit of totally losing control.

I leave the bedroom and head down the stairs. It's drizzling outside, so we can't enjoy our drinks in the garden, and

Van Helsing has settled in the leather armchairs in the sitting room.

"So where is she now?" he asks.

"At her apartment," I say, relaxing into the chair but keeping note of the time on the grandfather clock in the corner.

"So she doesn't live here yet?"

"No, though she spends most of her time here." Actually, Dahlia seems rather scared of her apartment. She doesn't say that but when she's talking about it, her heart begins to race and she looks unwell. I wonder if I am at fault for telling her that the area is haunted. She said she didn't believe in ghosts but she probably didn't believe in vampires then, either.

"It's just rather curious, don't you think?" he says after a sip. "Considering how when I was last here you told me that you were done with her."

"I never said I was done with her," I snipe at him. "I'm not that callous. I said I needed to end things for her sake."

"And for your sake too, don't forget." The way the doctor lets those last words hang in the air makes me know he's alluding to what happened with Lucy.

"Obviously my resolve is a lot weaker than I thought," I comment bitterly, placing my drink down on the table and fiddling with my cufflinks. It's an old tuxedo, complete with tails, though the cufflinks are new. Silver dahlias in bloom that I purchased from a trinket store just for this occasion.

"And so, have you had any contact with Saara and Aleksi?" he asks.

I originally invited Van Helsing out to Italy right after the night Bitrus and I went to Poveglia, when I drained that woman and murdered that man and they said I helped open a portal to Hell. I figured if Saara and Aleksi continued to be successful with that fabled book of theirs, then I was going to need more help. The two of them have Venice at their feet but with that book they could have the world. I also placed a call to my friend Absolon and his witchy vampire lover Lenore, but so far I haven't had a response.

Regardless, I need to assemble friends of mine in one fashion or another, to put our heads together and plan. It's totally possible that the two of them are full of shit and the faces in the water that Bitrus saw were just regular ghosts from the very haunted island, and that the masked plague doctors were just tall people in masks, and that the demons they talked about weren't anything at all. In fact, I'm holding onto that being true.

But then you factor in the people who have started to go missing, the people turning up dead from extreme "accidents" and the fact that the whole city is on edge these days, and you really have to wonder.

It's been enough, anyway, that I asked the doctor to stick around for a bit. He's been gallivanting around Italy, staying relatively close, but decided to come in to the city for the recital.

Because Saara and Aleksi will be at the recital.

We try to make a point of not having too many vampires around humans at the same time because it tends to alarm them in a subconscious way, but I heard from Bitrus that they'll be there because they obviously don't give a fuck. Me bringing Van Helsing might add to the mix, but since there will be drinks and music and the world these days already feels like it's holding its breath and waiting for something to happen, perhaps nothing will feel out of place.

It's not long before we finish our martinis and it's time to go. Not wanting to walk in the rain, I take my own boat and follow the canal behind my house as it leads to the Grand Canal and then down to the narrow slip of water that cuts in behind the conservatory.

There, someone takes my boat and ties it up (seems I

wasn't the only one who decided to arrive this way) and me and the doctor enter the building.

People are everywhere—teachers, students, friends, family, local musicians—dressed to the nines and gathered in various sections across the school, enjoying the prosecco the waiters are handing out until the recital starts and everyone will be called into the concert hall.

"Why don't you help yourself to a drink," I say, laying a hand on Van Helsing's shoulder. "I'm going to go find Dahlia."

I begin prowling around the first floor looking for her and when I don't spot her anywhere, I go up to the second. There are few people grouped here and there, mainly ogling the paintings and sculptures that are strewn about the school, but I don't see Dahlia.

I bring out my phone to text her, the only communication we have, and keep walking down the hall, but that's when I catch the scent of her. I would know her natural smell anywhere, like a spring meadow and honey.

I pause and turn around to see her coming out of the washroom and heading down the hall, not seeing me.

I take a moment to take her in from behind. She's wearing a one-shouldered burgundy gown made of silk, the fabric clinging to the full curves of her ass.

Fuck me.

I'm immediately hard and I start walking fast after her, so fast that in seconds I'm in front of her. A risky maneuver, but I don't think the few people on this level will notice.

"Val," she cries out in shock, trying to stop but still runs up into my chest. She tries to take a step back but I grab hold of her elbows, about to put my lips all over her.

"Not here," she says, glancing around anxiously.

I nod and look for an escape. I see it in the door next to us, the office of the cellist professor. He's obviously downstairs right now getting ready with his students. I should be doing the same, just my attention is a little more concentrated on Dahlia.

I try his door and the knob turns, unlocked. I quickly open it and shove Dahlia inside, locking the door behind us.

"What are you doing?" she cries out.

"What do you think? You're far too gorgeous to not have my tongue all over you."

"But the recital," she stammers, and I reach up and make a fist in her hair that's gathered in curls around the top of her head, flipping her around so that she's pressed against the door, the back of her head thumping against it. "My hair! It took me forever to get it like this," she says indignantly.

I kiss her hard, my fingers going through her hair and pulling out bobby pins so that her hair is loose around her shoulders.

"You're such an asshole," she says, punching me on the shoulder.

"Do you want your hair pulled or not, you little whore?" I growl at her before kissing her hard, making a tight fist in her hair again and giving it a sharp tug. She whimpers against my mouth, her tongue sliding against mine and I'm shot with the stricken need to consume her.

I can't get too carried away, though it's hard when my mouth slips down to her neck and I begin to lick and suck at her soft skin, the surest way to get her dripping wet for me. I hadn't fed on Dahlia since that first time in the Red Room— honestly I'd been too afraid—but I'm starting to need it. The hunger is becoming too much.

Not tonight, I remind myself. This is her night, not yours.

With that thought, I drop down to my knees and start shoving up her dress, my hands splayed against her thighs. I dip my head under the fabric and shove my face up into her, the scent intoxicating, her wetness already gathering on her inner thighs. She's not wearing underwear, which means she must have been thinking ahead.

"Val," she groans. "Please."

I don't need to be told twice, my tongue sliding up and down her slick curve, then teasing at her entrance. I put my hand on her hip and hold her in place, my other hand going to her ass.

I start to eat her out in earnest, my tongue lashing against her clit. She whimpers and groans, her body tensing as I push my tongue hard, forcing it deep inside her, her stance widening to give me more purchase. I moan, loving the way she tastes, how wet she is for me. I let my tongue stretch down so I can lick against her asshole, my saliva dripping down and making her wetter. I want to taste every inch of her, the messier the better.

"Oh god," she cries out.

I flip the dress over my head and stare up at her so I can watch her as she unravels before me, slipping a finger inside her. She clenches around me, her body wound up tight. I start to finger her fast and hard, and her back arches against the door.

She is so fucking beautiful like this.

"You're being such a good girl," I murmur. "I might have to reward you later." She groans at that and my mouth goes back to her cunt, my tongue lapping at her while my fingers pump in and out of her.

I can hear her gasping, her legs shaking, her body ready to go. I press my face hard against her, the need to taste her when she comes strong in me. I reach up and pinch her nipples and she comes, her body spasming against me, her cries of release loud.

"Oh god," she cries out.

I stand up and pull her to me, my mouth going to hers and kissing her hard, making sure she can taste herself while I fuck her with my hand, my fingers sliding in and out of her, slippery with her wetness. She whimpers and moans against me, her nails digging into my shoulders as she comes, her body writhing against the door and if I wasn't there to hold her up, she'd be falling to her knees.

"Jesus, Val," she says through a ragged gasp.

I just grin and turn her around, placing my hand between her shoulder blades and pushing her down on the professor's desk, shoving up her dress so her ass is exposed. I unzip my black pants and take my cock out, throbbing in my grip, painfully stiff.

I take in a shaking breath, trying to control myself, but then I spot the cello bow beside the row of cellos along the wall.

Suddenly I'm hit with a memory, the same one I've had before, with Lucy and me. I picked up a violin bow and...

I find myself doing the same now, picking up the cello bow.

"I know I said you'll get a reward," I say, coming back to her ass. With one hand I rub my cock against her sopping wet cunt, barely pressing in, with the other I brandish the cello bow. "But I was thinking you might deserve some punishment instead."

She glances at me over her shoulder, her red hair tangled and all over her face. Her green eyes wide. "What?"

"Trust me," I tell her, feeling déjà vu. "You'll like it."

I raise the bow and bring it down against her ass, spanking her with it.

"Fucking naughty little slut, aren't you?" I grunt.

She cries out and squirms. The way the bow made a light thwack against her skin, I wasn't expecting it to hurt, but it must because she hisses out her breath.

I bring it down again, a little harder this time and she seizes up, her legs shaking against the desk.

"More?" I ask. She just nods.

"You need to ask me properly," I coax.

"More, my lord."

I bring it down harder, completely sure this time that she'll like the pain. This time she lets out a deep moan that I feel in my toes. I bring it down over and over again, relentlessly, watching her body squirm and tense up in pain, her back arching and shoulders hunching in.

"Oh god!" she cries out.

"That's more like it," I murmur. "I'll be your lord and your god."

I bring the bow down harder, loving the way her pussy gets wetter. I rub my cock against her again for a moment, teasing her, and she groans, breathless.

Then I take the bow and press the end of the bow against her clit, so that the delicate horsehair strings are rubbing back and forth against her. She stiffens at the new feeling, then starts lowering herself onto it, and I take that moment to push my cock inside her.

Fuck, she's so wet I might drown right here.

"You like that?" I ask her, gently teasing her clit with the cello bow as I slowly pull my dick out of her, inch by agonizing inch.

"Yes," she hisses.

"Call me your lord," I remind her, quickly shoving back inside her, until I'm buried deep inside her, my balls pressed against her thighs.

"Yes, my lord."

"Would you like to come?"

"Yes, my lord," she says through a ragged gasp as I start moving the cello bow faster against her clit, playing her skillfully.

"Beg for it," I demand.

She cries out and squirms, her cunt clenching even tighter around me.

"Please, my lord, I beg of you, let me come, I need to."

I start to fuck her hard and fast, really ramming into her. I want to come so bad but she needs to come first.

"I need to come, please, my lord..." she gasps, and I feel myself start to lose control.

Oh shit.

I slam into her one last time, hard, and she's crying out. I pull the cello bow away, tossing it to the floor, and grab onto her hips and thrust into her hard, knowing I'm going to come, but I won't stop pounding her until I'm completely spent. My orgasm is deep, blinding, and intense as it rips through me, my cock twitching and throbbing inside her, the warmth spreading through my body, making my head spin as she milks me dry.

I keep my hand on her hip as I come down, watching her tight body as she finishes, her body moving against my hand, her beautiful hair all over her face as she throws her head back and cries out, coming against my cock. I lean back, my body shaking, my eyes clenched shut as I ride out the last waves of my orgasm.

I pull out of her, breathing hard, and watch as my cum spills out of her. Fuck, she's going to get it all over her dress. That's the last thing we need, people to notice cum stains when we're on stage.

I quickly dip my head down, running my tongue up her thighs and along her cunt, filling my mouth with it, the taste of our cum mixed together like the most decadent cocktail.

"Oh!" she cries out softly and in surprise as I swallow it all up, making sure she's been licked clean.

Then I lean over and grab her chin and turn her head to me. Her eyes are hazy and her mouth is open slightly, like she's just waking up.

I gently kiss her and slip my hand under her chin and kiss her again, slow and deep. I pull back and her eyes are still on mine. "My lord," she manages to say, giving me the laziest smile.

"My pupil," I say to her, zipping up my pants. "You have a recital in a few minutes, don't you forget."

Her eyes go wide. "You dick!" she exclaims, quickly getting off the desk and trying to fix her dress. "I'm going to be late."

I eye the clock on the wall. "We have two minutes."

She growls in frustration and pulls at the ends of her hair. "My hair!"

"Your hair is gorgeous. You're gorgeous. And you're going to do an amazing job tonight," I tell her.

She doesn't look like she believes me, worry on her brow.

"Come on, let's get you going."

I unlock the door and stick my head out to make sure the coast is clear, then we exit and hurry along until we're at the stairs. It's quiet down below and I think everyone is already in the concert hall. We're lucky that she's not up first but even so, we have to be there.

"You go first," I tell her. "Go to your seat with the others. I'll come in a bit."

She nods and turns to go but I quickly reach out and grab her, bringing her back to me so I can give her a searing kiss. "Good luck, my dove," I whisper to her.

"Thank you," she whispers back, then hurries along, holding the ends of her dress in her hands as she goes down the stairs, her wild hair billowing after her like a romantic heroine.

I wait a couple of minutes, making sure I look okay and my hair is fine, before I go down. The concert hall is packed, standing room only at the back, but everyone is still talking amongst each other in low murmurs and no one has noticed I'm late to come in.

Except for Van Helsing, who raises a glass of prosecco at me and goes back to the conversation he's having with another man.

I quickly go to my place alongside the other professors and wait. From where I'm sitting, I can only see the back of Dahlia's head and I can't imagine how nervous she must be.

The headmaster of the school starts it off by going on stage and giving a few introductions, and then the recital begins. For the next thirty minutes music fills the hall, almost all of it flawless, and then it's Dahlia's turn.

She goes up on the stage, looking so fucking stunning in that dress and I'm hit with how lucky I am to have her as mine. She takes her spot at the organ, slipping on her organ shoes while a violinist and celloist go behind her for their section of the piece. I don't think I'll ever look at a cello bow the same way again and I almost laugh when I realize we left the bow on the floor of the professor's office. He's going to be most confused when he picks it up.

Dahlia starts to play. She flows into the music and the music flows into her. It makes my heart soar higher and higher, swept away by the moment, by the emotion, until I come to a stunning realization.

I might love her.

And she's mine.

But not yours forever, I can't help but think, and all the joy in my heart is seized by a cold, strangling fist.

No.

Not mine forever.

CHAPTER 21

DAHLIA

I'M BEAMING.

There's nothing better than knowing you've just hit something out of the park, and from the way the applause is getting louder and louder, the pride I feel grows along with it. Magic may have increased my skill level on the organ, but I haven't used it for that since I got here. What I just played and how well I played it was a result of hard work and practice, and while I was so nervous earlier about being able to do the piece justice, I know I have. The string section accompanied me beautifully and together the music just seemed to take over the concert hall, coming straight from our hearts and our bones, perhaps fueled by the ghosts of centuries of performances in this very building.

Instead of demurely getting up and hurrying off stage, I stand up and smile at everyone in the audience, giving them a bow, feeling absolutely radiant. Moments like this have come infrequently in my life—I have to make the most of them.

I walk off the stage and Valtu immediately comes for me, his grin so wide and breathtaking. In his elegant vintage tux I get a vision of him at a party in the late 1800s and I'm stunned at how his iniquitous beauty transcends all decades.

"You were fantastic," he says, pulling me into a hug. "I am so proud of you," he whispers in my ear.

"Thank you." I'm tempted to tell him that people are watching us and they only know us as professor and student, but he pulls back and gives me an affectionate squeeze on the shoulder. He knows how we have to act. Besides we got a lot out of our system *before* the performance. Who knew I could be played like a cello?

I go back to my seat to be polite and watch the rest of the performances, but I can't stop glowing inside, and even though Valtu is standing further back in the audience, I feel his eyes on me the whole time. They never leave me.

This morning when I finally dragged myself back to my apartment to get ready after finding a dress, I was struck with the loneliest sensation. Being there, in that blank narrow space the guild controls, with just my suitcase, my crystals, potions, herbs, and blade of *mordernes*, that weapon that I once viewed as a partner and now view as a leash, I realized I didn't want that life anymore. If being a witch meant I had to spend the rest of my life killing vampires under control of the guild, then I didn't want to be a witch anymore.

I want to quit.

I want to tell Livia and Bellamy that it's over.

I want to live my life with Valtu. I want to go to the school as a real person and figure out what to do with my life with him by my side. I want to make decisions that benefit me and what I want, not some misplaced sense of justice put in me by an organization that has controlled most of my life.

I just don't know where to start.

I know there are some things that need to be dealt with. I know that the book has to be found and I'm going to need Valtu's help for that. I know that I need to be able to kill Saara and

Aleksi, and I can't do that without my blade. So it's not like I'm quitting cold-turkey. I need to finish things for the sake of me, Valtu, and humanity at large, and not for the sake of the guild.

How these things are going to play out though, I have no fucking idea.

I have to take it one day at a time until my hand is forced.

Which means I'll have to continue pretending to be someone else.

If I let my guard down ever, if I ever tell Valtu that I'm a witch, do I think he'd still want to be with me? I don't think so. I don't think he would take all the lies lightly. He'd say that he never knew me this whole time, that I was just a fabrication. Even if I didn't tell him about my true purpose, he'd want nothing to do with me. I know him well enough to know he wouldn't kill me or throw me to the wolves, but at the same time he's a passionate and moody creature. He would feel the betrayal deeply, and he's unpredictable.

So, I'm kind of fucked.

But as I sit here at the recital, I push that out of my head because I just want to keep living this fantasy life forever.

Finally, all the performances come to a close and it's the after party. I get up, making small talk with my classmates, which normally kills me because I'm seriously bad at making small talk and always bring up the weirdest things instead. I crave interesting conversation instead of forced niceties, but my classmates know me well by now and they don't seem to mind if I'm yammering on about a random fact or if I abruptly walk away because I'm bored. Tonight I'm complimenting them on their performances because they all did so well, and eventually we find our way to the inner courtyard which has been done up in a million icicle fairy lights, fake snow on the tiled floor, candles flickering and dripping wax on candelabras. It's beautiful and moody, just like this city.

There's a lot of people here and everyone seems happy. The city has been so on edge lately that it's nice to see, and I think a lot of the revelers are letting their hair down. The students especially seem to all have drinks in hand that are quickly disappearing, and the relief at the recital being over is palpable in the air.

I look around for Valtu and see him speaking to a couple of professors, plus a tall, barrel-chested man with glasses and dark red hair, who I've never seen before. I don't want to disturb them, so I head over to the bar.

Stop dead in my tracks.

The woman in a wispy white gown standing in front of me dealing with the bartender is none other than Saara.

I'd recognize her build—and her ice-cold vampire vibes —anywhere.

If I had my blade on me, it would definitely be glowing blue and tingling for me to kill her. My palms itch.

I think about turning around but before I can, she does.

She gives me a blasé look, about to stride past me with her glass of wine in hand, but then she kind of pauses, quickly appraising me with a cocked brow, and a feeling of dread fills my chest.

"Oh," she says to me in a faux friendly voice. "You're Professor Aminoff's student."

I try to smile, try to breathe. Why does she know that?

"I am," I say, trying to move past her to order as the bartender gives me a look of impatience.

She reaches out and rests her fingers on my shoulder and it feels ice-cold and sickly, like some weird poison has leeched through my skin and into my veins.

"I really enjoyed your performance," she says. "Both of them."

Then she gives me a devilish smile and walks away, her

heels clicking on the tile. I watch her disappear into the crowd, afraid to take my eyes off her.

What the hell was that about? Both of them?

I give my head a shake and the bartender calls me over.

I order a negroni with a splash of prosecco in it, and end up downing most of it before I've even left the bar area.

That's when the tall red-headed man approaches me. He has a strange energy that I can't make heads or tails of at the moment.

"Dahlia Abernathy?" he asks, his accent slight and vaguely German.

"Yes?" I ask, my suspicions running all over the place since that weird exchange with Saara. Everyone feels like bad news now.

He holds out his hand. "I'm a friend of Professor Aminoff."

"Oh, are you a professor too?" I give his hand a shake.

"No I'm a doctor," he says. "Doctor Abraham Van Helsing."

I stare at him for a moment. "I'm sorry. Doctor Van Helsing the..." I lower my voice, "vampire hunter?"

He laughs. "Don't be foolish, I am no such thing. It's just a name." He clears his throat and gives me a quick smile. "Vampires don't hunt vampires."

"Ah," I say. "You're a vampire. I figured as such."

"You don't seem surprised."

"Val told me the signs to look for," I say, though that's a lie, it's just my vampire radar feels a little scrambled tonight. "I'm pretty good at picking them out."

"Did you know the woman you were just talking to was a vampire?"

I take a sip of my drink, nodding. "I did. She's pretty obvious. She's got all the bad vibes going on."

"You're right about that," he says and gestures to the side

of the courtyard by a large potted olive tree strewn with fairy lights. "Let us discuss this in a more private place."

We walk over there and I have to admit, I'm more than amused that I'm talking to Van Helsing. "So, like, you're going to have to explain to me because Val doesn't talk about his past very much, but how are you Van Helsing? Did you know Bram Stoker too?"

He chuckles. "Never met the man. But I was a dear friend of Val's at the time. When he met Bram in Cruden Bay and told his story, I was naturally a part of it. Well, I guess I shouldn't say *naturally*, I didn't think my friendship would come up, and I most certainly didn't think that it was worthy enough to be fictionalized in the greatest piece of horror literature of all time. And I really didn't think I'd one day be played in a movie by none other than the great Hugh Jackman."

I laugh at that. "Well, you don't look too different from him." I'm not flattering him either, Van Helsing is hot, and though he's wearing a suit, I have a feeling his body would rival Hugh's. But he's a vampire and that's usually a given.

"Oh, aren't you kind," he says warmly, a twinkle in his eye.

"So what was Val like back in the day? What was this, the Victorian age?" The only friend of Val's I'd met was Bitrus, but that was in the Red Room and I wasn't able to ask him any questions. Of course, I want to know Bitrus and Van Helsing too, but honestly I'm just greedy for any information about my vampire's lover.

He nods. "Val..." he trails off, his expression souring. "We had a few good years, the two of us in London. He had just come out of his shell—"

"His shell?" I can't imagine Valtu ever being introverted.

"He had a few years of...troubles." He squints at me. "Guess he never told you many details about that either."

I shake my head.

He sighs wearily. "Well, I won't overstep my boundaries here. Despite being known as Dracula, he can be very private."

"He did tell me about the women he loved and lost."

"You mean Mina?"

"Sure. And Lucy."

Funny. Now that I think about it, he never told me either of their names. It's like I just knew.

He frowns, eying me warily. "But you know that Lucy and Mina were the same person, right?"

"No?" I blink. "How?"

"She was reincarnated."

I stare at him for a moment, trying to let that info sink in. "She was reincarnated?"

"Saw it with my own eyes. When Lucy was dying, she made it clear she knew Valtu from the past. She used to be Mina. Valtu, of course, knew it right away. He knew it the moment he laid eyes on her. When he told me, I thought he was just seeing what he wanted to see, but he was right all along."

"And she died too? That's awful," I tell him, feeling all sorts of horrible for him. "I thought the reincarnation thing was just from the movie, I didn't know that actually happened."

"Wish that were the case," he says. He gives me a small smile and nods at my hair. "But now that he's with you, I see he definitely has a type."

"What do you mean?"

"She had red hair too. Exact same shade. In fact, I'd say you look exactly like her but..." he takes off his glasses and peers at me closer. "Very strange."

I swallow uneasily. "What?"

"I'm having a hard time seeing you. Like seeing you for who you really are."

"You probably need your glasses on," I tell him, that unease building.

"These aren't real corrective lenses, my dear, I'm a vampire," he says, raising his chin and putting his glasses back on. He squints at me again and wiggles his brows. "Most peculiar. It's almost as if the more I stare at you, the more you seem to become..."

Oh god. Please don't tell me my glamor is losing its grip. If he finishes his sentence by saying "a witch" I'm toast.

"How did she die?" I interrupt him.

"Which one?"

"Either one."

"Well, Lucy died in childbirth. Stillborn. Very sad. I did all I could but..."

It just keeps getting worse.

"And the other?"

"Mina? She had been pregnant too. It's no wonder that Valtu got his vasectomy, you can't blame the poor guy after all those tragedies."

"She also died in pregnancy?"

"Oh." He shakes his head. "No. She was pregnant, but that's not what killed her. She was beheaded. By her father. A Russian general. In fact, at that moment Valtu discovered he was a vampire, he fought the soldiers to try and save her but it was too late."

The doctor keeps talking but I no longer hear him.

Instead I see my dreams.

I see me lying on the ground in the dirt. My father above me in his military garb, calling me a whore in Russian. I see him put his boot on my stomach, aiming to kill what was inside.

My baby.

And then I feel it.

I know it.

I know it's Valtu that the soldiers are holding back, I recognize his screams, the terror, and he's trying to save me but he can't.

He can't stop my father from swinging that sword against my neck.

My world from going black.

Then turning bright.

These aren't dreams.

They were never dreams.

I fucking *died*.

I remember dying.

And just like that a whole life comes sliding into me, like negatives into a developing plate. I remember being Mina, growing up in Moscow, living a lavish but controlled and empty life, my mother dying early, other people considering me strange, spending so many of my days alone, with only servants for company, before my father got his position in the war and we left Russia. I remember meeting Valtu in the field and knowing it was forbidden, I remember falling in love with him, having sex with him, how he opened me up to a whole new world with our bodies. I remember the dreams and the hopes that I had for us, then I remember discovering I was pregnant. That my handmaiden ratted me out, that we were caught one sunny morning and I was killed and Valtu...Valtu...

Then another life comes slamming into me, like waking up and realizing the dream you had or a book you read was real all along.

I remember being Lucy. I remember being raised in England somewhere, I had a sweet mother who was very weak, I had a dear sister who died in childbirth, I went to school, I had friends, I had money, and I met Valtu at the British Museum.

Suddenly I look at Van Helsing and I know.

"You were there," I whisper, the images flooding my brain now. "You were there."

He was with Valtu that first meeting in the new exhibit, Eastern art, and he was there. After that we would go to the opera together, Van Helsing was like a chaperone to us, and then he was the best man at our wedding, and then he was my doctor when I was pregnant, and he took out the baby and—

"Oh my god!" I cry out, bending over and clutching my stomach.

"Dahlia, are you alright?" the doctor says, putting his hand on my back.

I need to get out of here. I'm Dahlia but I'm also Lucy and I'm also Mina and I don't know what to do.

"I'm going to be sick, excuse me." I push past him and hurry to the woman's washroom on this floor, relieved when I find it empty.

I take the furthest stall and drop to my knees, vomiting up the negroni. It does nothing to stop the flood of feelings and emotions that pour through me, all the moments and scenes, the trauma, so much fucking trauma.

I throw up until I'm dry-heaving, then I flush and sit back against the toilet on the floor, my head in my hands, trying to make it stop. I'm dizzy and exhausted and I feel like I'm on the world's worst drug trip.

I remember it all.

All of it.

I am Dahlia and Lucy and Mina.

I am three different women in one.

Three different lives in one.

And Valtu...

Valtu.

Oh my god.

Valtu.

He's not some man I just happened to fall in love with.

295

He's a man I've already loved.

I've carried his child twice.

I was married to him.

I've died by his side.

And he's here.

I found him again like I promised him I would.

Suddenly I get to my feet and burst out of the stall, putting my head under the tap and rinsing out my mouth, then splashing water on my face in an attempt to gain clarity, and when I look back in the mirror I see myself across three different centuries, my outfits and hairdos changing and evolving but my face staying the same.

"Are you okay?" Margaret, the girl from my class says. I didn't even notice her standing beside me at the sink.

"I think so?" I tell her.

Then I run out of the bathroom, needing to find Valtu.

I bump into him right away.

"Are you okay?" he asks me, holding onto my elbows, his eyes searching my face with concern.

Oh god, Valtu.

My lord.

I place my hands on his face. "I'm okay. I'm here. Don't you see who I am! I'm here, I found you, I found you Val! I said I would!"

He looks taken aback, gently places his hands over mine and lowers them so that no one around is too suspicious of our relationship. "I was looking for *you*," he says. "Van Helsing said you were talking and you suddenly got sick."

I stare at him, giving my head a slight shake in disbelief.

Why doesn't he...?

And that's when it hits me.

It's like what happened with the doctor. He can't really see me. He's never been able to. This glamor hides who I really am, and it only works on vampires. I look familiar to them but they can't physically see me as Lucy. They can't see me for who I really am because the glamor doesn't let them.

"What color are my eyes?" I suddenly demand.

"What? Green. They're green."

"And my nose, I have this bump on it right? Right?"

"I love that bump," he says quietly.

"And my hair?"

"Red," he says, eyeing me uneasily. "Did someone slip something in your drink? What's happening in your head?"

"You can't see me?"

Now he looks concerned. He straightens up. "I'm going to take you home."

"I'm fine," I tell him.

But I'm not fine.

Valtu sees me but he can't connect me to Lucy or Mina.

He won't know it's me until I lose the glamor.

But if I lose the glamor, he'll know I'm a witch.

Specifically of the vampire-slaying variety.

I can't tell anyone, I can't tell Livia because then the guild is going to come after me, knowing I've been compromised.

What was I saying earlier?

Oh, yeah.

That I'm fucked.

CHAPTER 22

DAHLIA

I DON'T ARGUE when Valtu wants to take me home, but I'm only going back to his home, not my apartment. All that distance I felt between me and my slayer life, even before the evening started, has tripled.

He takes me by the arm and leads me down a corridor to the back of the conservatory where there's a small dock with a bunch of boats tied up. He takes me to his and helps me in and then we putter off down the narrow canal behind the school until we get to the Grand Canal, passing through the mist and fog. If he's worried about people thinking we're heading off somewhere together, he doesn't show it.

We don't speak, letting the space fill with the sound of our motor, of the passing boats and vaporettos, the sloshing water, the music drifting in and out of different calles as we pass them by. By the concerned looks he keeps throwing my way, I know he's worried about me being sick.

As for me, well, I do feel ill, but not in the way he assumes. I'm overwhelmed to my very core. It's one thing to live one lifetime, trying to dig up old memories that have been buried by time. It's another to have lived two others in two different periods of civilization and to have them all collapse on you at once. I feel like I'm drowning in a million different versions of myself, even though in reality there're only three.

That I remember, anyway.

Could I have been anyone else before Valtu?

How does reincarnation work anyway?

When I die again one day, will I come back in this body during another point in time? Can I ever appear in people who don't look like me? Can I be a boy? Can I be another race? Or am I forever doomed to have this face?

Not that I've ever taken issue with my face. I suppose there is some comfort in knowing you always look the same, give or take weight loss and other changes during the different lives. I was rather plump in my life as Lucy, obviously because I had a lot of access to rich foods, and luckily both me and Valtu liked that extra weight. I was underweight when I was Mina, because my father liked to starve me, even though there was enough food to go around in a general's family. And today, well, I'm somewhere in between. But in the end, still me.

Still me and Lucy and Mina.

Dear lord, Lucy and Mina. Bram Stoker wrote about *me*.

Okay, well at least my names were used for his characters, though they were nothing like me.

What a fucking trip this is.

The funny thing is, the concept of past lives isn't new for witches. I've heard of others remembering their past lives here and there, but none of it seemed very concrete or fully formed. I have to wonder if I'm an anomaly and, if so, why? What is it about me that makes me keep coming back? Do I have unfinished business or something?

Or is my business Valtu?

Perhaps I keep coming back because each time we haven't

been given the chance to make things right, for our love to get a chance to last.

"Almost there," Valtu says as he takes the boat down another narrow canal that leads to his place. "How are you feeling? Being on a boat can't help, can it?"

I shake my head. "I'm doing okay."

He gives me a sympathetic smile and is about to say something else when his eyes narrow at something over my shoulder.

I turn around to see something big and long and dark slipping into the water a few yards in front of us. It goes in with a splash and disappears into the inky depths.

"What the fuck was that?" I gasp, quickly remembering that my current life is full of all kinds of crazy shit. I quickly shuffle back from the edge of the boat, just in case whatever it is tries to pull me under.

You know what it is.

The bad thing.

"River otter," Valtu says.

I look at him over my shoulder. "Are you nuts?"

He presses his lips together and doesn't say anything.

God damn it. It's like the universe is trying to keep me in my current role. I have to get that fucking book back before this shit gets worse, then I guess I'll figure out how to eventually reveal to Valtu who I really am.

Luckily, we get back to his place without a demon capsizing our boat, and the moment we step inside his back doors, I calm down a little. I don't think his house is protected by any wards, not like the ones I have currently around my apartment to keep those bad things out, but I always feel safe and protected here.

"Do you want me to make you tea?" he asks, looking so adorable and yet dapper all at once in the tux and I'm only now realizing that I've seen him wear this tux before. To my twenty-third birthday party in London, a month after we got married. The love I felt that day...

"Valtu," I utter, suddenly so overcome that tears flood my eyes.

He stares at me in confusion, mid-reach for the kettle.

I stride over to him and grab his face, my palms pressed against his cool cheeks, his stubble scratching my skin. "Fuck me," I whisper, staring deep into his eyes. Oh these eyes, how dark and rich they are, as they've always been. I've lived so many lives staring into these eyes.

He raises his brows. "So, no tea then." Then he gives me one of those beautiful smiles that look like the heavens are shining down on him and he kisses me.

I could always count on him to oblige me.

Especially when it came to sex.

Our kiss deepens and I feel like I'm kissing for the first time, the first time with all my lives and memories. It's been so long that I've been without him. I had him and lost him as Mina, I had him and lost him as Lucy, then I became Dahlia and I had nearly thirty years without him in my life, and now he's here and I'm here and that's a fucking miracle in itself.

I kiss him with everything I have. All the love for him I have, all the sorrow, the loss, the missing him without knowing I was missing him.

"Dahlia," he whispers against my lips, groaning as I reach down and run my hand over his cock that is pushing against his tuxedo pants like a tent pole. "You are a firecracker tonight."

He breaks off into a guttural moan that sends shockwaves through me.

"You better take advantage then," I tell him as his mouth goes to my neck, licking and nipping and sucking.

This is the first time I'm with him as Lucy and Mina knowing he's a vampire, and I want him to feed on me. I want them to know what it's like to have that feeling of total submission.

"Hold on," I say to him and I lean over, swiping a knife out of the knife holder on the counter. "I have a request."

He eyes the knife. "You want me to cut you out of your dress."

I consider that, sawing my jaw back and forth. "Only if you let the knife go a little deeper."

His black brows knit together. "What do you mean? You want me to cut you?"

"I want you to feed from me."

His eyes blaze as he shakes his head. "Nope. No. Not here without anyone to stop me. Don't you remember what happened last time? We had a whole room full of people watching me and I still almost killed you."

I chew on my lip for a moment. "Can we compromise? What if you just had a taste?"

He growls at me and kisses me again, pressing me against the counter. "How about you stop making requests and let me be in charge. You want to feel pain and danger, I can bring you that, my dove, but I will not feed from you."

And at that he picks me up like he's a caveman taking a captive woman back to his den. He carries me to the bedroom, my clothes coming off as he kisses every inch of my exposed skin, my dress falling to the floor.

He lays me on the bed and I writhe naked on top of the covers, watching in desperate anticipation as he quickly shucks off his tux in hurried movements, wanting nothing more than to feel his hard cock inside of me.

I want him to fuck me now that I remember everything.

Now that I am not just Dahlia, but everyone else.

Still me.

Just me with a deeper understanding of him.

A deeper love for him.

A love so deep that it transcends time.

A love so strong it lasts beyond death.

And he doesn't even fucking know it.

Now he's naked, standing at the foot of the bed, and I'm staring at him with new eyes.

"Are you sure you're okay?" he asks quietly, stroking his cock with a quick flick of his wrist. Such a magnificent animal, so much power and prowess.

"Never been better," I tell him, my voice coming out husky as my emotions go into overdrive.

He gets on top of the bed, his movements smooth but measured, like a prowling black panther, or a wolf stalking its prey. His eyes rake over my body, leaving goosebumps in their wake and shivers down my spine.

He gets halfway across me, his cock jutting out in front of him and primed at where I'm wet and open for him, then pauses, running his tongue over his teeth, his mouth curling into a smile. His gaze is eternally wicked.

Always has been.

"You want to see a magic trick?" he asks in a rough voice.

I look at him in surprise, not expecting him to ask that.

"Okay..." I say.

He braces himself over me on one arm while lifting up the other, holding his fingers in front of my face.

He stares at them. I stare at him, not sure what's about to happen. This can't be an actual magic trick, right? I mean he's not a witch.

Poof.

Suddenly every fingertip on his hand bursts into flames.

I jump, pushing back slightly against the headboard.

He laughs. "Don't worry," he says, gently waving his hand in front of me. "I'm in complete control."

"How are you doing that?" I ask, unable to keep my eyes

off the flames. His fingertips aren't sooty or burnt at all, yet the flames are flowing.

"I told you, magic."

"Like from a witch?" I pause, holding my breath as I wait for his answer. I've never said the word witch out loud yet and—

"Yeah," he says lightly. "But no witch that I know. A witch gave the spell to my friend Solon, he taught it to me. Speaking of, I just got a text from him earlier. He and his lover are going to be in town tomorrow. I told them I would put them up here, if you don't mind?"

He's still dragging the flames back and forth in front of my face. "Sure," I say. I'm not sure how I feel about meeting more vampire friends of his, especially one as notorious as Absolon Stavig, a vampire I've heard plenty about, but that doesn't really matter at the moment now that he's got fire in his hand and he's dangerously close to my naked body.

"They'd stay in a hotel, but these days I feel it's better for us vampires to stick together."

I frown, my gaze going to him. "What do you mean, these days?"

"World feels a little unsettled, doesn't it?" he says. "I don't mean to spook you, but there are some vampires in town that don't have the greatest of intentions."

He means Saara and Aleksi. Damn it I want to talk about them but I also want sex.

"Should I be worried?" I ask.

"Not at the moment."

Then he brings the flaming fingers toward my breasts. I shrink back a bit, trying to get out of the way.

"Just relax," he murmurs. "It won't hurt you."

"It's fire, Val," I tell him, wide-eyed. "That's what fire does. It burns. And that hurts."

"You never put your fingers through a candle flame before? Just that quick kiss of pain. No damage."

I gulp, bracing myself.

He brings his fingers over my nipple and I gasp, the burn hot at first, then sharp, my nipples hardening as he takes the flames away.

Suddenly my body is flooded with endorphins and I sink deeper into the bed.

"Oh my god," I say breathlessly.

"See, no damage," he says, leaning down and kissing my breasts, swirling his wet tongue around my nipple.

Fuck. I arch my back, chasing that sensation, my cunt throbbing for him.

"Do it again," I whisper, raising my hips, wanting him inside me.

He grins and takes his fingers to the other breast, passing the flames over my nipple until I cry out from the burn, then he soothes me with cool, wet passes of his tongue.

Dear god, it's good.

It's so good.

"I told you to trust me," he murmurs, moving down my body, bringing the flames on and off my skin as he goes. I groan and gasp at the sensation, the way it burns, the heat wickedly intense, then how he calms it with his mouth, leaving soft kisses and long licks until I'm wound up so tight I feel like I'm going to shatter.

Then the flames suddenly go out with a quick wave of his hand and he seizes my hips, gripping tight as he shoves his cock inside me.

"Oh god!" I yelp, my head going back against the headboard, making fists on the sheets as I'm taken by surprise.

He's so fucking big. I can feel every inch of him as he begins to fuck me, having to close my eyes and grit my teeth just to take it. But even with the pain there's pleasure, too, and I stretch around him, greedy for more.

"That's it," he rasps, his fingers digging into my hips, making me moan from the feeling. "Take it. Take my fucking cock, love. Let me feel you fucking take me from the inside."

I groan again, trying to push back against him, needing more. He pulls my hair, tilts my head to the side, and bites the side of my neck. I start to shake, my entire body tensing as he grinds his teeth into the flesh of my shoulder. He inhales, his breath shaking, and I think his fangs might be coming out.

Then he pulls back and when I look at his face, it's contorted with restraint. He wants to feed. He won't let himself.

"You know what I want to see?" he asks, his voice low. "I want to see my cum dripping out of that pretty little cunt," he rasps, leaning forward to bite my ear, making me shudder with desire. "Are you ready to give me that?"

"Yes," I moan, my hips bucking in time with his thrusts. "God, yes, I'm ready."

He grunts, gritting his teeth as he pushes himself harder and deeper inside me, and I can feel myself getting close. I dig my nails into his back and he lets out this deep, guttural sound that belongs to an animal, fucking me faster and harder, his cock rubbing all the right places, almost sending me over the edge. He leans forward, biting my neck hard enough to leave a mark but not break the skin.

Suddenly I'm coming, moaning loud, my entire body shaking as I let the orgasm take me. But he doesn't stop, and I want him to come while he feeds, I want that sensation again of his cock growing inside me.

"Please," I whisper to him, my pussy still pulsing around his stiff length. "Take from me."

"I might lose control," he says through a shuddering

breath, fucking me harder, his hips relentless as they piston against me.

"You won't," I tell him as I jerk from each thrust, my tits bouncing. "That's not how it ends for us this time."

He gives me an odd look that's quickly swallowed by a groan of pleasure, his eyes pinching shut, and when he opens them his pupils are bright red.

Bloodlust.

A giddy thrill rushes through me and I move my head to the side, exposing my skin, taunting him, teasing him.

"Feed from me, my lord," I whisper.

It was the right thing to say.

"Fuck!" he growls, low and animalistic enough to make the hair stand on my arms and then he bites me, fangs piercing the skin.

The pain shoots through me like I'm being electrocuted. It's such a sharp, deep pain that my vision blurs and I'm crying out, my fingers digging into the skin on his shoulders so hard that I know I'm drawing blood as well.

He grunts against my skin and I feel my blood as it's drawn from my veins, hear him swallow it down, only a few drops leaking to the bed beneath. He's latched on the way he was before, and I can tell he's slowly losing himself by the way his cock seems to expand while inside me, filling and stretching me until I'm so completely full.

"I'm still here," I whisper into his ear. "I'm still here, my lord. I came back for you."

I don't know if he really understands what I'm saying but it's enough that when I push my hand up on his shoulder, he unhooks his fangs and brings his head back.

He stares at me with the wild eyes of someone half-man and half-animal. A man with demons that I aim to keep at bay.

"How do I taste?" I ask.

"Like heaven," he says, his voice raw and edged with desperation. I feel the more he talks, the more focused I can keep him.

He's panting, his chest rising and falling hard, his hands trembling.

He pulls away from my neck, but only to slide his fangs over my left breast. He breaks the skin there and then I'm crying out again as warm blood spills over my breasts.

The pain just lasts a second.

All I can focus on is the pleasure. I clench around his growing cock and he moans, his entire body shaking, his tongue cleaning up the blood as it runs from a small bite on my breast.

"Look at me," I tell him.

He lifts his head, mouth bloody, eyes meeting mine just inches away. The red in his pupils is bright but flickering like a torch, and I know he's fighting to remain in control.

I wrap my legs around him, heels at his ass, and draw him in deeper. "Please," I gasp, staring up at him, begging him to fuck me hard. I want to feel him come inside me, I want to remember all the other times he's fucked me like this, so hard and wild and good.

For once he does as he's told and I don't have to beg. He's driving himself into me over and over again until I'm just a writhing mass of pleasure under him. Pleasure that only seems to grow and grow until I'm arching off the bed, crying out as I come harder than I ever have before.

My world explodes in starlight and crimson.

I never want this to end.

All my emotions from all my lives come crashing down at me and as I cry out his name, tears spill from my eyes and I'm sobbing, gasping, trying to make sense of everything all at once.

It takes him a moment, but he finally comes too, driving

himself deep inside of me, his cock pulsing against the walls of my pussy. I can feel the heat of his cum as it spills inside me and it's extra emotional knowing that the same seed led to me being pregnant twice before, though that won't be the case now.

And probably for good reason, knowing our track record.

I lay there in his arms, feeling his heartbeat slow down and the comforting sound of his breathing.

Then he raises his head and looks at me, running his fingertips over my cheekbone, sweeping through my wet tears. "You're crying." Then anguish washes over his brow. "I hurt you, didn't I? I took too much blood. I knew it, I tried so hard to stay in control and not—"

"No!" I shake my head. "No. You didn't at all. I'm just..."

Tell him. Tell him. Tell him.

He'll understand, he'll still love you.

But how do I know that for sure, when he doesn't even love me now?

What if I tell him I'm Lucy and Mina and he decides he won't let himself love me again because he can't stand to lose me again? Could I even blame him for doing so, for protecting his heart? I couldn't.

So I don't tell him.

I just give him a faint smile. "I'm just so in love with you, that's all."

The corner of his mouth lifts, his eyes playful. "That's all? Dahlia, my dove, that's everything, isn't it?"

He kisses me softly, tasting of blood. "That's everything."

CHAPTER 23

DAHLIA

DESPITE THE DRIZZLE and gloom of last night, the morning ends up being beautiful. I help Valtu with doing the laundry since he got quite a bit of my blood on the sheets and duvet cover from feeding on me, then I help him get one of the guest rooms ready for his friends from San Francisco that are supposed to arrive in the late afternoon. Since his house used to be a hotel, there are a ton of rooms to choose from and he selects one of the suites.

While we work together making it nice for them, I can't help but smile at him adoringly, to the point where I think I'm weirding him out a little. The thing is, I'm remembering being Lucy. I remember the times we had guests over at the house in Marylebone, how Valtu really sank into his role as Count Aminoff and turned into a thoughtful host. He always wanted everything right, from the black roses placed in their gothic-looking vases, to the orange-scented soaps in the bathroom. Everything about it screamed tasteful elegance, with a macabre touch.

Looking back, I realize all those guests that came over were vampires. I didn't know it at the time—he never told me he was a vampire until I was literally dying. I wasn't surprised though, even in those sad, final moments. I always suspected there was something strange and unusual about him. But since even as Lucy I had felt strange and unusual, I chalked it up to two misfits finding love with one another.

Actually, now that I think about it, the way I felt as Lucy, like there was something more to me that I didn't realize, and how out of time I felt, out of place with most people other than my closest friends who were a little odd as well, is quite similar to the way I feel today. How I've had a hard time getting people to like me, how otherworldly I feel at times, how I've gone through life feeling like I just don't belong, and I wonder how much of that is just me being neurodiverse and how much is actually my past spilling over. How can you not feel at least a *little* different from everyone else when you've already lived before?

After we finish with their room, we head downstairs and Valtu goes through his alcohol selection, bringing out only finest wines and spirits for his friends.

"Are you sure you don't want me to make them something to eat?" I ask, wanting to be put to use.

"They're vampires, love," he says, inspecting a dusty bottle of red he had deep in a cabinet. "We don't need to eat food."

"I know you don't *need* to eat food," I tell him, opening the fridge for something that would pass as snacks. Everything in here is for my benefit. "But I know you enjoy the taste of it. You and your garlic everything."

He grins at me and takes out another bottle.

"Do you mind if I get something together for them? I'd like to be a good host too." I quickly add, "I know it's not my house."

It's just, when we did have a house together, that was my job.

"I would be honored," he says, coming over to kiss me on

the head, then walking off with the wine, disappearing around the corner to the sitting room.

I stare at his ass for a moment, admiring it, then turn my attention back to food. Vampires aren't the healthiest of eaters so I'm assuming the carrot and celery sticks I have won't fly. Instead, I make a quick charcuterie board with some meats from a nearby butcher and a selection of cheeses. I'm finishing with a touch of red pepper jelly and a dollop of antipasto when I hear the grand piano being played from the other room, a rich, sad song that immediately makes me feel emotional.

I smile to myself, hit with yet another warm memory. The way he would play piano in London each evening as I sat there with a hot cup of tea, the sound filling the house with beauty. He was so good at playing everything back then, and obviously over the years his skill has only improved.

I place the board on the counter and then go to the sitting room.

"That's beautiful," I say, leaning against the doorframe and watching as he plays, his long fingers moving masterfully across the keys. "Who is that by?"

"A Dutch composer," he says, keeping his eyes closed as he plays. "Joep Beving. The song is called Etude."

"Let me guess, you knew him way back in the day." I don't know how he's been able to know everyone famous. I mean, I was alive in the 1880s too and I'm pretty sure Valtu is the most notorious person I know.

He smiles and glances at me. "I believe he was born in the 1970s. I don't know him at all. You know, just because I was born three hundred years ago, doesn't mean I don't keep up with music from today. I know all the new composers, and I happen to hear the radio from time to time."

I laugh at that. Valtu abhors the radio. If it's ever on he's quick to turn it off unless there is classical music playing.

Suddenly the doorbell sounds, a melodic but loud clang that makes my heart jump.

"They're here early," he says with a grin, getting up and strolling past me to the foyer. I stay behind him, always apprehensive about meeting new people but especially when they're vampires.

He opens the door and I'm immediately met with a blast of dark, ancient energy, making my scalp prickle and my hair stand on end.

Before me stands Solon, the purveyor of this energy and one seriously handsome dude, even by vampire standards. He's tall, broad-shouldered and square-jawed with piercing blue eyes and chin-length black hair similar to Valtu's, except his is straight and not wavy. He's dressed impeccably in a charcoal grey wool coat, black pants, sleek boots. While his energy certainly brings this darkness and a sense of him being extremely old and almost sanctified, I don't sense any evil in him. In fact, he seems quite calm and thoughtful.

I look to his woman, expecting the same thing.

That's not what I get.

She's a witch.

This woman is a fucking *witch*!

I stare at her for a moment, absolutely dumbstruck. A witch can always tell a witch, and that's what this woman is. She's stunning, young, with long honey-colored hair, dressed in a leather jacket and jeans, but she's a witch. Standing alongside her vampire lover. For one millisecond it gives me hope for me and Valtu.

Then she meets my eyes and though her eyes are hazel, the pupils in them momentarily flash red, her nostrils flaring.

And then I know that she's not just a witch.

She's a vampire, too.

Oh fuck.

And now she's staring at me, puzzled, trying to figure me

out, like she's trying to see past my glamor and then I see the moment when she lifts the veil and sees me for who I truly am.

Her eyes go wide.

They go angry.

As I said, a witch always knows a witch. She can see the glamor coating me like a shimmering cloak, knows I've been hiding my true identity.

Oh fuck, fuck, fuck.

"Solon, this is my girlfriend Dahlia," Valtu says, gesturing to me. If I wasn't staring at the witch-vampire in horror, I probably would have felt giddy over him addressing me as his girlfriend for the first time, at least in this lifetime. "Dahlia, this is Solon."

I shake Solon's hand, looking at him momentarily, trying to smile even though I'm holding my breath thinking that this girl is going to say something.

"And this is Lenore," Valtu says. "She's a vampire and a witch. We try not to hold that against her."

Lenore stares at me, then looks at Valtu, then back at me, probably trying to gauge if he knows the truth or not.

Finally she clears her throat, putting on a fake smile and says. "Pleasure to meet you, Dahlia."

"Yeah, I'm just a human," I say through an awkward laugh, hoping that Lenore takes the hint and doesn't out me right now.

"That's okay, we don't bite," Solon says, his accent lightly British. Then catches himself. "Well, we'll try not to."

"Come on in," Valtu says, opening the door wider. Solon and Lenore walk past me and Lenore stares right into my very soul as she does, her eyes burning me from the inside out.

Oh god. I am so fucked!

I follow them inside and they go with Valtu to the

kitchen and then out to the garden where Valtu has arranged the patio table and chairs in the sun. It's warm at the moment, the chill being held at bay thanks to lack of wind, but it doesn't really matter to them since they don't get cold.

I pause in the kitchen, not sure what I'm supposed to do. I should pretend to be a good host and get the platter I prepared out to them but I'm terrified, so terrified that I can't move, I just stand by the island and watch Lenore and Solon sit down.

Valtu comes back inside and gives me a quizzical look. "You alright, my dove? You look a little pale."

I nod. "Uh huh. Guess that sickness I had from last night is coming back."

He peers at me then walks over, taking his fingers and running them through my hair, disarmingly tender as he does so. "You're nervous about meeting my friends," he says softly as he stares down at me. "Or you're anxious because I introduced you as my girlfriend."

I manage a quick smile, suddenly aware of how little time I have before this all blows up in my face. "No. No, I loved that." I swallow. "But maybe I am a little nervous."

"They'll love you," he says. "I know Solon can seem a bit stoic, but he's the real deal. And Lenore, she was like you. Meaning a human. She didn't even know she was witch or a vampire until she turned twenty-one. Her parents hid it from her. They were vampire slayers, can you imagine that?"

Oh god, it keeps getting worse! Of course she can tell what I am.

"That's wild," I say absently.

"Come along outside," he says, guiding me toward the door until I'm outside on the patio, the sunshine bright in my eyes. Both Solon and Lenore have slipped sunglasses on their face.

I sit down across from them, trying to hide my galloping heart from them but of course they can hear it.

"I'll get the drinks." Valtu goes back inside the house and I'm alone with them.

"So, Valtu tells me that you're an organist, for the pipe organ," Solon says, giving me a charming smile. "Did you grow up around churches? It's an interesting choice for an instrument in today's world. Of course, when I grew up it was quite common."

"Not really," I manage to say, keeping my eyes glued to him because I'm too nervous to look at Lenore. "My parents weren't big fans of organized religion. I just watched a lot of horror movies over and over again as a kid. The soundtracks kind of got stuck in my brain. All that organ. I wanted to create those sounds, too."

Valtu comes back out with drinks and I suddenly get up, my chair clattering loudly on the patio tiles as it gets pushed back. "I need to get the charcuterie board, excuse me." I head into the house, trying to take deep breaths as I lean against the counter.

Okay think. Think, Dahlia, think.

Maybe call Livia? Tell her what's up. Maybe she'll have a suggestion on what the fuck I'm supposed to do, because short of just leaving and never turning back, I don't know what my options are.

Maybe she doesn't even know, I tell myself. *Maybe you're jumping to conclusions.*

Suddenly I hear the patio doors shut and feel a rush of cold at my back and my heart sinks like a stone.

She's here.

"Dahlia, right?" Lenore asks in a tight voice. "That *is* your name, right?"

I take in a deep shaking breath and turn around.

I'm on one side of the island and she's on the other.

Outside Solon and Valtu are laughing about something and gesturing wildly with their hands, not paying any attention to us.

"That's my name," I squeak.

"Does he know?"

Gulp.

"What my name is?"

Her eyes turn ice-cold, pinning me in place. I try to move but I can't.

"Does he know who you really are?" she says, her voice growing deeper. "Does he know that you're wearing a glamor, in disguise? Does he know you're a witch, a vampire slayer? Does he know that, Dahlia?"

I open my mouth to speak but she's quick as a wink. In one fluid blur she jumps right over the counter, clearing it and then slams me back against the refrigerator, her forearm against my neck. Jesus, she's strong and I can't fucking breathe.

"Tell me what you're doing here. You're here to kill him, aren't you? You're a slayer, you kill vampires, that's what you do. What happened, that you lasted this long, got him to fall in love with you, and you still haven't killed him yet?"

He's not in love with me, I try to say but can't.

"What is your end game? I know that slayers are sent on their missions from the guild. Why did they send you here? What has Valtu done?"

I cough and she lets up just a little.

"I'm not just a witch," I manage to say, my throat bobbing against her arm as I talk. "I am reincarnated."

Her head jerks. "What?"

"I'm Mina. I'm Lucy. I remember now. I was with him in his past."

She frowns. "You're the one? You're the one he lost

twice?" Then a hardness comes back over her eyes. "Fucking liar!" she practically spits in my face.

"I'm not lying! Please. Look at me. You know I'm not lying."

"You are," she sneers. "You were playing a role. Why did the guild send you to kill Valtu?"

"I don't know. You don't ask. You know how it works. You do what they tell you."

"Oh, I know," she says hatefully. "My parents left the guild and they've had a mark on their back ever since. Did you know that you were a puppet? A pawn in their game? Did you know that they pick slayers who are oh-so good at masking, pretending to be someone else, and then they kill their parents so that they're easily brainwashed, driven by blind vengeance?"

I blink, trying to push her arm off me but to no avail. "No. Vampires killed my parents."

She lets out a caustic laugh. "That's what they wanted you to believe. That's what happened to my mother, to my father. The guild said their parents were killed by vampires so that they would be in their service for the rest of their lives. Did you have a mentor show up at the right time too, take you in, fuel your rage?"

No. This isn't true. It can't be true. This whole life can't be a lie.

"You don't understand," I tell her. "That's not…that's not what…"

But that's when I know.

She's telling the truth.

I cry out, anger taking hold of me now, rage and shame, so much shame.

"No," I whisper.

Bellamy killed my parents. I know he did. He killed my parents and then pretended to be my family. He turned me into a monster. He turned so many of us into monsters, just ready to do their bidding.

"How does that feel, to give your whole life to an organization that used you from the very start?" Her eyes grow mean again. "But it doesn't matter now, does it, because had I not found out about you, you would have killed Valtu. You would have killed him and not even asked them *why*."

"No, no, I love him," I sob. "I love him. I wasn't going to do it. I only found out last night who I was, that I've loved him for all these lives—"

"You can drop the act," she snaps at me, pressing her arm harder.

"The fuck?" Valtu's voice booms behind us and I see him and Solon come inside the kitchen.

"What the fuck are you doing Lenore?" Solon exclaims and in a second he's right beside us, pulling her off of me.

I keel over, hand on my windpipe, trying to breathe.

"What the hell just happened?" Valtu asks. He places his hand on my back. "What is wrong with you?" he growls at Lenore.

"There's nothing wrong with me." She doesn't struggle against Solon's grip. "Why don't you ask her?" she snipes.

I feel Valtu's eyes on me. "Dahlia?"

I won't say it. I can't. I can barely speak, my throat feels damaged and I cough.

I straighten up and that's when the tears start to prick at my eyes. God damn it, I am so fucking sick of crying. I'm so sick of all of this, all of these lies.

I don't care anymore.

Go ahead and tell him, I say to Lenore inside my head. *Tell him what I am.*

And she hears me too. She raises her brow as she looks at me, then turns her focus to Valtu. I brace for impact.

"Your girlfriend is a witch."

Valtu's hand doesn't lift off my back, which I appreciate.

"What?" he whispers harshly. "She's not a witch."

"She's got a glamor on, that's why. She's disguised herself using magic. She says her name really is Dahlia, but I don't believe it. She was sent from the guild to kill you, Valtu."

Valtu takes his hand away.

Oh no.

I slowly straighten up and the tears start running down my cheeks.

The minute he sees that, his expression collapses.

I can feel the pain, the confusion, the hurt that's just starting to seep through him and it's only going to get worse.

"Is this true?" he asks me, his jaw tense as he tries to keep his emotions in check. "Tell me this isn't fucking true."

I open my mouth to speak but I don't know what to say.

"She's a vampire slayer, Valtu," Lenore goes on. "Corrupted by the guild just as my parents were. That's the only reason she's here in your life. To get close to you and drive the blade of *mordernes* into your heart."

He shakes his head in disbelief, but I can tell from the way his eyes harden, the way I feel his pain as the truth settles in, that he knows it's true. Maybe he's always known it's true.

Maybe that's the reason he never loved me.

He knew I was poison.

"They came up with this whole backstory for her too," Lenore goes on. "It's like a play, you know, a game. She says that she's your reincarnated loves. She said she's Mina and Lucy."

Solon makes a *tsk* of disappointment.

But Valtu.

He just fucking explodes.

Suddenly he's at me and he's pressing me up against the fridge now, but it's not an arm to my neck, it's his hand around my throat, and this time he aims to fucking kill me, his fingers squeezing me like a lemon.

"How dare you?" he cries out, spit flying as his hand crushes me further, the edges of my vision going gray. I reach up with my hands to pry his fingers off me but it's no use.

This can't be how it ends.

"How could you pretend, how could you do that to me?" he goes on, bringing his face right up to mine, and his pupils cycle between black and red and there's a blood vessel in his forehead that I think might burst. "Why did you have to do it? Why did you have to pick on *me*?"

The anguish in his voice is breaking me into pieces.

But I'm also being broken by his grip.

I open my mouth but I can't speak because I can't *breathe*.

"Why me?" he says, his eyes watering, his whole body shaking as he raises his hand higher and higher until I'm being strangled, feet off the ground. "Did they tell you what to say, how to act? I bet you were a very apt pupil!"

"Valtu," Solon warns him.

I try to pry his grip loose but I'm losing consciousness now.

"Valtu!" Solon yells, and now he's at us and he's trying to put himself between me and Valtu. "You're killing her."

"Maybe that's what she deserves!" he cries out. "I don't know who she is, she's nothing to me! It was all a fucking act!"

Solon pushes Valtu back enough that his grip loosens and I don't know how much time I have before I'm dead.

"My heart," I rasp against his hands. "My heart will always find yours."

He stills, his grip softening further. "What did you say?" he asks in horror.

Remove the glamor, I say to Lenore inside my head. *Please, let him see. I am too weak to remove the spell myself.*

My eyes close and everything turns cold and black, my body going limp as I'm pulled under, my feet still dangling above the floor.

Everything turns fuzzy as I hear Lenore whispering frantically the words of a spell, over and over.

"What are you doing?" Solon says to her.

All is black now.

"My heart will always find yours," I whisper again. I believe it. And when I drop dead here at his hand, when the glamor is finally removed, he will finally see.

I love you.

Please don't let this kill you, Valtu. I should have told you the truth.

As my heartbeat slows and slows and I slip into that black void I've faced so many times before, I feel the glamor rise from me, like someone's lifting a wedding veil from off my face.

"Oh my god," I hear Solon's voice.

I hear Lenore gasp.

And Valtu lets out the most heart-shattering scream.

The last sound Dahlia Abernathy will ever hear.

CHAPTER 24

VALTU

MINA.

Lucy.

Dahlia.

She's in my hand, my fist around her throat, the life leaving her eyes for the third time as long as I've been alive.

I instinctively let go and she collapses to the floor of the kitchen in a lifeless heap and I'm screaming, the sound being ripped from the depths of my chest. I'm just useless, frozen, a shell of a person, paralyzed by the sharpest horror I've ever felt, a hook around my heart, tugging and sawing until there's nothing left of me.

But there is something left.

She's lying at my feet.

Not breathing.

I drop to my knees, the paralysation giving way to panic.

No, no, no.

This can't be.

But it is.

She's lying there in front of me, her neck bruised thanks

to my grip, the rest of her skin milky pale. That nose, those lips, that hair.

It's like a dream where you're trying to remember who someone is in it, their face always changing, and then when you see that person the next day, it all slides into place like puzzle pieces.

Dahlia is Lucy and Mina.

She always was from day one.

But why didn't she tell me?

Why is she a witch, a vampire slayer on top of it?

Why did she come back into my life only to die again, this time at my hand?

Because I killed her this time.

Just like I killed her the other times.

The children in her womb were a product of me.

This is my fault, too.

"No," I sob, pulling her toward me. I feel for a pulse on her neck, too panicked to stay in one spot for long. I twist around to look at Solon and Lenore. "Call Doctor Van Helsing!"

But Solon only kneels beside me, feeling for a pulse on her wrist, her neck, then finally puts his head on her chest, his expression grim. He doesn't even have to do all of that. We're vampires. We know when someone else is dead.

The silence is deafening.

"No!" I scream, pulling her up and cradling her in my arms. "No, this can't be happening, this can't be happening!"

I look to Lenore. "I don't understand!" I scream until a sob tears through my chest. I close my eyes, the tears pouring down my face.

Dahlia is my one true love.

Mina/Lucy had found me again, found my heart again, just like she said she would and I...I...

"I don't understand either," Solon says softly. "Why was she trying to kill you?"

"She wasn't," I whimper. "She would never. She loved me." She was just hidden so well. Even when I was drinking her blood, she always felt hidden from me. I couldn't get anything from her but feelings, and the feelings were that she truly loved me.

"She said she didn't know," Lenore says. "I'm so sorry Valtu, I just saw she was in disguise and she was a slayer. I didn't know she was…"

I stare at her through my tears, her face blurred. I'm so angry at Lenore right now. So angry. But that will do nothing.

"What did she tell you?"

She looks pained, pressing her fist to her mouth and wincing. "She said she only learned last night that she was reincarnated. She only remembered then."

I think back to last night. When?

Oh, God.

Van Helsing said she felt sick after he told her what happened to Lucy and Mina. Then she went to the washroom and when she came out…

"I found you Val, I said I would," she had said, staring at me like I had been lost to her for a very long time. There was so much love and amazement in her eyes, I didn't know what was happening. Then she started asking me what her hair color was, her eyes and…

"Your hair is red like Mina's," I whisper to her, my words ragged. "Your eyes are green like Lucy's. You are my dove. My lover. My everything."

I hold her tighter, but she's none of those things anymore because there's no life left in her body.

"She knew," I say quietly. "Last night she knew. God, why didn't she tell me?"

"Probably because she thought you'd kill her…" Solon says.

A fiery hit of rage stabs me and I roar at him, fangs bared, fuelled by so much anger and hatred for myself.

I did this.

I shake my head and collapse inward, like a dying star, the rage turning to the sharpest sorrow I have ever felt. I cover her with my body, like I did once before, as if I can protect her when I've only ever failed.

"I love you," I cry, shaking with the horror of it all. "I love you, Dahlia."

Because even though she was Lucy and Mina, she was also her own person and I loved her too. I should have told her. I wish I had known I wouldn't have the chance.

I'll never have that chance.

Unless…

I look up at Lenore, who is leaning against Solon and crying too.

"You can save her, can't you? You did it before. You're the only one who can turn someone into a vampire without turning them into a monster!"

Hope springs inside me.

She shakes her head. "It doesn't work like that."

"She's dead! You did it to Wolf's girlfriend, you turned her into a vampire and it worked! She didn't go insane, I met her. I saw her face-to-face. You can save Dahlia."

"I can't!" she protests. "It doesn't work that way, believe me. She has to be drained of blood, I have to get my blood in her heart."

"Just do it!" I jump to my feet and grab her, pulling her down to the floor with me.

"Valtu!" Solon yells.

I bring Lenore's wrist to my mouth and tear the veins open with my teeth.

She screams.

The blood spills everywhere, all over Dahlia's face, gathering on her lips.

I try to push her wrist to Dahlia's mouth and hold her there, but Solon is strong and he pulls Lenore off.

"Get a hold of yourself, Valtu. This isn't the way and you know it." He lowers his voice. "Is that even what Dahlia would want? You can't turn someone without their consent. At least, you wouldn't want to do that to your lover."

He's right. I collapse against the fridge and pull Dahlia to me once again, covered in blood.

She is so damn beautiful.

And I am forever broken.

"You'll see her again, Valtu," Lenore whispers, holding her wrist. "I'm sure."

"What if I don't?" I say. "What if it takes another hundred years again. Two hundred? Or never?"

How will I survive in this pain?

And what will happen to this world in that time?

What if I'm not even around?

"Maybe we should try and take down the guild," Solon says quietly.

Lenore and I both look at him.

Thinking.

"It won't bring her back, Valtu," Solon goes on, and though his eyes are soft, there's a glint of malice in them. "But it might feel good to find the people that made Dahlia this way."

"I'm down," Lenore says adamantly. "Revenge is my favourite hobby at this point."

Revenge.

I stare down at Dahlia's peaceful, bloodied face and kiss her for the last time. "I promise I'll get revenge," I whisper to her. "I'll get revenge on those who wronged you."

And that includes myself.

EPILOGUE
21 YEARS LATER

"YOU MUST BE GETTING NERVOUS, HUH?" Dylan asks me as he grabs a beer from the fridge. He's about to close it, then thinks twice. "You want one? You're almost legal after all."

It's rare my brother shows me any consideration so I should probably take him up on his offer. Besides, maybe a beer will help calm my nerves. No point denying how anxious I am about my birthday.

"Sure," I say as he hands me a can. I snap open the lid, relishing the feel of doing so. I had to get my gel nails removed because of tomorrow. Apparently they can be used as a weapon, so my parents made sure mine are cut short. The last thing I want is to accidentally hurt them.

"You're lucky," I tell my brother as I sit down on the sofa. A spring juts into my ass and I have to adjust myself. I'll be in this room for a few days and while my parents didn't want any of their good furniture to get damaged, they didn't want to lock me in a barren room either. Everything in here has been furnished from garage sales. In fact I think this sofa belonged to Brady Williams' family who live down the street from me. I kissed Brady one drunken night, maybe on this couch, as it happens with the boys in the neighborhood.

They never knew what I really was.

Or rather, what I was destined to be.

Not that the world thinks vampires are a myth. They don't anymore. They know they're out there, living among us, but as vampires are driven into hiding more, it's getting harder for the humans to come up with any proof.

My family are the only vampires around where I live, in Newport, Oregon. Sometimes I think we may be the only ones in the state, but my father assures me there are others. The Pacific Northwest has becoming a breeding ground for them now that so many places are becoming too hot for us to live in comfortably.

Tomorrow is my twenty-first birthday. It's the day I'll go through The Becoming. When I'll finally become a vampire. Though Dylan is a few years older than me, he won't go through it until he's thirty-five, so he has no advice to give me.

"You'll be fine," he says, leaning against the fridge. "Though that horny phase sounds pretty psycho."

Ah yes. The bloodlust and the just pure lust. In the fridge there are bags of blood for me to drink when my hunger makes me crazy, but before that I'll be tied down to the bed in the corner so I don't go insane with needing to come. It's definitely the part that everyone always talks about, and let me tell you, talking about it with your parents is all sorts of embarrassing.

That aside, they've both gone through the process so they assured me that no matter what I will be okay, and when I'm finally out on the other side, I will feel better than I ever have before.

"You'll finally feel like yourself," my mother said and that's the part I'm looking forward to the most. Even knowing that

I would fully transform one day, I spent my life feeling like there was something wrong with me. I just didn't fit in. I was always different and no matter how hard I tried to fit in, I just never could.

But in a week or less, I will emerge from this sound-proof garage turned vampire transition den, and *finally* feel at peace with the world.

"I'd rather not talk about the horny phase with my brother, thank you very much," I scoff at him.

He shrugs. "Well there's always the vampire porn sites that can tell you about it. Do you feel any other changes yet?"

I give him a steady look of disgust.

"I mean otherwise," he says with a raise of his hands. "Jeez. I mean like, cravings. For blood."

I take a long swig of my beer and nod. "Lately all I want is meat, the more raw the better. And the world is starting to feel a little different, you know? Clearer. Brighter."

"Well tomorrow you're gonna step into this room as Rose Harper, pain-in-the-ass sister, and leave it as Rose Harper, bloodsucking monster."

I laugh. "Probably not. You know how puritanical mom and dad are about feeding."

Vampires need blood to survive. In the recent past, vampire clubs and feeding bars were common. They still are, but they're harder to find because of some shit that went down in Italy a long time ago.

Thankfully for vampires like us, who don't live near the cities, we have become users of both blood bags and a drug that makes it so we can get nourishment from old blood, even animal blood. When it's supplemented with regular human food, people, like my parents, don't have to go out anywhere and kill people to survive, or live close to the underground clubs, which are usually sex clubs at the same time.

We move around a lot, though. We have to. People get

suspicious. We've lived in Newport for about five years and that's the longest we've ever been anywhere. We'll have to move on somewhere else before people realize that my very young-looking mother and I look the same age.

I have no idea where we'll go next. Maybe I can convince them to take me to a city. Or maybe I'll just go off on my own. See the world, that sort of thing. I'll stick to cooler climates though. With my fair skin and red hair, the sun isn't a friend of mine.

"Well, here's to you then," Dylan says, coming over and hitting his can of beer against mine. "I hope you turn into the bad-ass you were always meant to be."

I laugh. "That might be the nicest thing you ever said to me."

He laughs and we drink up.

❧

"ROSE, HONEY? CAN YOU HEAR ME? DO YOU KNOW WHO I am?"

I buck against the restraints, opening my eyes.

I'm staring at the roof of the garage and for a moment I wonder what the hell is going on in here. Why am I...

But then it hits me.

The Becoming.

I'm going through The Becoming.

Least I think I am.

How long have I been here?

"Mom?" I say but my voice sounds foreign to me. I don't see her anywhere. I turn my head to see her coming toward me with a bag of blood in her hands, the fridge door open showcasing a row of blood bags and my brother's beer.

"Hey sweetie," she says. "It's time for your first sip."

I swallow, suddenly painfully thirsty, my throat as dry as a desert. My stomach gnaws at itself like I've got a ravenous beast inside me, eating me from the middle.

She stops beside me. "There you are," she says brightly as she smiles down at me.

"What happened?" I ask, looking around the room, though my attention is brought right back to the blood in her hands.

"You went through your first stage. You know. The lusty one. We thought you would have broken through the restraints already and gone for the blood but you haven't yet. That's okay. That's a good sign. Means you didn't get a chance to trash the room. Your hunger is more civilized."

I stare at the blood in the bag, the rich crimson.

She holds out a pill. "Open your mouth."

I do so and she places the pill on my tongue.

"Chew."

I chew. It tastes like fake cherry, a taste I used to tolerate but now it makes me want to vomit. But if I don't have it then I won't be nourished by the blood and since it will be my first feeding, it's extra important.

"Good girl," she says. "Now I'm going to untie you and give you the blood and leave you be. There's more in the fridge there if you need it." She leans over and kisses my forehead while undoing the leather straps around my wrists. "I am so proud of you."

Then she leaves the room rather quickly.

I slowly sit up. I feel like I have the world's worst hangover and I ache between my legs. I know that I was restrained, so I hadn't done anything to myself and this is just a leftover from days of being in the lust stage. Thank god I don't remember any of it.

As for the rest of me, I do feel different. My skin is extra sensitive, my eyes, my senses feel like they're working overtime. But I couldn't say I feel like a vampire.

I eye the bag of blood beside me.

No, this is what will bring that feeling on.

I take a deep breath and then pick up the bag.

I raise it up above my head.

Weeks ago I would have looked at the blood in disgust.

Now I see it as a gift from God.

I open the valve, put it to my lips and drink.

It hits my tongue and my entire world changes.

I was expecting the usual taste of blood, the metallic pennies in your mouth thing. And maybe it does still taste like that, but suddenly having a mouthful of pennies is the most delicious thing I have ever tasted. It's all I ever want, for the rest of my life.

I drink and I drink and I drink, the blood flowing down my throat, filling me but not filling me, and I've almost drained the bag when suddenly my head explodes in a flurry of stars and pain.

I scream. "Fuck!"

Drop the bag and grab my head, my fingers digging into my scalp.

Is this part of it?

Is this—

But my own thought ends in my brain because suddenly I'm flooded with a million different images, all of them awful, all of them bringing me pain.

I see myself on the ground, staring at a crowd of soldiers holding back someone I know is my lover, while my father brings a sword down on my neck.

I see myself lying in bed with a big belly and covered in blood, staring into the dark eyes of the man I love.

I see myself in that same man's grip, his face contorted in rage as he drains the life out of me.

I see all my deaths.

The deaths of Mina.

Lucy.
Dahlia.
I remember everything.

THE SEQUEL TO BLOOD ORANGE IS BLACK ROSE
—releasing December 29th 2022. You can preorder it HERE.

To keep up-to-date with me, please follow me on Instagram or Tik Tok (authorkarinahalle). I'll have some signed special edition hardcovers of these books coming soon too, so you don't want to miss out!

AN EXCERPT FROM NIGHTWOLF

A VAMPIRE ROMANCE

The drive from Garberville to the coast is about an hour through winding mountain passes flanked by towering redwoods. We don't see many cars on the way, making me feel more and more isolated the further we go. With the daylight fading, I just hope we make it to the house before it gets dark. Wolf may have no trouble seeing in it, but I at least like to know where we're going.

But eventually the trees open up and I start to see more sky and glimpses of the ocean over the tops of the redwoods below, everything glowing orange and gold with the coming sunset. We pull off the winding main road and start our descent. To my relief there are some houses around, though they all fade away when we approach a wooden gate that says "Dead Man's Point" on it.

"Really?" I ask as Wolf slows the car. "That's the name of this place?"

Wolf grins. "Well, he's not going to flat-out call it Vampire's Lair, is he?" He reaches across and opens the glove compartment and I breathe in the scent of his hair because I'm creepy like that. If he notices he doesn't say anything and brings out a remote, pressing the button so that the gate swings open.

"Fancy," I remark as we drive through.

Then I gasp.

As we come through another section of trees, suddenly the house appears before us, perched on what looks like the edge of the world. It's a huge, sprawling place, surrounded by dry grass that moves in the breeze, shining in the sunset like liquid gold. They remind me of Wolf's eyes. And beyond the estate is the ocean, that endless Pacific, with the sun heading for the horizon.

"Wow," I say as we park the car. "I need to get a picture of this."

I quickly grab my purse with my phone and get out of the car, running around the house to try and get the best view.

"We can make it to the beach if we hurry," Wolf says, right beside me.

He reaches out and grabs my hand, holding it tight, then leads me down a stony path between the grass until we come to a cascading set of wooden stairs. It's a long way down the cliff to the curve of beach below and the frothy waves that shine rose gold, but Wolf holds my hand the whole time.

I'm not sure if Wolf has ever held my hand before, not like this. Not with such a strong grip, not with such assurance.

And when we finally reach the bottom, our boots sinking into the soft sand, he doesn't let go. He keeps holding on, his cool palm against my warm one, ice and fire, leading me to the middle of the beach until he seems certain that he's found the best spot to take pictures.

"There," he says, awe in his voice.

I expect him to be looking at what I am, the pounding waves that send metallic gold into the air, fill my ears, the sun that is now melting into the horizon.

But he's not.

I turn my head slightly and up and he's staring down at me.

He's looking at me like I'm the sunset.

After every single amazing sunset Wolf has probably seen in his long life, he's looking at me like I'm a brand-new experience.

My heart skips until there's a thunderstorm in my chest.

Yeah, there's something happening between us. I don't think we can stop it, even if we wanted to.

God, I hope he doesn't try to stop it.

"Going to take a picture?" Wolf asks me.

I shake my head. "I don't need to."

I squeeze his hand.

He squeezes mine back.

Then he looks to the sunset and we both watch as it dips below the horizon, waiting for that green flash that comes and goes by the time I've blinked.

"You know what we should do now?" Wolf asks me.

Oh god. I could think of a million things, and I don't have the guts to say any of them.

Yet.

"Get drunk?" I ask. Cuz that would help.

He flashes me a grin that makes his dimples deepen and my legs feel weak. "You read my mind."

Then he finally lets go of my hand as we head back up the stairs to the house.

By the time I'm at the top, I'm breathless, my thighs burning, lungs aching, while Wolf seems even more energized. We grab our bags from the car and bring them into the house. It's even more stunning inside, like a mix of a mountain lodge and old-timey elegance. Lots of antiques and velvet paintings and sculptures that look expensive and rare, but with exposed beam ceilings, heavy wood furniture, and sheepskin rugs throughout, plus a massive stone fireplace right in the middle of the living room, the kind you would see in a ski lodge.

"What room are you taking?" Wolf asks me, sounding innocent enough.

Oh. *Oh*. I see. Well, of course we would each get our own room, just because we held hands on the beach and he stared at me instead of the sunset doesn't mean we're going to start sharing a bed—and then some—together. This house is huge and doesn't lend itself to the much-coveted *only one bed* situation. Unfortunately.

"Oh, uh," I say, looking down the lengthy hall and then up the stairs. "I don't really know. Doesn't matter, I'm sure the bedrooms are all the same."

"You at least need one with the view of the ocean," he says and gestures for me to follow him up the stairs. He brings me to the first bedroom on the west side. It's not huge but it has its own en suite, and the view over the ocean is phenomenal, even with the darkening sky turning purple and gray. Waking up to that tomorrow is going to be heaven. It would be even more so if Wolf shared the room with me.

Alas, the room he picks is two doors down, as if he's purposefully putting distance between us.

I start putting things away, use the bathroom, and take a moment to stare at myself in the mirror and breathe. It feels like I haven't been breathing since we left the city.

I don't look my finest. Solon was kind of right when he said I look like shit. My eyes are puffy, creating dark circles under them that even the strongest concealer isn't masking, and my eyes themselves look kind of wild, the violet in them brighter than normal. My hair is tangled from having the window down in the car, and I should probably take a shower because I've got that stale road-trip smell all over me.

And I'm nervous. I can't remember the last time I've been

nervous around Wolf, but I am, here and now. All these years of just burying my feelings, some of which I haven't even come to terms with yet, of living with a crush that's been building and growing—it feels like it's all coming to a head. Like there's a storm brewing between us that's about to take us both out. A storm of destruction, maybe, but something neither of us can avoid.

And the conditions for the storm are more than right.

"It's just Wolf," I whisper to myself in the mirror, trying to find the courage I normally don't lack. "Stop being so dramatic."

I take in another deep breath and then raise my chin to my reflection. Then I step out of the bathroom and poke my head out of my room.

"Wolf?" I call out down the hall, about to tell him I'm going to take a shower.

"Come down here," he says, his voice coming from the first floor.

Curious, I shut my door and head down the grand staircase. The fire in the fireplace is already large and crackling, no doubt caused by a snap of Wolf's fingers, and I walk around it to the kitchen.

The kitchen is huge and Wolf is leaning on the quartz-top island in the middle, the sleeves on his olive green Henley rolled up to his elbows, showcasing his massive forearms. But that's not the only thing impressive in front of me. On the island is an elaborate spread; lit candles, an extravagant charcuterie board piled with juicy strawberries, grapes and fleshy figs, fresh cheeses, meats, different types of bread and crackers, spreads and jellies, all flanked by an array of hard liquor and vintage wines, the kind that Solon keeps locked in a cellar.

"What the hell? Did you do this?" I ask him.

He shoots me a sheepish grin. "I'm starting to think I

should have. No, Emilio did this, the groundskeeper. Must have set it up right before we got here."

I come over, looking for the juiciest strawberry on the board. Everything looks perfect and professional. "Looks like he was planning for a romantic weekend."

I stick the strawberry in my mouth, sucking back the juice. Oh, it's sweet.

Wolf watches my mouth intently, clears his throat. "Looks like."

I meet his eyes for a moment and see a hint of a smile in them. Then he jerks his head toward the French doors at the side of the kitchen. "Did you see that?"

I finish the strawberry and go over, peering through the glass. There's a deck outside that seems to stretch over the edge into nothing, a hot tub in the middle of it. The lights in it are on and the steam rises in the air invitingly into the night sky.

"Oh my god, I didn't know he had a hot tub," I practically whine, my hands against the glass in yearning. "I would have brought a bathing suit."

"So?" Wolf says from behind me. "Shouldn't be a problem."

I turn around to face him just in time to see him pulling his Henley over his head, his abs and chest and arms on full display.

I stop. Stare, in open-mouthed awe. I can't help it.

He throws his shirt on the floor, then he removes his jeans until he's just in a pair of gray boxer briefs and...

Oh my god.

Oh. My. God.

I've never seen Wolf in this state of undress before and *oh my god* is the correct phrase to keep muttering to myself because he truly looks like a god. Nordic, Roman, Greek, Chris Hemsworth, all of them are apt.

Somehow he looks even bigger and taller than he does with clothes on. His legs are *long*, the thighs that I felt earlier are massively muscled and powerful. A half-hard cock is clearly outlined in his briefs and if that's not him in full capacity, then I may want to rethink about riding him because I think it would kill me when erect.

His waist is narrow, with those sharp Vs on his hips, like arrows pointing to his dangerous dick, his abs are rippled and defined without an ounce of fat, and his chest is this wide, hard expanse leading to impossibly rounded shoulders and thick biceps. You know all those ropey muscles around the neck and the arms and the shoulders that those insanely fit celebrities have? Yeah, he has them too. Except his don't come from steroids and a diet of cod and broccoli.

"Close to what you imagined?" he asks with the cockiest grin.

I open my mouth and close it again, trying to find the words. "Better," I admit, no use in denying it. "Much better." I clear my throat. "But Wolf, you can't just go around taking your clothes off like that without any warning. You could kill a woman dead, on the spot."

A quick glance at his face shows that grin getting wider as he lets out a laugh. Then his eyes tighten, a heat flashing through them, as he focuses on me. "Then make it even. Take off your clothes," he commands, his tone more serious than playful.

Mild horror runs through me. "I'm not taking off my clothes!" I shriek.

He grabs a bottle of red wine off the counter and two wine glasses, his mouth twisting with amusement. "Since when have you ever been bashful?"

"Since you took off your clothes! I can't be almost naked next to you, a vampire, whose body has been blessed by some dark god. I'm just so terribly human."

"*Beautifully* human," he says, his voice going low. "Now strip down. Grab an extra bottle of wine. And come join me."

Oh shit, is he trying to compel me? Because, as I watch his tight, rounded, gorgeous ass go through the doors and onto the deck, I'm already grabbing the hem of my shirt and lifting it over my head. I pause for a moment, my heart thundering against my ribcage, then think *fuck it*. I'm going for it.

I unzip my jeans, take off my socks, until I'm standing in the kitchen in just my bra and underwear. Thank god they match, black and lacey, though I'm starting to wish I wasn't in a thong.

Even though I can't see Wolf outside now, I know he can see me, my body lit by the candles and the mood lighting of the kitchen. I straighten my shoulders and fling my hair over my shoulder, sucking in my stomach as I grab an extra bottle of wine. I'm a curvy girl but I don't have too many hang-ups about my body because the men I've been with all seem to enjoy the hourglass figure with extra padding. In high school I had my insecurities about being bigger than a lot of the popular girls, especially my ass and bust, but once I graduated and met men who knew what they wanted, I learned my body is a powerful weapon.

But right now, in my underwear in the kitchen, feeling the heat from his gaze all the way from outside, I feel like he has the bigger weapon, and I don't mean his dick. In all the fantasies I've had about Wolf, and I've had a lot, I forgot about that anxious, fluttery feeling that comes with baring your body to someone for the first time. I feel so *vulnerable*, while he isn't. I'm not sure he ever is.

So, I put the wine down for a moment, slide a bottle of whisky toward me, pop the top, then proceed to take a large gulp. And then another, until I'm coughing and it burns like hell. There. That should help.

I grab the wine again, take a deep breath, then head out the door.

Outside it's freezing, the wind whipping up from the ocean and messing up my hair. I let out a little squeal from the cold, and then scamper across the deck toward the hot tub, fully aware that Wolf is watching my every move, which includes my boobs bouncing all over the place. Should have worn a more supportive bra.

"You know, I never thought I'd be sharing a hot tub with a vampire," I tell him as I step over the side of the hot tub and ease into the water. I try to look graceful doing so, but I nearly fall in. I yelp, water splashing around me, and Wolf grabs the bottle of wine from me at the last minute.

"Seems like you've never been in a hot tub before," he says with a laugh as I try to right myself. The water is so unbelievably hot that it makes me shiver. I shove my hair back from my face, finding a spot close to Wolf but not so close that I'm all up in his face. "Must be the whisky," he adds.

"You saw that?" I ask.

He gives me a quiet smile, his eyes glowing in the hot tub lights. "You know I was watching."

A thrill runs from my head to my toes. He's got me there. "And was I as you imagined?" I ask playfully.

His smile deepens as his eyes drift over my breasts, leaving licks of heat in their wake. "Even better."

I'm blushing now. Or maybe it's the hot water. "Well, you're the one who suggested we get drunk. I was just getting a head start."

"Actually, *you* are the one who suggested it," he says, reaching behind him to the ledge along the tub. He hands me a wine glass, then takes the corkscrew and pops open a bottle of red. In the dim light outside, I can barely make out the label, then I realize it's because the label is so old and faded. It must be at least fifty years old.

"Wow," I comment. "I've never seen us serve this at Dark Eyes."

"Must be from Solon's private reserve. If you think the cellar back home is impressive, you should check out the one here." He pours the wine into my glass, the liquid a deep shining ruby that makes my mouth water.

"So, how many times have you been here?" I ask as he pours himself some. "I don't think I've seen you come up here since I started working for you."

"You don't work for me, Amethyst," Wolf says, practically scolding. "*With* me. I'm not your boss."

"You're a centuries-old vampire. It's hard *not* to think of you as my boss sometimes," I admit, running the glass under my nose, smelling earth and cherries and violets.

"I don't know about that. I've seen the way you look at Solon. With such reverence and respect."

"He saved my life," I say quietly.

"I know," Wolf says. "Thank god for that."

"I think I look at you the same way."

He looks at me for a moment, thoughts turning behind his eyes. "No, you don't."

"Then how do I look at you?"

He rubs his lips together, still staring at me. "I used to think you looked at me like an older brother."

I wince internally, because I *definitely* don't see him as that, and never have. "But not anymore?"

"No. Not anymore."

I want to pry, to ask for specifics, but if he's not offering it up, then I might just make things really awkward and I don't want to deal with an awkward moment when I'm already half-naked in a hot tub with him.

"How come I never see you feed?" I ask him.

He blinks at me, the subject having gone sideways. "What?"

"I just think it's odd," I say, having a gulp of wine. It tastes heavenly. "I run the feeding room from time to time, I've seen what goes on in there. I've seen Ezra feed sometimes. But never you."

"Or Solon."

"Solon has Lenore. And before that he would bring someone to his room."

"Then I'm the same."

"But I never see you bring anyone to your room," I tell him. And that's the truth. I know Wolf is no virgin—I've heard Ezra talking about certain vampires in the near past and the far past. But I've honestly never seen him take anyone to his room, to feed or to fuck.

"You really are curious, aren't you?" he asks, thankfully sounding more amused than annoyed at my endless prodding. I nod. "Well, I do feed in my room. And sometimes I feed in the middle of Dark Eyes, when you're talking to me. I do it from a glass."

My eyes go big. "Wait. You mean sometimes when I think you're drinking wine, you're actually drinking blood?"

"That's correct," he says, having a sip of his drink. He raises his glass at me. "Don't worry, this is still wine."

"Well, who donates it?"

He tilts his head. "I don't know. I'm not particular. Some human from the Dark Room. That's all it needs to be."

"But..." I begin, trying to wrap my head around it. All those times I've seen him drinking wine, how often was that someone's blood? I don't know why I'm finding this all so intriguing considering, but I do. "Like, you don't prefer a certain person? What about the taste? Doesn't that differ?"

"It does, but it hasn't ever mattered to me. A vampire's relationship with blood is a personal one," he explains. "It can be complicated, just as food can be complicated for some humans. Some vampires enjoy inflicting pain as they feed.

Others find it too intimate and prefer to drink via a vessel instead. Others find it sexual, no matter who the donor is. Others still will only feed off certain types of humans, and some barely think about blood at all and only take enough to sustain themselves."

"And you're the one who finds it too intimate?"

He shakes his head, his lips pressed into a hard line for a moment. "No. I fall into another category. The one that loses control."

"Like Solon," I suggest. "Lenore told me that he was so hesitant about feeding on her at first because he was afraid the beast would come out."

"No, not like him. Solon never lost control while feeding because he was hungry. He lost control because of fear or emotions and that led to the beast. For me, after I go so long without it...I get ravenous. Insatiable. I get..." he pauses, his eyes going dark. "Violent."

If that was meant to scare or disturb me, it hasn't. "Have you thought about maybe not going so long between feedings? This sounds a bit like a binging-purging thing. You wouldn't be so hungry if you ate more often."

He lifts a shoulder, his eyes gazing at the water, lost in thought. "I don't know. Even with a glass of blood it's hard to restrain myself. By the time you usually see me with a glass, I've already had several. Sometimes I think I restrain myself out of punishment. Or maybe I..."

"Maybe it's so ingrained in you from when you were growing up, after your father died, that it's stuck. Like those people who lived through the depression and ended up clipping coupons and stocking up on soup for the rest of their lives."

"Could be," he says, finishing the glass of wine in one go. Some of the scarlet liquid spills over the side of his mouth, making it look like he's drinking blood. Another thrill runs through me, shivers from the inside out.

"I would love to see you feed," I say, without meaning to. "Not from a glass, from a human."

He eyes me as if he's surprised I said that too. "I don't think you do."

"You could feed on me."

He swallows hard, shaking his head. "I wouldn't. I would never."

"You mean you've never thought about it?" I ask, my tone both playful and serious. "About biting me, feeding on me."

Fucking me...

He stares at me, his look growing more intense by the second. He may have not heard that thought, but he felt it. He adjusts himself, as if uncomfortable.

"I'm a vampire, Amethyst. Of course, I've thought about it." He closes his eyes, breathing in deep through his nose. "But it would be violent."

"Maybe I like the violence of it."

His eyes fly open, piercing me in place. "You wouldn't like that."

I don't know if it's the whisky, the wine, the hot tub, or all these years of build-up, but suddenly I move forward through the water, placing my hands on his shoulders, his skin feeling extra cold compared to the hot water. "I don't think you know what I like," I tell him. "Or what I want."

His focus goes to the swell of my breasts, which are practically in his face, then up to my chin, my mouth, my eyes. "I'm starting to get the idea," he murmurs.

A sly grin spreads across my face, feeling fully empowered now. I move so that I'm straddling him, my soft thighs on either side of his hard ones. I know I'm being bold now, my bashfulness having dissolved in the hot water, and I'm taking a chance with him because even though he's giving off all the signs, I still don't know for sure if this is what he wants. We're at a point where we could turn around and go back to being just friends, zero benefits, and our relationship could still be saved.

But there's a line that can't be crossed and I'm stepping over it, one foot down on the other side, waiting for a signal from him to follow through.

"As I said before," he says in a gruff voice, his hands skimming down the sides of my waist, his eyes glued to my parted lips. "You're a tease."

Oh baby. I give him a wicked smile in response, straddling him deeper until I can feel the long hard length of him pressing up against me, only thin wet fabric between us.

My god.

I can *feel* him.

I can't believe this is happening.

"Did you ever think that *you've* been the tease in this situation?" I manage to say.

He tilts his head, appraising me, gaze flicking up to meet mine. "In this situation at the moment?" His voice is even lower now, making my nerves dance. His eyes sharpen with intensity. "I'm definitely not teasing."

And at that, he brings his hand over my stomach, sliding his lengthy, strong fingers down beneath the band of my underwear, and fucking hell am I glad I got a bikini wax a few weeks ago because his finger slides over my clit and I immediately gasp.

Holy jeez.

That line that I was crossing? He just pulled me right over.

"Definitely not teasing," he says again, biting his lip as he stares at me. I swear to god he can make me come with just his eyes, so having his fingers swirling over my clit is just icing on the cake.

"Fuck," I whisper, my head going back as I push my hips down, trying to get more friction in the water, more pressure. He responds in kind, rubbing his fingers harder, though the movement is still so slow and deliberate that, yeah, it feels like teasing still.

"Do you like that?" His voice is rough but also quiet, hopeful. His other hand comes up and cups the side of my jaw. "Do you want me to stop? Or do you want more?"

I manage to swallow, staring deep into his hooded eyes as he holds my face, the pressure of his fingers as strong on my chin as they are between my legs. "What do you think?" I say thickly.

"I think you're a girl who always wants more," he says, running his thumb over my lips. "Deserves more."

Jesus.

I delicately bite the tip, sucking on it for a second, watching as his pupils dilate.

Oh, he knows exactly what I want.

He sucks in a harsh breath through his teeth as he pushes his finger further down, the pressure increasing against me until I feel like I'm hot lava under his skin. Slowly, he pushes his finger up inside me and I'm immediately clenching around him. Damn, he has large fingers.

Damn, I want more.

When I dreamed about doing this with Wolf, when I imagined the first time we were intimate, I always pictured it happening in a drunken tear-your-clothes-off, fuck-on-the bar type of moment after a long shift in Dark Eyes. But this, this is like a luxurious dream. It's like being on drugs, in an alternate universe, floating among stars. And the setting is half the experience, being in the hot tub out beneath a dark endless sky brimming with so many stars that it looks like someone sprinkled too much icing sugar.

But Wolf, he handles my body with such skill and assurance, it's like he's been waiting for this for ages and has no problems taking his time. As he pushes a second finger inside me, adjusting his large hand so that his thumb presses on my clit, he watches me closely, intently, studying the way my face responds to the pleasure, the little noises that escape from my lips.

"I've had this secret obsession with making you come," he says, leaning in to place his mouth at the soft slope where my neck meets my shoulders. The feeling of his lips there sends a violent shiver down my spine.

"That's funny," I say through a gasping breath. "I've had a secret obsession with you making me come as well."

I feel him smile against my skin. "I don't think it was much of a secret."

I tense up and he pulls back, grinning at me.

"You mean you've known how I felt about you?" I ask, breath hitching as he slowly slides another finger over me.

"I told you I knew when you were staring," he says. "Suddenly you weren't looking at me like an older brother anymore."

"And there I thought I had an air of mystery about me," I grumble, adjusting myself on his hand, wanting him deeper.

"You're a lot of things, baby," he murmurs roughly.

Baby. He just called me *baby*.

I think I might die.

"And fucking greedy is one of them," he goes on with moan as he pushes two more fingers inside me, practically fisting me.

"Fuck." I gasp loudly, my body squeezing around him. His fingers feel as good as any cock I've ever had. But I know his cock would feel even better.

"I dreamed about what you'd sound like too," he adds, his voice taking on a silken tone. "You sound better than in my dreams."

"Doesn't seem fair that this is a one-way street," I tell him, trying to reach down with one hand to grab his cock, guide him to me.

He plunges his free hand into the water and grabs my wrist firmly to stop me. "This isn't about me."

"You think I want your cock inside me for *your* own pleasure?" I say, my eyes pinching shut for a second as his fingers fuck me deeper. "Oh, no. That's all about me, too."

He grins. "As I said. Fucking greedy."

To punctuate his words, he thrusts his fingers in harder, bending and curling over all the right spots, the pressure inside me building like a river at a dam.

"Wolf," I whimper, my body starting to shake.

I try to hold back, try to keep myself from going over the edge. I want to come like crazy, but I'm afraid it's too soon, that this might be it. I want this to last forever. What if this is all I get?

I bite down on my tongue, gripping his shoulders, trying to meet his eyes.

Fuck, he's so beautiful.

And he's staring at me like I'm some goddess from above.

"That's it, baby, look at me when you come," he says in a deep, gruff voice, and then I'm letting go, into the freefall.

I come hard on his hand, rocking my hips into him, his fingers diving deeper, leaving no inch unexplored. I cry out, a string of expletives that ring out across the night, and it feels like my soul is being torn in a million little beautiful pieces, softly floating down from those stars.

Holy shit.

I mean, *holy shit.*

What the hell just happened to me?

I gasp for breath, my body still quivering over his, and he's smiling like he's the king of the fucking world. He grabs me by the waist and moves me over so I'm sitting on the bench, my head back along the edge of the hot tub, the black sky swirling above me.

I can't believe Wolf just made me come.

That he finger fucked me.

Wolf.

My Wolf.

This was not at all what I thought the day would bring when I woke up this morning.

That's when it dawns on me. He just fucked me with his hand and we haven't even kissed yet.

I open my eyes, my vision momentarily blurry as the alcohol and waves of the orgasm are still making my world spin. "Come here," I murmur, reaching up for his face which is just inches away, my fingertips running over his beautiful bone structure. I try to pull him closer, to finally kiss him, but he just starts slipping downward.

"Where are you going?" I ask, though it becomes obvious from the way he parts my legs, the dancing look in his eyes as he sinks deeper into the water. "You're going to drown."

He smirks at me. "I won't."

His head disappears under the water.

His hands grip my inner thighs, pushing them apart.

I'm still throbbing, my body on fire, and I know I'm too sensitive, but the moment he pushes the wet fabric of my underwear to the side, I suddenly realize I could go again.

Oh, I could go again and again.

And, apparently, so can he. He doesn't hesitate, he just jams his head between my legs and starts assaulting me with his tongue until my thighs are gripping his head and my eyes are rolling back.

Now, I've had sex in a hot tub before. And I've obviously been fingered in a hot tub before. But I've never had anyone go down on me in a hot tub before, and for all the normal reasons, including the fact that it's over a hundred degrees, and also the person would drown in less than a minute.

But Wolf isn't a human. The heat doesn't bother him to the same extent, and he can hold his breath forever. I don't even think he *needs* to breathe at all. Maybe oxygen is like a treat for vampires, I don't know.

What I do know is that this is blowing my fucking mind. Even in the water, which is usually desensitizing, his tongue is rough and strong, delivering all the right friction as he licks me up and down, sucking my clit between his lips, plunging his tongue deep inside.

Good lord, getting eaten out by a vampire is the way to go. If this is what it feels like in a hot tub, I can't imagine the sensations when we're dry. I already feel like my circuits are overloading and I have to grip the edge of the hot tub, my fingernails digging into the material, in order to keep from going mad.

"Oh god," I cry out, the skill of his tongue unparalleled as he swirls and circles my clit in hard passes that make my lips tingle. "Fucking hell."

It's weird too that he can't hear me, can't hear my moans and little cries, it's almost like I'm getting off on mute. But then I realize he can hear me. The louder I moan, the harder he goes at me, sucking my swollen flesh between his lips until I'm so close to coming again I can taste it.

It's his heightened supernatural senses. He can hear me, feel me, he probably knows exactly when I'm about to come just by listening to my body. It speaks to him without me knowing it.

And it tells him exactly what I want.

His tongue lashes me, mouth moving hard and fast, ravenous, and even though he's not feeding, he's feasting on me all the same. The hot, thick pressure in my core is molten, spreading throughout me, and my nerves feel like they've been stretched like a tightrope, moments from snapping, and, and...

"Oh, fuck!" The cry rips out of my throat, something deep and dark and primal, and I'm writhing on Wolf's face, the water splashing over the tub as I thrust my hips up, helping his tongue fuck me deeper until I lose all control.

I come so hard, I'm slipping down in the water, gasping for ragged breath, trying to hold myself up, yet succumbing to oblivion as my limbs jerk and shake, as if my mind has been pried open and the contents won't stop spilling out.

The water goes above my head.

Then everything goes black.

NIGHTWOLF is available in Amazon KU here and in paperback.

ACKNOWLEDGMENTS

Biggest thanks goes to the readers for picking up this book and for helping me make vampires cool again (I mean, they've always been cool to me ;).

I know when I was promoting it I said it was a standalone but I realized these characters have so much story to tell. When I got to the epilogue the first time around, thinking this was just going to be a big book, I realize it was going to be two whole big books and that epilogue needed a whole book of its own.

I hope you enjoyed Blood Orange this spooky season or whenever you picked it up. And don't worry, the sequel, Black Rose is coming December 29th 2022 and I am SO excited for it! It's all about revenge, baby.

If you happen to make a fun Tik Tok, please tag me (link on next page) and in case you're curious who my muses are, Professor Valtu Aminoff has always been Aidan Turner (and that was even before I saw him as a vampire in *Being Human* *bites fist*) and Rose Leslie for Dahlia (and Lucy and Mina and Rose).

Special thanks to Laura, Hang, Chanpreet, Sandra, Anna, Kathleen, Jenn and the SB team, Rachel, Jay, Ali, Taylor and everyone at Root Lit, my mom, and of course Scott and Bruce.

ABOUT THE AUTHOR

Karina Halle, a screenwriter, former travel writer and music journalist, is the *New York Times*, *Wall Street Journal*, and *USA Today* bestselling author of *The Royals Next Door*, *A Nordic King*, and *Sins & Needles*, as well as over seventy other wild and romantic reads. She, her husband, and their adopted pit bull Bruce, live in a rain forest on an island off the coast of British Columbia in the summer, and in sunny Los Angeles during the winter months.

www.authorkarinahalle.com

Find her on Facebook, Instagram, Pinterest, BookBub, Amazon (and click here for Tik Tok)

f facebook.com/authorkarinahalle

⊙ instagram.com/authorhalle

⦿ pinterest.com/authorkarinahalle

BB bookbub.com/authors/karina-halle

a amazon.com/Karina-Halle/e/B0050KE63C/ref=dp_byline_cont_pop_ebooks_1

ALSO BY KARINA HALLE

My Life in Shambles

Discretion

Disarm

Disavow

The Royal Rogue

The Forbidden Man

Lovewrecked

One Hot Italian Summer

The One That Got Away

All the Love in the World (Anthology)

Romantic Suspense Novels by Karina Halle

Sins and Needles (The Artists Trilogy #1)

On Every Street (An Artists Trilogy Novella #0.5)

Shooting Scars (The Artists Trilogy #2)

Bold Tricks (The Artists Trilogy #3)

Dirty Angels (Dirty Angels #1)

Dirty Deeds (Dirty Angels #2)

Dirty Promises (Dirty Angels #3)

Black Hearts (Sins Duet #1)

Dirty Souls (Sins Duet #2)

Horror & Paranormal Romance

Darkhouse (EIT #1)

Red Fox (EIT #2)

The Benson (EIT #2.5)

Dead Sky Morning (EIT #3)

Lying Season (EIT #4)

On Demon Wings (EIT #5)

Made in United States
Troutdale, OR
06/25/2024

20450503R10228